Flame Of
Courage

Flame Of Courage

Connie Monk

PIATKUS

First published in Great Britain in 1992 by
Judy Piatkus (Publishers) Ltd of
5 Windmill Street, London W1P 1HF

**The moral right of the author
has been asserted**

*A catalogue record for this book is available
from the British Library*

ISBN 0-7499-0153-5

Phototypeset in 11/12pt Linotron Times by
Computerset, Harmondsworth, Middlesex
Printed and bound in Great Britain.

Chapter One

Last night she'd left the car parked half way down the long drive so that her early start wouldn't disturb Grandam. The stars were like jewels in the dark sky as she switched on the engine and drove slowly out through the huge wrought iron gates of Bullington Manor – left open in readiness – then down the narrow lane through Newton Dingley village and on towards the Oxford road.

To Katie O'Hagon this was a Red Letter Day. She'd been in England just over a year, she who'd come from Canada for six months, getting to know her mother's family, living the dream that had been with her all through childhood. Six months had stretched so easily to eight, to ten, to a year.

'Why are you so keen to run away from us?' Lavinia Matheson had wanted to know when Katie had talked again of going home.

'Do I sound keen to go, Grandam? Oh, but I'm not. Of course I miss Mom and the others, but it's a healthy sort of miss. I can't just drift on here for ever, though. Holidays are special because they are holidays, I guess. I ought to be doing something positive. I'm nineteen – it's time I was carving a future.' The thought of it was exciting, as exciting as it is to any girl who feels the world is waiting to be discovered. In Katie's case, growing up on the edge of the Albertan prairie, the star that had guided her had been set firmly over England. For her eighteenth birthday her great-grandmother, Lavinia Matheson, had turned dreams to reality in the shape of an airline ticket.

Lavinia had long passed the time of life when she was afraid to show her feelings. In August she'd be ninety-five. For her, most physical pleasures had become no more than memories; emotion was the only outlet left for the energy that mentally was still strong in her. She'd listened to Katie, she'd watched her, she'd loved her, and above all she'd dreaded the day she'd have to see her go away.

1

Katie had had no idea, on that April day last year when her mother's parents had met her from the plane, that this would happen to her. They'd driven her to their home in Sycamore Avenue, Brimley, the house where her mother had been brought up; they'd welcomed her; she'd been excited and happy to be with them – for all of them it had been the fulfilment of a dream. Her grandparents, Kate and Rupert Bradley, had taken her to London, to Windsor, to Cornwall, everything had gone as she'd planned. Then, in July, she'd come to Bullington Manor, home of the Mathesons for more than two centuries, and found herself a member of a family who all looked to the great old house and its history as their anchor. Bullington? Or Grandam, Lavinia Matheson, her great-grandmother, a woman whose spirit touched her own? Summer had given way to autumn, autumn to winter, 1961 to 1962. Still she'd stayed, the months slipping by.

The stars had lost their brightness, the sky no longer looked like black velvet, the first hint of dawn was already touching the eastern horizon. She slowed down as she approached a junction and read: 'Oxford 5'. Five more miles and Nigel – second cousin Nigel, is that what he'd be in this jungle of relatives she's discovered? – would be waiting for her. He'd promised to wave her down before the road she was travelling took her into the city. Back home in Alberta she'd read everything she could lay her hands on about England, its traditions and its customs; but this was one she'd missed. The First of May in Oxford, Magdalen's May greeting to the dawn. It was Nigel who'd told her about it, had described how, as the clock struck five and the first colours of dawn lit the eastern sky, the choir on the tower of Magdalen College rent the silence with their May Morning Hymn. To Katie, coming from the New World, it held all the mystique she craved. Now, as she neared the city, in her imagination she saw the first golden rays of the rising sun reaching out to the dreaming spires. It had to be more vivid than reality, larger than life, something that would stay with her when she was home again in Alberta.

There he was! On the early morning empty road he'd recognised the sound of the Manor car, and was waving to her to stop.

'Hi!' There was nothing in her greeting to hint at the way her heart was pounding with excitement. Excitement at the sight of Nigel, or in anticipation for all that lay ahead when they reached Magdalen Bridge? Perhaps it was all one.

'I was afraid you'd oversleep,' Nigel Matheson grinned.

'I set the clock and put it under my pillow. But I didn't need it. I was too excited to sleep at all – well, hardly at all.'

'And me. Move along the seat. I'll drive from here, I know a good place to leave the car. We've the best part of half an hour.' She slithered along the bench seat and he got in behind the steering wheel. 'This is great, Katie! A perfect morning for it too, there hasn't been a sign of cloud all night. It's something I've never missed since I've been up at Oxford. I'm glad you're here to come with me for my last year.'

'Me too. Having you here already, part of the university, I feel I sort of belong, that I'm entitled to share in it.'

'And quite right too.'

Later, as they stood on Magdalen Bridge, he watched her. This was the third year he'd listened to the dawn hymn. He'd been moved not so much by the sound as by the feelings of continuity. Now he gazed at Katie, her curls like burnished gold in the first light, her blue eyes luminous with what was surely a hint of unshed tears. What did it mean to her, this 'cousin' from the New World? As if she were suddenly conscious of his scrutiny, she turned towards him and slipped her cold hand into his. High above them on Magdalen Tower the voices were raised in exaltation. That the choir sang in Latin added to the wonder of the hour. There was no need to understand the words. For Katie all the praise and glory was in the soaring voices. It was springtime; this was England; she felt herself drawn into the mystery and magic of the dawn of the day, the heralding of spring; it was part of the heritage given her by her mother but, more than that, she belonged because of the spirit of Bullington, the natural welcome of the Mathesons and because she was with Nigel.

Soon it was over. Had she imagined the aura of gold that had shed its light on the ancient stone of the buildings? Already, in these few minutes, the wonder was fading, this first day of May no different from any other.

'I'm free all the morning,' Nigel told her, 'you can stay awhile can't you?'

'Sure, I don't need to rush back to Bullington. But, Nigel, I want to remember it here on the bridge just like it was.' She shut her eyes tight, as if that would explain what she meant. 'See, already it's almost properly light, an ordinary day sweeping it all away. Soon there'll be lots of people rushing off to work. It'll be no more than just any old day, not special – magic.'

'You wait here and watch the river, that won't burst into sudden activity. I'll get the car. We'll be out of Oxford before it's opened its eyes and stretched itself.'

An exaggeration and they both knew it. Already cars were crossing the bridge, heading towards the south side of the city and beyond. The bread and butter of the area came from the motor industry.

There was a practical streak in Katie that loved to think of the two faces of Oxford, each so vital. But the mystique of the last half hour elbowed practicality out of the way.

In no time he was back, reaching across to open the car door for her to get in beside him.

'I know just where we'll go. Best bacon and eggs for miles around. We'll take the Abingdon road, drive over the downs. In fact, tell you what I'll do, I'll come right back to Bullington with you afterwards. This place I know is on the A4, not terribly far from there.' He settled comfortably behind the wheel. He'd imagined they would have spent the morning in Oxford, then she would have gone home while he went to join his tutor, ready to immerse himself in a discussion on the repercussions of Gladstone's economic policies.

Suddenly none of that was important.

'Will you have time to get back to college?' she queried.

'Highly unlikely,' came the laughing reply. 'So unlikely that I shan't even try.'

'I ought not to let you skip lectures on my account. Grandam was telling me how important this final year is for you. Your exams are almost here, aren't they?'

'My theory is that what I haven't absorbed in three years isn't going to penetrate my thick skull now.' It was said with such confidence, clearly he wasn't worried by thoughts of failure.

'You'll get your degree OK?'

'I suppose I'm lucky, I've been studying a subject I enjoy. But, to be honest, Katie, I've never flogged myself to death over things that don't interest me. I think I'll get my degree – but how good a one, who knows?'

'Then what? Will you teach? Will you write?'

'God forbid – on both counts. Looking into the future there's no doubt what I'll do – I'll do it well and it'll take all my time.' He didn't elaborate. It was as though he expected her to understand.

'Not teaching? So what else is there? Back home, that's about the usual thing for folk who major in history. Politics? Are you going to try to get into Parliament?'

'Think, Katie, think! An estate like Bullington is a full-time job of work. Don't you see? Grandma – or Grandam as you call her – she can't be there for ever.'

She wouldn't let herself picture Bullington without Lavinia. She rushed into words, anything to draw him on to another track.

'But there are lots of family so much older than you. To be honest, I've never got some of them sorted out. Second cousins, great aunts and uncles . . . Back home it was all so simple. Except for Mom's

4

Aunt Eva Bradley in Calgary, we're just one house of people, all of us living at Higley Creek.'

'Lots of family older than me, yes, but none of them likely to inherit Bullington. You see, Grandma had two sons. Jonathan was the eldest but he was killed in France in 1915 or thereabouts. Charles was the other – my grandfather. He had two sons, Christopher was the elder, that was my old man. Luke, the younger, skedaddled off to New Zealand just after the last war, married out there and is doing very nicely on a sheep farm that could swallow Bullington without noticing. I was still at prep school when my grandfather and my parents were killed – in a plane crash coming back from France.'

'I remember when the letters from home came and Mom heard about it. I remember thinking how dreadful for you, not much older than me and losing you mom and dad and having to go to live with your great-grandmother.'

'Now you know her you won't feel so sorry for me. Of course I felt rotten losing them, they were great. But Bullington has always been – well, it sounds corny but it's no more than the truth, it's always been the centre of the universe as far as I'm concerned. When Grandma gets her call up yonder, inevitably Bullington must fall to me. Grandma knows she can trust me to make a good job of it.'

In the brief glance she gave him, Katie seemed to see him anew. Not just a fresh-faced, good-humoured friend; it was as if she glimpsed into the future, to a time when he would be squire of Bullington. But none of that would happen until Grandam was no longer there. Nearly ninety-five years old, yet still as much in command of the running of the estate as when she'd been widowed over forty years ago. These days a good deal was done from her armchair; when she wanted to visit the stables or the gardens, even when she wanted an hour's thinking time by the lakeside, then she had to be pushed in a wheelchair. But her eyes were as bright as ever, there was little that Lavinia missed. Katie shied away from picturing Bullington without her.

'Time doesn't stand still.' He must have seen into her mind. 'I don't want that day to come any quicker than you do, but nothing stays the same for ever. You asked me what I meant to do with my degree, what sort of a career I'd mapped out. She's a very old lady, Katie. You may think it's presumptuous of me even to suggest it, but I've always had the feeling that Grandma is avoiding Saint Peter's eye until I can be at Bullington for keeps. She's a great lady – and she has the willpower to match.'

Katie believed he was right, but she wished they hadn't talked about it. To accept vaguely that 'one day' Bullington would be his was one thing; the suggestion that Grandam was only waiting for him to relieve her of her responsibilities was harder to take.

He went on: 'The pity of anyone of her age dying is the fund of memories that is lost. Do you realise, Katie, when Grandma was born it was 1867? She came to Bullington as a young bride in the eighties. If only we could all see the pictures that must be imprinted on her mind, the changes in the world all around, yet through it all the core of continuity at the Manor. You felt it too, I know you did. It lays a claim on one.' Young, eager, fun-loving, that's how Katie had seen him. This unexpected glimpse of another side of him must have stemmed from that traditional rite on Magdalen Tower.

'I don't want to think of Grandam not being there. I'll be back home by then. And I want to remember Bullington just as it is.'

'Just as it is is how it will be, that much I promise you.' Then, with a sudden return to his normal cheerful voice: 'And now, Cousin Katie, we are approaching the finest bacon and eggs in the county. Proof? Why else would every lorry driver belt like mad to reach it? See the evidence?'

'Over there? In that long sort of shed place?'

'Sacrilege, woman! It may not look like the Ritz – indeed some of the customers could strike you as travel-soiled! But my friends and I have been frequenting it since first we could take transport on the roads.' Drawing up between two lorries, he jumped out and came to open her door. 'Allow me, madam. I say, but these chap's are going to get more than eggy-bakes to feast their eyes on this morning.' He let his gaze travel from the top of her golden-brown curls to the tip of her high-heeled scarlet shoes. Slight, slim, yet completely feminine in the soft curve of her bust, the small waist and legs that would certainly take minds away from crispy bacon, Katie was a picture. The new style above-the-knee flared skirts which had appeared on the fashion plates and were just beginning to nose their way into the High Streets might have been designed especially for her.

No wonder Nigel was proud to make his entrance with her! With a flourish he offered her his arm.

'Fair Cousin Katrine, allow me to escort you to your table.' Then, with the infectious chuckle she'd come to know: 'And if some dirty devil's slopped his mug of tea over it, allow me to mop it up for you.'

The shadow cast by a Bullington Manor without Grandam was lifted. It was always such fun with Nigel.

And that was the pattern for the rest of the day. He came back to the Manor with her, needed no persuasion to stay to lunch, then in the afternoon the family car was on the road again. This time Nigel was at the wheel with Lavinia beside him; Katie on the edge of the rear seat, her elbows on the back of the front bench and her head almost level with theirs.

Lavinia was enjoying her unexpected outing. Her eyes bright, she looked from one to the other seeming to draw her own strength and pleasure from being with the young ones. She was wide awake, she listened, she missed nothing.

Having deposited Nigel in Oxford, Katie took the wheel and as she drove home talked about the May Day celebrations. She knew she didn't have to explain to Grandam the atmosphere, the wonder of sight and sound, any more than she had to spell out the contrast of breakfast at 'Joe's', nor yet the fun she and Nigel had had.

And, not for the first time in her life, Lavinia silently laid her plans.

With her arms clasped around her drawn up knees, sitting on rough grass that was thick with the wild flowers of spring, Katie watched the still water of the canal. Not a human sound to be heard, just the gentle drone of bees as they hunted for the sweet nectar, persuaded by the sudden warmth that summer had come. Behind her Cleo, the piebald mare she'd come to look on as her own, nibbled at the bounty nature provided, and occasionally stamped a hoof as if a gentle reminder that they were nearly two miles from home.

'OK, old lady.' Katie stood up. 'I guess you're right, time we were heading back. Here, see what I brought for you.' A carrot to munch and Cleo was suddenly in no hurry to leave. Katie waited until the last juicy shred had been swallowed, then mounted for the homeward ride. It was later than she'd thought. Instead of returning the way they'd come, she'd take the quicker and less attractive route, a quarter of a mile or so along the towpath, then up the lane that edged Redman's Paper Works, across the main London to Bath road, along Corder Lane to a seldom used gate into the eastern end of the grounds of Bullington Manor.

With Cleo at a smart trot she was into Corder Lane, about to round a blind bend in the road, when a car came towards them. A lesser rider would have been in trouble! Whatever sort of a mad driver would take a motor car down a narrow country lane at that speed? Whatever sort of driver would see the approaching horse and rider only yards away and stop with a squeal of brakes and a stalled engine?

'You crazy coot! She might have bolted!' Angrily Katie turned on the stranger, at the same time soothing Cleo with a gentle hand.

'Katie O'Hagon! If I didn't know it from the look of you, I'd know it from that voice of home.'

Bad driving was forgotten. 'Home,' he'd said. Perhaps the average Englishman would have known no more than that he came from the

7

other side of the Atlantic. But to Katie – and to the stranger – the western provinces of Canada had a tone of their own.

'Sure I'm Katie. But I don't know you. Did they tell you at the house that I was out riding? Where have you come from? Are you a friend of Grandam's – or of Nigel's?' Yes, that must be it, he must be a student from Canada.

'You don't remember me? No, I guess you wouldn't. We were only kids – well, you were hardly worthy of being called a kid even. Dylan Kitashee.'

Kitashee? An Indian name, surely. His appearance was in keeping, except whoever saw an Indian with eyes like that?

The young man at the wheel of the car had eyes of the most startlingly light blue she'd ever seen, eyes fringed with lashes as black as his hair. Even in the height of summer, no tan could give him a complexion like that, and it wasn't even summer yet. Olive? Darker than olive? So too were the hands that still rested on the steering wheel. It took only a second for her to take in the picture of him, involuntarily to remember a day last autumn when she'd helped harvest the walnuts, the stains on her fingers afterwards. That's how he looked, she decided. Dylan Kitashee?

'I don't remember. Did you come to Higley Creek? When you were a child, you say?'

'Sure I did. And before that. It's from Kilton Down that I remember you. Can you recall when you lived there?'

'Not really. Of course, I remember the folk. Mom and I used to go over there sometimes from Higley.'

The same as with all children, there were some incidents that left an impression. And one of those was pricking her mind now, something that she *almost* remembered.

'Dylan Boy,' he prompted.

'I sort of get something of a picture. The boys and me . . . the woodshed. There was someone older . . . I remember there was someone . . . but I don't think it was a youngster like us.'

The young man laughed.

'You must have been about three – from that size I guess I'd have seemed all of the man I believed myself to be. I'd have been about eleven that summer!' His blue eyes laughed up into hers as she sat mounted by the car. 'I remember that day too. I was chopping the wood for Lottie, and you kids were supposed to be stacking it in the woodshed. But you just sat right by me. "I'm busy watching, Dylan Boy", that was your excuse.'

At the back of her mind was a golden haze of memory, hardly more than a certainty that there had been *somebody* who, little more than a baby though she'd been, she had held in godlike esteem. His words alone might have stirred some of the memories buried in childhood, but it was his eyes that drew her. She felt she was seeing through a lifting haze, that somewhere beyond it the sun was shining.

'You took me on your horse, didn't you? Was that you? Am I dreaming it? Was that the same day?'

'No, that was later. Sure, I used to ride with you. That was before the accident. You remember your father?'

'No. I don't remember much at all before I went to Higley Creek. I can't even think of a time when Mom wasn't married to – well, I call him "Dad", I think of him as Dad.'

She'd heard about it, of course, picked up a snippet here and another one there, until finally she'd asked Lottie, her mother, what had happened. It had been during the war, back in 1942, that her parents had been married: Lottie, who'd grown up in that house in Sycamore Avenue, Brimley, and Neil O'Hagon, a Canadian soldier. He'd taken her back to Kilton Down, the cattle breeding ranch he worked with his cousin and family in Alberta. Katie had been two when she and her mother had gone to Canada, the war just ending. She could understand now some of the things that she wouldn't have questioned then: how hard it must have been for a girl from that sheltered home in Brimley, a girl who'd spent glorious months each summer at Bullington Manor, to find herself in the rough and ready household of the O'Hagon's. She could even understand the things that had never been spelt out to her: round-up time, Neil O'Hagon and the other men walking the great herd the miles to auction – just one woman going with them, a half-breed Indian. No one had ever told her the details that led up to the fight that had brought about the change in their lives, but she knew that it had happened after the auction and the annual binge that was part of it. Neil O'Hagon and his half-wit uncle had gone back to the Indian woman's cabin, there had been a fight. Everyone said that Uncle Donald adored his nephew, yet it had been he who had run the knife into him. So Neil had been killed and, after the Inquest, Donald had been taken to be kept under lock and key in a mental home and the Indian woman had gone away. To Katie it was as if life had started somewhere around that point. She knew that she and her mother had left Kilton Down and for a while had been in Calgary with Aunt Eva, she knew it because she'd been told. But for her, conscious memory began after that, when they were at Higley Creek, only a few miles from Kilton Down and yet so different.

A kaleidoscope of all these things flashed into her mind, all these and Higley Creek too, with Ramsey McFee – or 'Dad' as he'd so truly become – and Lottie married.

9

'I do remember. Well, I remember a bubbly sort of feeling of excitement when you took me on the horse. Feelings – they're what stay with you, aren't they? Not events themselves. I remember a moment when I felt like a queen, sitting high on the horse.'

'You often sat in front of Lottie.'

'Yes, I know.' But it wasn't riding in front of her mother that had elevated her to the ranks of the gods. How blue his eyes were. They seemed to look right into her, gave her a sensation that she'd been here before.

When she'd first come to Bullington Manor she'd had just the same feeling. Nothing was new and strange, it was as if it had been waiting for her to come back. And now this dark young man was nudging life back into memories that had been buried for years.

'What are you doing over here?' Talk of the present, two strangers both far from home, two adults who'd grown distant from the children of so long ago.

'I'm over here on business, I'm at Redman's Paper Works. It was there that I heard about you. Clifford McNaughton told me he'd met someone at the big house, a girl over from Alberta. He told me your name –'

'Mr McNaughton came to dinner last night.'

'Sure, he told me. You're staying with your grandmother, he said.'

She nodded. 'Grandam's my great-grandmother actually. I've been in England more than a year. I was going home, but Grandam's having a big party for her birthday. I think Mom and Dad are coming over for it. I shall wait for that. How long before you go back?'

He was from home, it seemed to unite them. She told herself that was why she found herself inviting him to the Manor for dinner the following evening.

'I'm not late, am I, Grandam? I just met –' Katie raced into the dining room, talking as she came. At Bullington Manor lunchtime was twelve-thirty, five minutes ago. Seeing a visitor, the words died on her lips. She'd been looking forward to telling the old lady about her meeting with Dylan Kitashee, she was excited at the thought of his coming to dinner tomorrow. A glance at their lunch guest and her smile vanished. No, not true. It didn't vanish, but it changed, lost its spontaneity.

'Here she is, Mr Hickstead, this is Katrine. Katie, my dear, Mr Hickstead came to discuss one or two legal things with me. He'll be taking lunch with us.'

Black jacket and pin striped trousers, his thin hair a nondescript grey, his half moon spectacles adding years to the fifty or so he had to his credit, yet when he smiled Katie understood why it was Lavinia put her trust in the solicitor who'd dealt with her affairs for more than twenty years.

'Miss O'Hagon, I'm delighted to meet you. You are enjoying your visit to England?'

Lavinia threw a surprised look in his direction. Visit to England, indeed!

'I've loved every bit of it. Did Grandam tell you, I'm staying on until after her birthday in August? That'll be sixteen months I'll have been here, and I only came for six! I'll go back home sounding as English as all my cousins.'

'There's a good deal of England in you, every bit as much as there is Canada.'

And that sent her mind full circle to where it had been when she'd charged into the room.'

'Grandam, I just met someone from home!'

Using her two walking sticks, Lavinia pulled herself from her armchair to stand very tall and straight. That always helped her get her footing before she walked to the table.

She made sure she was safely balanced before she replied: 'A handsome young feller, hair as black as jet?'

'That's right. He said he'd called here, but he hadn't seen you.'

'I was with Mr Hickstead. We looked out when we heard him come racketing up the drive. Mr Hickstead and I were discussing matters of business. I told Hawkins that on no account was I to be disturbed. Could hardly have failed to be, eh, Mr Hickstead? Driving as though he were on Brands Hatch, then a screech of brakes! I looked out, of course. Now then, Mr Hickstead, if you'll take the seat over there. You ring the bell for them to serve, Katie dear.'

'I've asked him – Dylan – to dinner tomorrow, Grandam. That's all right, isn't it?' She knew it would be. If there was one thing Lavinia liked it was company in the evening.

'Dylan, you say?' Lavinia drew her brows together in a frown. 'Dylan . . .' Now why should that name ring a bell? No, it didn't ring it, that was the sickening part about getting old. The bell was there, it was swinging, but not enough for it to ring and disturb something that slumbered deep in the cotton wool of her silly mind! 'You say he's a friend from home? Someone Lottie and Ramsey know?' Would that give her a clue?

'Mom might remember him. Well, of course she would. But I was too young when we were at Kilton Down. I've just got a hazy feeling. He's over here on business with Redman's, he said Mr McNaughton mentioned being here last night, said something about me – because I

11

came from Canada like him, you see. I bet he was surprised when Dylan knew my name!'

'Dylan who? What's his other name?'

'Kitashee.'

'Ah, Kitashee – over here on business. What a rum world this is turning into.'

For the first time, Katie felt herself distanced from the old lady she's come to love so dearly. Sheltered by generations of security and comfort here at Bullington Manor, what could she know of the struggle of the Indians back home? What did she know of their pride, their ancient traditions, their beliefs steeped in nature? This morning Dylan hadn't talked about his own background, but Katie had recognised the mixed blood in him. Sitting here at the lunch table she felt her hackles rise in his defence; not just his but all his people, all of them her own countrymen.

'I don't understand your meaning, Grandam?' Unflinchingly her gaze met her great-grandmother's. She spoke politely enough, but there was a challenge in her words. Lavinia recognised it and her eyes were the first to look away.

'He'll be very welcome, my dear. Of course, your friends are welcome, you know that.'

The moment passed. Talk turned to Mr Hickstead's family, then to Nigel. Lavinia was cross with herself.

She put me in my place, and I deserved it! I'll make it up to her tomorrow when he comes, I'll show her I didn't mean to sound so superior. Perhaps Nigel could find the time to drive down from Oxford, he's always such a dear, so friendly. She'll see I didn't mean to sound condescending towards the young man. Dylan . . . no, of course I've never heard his name, why should I? Kitashee . . . Well, I'd not forget that in a hurry. It's just that – I seem to half think there's something. Oh, damn getting old! Old and stupid. Best to talk about what's going on in the world today, I haven't had time to let that slip through this sieve I like to call my mind!

The next evening Dylan Kitashee was received with all the courtesy Bullington Manor would have bestowed on royalty. Playing host at Bullington was more important to Nigel than the work he'd meant to catch up on in his rooms at college.

'You've come across to Redman's, Grandma tells me. From where Katie's people are in Alberta, I suppose? What's the connection with the paper works?' Nigel looked at him with frank friendliness, encouraging him to talk.

'I've been away from Alberta for many years,' Dylan said. 'It was chance put me in touch with Katie – the Katie I remembered was just a young kid. I'm in British Columbia these days.'

'Vancouver?' Nigel floundered in his mind, trying to pull together all he knew of the province.

'No, way up north from there. A town called Wyndhamslake. Maybe you won't have heard of it, but it's growing, being put on the map by the timber industry. Its a huge forestry district, the annual cut is a billion and a quarter board feet, and Wyndhamslake is the centre of it.' He spoke with enthusiasm.

'Sounds like a lot of wood. Aren't they killing the goose that lays the golden egg?'

Just for a second Dylan frowned, unsure of the expression. Then: 'Sure, now I see what you mean – destroying the forests, you think? That's gone on a lot in the past, but not now. They're careful. They operate a plan to replace what's felled. Reckon we'll always get wood.'

Lavinia listened, looking from one to the other.

Katie listened, her gaze on Dylan. The fog between her and her early days in Canada was thinning almost enough for her to remember – then, when she thought it was within her grasp, closing down again, leaving her looking on a handsome stranger. One thing hadn't changed: now, as so many years ago, she was "busy watching Dylan".

'And Redman's?' Nigel prompted.

'There's more to forestry than planks of wood,' Dylan laughed. 'A lot of the spruce is thin stuff, not the quality for the sawmills. That's where I come in – and Redman's Paper Company. Together we're working on forming a pulp and paper company. I'm employed by Timber Products of Wyndhamslake. The project is to form a partnership with Redman's, to build a new pulp mill back home and ship the pulp over to them here.'

Lavinia looked at him with a new respect. It seemed a responsible post for a man of his age – for, from her advanced years, he seemed hardly any older than Nigel. He was no fool, though. What he said about the forests, about this town that was the centre of the industry, even at her age she found it exciting. Something that was building for the future, looking forward. Plenty of grit, that's what she liked to see in a man. He must have needed it too to have risen so high in the company. For Katie could try as much as she liked to pretend otherwise, but the world was a hard place if your face didn't fit. But he was handsome by any standards with his high cheekbones and firm jaw. And those eyes, the blue of a winter sky, piercing eyes that seemed to look at you and through you.

Lavinia let her mind wander free. From one to the other she looked at them. Dear Nigel, such an open smile, the world was his friend. And Katie, darling Lottie's Katie, with her tumble of light brown curls, that dimple in her left cheek . . . she wished she could tell Katie her secret, she wished she could see the expression in those dark blue eyes . . . but she couldn't, she could tell no one. Young people, all of them with so much living ahead of them . . . Lavinia's head fell forward. Just for a minute she slept, her dinner forgotten. Around the table the chatter continued, they all pretended they hadn't noticed.

'Dylan,' Katie had a sudden idea, 'I bet you haven't ridden since you arrived.'

'Correct. Some people sit naturally behind the steering wheel of an automobile. But not me. Give me a horse any time.'

As suddenly as she'd fallen into sleep Lavinia woke, sitting straight, eyes wide open as if to defy them to have noticed her lapse. And perhaps she hadn't slipped so very far below the surface of consciousness, for waking with a start she joined in the conversation.

'Then I will,' she told Dylan. 'Any time you care to exercise one, I'll give you a horse gladly. Bullington has always been proud of its stable. It's many years since I've sat a horse. What a joy it was. I remember when the hunt used to move off from the Manor here. Ah, what days they were! What chases we had! I can hear it now, the huntsman's horn, the baying of the pack. Great days! Long time ago . . . so long ago.' Then, pulling her mind back to her visitors: 'But Bullington's still proud of its stable. Sometimes when the Matheson tribe come home – and it is a tribe too – they're keener to see the horses than they are to see me.' But she beamed with satisfaction as she said it. They were as they were, and clearly she wanted them no different.

'I ride every day,' Katie told him, 'I could show you the best places if you like.'

'Tomorrow?' Then to Lavinia: 'I'm obliged to you, Mrs Matheson. More than any other thing I've missed the feel of a saddle under me.'

As he spoke he inclined his head. There was something gravely courteous in his manner. Yet at that very moment the light seemed to pierce the fog in Katie's mind, and memory stabbed. She remembered a feeling of inadequacy when she'd known she was too small to be able to help the boy in the starchy-looking bed . . . surely it must have been him, turning his head away so that no one would see the tears in his eyes? When was that? And where? A row of beds, perhaps a hospital . . . It was all so vague. The only thing that was clear was the need she'd felt to make him happy, the ache in her that she'd not known how to let him know he was loved.

14

Lavinia kept early hours and Nigel had to drive back to Oxford, so the party broke up in good time. Katie went down the front steps to where the cars were parked. She arranged to meet Dylan in the lane by the east gates at six o'clock in the morning (that should prevent the roar of his arrival waking the whole household!), she'd ride Cleo and lead Black Knight ready for him. Then she waved them both on their way, Nigel to move at a steady pace down the long beech-lined drive, Dylan to follow, alternately over-revving the engine and braking, reminding her of a day when first she'd been learning to drive. Out with her mother, they'd stopped for gas, then feeling herself very grand and grown-up she'd pulled away from the filling station in a series of jolts. 'Hang on there,' the attendant had called after her, 'what's that I put in your tank? Kangaroo's milk?'

Tonight she was glad to get to her own room. She wanted to lie isolated by darkness, sure that somewhere in that void she would reach out to what was evading her. If when she'd been a small child at Kilton Down she'd known Dylan so little, how was it that after all these years she could remember the hollow ache inside her at the sight of his tears?

15

Chapter Two

Lavinia was certain there was something she ought to be able to remember. Here in the quiet privacy of her room she would find a way to whatever it was that was teasing the back of her mind. Tonight she'd not let her thoughts ramble, she'd concentrate. She'd make herself recapture things Lottie had told them about the people she'd known at Kilton Down. She'd think herself back to the time of her own visit for Lottie's wedding to Ramsey. Kitashee? Dylan Kitashee? But already she was forgetting her intentions, her thoughts were being diverted.

At her age one of life's remaining physical pleasures was to lie, warm and comfortable, in her soft bed and let her spirit wander where it would. To years when she'd been young, before the turn of the century, when Clifford had brought her here to Bullington Manor as his bride – all of it so long ago, and yet engulfed in the gentle darkness the long span between seemed to vanish. Then there were their children. She could almost hear the clatter of them running down the stairs from the nursery on the third floor. Her lips softened into a smile as she gave rein to her imaginings. Jonathan their firstborn . . . the old wounds of loss had healed with the years. When he'd been killed on the Somme, he and thousands more young men, 'the cream of youth' people had said, she'd believed her bitterness could never grow less. Now she was nearly ninety-five, she never asked herself what she expected of the step she must soon take, but she was filled with the quiet belief that somewhere her spirit would be with Clifford's, and together they'd be united with Jonathan and Charles. Jonathan had been only twenty-four when he'd been killed; Charles, their second son and Nigel's grandfather, had lived more than twice as long. Yet age had no place in Lavinia's nocturnal thoughts, only the anticipation that soon she'd be with them again.

Then her wandering mind moved on. Hester, her eldest daughter, *she'd* had her own griefs, widowed in that same war after only a brief

16

marriage. But Hester was strong; Lavinia might not admit it, but as time had gone on she'd grown a little intimidated by her. Then there was Kate, the youngest, always the delicate one – no one could ever be in awe of Kate. Again Lavinia smiled, but this time her eyes were a light with laughter. Timid, gentle Kate – with a will like iron and the ability to cajole everyone into bending to her wishes! Even as a child that's the way she'd been. And Rupert, that ninny she'd married, seemed to expect nothing more from life than to be a doormat to her. Three good children Kate had had – but of them all Lottie had been the darling of Lavinia's heart. How 'the ninny' had ever sired her she didn't know. Such a dear, jolly child! What a fuss Kate had made when the girl had married that Canadian and gone off to make a new life. Ah, well. Lavinia's smile faded. She knew as well as any of them the heartbreak it had been. But she'd kept her sadness to herself, and had made sure that Lottie had the wherewithal to keep her independence when the time came that she needed it.

Tonight it was Lottie who was uppermost in her mind. What sort of a life had she had, taken from Kate's gentle upbringing and hurled into the rough and tumble of that western home? Whatever the marriage had been, one good thing had come out of it. Katie . . . who'd come to England for six months holiday and stayed for more than a year. Katie . . . who brought joy into the house. Lavinia knew she was being fanciful, but it seemed to her that Lottie had sent Katie back to them as if to compensate for the void her own going had left.

Age does strange things to a mind, it telescopes time. To the old lady lying there with her memories it seemed only yesterday it had been Lottie who rode in the point to point or sat with her by the lakeside, somehow part of the unchanging scene. Katie . . . Ah, that reminded her of what it was she'd set out to think about. This handsome young man, eyes such a striking blue in his dark face. Dylan . . . Dylan . . . She was still reaching into the shadowy memories when she fell asleep.

Dylan heard the sound of the horses. Katie was coming. He'd been waiting for some minutes outside the closed east gates, although it wasn't yet six o'clock. He'd drawn the car off the lane, parking it in the entrance to the drive.

'I thought I'd have to wait for you,' Katie greeted him.

'I thought the same about you.' In repose it would have been difficult to guess his age (Twenty-five? Thirty?), his expression so solemn, thoughtful; yet when he smiled, as he did now, his whole countenance was transformed. His teeth, white and even, looked strong, a strength reinforced by the bone structure of his lean face.

17

'Late, on a morning like this? Just sniff the air, Dylan, all fresh and new. This is my very favourite time of day, I've always loved the early mornings.'

He swung himself into the saddle, the easy grace of his movements reminding her of what he'd said last night about cars not being for him. That sure action confirmed the rider he'd be; she felt she'd known already. As they rode she found it hard to keep her eyes off him.

Not because of who he is, not even because of this funny feeling that deep down he's not a stranger. No, it's because it's pure joy to see him in the saddle. He's lithe, he makes me really know what the word means. It's as if all his movements are natural like an animal's – a panther, a cat. Poetry in motion – watching him makes me understand about that too. Not in a car though! Her eyes lit with silent laughter as she thought of him at the steering wheel. I've never seen anyone so out of tune with a car.

They'd reached the edge of the downs, or the Common as it was known locally. With a quick look back at her he put Black Knight into a gallop. Katie wasn't going to be left behind! Oh, the joy of it, the wind blowing through her hair, the clear sweet smell of morning, the pounding of the horses' hooves.

Later they stopped, high on the open grassland, looking over the wide countryside, Newton Dingley little more than a distant church steeple, the canal a ribbon of silver.

'Dylan, tell me about the things I can't remember. Why did I know you at Kilton? Were you a neighbour or something?'

'I belonged to the settlement out beyond Radley. Round-up times my mother used to work at Kilton Down bringing in the cattle. Your Grandmother O'Hagon was pretty good to me. I used to be left at the house, they seemed to expect that I would be. When you're young you don't work things out. You take it as it comes, I guess.'

"The settlement" he'd said. That must be the Indian settlement. Wasn't there where her father and uncle had been on night of the fight? Could it have been Dylan's mother they'd been with? She didn't ask.

'Were you ever in hospital? There was someone . . .?'

'That was a bit later. My mother moved away and I had plans to stay behind. I must have been a wild sort of kid. I could pretty well keep myself going with what I could catch in my traps – or so I thought.'

'You mean she moved off and left you?'

He shrugged. 'As things were I reckon she thought she was doing me a favour.' He didn't elaborate, and something in his manner prevented her delving.

18

'So what happened? Anyway, how about school?'

'Up till that point they'd not had much luck in dragging me in to the school in Radley.' His face took on a closed-in look as he remembered. 'It was Ramsey who made me see it was a challenge.'

'Ramsey? You mean Dad?'

'He talked to me like no one ever had, influenced me more than any person before. Yes, that was me in the hospital.' Again that smile that started in his eyes before it reached his mouth. 'And you know something else? It was you, Katie, who got me there. I was fishing down by the "cut backs" – it was during the period I was living rough. You were on the path at the top with Lottie and you saw me. I heard you shout to her, something like: "Look! there's the Dylan Boy." And before she could stop you you came slipping and sliding down the slope – you know how steep it is – there was no way you could hold yourself back, you went straight into the river. I got you out, but there was a rockfall – oh, nothing really serious, just gave me an unlucky hit and knocked me out. You probably don't remember.'

'Sort of, I do.'

'Come on, let's ride. Forget the past. The only important thing about any of it is what use we made of it, whether we let ourselves take what got dealt or whether we shaped it the way we wanted.'

By now they were moving forward at a steady trot. She could feel that he was about to put Black Knight into a canter. Talking wouldn't be so easy then.

'Well, you must have done that. You say you played hookey and didn't go to school, but you must have studied something and done better than most or how is it you're sent over here for this wood pulp company you work for?'

'I must have been eleven or twelve when Ramsey made me see. I could read and write, I knew about dollars and cents – not that I had much contact with them! The kids from the settlement went in to Radley to school. You wouldn't understand. It was as if having a white skin put you in a magic circle. We were outside it.'

'But that's awful! I went to that school. Were we like that to the children from the settlement? Children keep so much in their own groups – them as well as us.'

'There! Even you! "Them . . . us".'

'You know I didn't mean it that way. Dylan, I'm sorry –'

'Sympathy!' He spat the word. 'I didn't want it then and I don't want to hear it now. It was Ramsey who made me see what a fool I was being, playing hookey, running away from the contempt I could feel in that schoolhouse. He didn't show me gushing sympathy for being what I was, he pointed out the commonsense of doing something to help my people. Outsiders couldn't do it – oh, they might treat them to hand-outs but only one of their own sort could earn respect for them. Until Ramsey talked to me, no one made me see how important it was – that if I wanted to see things changed, then I needed learning to do it.'

'All society can't be the same, can't even want to live the same sort of lives. The ethnic Indians have their own culture. What did you want to change?' Yet surely she knew what it was he meant.

'If you'd been born of an Indian tribe you'd not ask me. My people have a history to make us as proud as any – prouder than those who plundered what by rights was ours. The moon shines as pale on my people as on yours, the stars shine as bright. Ramsey made me see I had a duty to learn all I could, not to be content to do as well as those white-skinned rivals who shunned those of my people, but to do better, to take up the challenge for those who couldn't do it for themselves.' Here spoke the fighter, the man with a mission.

'Seems you did that, Dylan. You must have climbed pretty high in your business.' She'd heard the bitterness, even hatred, in his tone. It set him apart from the boy she almost remembered. 'Race you to the copse.' And without a backward glance she was off. She wanted to find again the gaiety of the morning, she wanted to share with him the carefree freedom of the empty downs, the two of them held together because they were both Canadians – not one a half-breed Indian, shouldering all the injustices meted out to his race and the other an Anglo-Saxon, descended in part from English gentry.

It seemed he too wanted to put the past behind him, let the moment be enough.

As they arranged to meet again at the same time next morning she was struck by the realisation that she'd never experienced this feeling before. Excitement? Eagerness? A sort of wild confused longing for something out of reach? No, not quite any of these things. Elation that lifted her apart from the normal things of living. Tomorrow . . . same time tomorrow.

In the fog at the back of her memory was a small girl's hero worship. But that could have nothing to do with the man life had made of him, the woman she'd become.

Lavinia had gone to sleep with the question on her mind. In the early light of morning she half woke, sure there was something that last night had eluded her. For a second it was clear. Dylan Kitashee . . . Rosie Kitashee . . . everything was clear. In another second it was gone again, memory was lost. She'd always acknowledged herself to be a sentimental hoarder as far as Lottie was concerned. In all the eighteen years every one of her letters had been kept. The long shaft of morning sunlight streamed across the room, throwing its beam on the cupboard where the letters were kept. In there would be the missing piece to the puzzle.

'Up at the house they'll be relieved to see you back, Miss Katie,' Jo Dibbens, the stableman, met her as she rode into the yard. 'You leave the horses to me and scuttle indoors soon as you can. Seems the mistress has had a fall. The doctor's been with her some time. They're waiting for the ambulance so Jenny just came across from the kitchen and told me.'

Katie didn't wait to ask questions, she dismounted and passed both sets of reins to him then ran towards the house. Two at a time she took the wide steps leading to the front entrance, then across the marble-floored hall and up the elegantly curving staircase to the gallery above. Reality had caught up with her, planting her feet on the ground and leaving no room in her mind for confusion or elation. Grandam had had a fall. At her age bones broke easily. That was what reason told Katie. Yet her mind wouldn't listen to reason. Just as she'd shied away from Nigel's talk about a Bullington Manor without Lavinia, so now she wouldn't let herself face what a fall might mean to a woman of nearly ninety-five.

Knocking and entering in one movement, she ran into the bedroom.

'Grandam? What did you do, Grandam?'

On the bed the old lady lay, like a stranger, one side of her face sagging, the eye closed, the corner of her mouth pulled down. The other eye was open but stared blankly at the ceiling.

'Miss O'Hagon,' Doctor Holsworthy turned as he heard her, 'I'm glad you're back. I've telephoned for an ambulance. I'm afraid she won't recognise you. Perhaps I could have a word outside.'

The patient wouldn't have been aware of what was said, but he'd had a great liking and respect for the matriarch of Bullington for many years, and couldn't bring himself to speak about her as if she weren't there. So outside the bedroom door he told Katie as much as he could, which was that Lavinia had had a stroke. She must have got out of bed during the night. When she was found this morning she'd been half way across the floor, her sticks lying nearby. When she fell he didn't know, but she'd been very cold. A woman of less stamina wouldn't have lived. However, his examination had told him that she'd broken her hip, so easily done when bones became brittle with age.

'But she looks so strange.'

21

'The stroke has taken the use from her right side. You notice the eye is closed, the face slipped. As I say, she is a remarkable woman, one mustn't assume there'll be no improvement. But at present all we can do is be thankful that she is unaware of what's happening.'

Back in Lavinia's room Katie looked down at the old lady. At that first sight the change had come as a shock. But now, knowing what had happened and what had caused the unfamiliar expression, it was easy to see the Grandam who meant so much to her. She took her left hand, a hand that seemed no more than bones covered with wrinkled skin, the rings she wore even at night only held on by the fact that her knuckles were disproportionately large.

She tried to take in what the doctor was saying: hospital, X-rays, intravenous feeding . . . It was Grandam he was talking about. Katie bent over her. Surely she could see?

But if Lavinia could she gave no indication of it.

By mid-morning the ambulance had taken her. These days Bullington Manor employed no more than half the staff it had kept in times gone by, but from Mrs Moggs the housekeeper, to Jenny the kitchen maid, to Bill Huffkin the under-gardener, there wasn't one who didn't watch the vehicle's slow progress down the long drive.

Katie telephoned the family. Could it have been only last evening that Grandam had talked about them to Dylan? '. . . when the tribe come . . .' Now the tribe must be told. She was glad to be able to do something useful. By the time they could travel to the hospital where she'd been taken perhaps her broken hip would have been set or pinned or whatever they did to bones that were too difficult to plaster, and she would have started to come back to them. The doctor had said that many people did recover. That at ninety-five everything must be weighed against her was something that Katie wouldn't even consider.

Lavinia had had four children. Only two were left. Hester, Katie's great-aunt, lived in Warwickshire in the dower house of Claygate Hall, her late husband's family seat now in the charge of her son Alistair and his wife Claudia. Then there was Kate, Katie's grandmother. There was no ancestral home for Kate Bradley, married to a retired chartered accountant in the small town of Brimley, the whole of her married life spent at number 14 Sycamore Avenue. Built in the first decade of the century, it was a solid family house with six bedrooms and a garden large enough to have boasted its own tennis court in the days when the young Bradleys had been living at home. In fact last summer, with the event of Katie coming from Canada, Rupert, Kate's husband, had marked out the court and even bought a new net.

First Katie called Claygate Hall and Alistair was fetched to the telephone. She always felt that she should stand straighter than straight when she spoke to him, she was never at ease with his clipped way of speaking. Recently he'd retired from a career in the Army, having risen to the rank of brigadier. Now he listened to what she had to tell him, his manner efficient and unemotional as he asked for details of where Lavinia had been taken, and the telephone number of Dr Holsworthy – which Katie felt was a slur on her own capability to explain the situation.

'I'll drive Mother down as soon as I've had a talk with Holsworthy. You'd better see rooms prepared in case we come to Bullington. It will depend on what we find when we get to the hospital. Have you spoken to Aunt Kate yet?'

'To Granny? No, I rang you first. Next I'll speak to Nigel, if I can get hold of him. Then I'll ring Granny and Grandad. I know she'll be dreadfully upset.'

Of them all, it was her grandmother she dreaded telling. She'd known that at Claygate Hall they'd deal with the practicalities, accept the news without emotion; even Nigel, who cared more for Lavinia than for any living person, would rise to the occasion with the same fortitude. But Granny? Her heart ruled her head. It wasn't in her nature to be able to hide her grief. Katie would have given a lot to have spared her, but there was no escaping.

'Humph.' Not much more than a grunt, but it told her just what Alistair thought. 'No doubt she'll turn the taps on. I hope she pulls herself together before your grandfather takes her visiting the hospital.'

Katie sprang to her grandmother's defence.

'After all it is *her* mother. You can hardly expect her not to feel anything!'

'No bigger abomination than a weeping woman. Better by far to size up the situation and decide the best constructive use one can be. Well, my dear, I'll leave you to handle your grandparents. I'll go across to the dower house and see Mother. At least I know I shan't get histrionics from her.'

'Hey, that's a rotten –' But the click at the other end of the line told her that Alistair had gone.

Next she tried to contact Nigel but he wasn't obtainable so the best she could do was leave a message that he should ring her when he came in.

Histrionics indeed! Her uncle's criticism still rankled as she asked the operator for the Brimley number and waited for the sound of Kate Bradley's voice. She was prepared for tears, panic, and had nothing but sympathy for her grandmother. Of course it would be a shock to her. Because Grandam had weathered so many storms, had outlived members of the family far younger than herself, it was impossible to imagine her not being there.

'Your grandfather isn't even home. Fancy, hearing news like this when I'm all by myself. Just when I need him with the car.' Kate didn't have to see her to know she was crying, the tears were in her voice. 'It's Thursday, his day for the Rotary Club. Oh dear, oh dear. You say Mother doesn't recognise anyone? But she'd know *me*, I'm sure she would. Oh dear. We'll get to the hospital just as soon as we can, Katie. Listen to me, dear, if Mother isn't at Bullington Manor there's no point in your staying there on your own. Drive back here to us. Your room's ready. You know how much we both want you to be here.'

'No, Granny, I'll stay here. They may not keep Grandam long. Once they've done whatever they have to do to her hip, they may let her come home. She'll be glad to have me, I can do things for her.'

'If they let her come home, and I can't think they will,' Kate croaked, the sound bringing Alistair's words back to Katie, 'but if she does get back to Bullington it will only be if she has nurses to care for her. There won't be anything for you to do. If anyone needs you, Katie, it's me. I'm alone in this house hour after hour. I'd look forward so much to these first summer days, imagined you taking the old bicycle out – remember how you enjoyed it all last year, bluebell time . . .' Her words were lost as she swallowed a sob that rose in her throat.

'I'll come back soon, Granny. I must see how Grandam goes on first though. If we engage a nurse I expect she'll soon be home, don't you?' It was herself she was trying to reassure. 'Then you could come here to stay. Isn't that the best thing?' Then, turning the subject away from a return to Brimley: 'I've spoken to Uncle Alistair, he's telling that side of the family. I couldn't get hold of Nigel so I left a message for him to ring me. When he comes to Bullington, Granny, I don't want him to find no one here. She's been his family for so long.'

Had they been together talking instead of thirty-five miles apart then she might have followed the workings of Kate Bradley's mind.

'You're right, dear, Nigel will be dreadfully worried when he hears the news. You stay there and keep him company. You two get along very well, I know you do. Mother has so often spoken of your being together. It pleased her so much.'

'Sure we do, I like Nigel lots.'

'And Bullington – what was the expression I heard you use? As if subconsciously you'd remembered it since you were a baby. Yes, you stay and wait for Nigel, he'll be glad to have you there.'

24

'He was here only yesterday. We had someone to dinner, someone who's over from British Columbia, visiting Redman's.' She started to explain about Dylan.

But the last thing her grandmother wanted was to hear about a visitor from the other side of the Atlantic. Canada had claimed Lottie and had taken Katie, the baby she'd adored, away from her; until last year when Lavinia had sent an air ticket for her eighteenth birthday Katie had been lost to them since she was two years old. No, she didn't want to listen to the details of someone visiting from British Columbia.

'And Nigel came home especially to play host?' Well now, that was encouraging. Even upset as she was with this dreadful news about her mother her imagination was leaping ahead. 'Quite right that he should, of course. Oh dear,' with another sniff, 'however well she may rally, it can't be for long. One thing is certain though, she'll be content to know she need have no worries over Bullington's future, not with Nigel there.'

'Of course she'll get over it, Granny! Dr Holsworthy said that her constitution is incredibly strong.'

'I do wish your grandfather would come home. I think I shall telephone to the Tudor Rose – that's where he and his Rotary Club friends meet. When he hears how upset I am he won't wait for lunch, he'll come home and drive me to the hospital. It's not the same for any of you others. After all, she is *my* mother. And soon I won't have her. Both of them gone – her and Father too. It's like the end of an era to think of her not being there.'

'I'm not thinking of it. She's not gone.' Kate spoke defiantly, as if her own strength would help Lavinia.

Misunderstanding her tone, Kate's snivelling turned into full-blown weeping.

'I can't expect you to know what I'll be losing . . .'

'I'll ring off, Granny, so that you can get on to the Tudor Rose like you said. When you've been to the hospital you will telephone me won't you?'

The conversation left Katie feeling out of tune with her grandmother – and with herself too for not having more patience.

It seemed like hours since she'd watched the ambulance make its steady journey down the drive but, looking at her watch, she saw it was less than thirty minutes. There could be no news for ages. She needed activity. She wished she could go out, walk to the lake perhaps, but until she'd spoken to Nigel she must wait near the telephone. She felt so helpless.

The sound of a car sent her to the window. Even before she recognised him she knew from the sound of the engine who it was.

25

Dylan! Breaking violently he brought the car to a sudden standstill at the same time as opening the door, ready to jump out. Two at a time he leapt up the front steps. Built in the mid-eighteenth century Bullington Manor had all the elegance of the period, with wide stone steps leading to a magnificent entrance. Dylan saw none of it – all he saw was Katie waiting for him in the doorway.

'What happened? I was afraid you'd had a fall after I left you. Someone said an ambulance had come from here? I thought . . .' Looking at her, his tone changed. Gently he led her across the great hall and through the open door into the morning room, then turned her round to face him. 'Katie, don't cry.' He pulled her towards him.

Katie didn't cry easily. So why now?

'It's Grandam,' she sniffed, feeling in the pocket of her breeches for her handkerchief. Briefly she explained. But she hadn't cried when she'd telephoned around the family. It was as if being with Dylan had melted away all her reserve. Just to be able to stay like this . . . he didn't loosen his hold, she didn't try to move away. 'Everything was perfect there on the Common, and all the time she must have been lying on her bedroom floor, all alone, cold, not knowing.' His chin was caressing her forehead, she felt the touch of his lips on her hair. How could she feel this wild joy? Why was she crying? Was it unhappiness or were tears some sort of a safety valve for the emotion that tugged at every nerve in her body? Her cheeks were wet with tears, her eyes were bloodshot, she knew they were as she raised her face to his. Then everything else was forgotten as his mouth covered hers and her lips opened to his, hungrily, clinging.

And just as suddenly, reason returned.

'No, don't. We hardly even know each other. It's because of Grandam, it's thrown everything. Dinner last night, a ride this morning – we're strangers. Let me go!'

His hold loosened, but his hands were firm on her shoulders.

'Us – strangers? Katie, what's time got to do with how well folk know each other? When I was told an ambulance had driven out of the gate here, I guess I knew in that moment just how well you and me know each other. Not just the few hours now, not even the time you say you can't remember properly when we were kids, but all the time in between too. I figure that your memory might have let go of things, but your heart hung on to them.'

It was crazy, she told herself. Yet she wanted to believe that what he said was true, never in her life had she wanted anything so much. But it was madness.

'I want just to think about Grandam.' She was being a coward and she knew it.

26

'And so you should. And while you're thinking about her, just be sure that what I say is true.'

'The family are coming,' she said apropos of nothing. 'Uncle Alistair will be bringing Great-Aunt Hester, perhaps others too. Nigel's sure to come home.'

'You can't run away, Katie. Neither can I. Just as surely as the sun and the moon have their place in the firmament, so we have ours here on the earth, together.'

'How can you talk like that? Two days ago we'd only just met!'

'I am saying that it is ordained that we belong together.'

The shrill bell of the telephone sounded in the hall.

'That'll be Nigel.' Relief mingled with regret. She was floundering out of her depth, yet just beyond the reach was something – something that vanished with the interruption.

'I'll go. Today you belong to your family. Tomorrow at six o'clock you will be mine again.'

As she explained to Nigel what had happened she heard the roar of the engine, then the tyres on the gravel drive. Dylan had gone.

"The tribe" never waited to be invited to Bullington. Lavinia liked to think of it as home to all of them. Children, grandchildren and then great-grandchildren had all sailed their toy boats on the lake, discovered the best trees to climb, organised tournaments on the tennis courts, ridden in the local gymkhanas – in fact, felt they had a rightful claim on the place.

Alistair drove his mother to the hospital, arriving just as Rupert Bradley was taking a tearful Kate home to Brimley.

'There's no point in staying,' Kate sniffed. 'Can't believe it . . . Mother . . . it's as if she's breathing but not really living at all.' Today she didn't resist Rupert's hand holding her elbow.

Kate had been the youngest, she'd taken it for granted that she should have been thoroughly spoilt by the rest of the family. Now she turned her brimming blue eyes on her elder sister.

'I take it you've talked to someone in authority?' Hester spoke to Rupert. But she'd known her brother-in-law for forty-four years, long enough not to expect anything decisive from him. Sometimes she'd reprimanded her mother for referring to him as "the ninny", but in truth her own opinion of him was no higher and she turned a deaf ear at Claygate Hall where he was nicknamed "Drupert".

'There was only a young nurse,' he explained apologetically. 'I did ask her if the Sister was available but I'm afraid she wasn't in her office.'

'I knew you were coming, I knew you'd see to things,' Kate brushed his words aside, 'and with Mother as she is there's nothing we could do. She doesn't even know. It's awful.'

'We'll go in and see what can be arranged. In Clementine Ward, you say? Leave it with me. I'll telephone you later. You'll be going back to Brimley, I suppose, it's easy enough for you to visit from there. I shall stay a while at the Manor.'

Kate nodded. It would be all right now. Hester had come to take control.

As Rupert opened the car door for her she mumbled her thanks but the look she turned on him held no sign of gratitude. It told him that once again he'd let her down. They'd been the first of the family to arrive at the hospital, he'd been the first man, and what had he done? Stood helplessly at the end of the bed . . . meekly accepted that there was no doctor available for him to talk to . . . gone to look for Sister and come back without finding her . . . let the decisions wait for someone else. Kate was humiliated by his inadequacy.

He drove silently back to Brimley, aware that again he'd disappointed her.

No one refused Hester. She told the young nurse she wanted to speak to the Sister; the Sister was found, Hester was taken to her office. Enquiring the name of the consultant in charge of Lavinia's case she was given not only his name, but it was suggested she might like to talk to him.

'He is still in the building. If you care to wait in here, I'll see if I can find him to have a word with you.'

'I'd appreciate that,' Hester thanked her. So she did appreciate it, but the suggestion didn't surprise her. She would have expected nothing less.

Ten minutes later it was all settled. Had it been left to Alistair the end result would have been the same, but Hester wasn't a woman to shirk her responsibilities. Her mother was to be taken to Sydney House, a private nursing home run by Mr Osborne, the consultant. Here she would have every care and comfort until she was considered fit to return to Bullington. That Sydney House was about mid-way between the hospital and Brimley was a bonus, it would make visiting so much easier for Kate.

Alistair returned to Claygate Hall, leaving Hester at the Manor until her mother was settled in her new surroundings, if "settled" was the word for anyone as unaware as she was. They all went to see her, even Nigel to whom acquiring his degree was less important than filling the role he already felt was his at the Manor. One after another they spent hours with her. Kate wept over her; Rupert hovered anxiously, ready to be of use if he was called on; Katie talked to her, sure that at some stage there would be a flicker of recognition; Hester did *The Times* crossword puzzle, checking between each clue that there had been no change.

Wet or fine, each morning at six o'clock Katie rode to the east gate, leading Black Knight. Neither she nor Dylan had referred again to those few minutes at the Manor. The sun and the moon had their places in the firmament – but that her place and his were pre-destined together might have been a dream conjured up in her imagination.

It was meeting Katie coming out of Sydney House that Kate tried to persuade her to come home to Brimley.

'You stayed at the Manor to be with Nigel – and that I could understand. But he's back at Oxford most of the time, I know he is, I've talked to him here at the Nursing Home. It's not fair that Hester gets your company. You're not *her* grand-daughter, you're mine. I know Mother gave you your ticket to come over, but she did it for my sake because she knew how much I wanted you with me. Come home to us, Katie. Soon you'll be wanting to be off back to Canada. All the years I dreamed of you coming to be with us and it'll be over and you've spent so much of your time at Bullington. I can understand it, of course, there's more for you there than in our little place –'

'Oh, Granny, what rubbish you talk. You know it's not like that. I promise I'll come back to Brimley very soon. It's just . . .' Her voice trailed into silence. There was so much she wished she could say, but something warned her against it. Her grandmother was too worried and upset to understand.

So not for the first time Kate Bradley let her hopes wander down the wrong track. Any day Nigel would be home at the Manor, finished with Oxford for good.

The next afternoon, though, it was Hester who told her: 'Katie won't be coming today. She's gone to London.'

'But I saw her yesterday! She didn't say. I wish she'd told me. I could have gone up with her, I would have loved that.'

'It was arranged quite suddenly. You know what these young people are.' Always confident herself, Hester had no doubt that Katie would be equally capable of looking after her own affairs. 'Last night she had a 'phone call. A friend over here from Canada, she said. She'll be home tomorrow, I believe.'

'I have an early meeting with someone in London in the morning, so I shall travel up tonight. It means I'll have to miss our ride tomorrow,' Dylan had said to Katie when he'd phoned yesterday evening. Then a

29

pause. Had the idea only that moment occurred to him? 'Katie, I'll be free soon after lunch. Come up and meet me, please? The city is not for me, but it's unfamiliar to us both, we could discover it together. Please.'

'To meet in the afternoon. We'd not have long.'

'I'll reserve a room for you at the hotel.' She'd known he was unsure of himself, she could tell by the way he spoke. 'Please, Katie. A room for you and a room for me. I promise you.'

If he'd said nothing about the two rooms she would have taken them for granted. But the fact that he felt he had to reassure her had made her heart beat faster, had carried her forward down the slippery slope she'd already started on. Just the two of them, strangers in London, but not strangers to each other.

'Where shall we meet?' She'd given him her answer.

London hummed with excitement. It was a city for the young in this summer of 1962, a city that made Katie and Dylan conscious that that was what they were – young, carefree, untrammelled by sober responsibility. She'd wanted them to see London together, two Canadians on a journey of discovery. She'd not imagined it could be like this; as if here amongst six million strangers they were suspended in time and place, these hours together having no connection with their roots across the sea, nor yet with Bullington, with Redmans, with career or family.

She'd been to London before, there had been visits with her grandparents. They'd taken her to the National Gallery, to Westminster Abbey and St Paul's Cathedral; with them she'd waited in the crowd outside the gates of Buckingham Palace to watch the Changing of the Guard and taken a steamer trip downstream from Westminster listening to the guide as he pointed out the modern Festival Hall and the ancient Monument that marked the place where the great fire of London had started. Now today with Dylan she remembered those other occasions as colourless – then was ashamed of her thoughts. Of course she'd enjoyed it all, it had been the realisation of a dream to see all those things. But this was different! Boutiques crowded with clothes, clothes for the young . . . the beat of music tempting one inside . . . music that belonged to today, to youth.

In some dimly lit cellar bar they danced the evening away. The music came from a group of four young men, two with guitars, one with a bass, while the fourth was a drummer. It was the drummer who set them dancing with such wild abandon, his beat never faltering as he built to a frenzied climax. Katie and Dylan were caught up in an emotion that found expression in dancing. Twenty years before and a quickstep would have held all the same passion; but theirs was the generation of 'the twist'. Shoulders, waists, hips, arms, legs, they danced with their whole bodies, touched, moved apart, together again, twirled, swayed, rocked, wriggled, excited by the motion and the pounding of the drumbeat. And like youth of every age, they were sure they were discovering something new. She wanted the evening never to end.

But end it did and they found themselves outside in the July night. All around them was noise, people being turned out as the doors were shut. In that dimly lit, brick-walled room, they had all been part of the scene; out here, by common consent, Dylan and Katie moved away. He hailed a cruising taxi and they were driven to Westminster Bridge. Here was another London. Nowhere is ever quiet in this city that never sleeps, but standing looking over the parapet into water that glistened with reflected lights, the scene belonged just to them. Traffic hurried by, even pedestrians passed without curiosity, there was nothing new or interesting in a courting couple in the shadows between the lights on the bridge. Katie's world stretched as far as Dylan. In her mind she still heard the echo of the drumbeat, the throb of the guitars.

Since the morning when Lavinia had been taken away in the ambulance he'd not kissed her again; the memory had the quality of a dream. Until now. She was drawn close to him, pulled as if by some magnetic force. Vaguely she was aware of people walking past them on the footpath, too disinterested even to notice the young couple locked in each other's arms: the beauty and the sadness of a big city, the joy and the loneliness.

In those moments they both knew the second room wouldn't be used. Tonight was their own. What was it he had said to her about the sun and moon having their rightful place in the firmament, just as here on the earth so too did they, together? Vaguely she was surprised that she had no feeling of guilt for what she knew was ahead of her. Just for a second she thought of home at Higley Creek, her mother, Ramsey – or Dad as he'd become; she even thought of Lavinia, and in a distant way of Nigel. But all of them were far away, they couldn't come between her and Dylan. The day had belonged just to them, and so would the night.

'When I go home I shall take you with me,' he told her as the pale dawn lightened the patch of sky they could see through the hotel bedroom window.

'I know. Of course I shall come with you.' She'd never been more certain about anything. 'When, Dylan? Mom and Dad are coming next month, they'd planned it for Grandam's birthday. I don't want to tell the others until we tell them. Do you mind if we keep it a secret?'

'It's not important. You know and I know. Nothing can alter what is ordained for us. So, my Katie, we will keep it our own secret if that is the way you want.'

She stretched luxuriously.

'Want? I don't think I want a single thing. I've never woken up feeling like this, it's frightening that everything is so perfect.'

He laughed with a sudden change of mood, moving towards her. 'Not want? Oh, but you do, you want what I want. Don't you? Don't you?' He knew she did.

Last night she had felt their first coming together in love had been holy, blessed and guided by an unseen spirit; later, reaching out to each other, isolated by darkness, they had been driven by passion straining towards the goal they knew would bind them. This morning there was love, there was desire, but there was laughter too. And she was glad. All their moods, all that they were, belonged to each other.

By afternoon they were back on the platform of Newton Dingley Halt. Their twenty-four hours was a bubble of perfection, floating out of reach nothing could ever destroy it.

For many years it had been tradition that Newton Dingley Summer Show and Gymkhana should be held in the meadows of Bullington Manor. As long ago as January the Show Committee had held a meeting setting the wheels in motion. There was no thought that plans should be changed at this stage.

'I won the cup last year,' Katie told Dylan. 'When Mom was a girl she always used to ride here, she had the cup, oh, way back, somewhere in the thirties, and she had lots of rosettes. We'll both enter, shall we?' And even as she said it she knew that if Dylan took part no other man would stand a chance.

The day of the Show was suddenly warm, coming after outbreaks of rain. The gates to the meadows were bedecked with bunting; the Newton Dingley Band had set up their music stands in the usual place at the far end, away from the gymkhana ring; at one stand was a leather worker from East Hagley, a neighbouring village; at another a display of tatting put on by members of the Women's Institute; then there were jams and pickles made by the Young Wives' Club to raise money to send a party of children to the seaside for the day; from Millbrook Farm a stall of cheeses; from a firm of glass makers a demonstration of glass blowing; the local scout master was calling through a loud hailer encouraging folk to 'Roll a Penny down to Win

– every penny you lose helps towards the new scout hut'. On the southern end of the field a queue waited outside the fortune teller's tent. They all knew that under Madame Estelle's heavy disguise – which was uncertain whether its origins were oriental or Romany – lurked Edith Briggs from the butcher's pay desk, but to admit it would be to spoil the fun! And the tea tent, that was a sight and smell like nothing else: the warm, damp grass inside the marquee, the steaming urns, sandwiches with their corners already curling, home made cakes an example of the varying degrees of talent in the village, the clatter of plates and a constant jabber of voices.

'You want some tea?' Dylan sounded surprised.

'Not because I need it. It's just that I want to be in here – just sniff it, Dylan.' Then, when he carried their tea and two rock cakes to their table: 'Get the feel of it, we both must. Next year it'll all be happening just exactly the same, but we shan't be a part of it. Have you ever seen anything like the Show? I came last year. There was a thunderstorm in the middle, but people put tarpaulins over their stalls and rushed in here to shelter. Then when it was over everything carried on just as if nothing had interrupted it.'

'You will miss all this, Katie.'

'Yes. But now I've seen it, I'll always have it. I read a notice in a magazine the other day, it was some silly article about slimming and the heading was "We Are What We Eat". That may·be true, but "we are what we experience", "we are what we see". I guess all this will always be part of me. And you too Dylan.'

'I shall remember it, yes. But part of me? I look at it – I do not feel it, here.' He tapped his chest. 'This is not where I belong. Nor you, Katie. You belong with me.'

The air was heavy with the sweet smell of the grass; across the meadow came the sound of the Newton Dingley Brass Band. 'I Could Have Danced All Night', the song everyone was humming this year.

'Oh! That's the children's event Mr. Harkin's announcing. It'll be us soon. We must get ready.' Katie was already on her feet.

Nigel was mounted and waiting at the entrance to the ring as Dylan rode out on Black Knight. There were six other men, young farmers, older farmers' sons and the owner of the local riding school. But from the outset there was no competition. As the bar was raised one by one they fell out. Only Dylan was left, he and Black Knight taking each jump with the same graceful ease.

'Bravo,' Nigel congratulated him, but there was no smile in his voice. It surprised Katie; she'd known Nigel beaten at tennis, she'd seen the visiting village team's fast bowler get him out for a duck, but his good humour had never faltered.

It was late evening by the time the Show was packed away for another year and Dylan had driven off bearing the cup. And it was Hester, not Nigel, who said to Katie what had been in all their minds.

'Riding is in his blood, I dare say. As I heard someone saying, we ought to have had archery laid on for him. He must be adept with a bow and arrow.'

It was all too much for Katie.

'Well, you'd better all get used to him. I'm going to marry him!' It was the first time she'd actually put it into words. No wonder her anger evaporated at the sound. 'We're only waiting until Mom and Dad come before we tell folk. They're fond of Dylan, they always were.' Silence. 'Don't you tell them first will you, Aunt Hester? I've got it all planned. I'm going to take them to the White Swan where he's staying then see if they recognise him after all this time. Promise me that you won't tell Mom he's here and spoil it.'

'I won't mention him to your mother. But don't get your hopes up. You're building trouble and heartbreak even to consider it. What Mother would say if her mind was clear enough for her to understand, I hate to think.'

'Grandam made him welcome here. She's never mean-minded.'

Hester's straight back became even straighter. But she said no more.

Katie drove to the White Swan. She and Dylan had supper in his room. It was something she often did. Here, with him, she stamped down the echo of Hester's warning; in his arms it had no power.

Lavinia was making some progress. Her consciousness had returned, even her face was restored to normal, but her speech was barely intelligible and it was impossible to tell how much she understood. No one put into words what they feared for her future. At her age it was clear she would spend the rest of her life helplessly bedridden, for Mr Osbourne had said an operation to pin her hip was out of the question.

Two days before Lottie, Ramsey and the family were due to arrive from Canada, an ambulance drove slowly and carefully in through the Manor gates. Lavinia was home. She still couldn't make herself understood, but the smile that played around her mouth and eyes told them that she was content, she knew where she was.

Everywhere there was a bustle of excitement. The "tribe" were about to gather, Bullington was making ready to receive its own. And Katie's excitement kneww no bounds. It was fifteen months since she'd said goodbye to her people at Calgary Airport, that in itself was enough to give her this bubbly feeling of anticipation. But it was more than that. She was confident that they would love Dylan, of course they would. All those half-forgotten images of childhood told her she had nothing to fear.

Kate and Rupert arrived at Bullington the day beforehand so that her grandmother could have a few hours with Katie before the family arrived and swamped her.

'Surely we'll bring them to Brimley first? This was Lottie's home.' Rupert had been surprised when she'd told him her plans.

'Here? Really, sometimes you do talk such nonsense. Ramsey has nemver been to England, I want him to have a good first impression to remember. Bullington was always my home, it's where the family should be.' And as if her words weren't enough, she made her point even clearer by the way she glanced around the sitting room of number 14 Sycamore Avenue. For forty-four years she'd been Rupert's wife and this had been her home, yet she'd never come to accept it. She was a child of Bullington Manor, at heart a Matheson still.

They'd been at the Manor an hour or two, Katie had walked to the lake with Rupert, Kate and Hester were sitting one on either side of Lavinnia's bed. The old lady looked from one to the other. She seemed pleased to have them with her, each holding a hand as she lay there.

'All this time it's been *me* who's been fretting to see Katie. And what happens? She drags Rupert off and here I am left alone again. It's always the men who get made the fuss of.' How was it that even when she spoke in that whining voice, Kate still managed to look pretty? The two sisters were so different. Hester was nearing seventy, a woman whose looks were due more to elegance and bearing than to features; Kate, six years younger, slim, slight, her once blonde hair colourless rather than grey, her skin as delicate as a child's and her eyes as clear. She had always been the beauty of the family, conveying an aura of gentle innocence.

'She's spoken to you about this Canadian friend, I suppose?' As soon as she asked it Hester could tell from Kate's expression that she had not been taken into the girl's confidence. She had a duty. As a grandmother Kate would feel she'd been responsible for what sort of friends Katie made here in England. 'No, I see she hasn't. Then I think it's up to me to warn you. She wants to tell Lottie herself, made me promise not to say anything to her when she arrives. But I've made no such promise to keep my silence with you.' Then, in a whisper: 'Half Red Indian! Here in Newton Dingley. She means to marry him.'

The two women leant towards each other, neither of them noticed Lavinia's agitation, the way she opened her mouth trying to say something, the way she looked towards the cupboard where her letters were kept. And neither of them heard footsteps along the thickly carpeted gallery outside the half open door.

For Katie to come to join them was natural. Having Rupert and Kate here seemed like the beginning of all the excitement. By now her parents would be at Calgary ready for their flight, tomorrow they'd be here. She hadn't heard what they were talking about as she came towards Lavinia's room, but there was something in their whispering tone that halted her, her hand already raised to push the door open.

'Even his name,' Hester was saying. 'Kitashee! Dylan Kitashee! Katie Kitashee! Can you imagine? The trouble that fell on the family when you and Rupert allowed Lottie to marry that dreadful Neil O'Hagon and go off to Canada! If it hadn't been for that –'

How dare she talk like that! Katie squared her shoulders ready to do battle. But her grandmother's answer stopped her. What did she mean?

'Dear God in heaven! Katie will have to be told. Should I do it? Or wait until Lottie gets here?'

'I don't understand . . . I've already given her my views, said how impossible such a match –'

'No, you don't understand! How can you? None of you have known even half the trouble brought by that ill-bred, uncouth man. Trouble and tragedy have dogged me all my days – what have I done to deserve it? Now this! Was I such a bad mother, is that why she wouldn't listen to me? I told her what he was – and I was right.' Listening, Katie frowned. She couldn't really remember her father, she supposed he'd got into bad company and that's how he'd got into the fight that had killed him. But it was years ago – and why dig up all the old arguments and hold them against Dylan? They weren't being fair. Once Mom got here they'd understand Dylan wasn't a bit like that. 'There was no morality in him. Red skin or white it was all one to him with his filthy animal lusts. Lottie only told us that his half-witted uncle had knifed him in a fight. It wasn't until we went out there for her wedding to Ramsey that I stumbled on the truth – that Rosie Kitashee had been his mistress. He must have sired her son when he was hardly more than a child himself, disgusting animal that he was! Knifing was too good for him. And now this! All the years I've looked forward to her coming home, even now his shadow has to fall.'

Katie had to get away. Silently, on the thick carpet, she crept to her own room. Perhaps she'd heard it wrong. But she hadn't, she'd heard every word . . . Neil O'Hagon's son, her own father's son! It wasn't true, it couldn't be true! If he were her brother, how could she feel this sort of love for him?

36

By the side of her bed she sank to her knees, her face against the eiderdown as if that way she could escape.

It can't be true, she must have got it all wrong because she hated my father so much. She wanted to believe the worst of him. Yes, that's what it was. Please, please, let that be what it was. Mom'll tell me the real truth. If this Rosie woman, Dylan's mother, if she was my father's mistress – well, that's not Dylan's fault and mine. Please let it all be lies. It must be lies. Mom would have told me.

Round and round in her mind it went. If only Dylan were here. But this evening he was away in Oxford. Tomorrow she'd know the truth, tomorrow everything would be clear again, tomorrow Mom was coming.

Chapter Three

'Mom, Dad said I'd find you here. I've come to talk with you.'

'Eighteen years since I last saw it all.' Lottie stood gazing out of the window, she might have been speaking to herself. 'But look at it. Nothing has changed. The view across the park, sloping away down to the lake. I can't see the lake, but I know it'll all be there waiting for me. Just the same . . . Oh, Katie, you don't know how often I've pictured it. If only we'd come just a bit sooner, before this happened to Grandma. Does she realise I'm here, do you suppose? She must do, mustn't she? I'm sure she must – her eyes tell me she does.'

'Mom, I've got to talk with you!'

At the urgency in Katie's voice, her mother turned away from the parkland view and held out her hands. She looked hardly more than a girl herself: slim (back in Alberta where she lived she'd been de-scribed as 'put together real neat'), short hair of rich chestnut brown, hair that sprang into natural curl, and eyes just the same shade. But the youthfulness came from something within her own optimistic nature – that and the fact that she found life a happy thing.

'Oh, but it's good to see you, Katie. You've loved being here? Of course you have, I could tell it from your letters. Come and tell me about everything. Let's sit on the bed and talk together, just like back home.' Then, with a laugh: 'Before the family find where we're hiding out.'

But there was no answering laugh from Katie.

'Mom, there's something I have to know, you've got to tell me the truth. Promise me. I want to know everything there is to tell about Dylan.'

'Dylan?' Lottie looked puzzled. 'But why? Whatever's made you ask about him? You were only knee high.' Then, picturing the little girl Katie had been: 'But if ever there was a case of hero worship! Fancy your remembering Dylan after all this time – and here, so far away.'

'I want the truth, Mom, nothing hidden. I've got to know. It's important.'

It was the emphasis on those two words "It's important' that warned Lottie. What sort of slander against Neil O'Hagon had been fed to Katie here in England? In a flood the memories crowded back: the opposition she'd battled with from the family that she could have fallen in love with him – "an uncouth cowboy"; she could still hear the contempt in their voices. It was sixteen years since he'd been killed. They had no right to blacken his name to the daughter who'd been too young to remember him!'

'Don't let's rake over old ashes, Katie. My family didn't want me to marry Neil, and tried their hardest to stop it. I guess he didn't fit into the pattern. You can understand that now that you've been here. But they've no business spreading gossip about him and trying to blacken his name – and to you of all people! What have they been telling you about Dylan?'

'Never mind what I've heard. Mom, I want the truth and there's no one else I can ask. If my father had an affair with Dylan's mother, that's nothing to do with me or with him, is it?'

'Sure I'll tell you the truth. You're not a baby, you're old enough to hear it and not feel bitter against Neil. It all happened long ago, long before the war brought him to England. You've got to hang on to that, Katie. Whatever was between your father – your real father – and Rosie Kitashee happened when he was only a boy. She had a son, Dylan. But we can't blame Neil for things that happened before he even met me. They've got no business to try and poison your mind.'

Katie's mouth felt dry. Please let her tell me I've got it all wrong, let her tell me it's just rumours, lies . . . If only she'd written home about Dylan, told them that she'd met him again. But these months of summer had been so perfect, she'd hugged her secret to herself, delighting in imagining the moment when she brought him face to face with her people.

'No one's told me anything about him – they none of them ever talked about my father.' She held Lottie's gaze firmly, her words coming out louder than she intended. 'Dylan is in Newton Dingley. Mom, I want to marry him. I'm going to marry him.' Was it defiance or fear in her voice?

'It's not possible!' By contrast Lottie spoke in little more than a whisper. 'Don't you understand what I've been telling you? Katie, Dylan's your half-brother.'

The silence lengthened between them. And as those seconds ticked by, Lottie came nearer than ever before to understanding something of her own mother's fears all those years ago when she'd brought Neil

O'Hagon home to Brimley. Her own words echoed, the same words as Katie had spoken just now: 'I want to marry him. I'm going to marry him.' Memories that had been buried for so long . . . Only now, a generation on, could she realise that her parents' hostility to Neil had been rooted in fear – fear for her own sake and for theirs too, that she would be lost to them. At the time she hadn't understood, she'd over-simplified their reaction, seeing their treatment of him as disparaging, shamed by their unconcealed contempt. In a sudden flash of understanding she saw the deep hurt their attitude had hidden.

But now they'd all moved on a place; here she was, looking at her darling Katie, knowing she must hurt her, knowing life would hurt her – and aware of an unexpected rage against Dylan. How dared he do this! Did he profess to love Katie? If he cared about her at all, then he'd not have let it happen. They could have been friends, they could have picked up the threads of childhood and he could have guarded against it growing into anything more. But marriage! Even if Neil hadn't made it impossible for Katie and Dylan to make a life together, there was so much else that stood between them! The very idea of it was preposterous! Custom, creed, upbringing, education – and again the ghost of the girl she'd been twenty years before proudly bringing home the handsome Canadian only to hear her mother refer to him as uncouth, coarse, ill-bred, ignorant . . .

And uninvited into her mind followed other pictures: Katie toddling around after the beautiful Indian boy, open adoration in her eyes; Rosie Kitashee moving away and Dylan left behind, fending for himself, living from what he caught on his fishing line or what he took from his traps in the forest; Ramsey bringing him to Higley Creek, prepared to make a home for him; Dylan, like a wild bird brought to live in a cage then disappeared, run away. It had been Ramsey who had gone to the settlement in search of him, and who'd arranged for him to be taken to join Rosie who by then was living somewhere across the Rockies in British Columbia. All of it almost forgotten, buried beneath the happiness she'd found in her life with Ramsey. And now Dylan was back. He'd lifted the lid from Pandora's box, letting all the unhappiness of their yesterdays reach out to today.

'Mom, someone ought to have told us.' Katie's voice was small. She didn't cry, she didn't argue. Shadows under her eyes told of the sleepless night she had had.

'Us, you say? *Dylan* knows the truth as well as I do. He was in Court to hear it, the same as I was. When Neil was killed there had to be an Inquest. That's when it call came out. The accident happened at Rosie's cabin, she was trying to come between Neil and me –'

40

'You mean, you were there?'

'No. I told you, we heard it all at the Inquest. Donald – Neil's uncle – well, you know about him even if you can't remember him, he wasn't like other people, he was some sort of a half-wit, but he adored Neil. He got the knife and meant it for Rosie, but as he lunged forward Neil must have tried to stop him. Dylan was there, he saw, he ran for help.'

'But that was awful for him, Mom. And he had to tell them about it in Court? But that still doesn't make him my brother!'

'No, I'm just telling you what happened that night. Up until then Dylan had just been looked on as her illegitimate son – although afterwards I realised that the O'Hagons had all had their suspicions. That night she and Neil quarrelled, she threatened to tell me about the boy being his – I don't know all that went on, but I do know that much. Dylan must have heard it. Then in Court, under Oath, she said it all again, named Neil. The whole thing came out. And you know what happened after that: Donald got locked away in some mental home; Rosie was cleared of having any part in Neil's death, but she left the settlement and went west. It was only afterwards that we came upon Dylan living rough – he was a sorry sight. Ramsey brought him back to Higley Creek.'

'I know all that part, Dylan told me. Mom, you say he heard all this, he knows who his father was? But he can't have taken it in – he wasn't very old. He doesn't know. I swear he doesn't know. Anyway, if he was my father's son, why didn't Grandma O'Hagon give him a home at Kilton Down?'

'I guess they felt pretty bitter, all of them. Neil dead, Donald locked away. You can't wonder they didn't want any more dealings with Rosie Kitashee after all that had happened. Craig was running Kilton Down, he had sons of his own, younger than Dylan; he probably saw him as a threat. Rosie used to help on the ranch at round-up time, and Molly always had Dylan at the house. Rosie must have expected they'd take him in when they knew who he was. I suspect when she left him she took it for granted that's where he'd go. But when they didn't, there was only me. He was Neil's boy, I couldn't leave him with no one to care for him. I guess it was because Ramsey knew how I felt that he fetched him back to Higley Creek.'

'He told me about being brought there. But I don't seem to picture him home with us – just occasional flashes, and I'm sure it was when we were at Kilton Down. Yet I was younger then.'

'He started to go to school each day; he helped Ramsey outside; but he never – never – I don't know, never opened up. It was as if he couldn't let himself be one of us. Maybe that's why you can't picture him there, he never really belonged. It was like catching a wild animal out there on the mountains and taking it to live in a zoo.' They were sitting side by side on the bed. Now Lottie turned to look at Katie, her brown eyes troubled. 'Sometimes a brother and sister have that special relationship, something in their genes that draws them together. Can't you see it as that?'

'He *doesn't* know. You must be wrong. Anyway,' and with a sudden change of mood she turned to glare defiantly at her mother, 'what's to say that it's not you who's made a mistake about what they said at the Inquest? You must have been upset, shocked by it all, you probably got things wrong. He'll tell me the real truth.'

Lottie shook her head, reaching out to take Katie's hands. 'Do you think I like having to tell you? It's the truth, I swear it, Katie. You've go to put him out of your mind – at least you've got to forget that you thought of him as a boyfriend. See him just as –'

'You don't know anything about it!'

'I know this much. You met when you were both thousands of miles from home, so of course you were drawn to each other. But even if he weren't Neil's son, marriage would be impossible. You can't take two people with different cultures, different values, different interests – you just can't do it, Katie.'

'But wasn't that what you did when you married your Canadian soldier? I bet Granny tried to stop it – I know she did! But you didn't listen. Old people always think they know best!' She wanted to wound, but as soon as she'd said it she was ashamed. 'Oh, Mom, I'm sorry. Don't lets you and me fight.'

The jibe surprised Lottie. Old? She wasn't even forty! But perhaps parents are never seen by their children as anything else. It hung between them for a moment before she swept it away, ignoring it.

'Marrying Neil wasn't the same at all. His grandparents came from Ireland. His wasn't a different culture. I loved Dylan when he was a boy, honestly I did, and felt sorry for him, having that dreadful woman for a mother. But he's her son. She gave him his background, he belongs to *her* people, her sort of life. He could never be right for you, even if Neil didn't come into it at all.'

'Mom, that's a hateful way to talk! I love him. He loves me. All right, his skin isn't as pale as mine, but are you saying he's the worse for that? Even Grandma hinted at it when he was coming to here to dinner. That was before she met him. He's proud of his Indian breeding and why shouldn't he be? I'm proud of it for him! It makes me sick . . . you make me ashamed.'

'Of course he's proud, and so he should be. Just the same, you don't mix red wine and white. Oh, Katie.' She pulled the girl into her

42

arms, stiff and unrelenting. 'Love him as a special friend, as a brother.' Then, another thought striking her, she drew back, suspicion sending her thoughts off at a sudden tangent. 'If you've known each other long enough to talk of marriage, then why ever didn't you write to us about him? Whose idea was that? Did he tell you not to? Was that why?' Dylan had no cause to love the O'Hagons, but surely he wouldn't take his revenge through Katie?

This was Lottie and Ramsey's first evening. Katie had been keen for them to meet Dylan as soon as they arrived, but in fact he was dining at the Bell, a hotel some ten miles away on the Bath road. The business he'd come over for was already completed. This social evening with the company director of Redman's and his wife was by way of a farewell. Katie had been childishly disappointed at the thought of waiting another day before, like a magician, she could produce him.

Around the dinner table at Bullington Manor the family gathered that night. Hester, elegant in black relieved only by a long rope of pearls knotted on her austere bosom, her iron grey hair coiled into a bun in the nape of her graceful neck; Kate, the natural curls of her once blonde and now colourless hair combed with special care to frame her sweet face, her cheeks pink with pleasure that she should be here in her favourite place and surrounded by the people she loved most (tonight she wouldn't let the thought that Lavinia was watched over by a nurse, a prisoner in her worn-out body, cast a shadow), her mouth set in a half smile as she looked around her with satisfaction; Rupert, her husband, his grey hair thin enough now to see the top of his head, his shoulders stooping, "the ninny", "Drupert", names tagged on him by the Matheson tribe who knew him to be weak and indecisive – yet had they looked a little deeper they might have understood him better; Ramsey, a man of the open spaces yet somehow fitting into the scene with ease, a gentle man but never a weak one; Nigel, his fair hair well cut and groomed, turned to gold by the lights of the candles set in the two silver candelabra on the long table where he presided at the head.

He, too, was enjoying the evening. There was nothing he liked better than to draw the family together here at Bullington Manor, the pivot on which his own life revolved. To him it was as if they were all spokes making up the wheel, this the axle that held them; and he, all his strength rooted in Bullington and given back to it, was determined that with Lavinia giving up her hold nothing would change. Tomorrow "the tribe" would gather in readiness for the birthday celebrations. Hester considered the idea macabre but for once she kept her

43

thoughts to herself. It had been Lavinia who had decided that August 17th should be marked by a gathering of the family; to change the plans she'd so carefully laid would be to over-ride her while she was unable to voice her wishes. And even Hester wondered whether the atmosphere of a houseparty might break into the old lady's consciousness as the hours they'd all spent sitting at her beside never could.

The seventh at the dinner table was Katie. Around her was the buzz of voices, English voices and Canadian too. This is the evening I've looked forward to, Mom and Dad here – Dad? If only he were my proper dad, not that hateful soldier Mom took up with! Is that wicked, thinking like that about a man I can't remember, a man I must have inherited my own genes from? And if I've got his genes, so has Dylan. Mom must be wrong about him knowing, he can't have understood what they were saying. But he wasn't small, he was about eleven, he told me he was eleven when he used to come to Kilton . . .

'Aren't you hungry, dear?' Her grandmother smiled lovingly at her across the table. 'It's all the excitement.'

'Yes, I expect it is. I'm not really hungry. I've got a bit of a headache.'

'That's something I know all about! My poor head has been the plague of my life. The least upset, the least over-excitement, and there's nothing I can do but lie down in a dark room. Your grandad would tell you how I've suffered.'

Rupert nodded obligingly, the look he rested on his delicate little wife sympathetic. Listening, Lottie watched them. Nothing had changed. She'd thought the years had altered them, but the outward signs of age went no deeper than the surface. Her mother's headaches, so often disguising her dominance over the household, and her father's never failing sympathy – all of it just as it always had been. She'd grown up accepting the way things were without question; only later when the headaches and tears had been brought on by her own fight for freedom had she been irritated by them. Now, looking from one to the other of her parents, she willingly let herself be wrapped in the warmth and security of being with them again.

'If I were you,' Kate was saying now, 'I'd go to bed early, pull down the blinds and close the curtains, cut the light out of your room. Sleep will put you right. We'll all be here waiting in the morning and you'll be bright for the day. I've thought all day how drained you've been looking. It's over-excitement.'

'Go to bed early, with Mom and Dad just arrived!' Katie forced the laugh the suggestion deemed to demand.

Knowing what had passed between Lottie and her daughter, it was Ramsey who eased the way for her to escape.

44

'My guess would be that Lottie plans to spend the evening sitting with her grandmother – and as for me, Nigel is driving me around the home farm before the light goes and introducing me to the manager. I'm looking forward to a talk with him.'

'Seems I'm redundant,' Katie tried to joke. 'Perhaps you're right, Granny. I think I'll slip away and get that early night. Can't let the side down tomorrow when the rest of the folk arrive.'

'That's right. Your mother will be here more evenings than one. But I did think, after all the years since she and I have had an evening together, that she might have spared this one to *me*. Don't rush away to Mother, Lottie. She can't appreciate being with you like I do. If you knew the hours I've spent by her bedside, and Hester too of course –' as an afterthought ' – and it's been wasted on her.'

'I'll take that chance. Give me ten minutes with her, Mum, then come up and join us. We'll have our talk and maybe she'll feel she's part of it.'

Katie was free to retreat to her room. Through dinner she'd tried to keep her mind on the conversation at the table, now she let her tangled thoughts have full rein. It was a relief not to have to act a part and yet, faced with the silence of her bedroom, there was nowhere she could escape the truth that had to be faced. At the time of the Inquest Dylan had been eleven, maybe even twelve. It couldn't have been that he'd not understood. Anyway, the scene must have etched itself indelibly on to his memory. So why had he said nothing? Had he been wanting just to use her, a meaningless affair to wile away his months in England? Wasn't that what her mother had hinted at when she'd suggested it had been *his* idea to say nothing about their meeting? No, she wouldn't believe it, she couldn't believe it. Anyway, where would have been the point? How much easier to tell her all he knew, let their friendship grow as it would have done knowing themselves to be brother and sister. Friendship? More memories. She pressed the backs of her hands to her cheeks, her eyes tight shut. There was no escape from the pictures that crowded in on her. Letting herself drop to sit on the edge of the bed, not for the first time she re-lived those hours. Until now, whenever she'd tried to rekindle the joy, the exaltation, she'd found in their love (She? Oh, but surely it had been the same for him?) she'd been so sure of the rightness of what they'd done, she'd believed that as their bodies merged so too did their spirits . . . and all the time he must have known this dreadful thing!

There was a light tap on her bedroom door.

'Can I come in, Katie dear? I won't talk if you want to lie quietly,' came Kate's whisper. Her evening wasn't turning out a bit as she'd hoped. Hearing the pleading tone, Katie felt a pang of guilt. She knew how disappointed her grandmother had been that Lottie hadn't wanted an evening just with her.

'I'll get to sleep quicker on my own, Granny. You don't mind, do you? And, Granny,' in a conspiratorial whisper, 'tell Mom I don't want to be disturbed, will you?'

She knew that would help to salve Kate's hurt at not being allowed in.

About five minutes later she'd heard the door of Lavinia's room open and close, heard Nigel taking Ramsey off to meet the farm manager. With her shoes in her hand she stepped lightly along the carpeted gallery, keeping well back to the wall in case anyone should be in the large hall below. Then down the back stairs and out through the side door.

She had to see Dylan. She had to tell him what she'd found out. Perhaps she'd been right when she'd suggested that her mother had been too shocked to get the facts right; but it was more likely that Dylan, frightened by the whole chain of events, had been running away from the truth just as he'd been running away from everything else when Ramsey had brought him back to Higley Creek to stay with them. Yes, that must have been what happened. His child's mind had rejected the whole thing. The picture of him in that hospital bed sprang to mind. Poor little boy, hiding his tears . . .

Once in the car she sped down the long drive without a a backward glance. Only one thing was clear: she had to talk with Dylan. Beyond that she daren't let herself think.

Lottie sat on the edge of Lavinia's bed. She bent forward, her face near to the old lady's.

'Grandma, you *do* know I'm here, I know you do.' She took the powerless, boney hands in her own, almost willing life and warmth into them. 'Remember how we used to talk by the lake?' Even as a young child she'd known all her secrets were safe with Lavinia; then, as she'd gone into her teens, no subjects had been barred between them. The age difference hadn't been a barrier – rather it had formed a bridge, a place where they met, where Lavinia remembered the dreams of youth and where Lottie was guided towards seeing from a mature viewpoint. 'I wish I could tell you – I wish I knew how to help her. Does she truly love him? Properly love him, I mean? But how can she, wouldn't nature stop her? You remember what happened, you've not forgotten. Neil and Rosie Kitashee – it's buried so deep now that I don't even feel hurt thinking about it. The sins of the fathers. How can I help her? She must feel so – so betrayed . . .' If

46

she'd been alone, so she might have talked to herself. Yet there was a comfort in opening her heart just as she always had to this very special person. For all that she chafed those still hands with the warmth of her own, there was no answering pressure on her fingers. There was recognition in Lavinia's eyes, though, Lottie was sure of it. She leant closer.

'Grandma?'

The left side of Lavinia's mouth tried to smile.

'You do hear me, you do know it's me.' And for the first time since this afternoon Lottie's mind was cleared of the problem of Dylan.

Another five minutes and a timid tap on the door told her her mother needed to be drawn into their magic circle.

'Come and join us, Mum. You take the chair, I'm happy perched on the bed.'

She was less happy when Kate dived in with the problem that was at the top of her mind, the very problem Lottie was wanting to escape. So often they'd seen things from differing angles, but here they were united in their anger at Dylan, at their fear that nothing could protect Katie from hurt. As they talked Lottie still held her grandmother's hands, still there was no answering life in them.

Three women, each of her own generation, each frustrated by her own inability to help one she loved from that fourth generation.

'If only you'd listened to us. You were so sure you knew best. We told you that that dreadful man could only mean trouble.' Kate's mouth trembled. 'Even now, after all these years, his shadow has to fall on us! Never look forward to anything, Lottie. To dream and plan is to court disaster! I should know! I looked forward so long to your being home with us – just like I looked forward to Katie being here in England. And what happens? She's spent months and months here, not with me at all. And why? Because of some hateful reminder of that coarse, horrible creature you gave up your family for. Even as a boy he must have been the same, like some prowling animal, lusting –'

'Mum, don't! Please, don't. Neil loved me, I swear he did. And I don't want all that to be dragged up again. Leave it. Oh, Mum, don't cry.'

'I'd looked forward to us all being happy together.'

Lottie tried to trample on the irritation that as long as she could remember her mother had been able to arouse in her, but she couldn't stop her sharp rejoinder: 'If you must cry, then cry for Katie – and for Grandma. Just think how long she must have been looking forward, too. Everyone coming tomorrow, her birthday the next day . . .'

She said all that, Kate sniffed into her lace-edged handkerchief, but neither of them noticed how the old lady tried to force her mouth to do her bidding, fought to turn those incomprehensible noises into some sort of message.

Katie drew up in the forecourt of the Bell. She longed to see Dylan – and yet at the same time she dreaded the moment. What would she feel? Until yesterday there had been nothing complicated in her emotions: she loved him; she wanted just to be with him; and when she *was* with him every instinct made her reach out to touch him, to be close to him. But that was yesterday. What about now, today? And, something she shied from contemplating, what about tomorrow, all the tomorrows?

Before she went into the foyer she looked through the window of the dining room. Perhaps they were still at the table, perhaps he wasn't alone? How could she face him in front of other people, pretending nothing had changed?

'Where are they? Didn't they arrive?' At the sound of his voice just behind her, she started guiltily.

'I was looking for you. I thought you might still have people here,' she stammered.

'They just left. I wanted some air. You didn't say – didn't Lottie and Ramsey arrive? You're on your own?'

'Yes, they've come. Dylan,' as if to stop them behaving with a will of their own she clasped her hands together tightly behind her back, 'we've got to talk about things.'

'I know. Tomorrow we'll sort it all out with your family, once you've had your fun and surprised them.' He put his arm around her shoulder as he spoke, his blue eyes teasing her.

Still her hands were clasped, her fingers interlocked. It took all her control to hold herself stiff. How easy it would have been just to relax, to lean against him, to pretend none of the last twenty-four hours had happened.

'Something's wrong,' he said, sensing her tension. 'Get in the car, we can talk better in there.'

She nodded. Behind the steering wheel she would be safe from his embrace, she could steel herself.

'Shall I drive somewhere?' Anything rather than say what had to be said.

'On up the main road a mile or so, there's a turning to the right. It takes us towards a track on to the downs. I found it this afternoon. There's nothing wrong at home, Katie? I had not thought you would escape to see me on their first night.'

She put her foot hard on the accelerator as if in speed she'd lose the devils that chased her. Along the main road, a turn to the right, and in another mile or two they were on the edge of the downs where she could pull off the lane on what Dylan accepted as just a track. Katie knew better, she knew it was part of the old Roman road. Riding on the downs she'd loved to follow it, thrilled to think that she was treading where men had trod for two thousand years; she'd been humbled by her own insignificance and yet aware that in every age the mark men made could never be wiped out.

'Let's get out and look at the night.' Already Dylan had the door open.

Say it now, before he touches you, before he turns you to face him in the soft light of the waning moon.

She couldn't let herself look at him. There was a leaden weight in her chest and her throat felt closed, as if no sound could come if she tried to speak.

She opened her mouth. 'Dylan –' Too late. His mouth covered hers, the words were lost.

He wasn't prepared for the way she suddenly pulled herself free.

'No! Don't touch me! Don't come near me!' He heard the panic in her voice. Only distance could give her the strength to tell him. 'I've told Mom – about us.'

'All that fuss you made about surprising them.' He laughed. 'Well, that's OK by me, Katie, it was your idea to produce me like I was magic, not mine.'

'Shut up. Just shut up and listen. Mom told me things – about you – about what happened when my father was killed.'

'Does that have to come between you and me? OK, it was Rosie who made the trouble. But, hell, Katie, how can I help that any more than you can help Neil's part in it? If he was playing around with Rosie it was rough on Lottie, but it was never our fault, yours and mine.' The only sign of his agitation was his distant pronunciation of each separate syllable. 'Let us forget it. Do not let us suffer for the mess they made. It will never be like that for us.'

'You don't remember?'

'I do not want to remember. I want it done with, forgotten. Katie, we are not like our parents – well, maybe you are like Lottie, but for the rest of them – let them go, forget them. *We* are the ones who matter. We belong to each other, we always will.'

'So you honestly don't remember? You don't know? Oh, Dylan, Mom told me it. Neil, my father – he was your father too.'

It was only seconds before Dylan spoke; it seemed a lifetime, the silence only broken by the hooting of a owl.

49

'No, it is not true, that old story! It was a lie. I had forgotten Rosie had ever said it.'

'How could you forget? Of course you hadn't forgotten! What sort of a fool do you think I am?' And this time as he reached to put his hands on her shoulders, she drew back as if his touch burnt her. 'Now who's lying? What did you think? That it was easier to pick up with me than find some English girl to amuse yourself with? What luck I rode along, the little girl out of the past – the little sister! Snooty lot, these English, maybe they didn't like the look of you!' Her voice trembled, she couldn't hold it steady but there were no tears.

His tone was cold as ice. Even anger would have been easier than this.

'You may be right. I am not a white man. I am not blind to the way I have been received here. If that is what matters to you then better for you to tell me honestly.' His chin was high. In the dark she could feel rather than see the way his gaze held hers, defying her to turn away. She was ashamed.

'I was just trying to be beastly,' she muttered.

'Does she really believe this tale she's told you, Katie? Or does she think it's a sure way of getting rid of me?'

'But it's true! Don't you remember the Inquest? I don't see how anyone could forget hearing a thing like that!'

'I remember it. Word for word I remember it. I remember looking at Lottie and the O'Hagons and feeling a strange sort of pride that I was one of them. Things would be different once I was known to belong to the O'Hagons. When Rosie said she was moving off it was because of what I'd heard that I wanted to stay around Kilton Down.'

Her legs ached as if they hadn't the strength to hold her. Over the last months she'd given herself to him – her body, her spirit, all that she was. And she'd believed, she'd never doubted. What was he saying to her? That all these months he'd known . . . She found herself kneeling, the ground hard under her knees. With so much else crowding her mind yet as the stones pressed into her skin she felt herself to be just one more traveller on this road that was a part of history, her sadness mingled with that that had gone before, her pain etched there for all time.

But it was only a momentary sensation then reality pulled her back. Dylan was kneeling in front of her, reaching out as she crouched away from him.

'Damn Neil O'Hagon, and damn Rosie too! How can you even imagine I'm your brother? I tell you, it was lies.'

'She swore in the Court that it was the truth. You were there, you heard her.'

50

'She told Neil the same thing, I heard her do that too.' He spoke patiently as if he were soothing a frightened animal, 'Rosie didn't see things the way you do. She found no wrong in using words the way it most suited her. She was frightened of losing her hold on him, she'd been his mistress for years. I knew that. They used to think I was asleep but I used to watch them. He wasn't the only man who came after Rosie. I had plenty of instruction.'

'Don't talk like that. It's hateful.'

'I want you to understand. That night she thought Neil was lost to her, that's when she told him about me. That way she would have kept him. Then there was the fight – you know about that. At the Inquest she lied. Is that so hard to understand? Since he was a boy Neil had been her lover. If he hadn't married the young English girl he would still have been alive, still have been her lover. Rosie must have wanted to hurt Lottie any way she could. And I think too that she wanted her freedom – from me, from anything that was a responsibility. So what better than that I should be taken by the O'Hagons? A reminder to Lottie that Neil had betrayed her, and a future for me all in one move. It's the truth, Katie. Rosie told me when I finally caught up with her in British Columbia.'

'And you believed her?' Katie heard the contempt in her own voice. 'A woman who could swear to tell the truth then lie to suit her own ends? You believed her?'

'Neil O'Hagon was not my father. Rosie used him to suit her own purposes right from the beginning. She was already pregnant, Neil eager beyond his years. He was only fourteen or fifteen, you know, years younger than her. Poor Rosie.'

'Poor? She was wicked! And if that's the tale she told you afterwards, what makes you think that wasn't to serve her own purpose too? Mom never lies.'

She felt her shoulders taken in his grasp, there was no way of escape.

'I said poor Rosie because even though she used Neil O'Hagon for her own ends in the beginning, in the end she was obsessed by him.'

'Please let me go,' she croaked. 'He was our father. Mom says she thinks the O'Hagon's always suspected it. If it's poor anyone it's her. Please don't hold me like that.'

'If the O'Hagons really thought that was the truth, why do you think they sent me away when I went to them at Kilton Down?'

In the dark she felt the prick of tears, this time not for herself but for the young boy he'd been.

'Mom says it was because you were a reminder of Rosie and the damage she'd done – and because Craig had boys of his own. He and

Neil, our father, used to run the place, but when Neil had gone it was Craig's – and one day his sons.'

For a moment he didn't answer. Katie thought that at last he'd accepted what she said, at last he'd realised that Rosie's word meant nothing. She wasn't prepared for his sudden movement, pulling her into his arms, gripping her so close that he seemed to force the breath from her body.

'You're mine. Before all the gods I swear no one shall take you away from me. We belong together, you know it's the truth. Oh Katie, Katie, when I've loved you, when we've lain close together, we've been one, one body, one soul.'

'Don't, please, don't! Don't hold me. Dylan, I don't want to remember, I don't want to think,' she sobbed. 'It was wrong, wicked, unnatural. I'm your sister. Even the animals don't . . .' His mouth covered hers. It had never been like this before. Desperately she fought to be free. Opening her mouth she tried to bite him; she dug her nails into the back of his neck. And all the time as she struggled she lost ground. Pushed from her knees, she was on her back, his weight anchoring her.

'You are my woman. Who do you believe? Me or them? I tell you, my father was *not* Neil O'Hagon.' Dylan was lying above her, his hands on her shoulders, his face only inches away from hers. 'You were mine. You are mine still. Always.'

Looking upwards Katie saw the shifting clouds move before the moon. 'The sun and the moon have their place in the firmament – we have ours on earth. We belong together . . .'

In that moment she forgot to fight. What was there to fight for? The future held nothing.

And in that moment Dylan moved his position. With one hand he pressed her against the hard stony ground. She heard what sounded like a sob catch in his throat, or was it just that he was breathing hard, as if he'd been running? Every instinct was to hold him, to comfort him – and then the truth hit her anew. Her brother! Now she realised why he'd moved his position, why he held her with only one hand. She felt her short skirt pushed away from her bare legs, she felt his hand.

'Let me go.' But she hardly had the breath to speak.

'I'll never let you go. Damn our parents! Our lives are our own, together.'

No, no, we mustn't, it's wicked, unnatural. Unnatural? But how can it be? Nothing can ever have been so right . . . I wish I could die, now, like this, just me and him.

52

'Now tell me you're not mine,' he spoke through clenched teeth, 'that I'm not yours. Go on, tell me, tell me if you can. You can't. You know I'm right.'

There was a wildness in his lovemaking, an urgency, as if all the devils in hell were chasing him. 'Katie, say it, love me, say it. Now . . . now . . .' As he cried out she looked again at the moon, riding now in a patch of clear sky as the next clouds threatened it. In seconds it would be hidden; in seconds, too, the horror would be with them. But nothing could take this from them.

Then the moment was gone. The sharp stones she was lying on pressed into her flesh, there was nowhere to run from the truth. She felt crushed by his weight.

'I can wait until the end of the week. Katie, come home with me. Lottie's got it all wrong. Who do you believe, me or her?'

'Mom or a woman who'd lie when she's sworn to tell the truth, you mean? Get off me, Dylan. Please.' It was difficult to breathe, let alone speak. He didn't resist. Of the two it was Dylan who retained a kind of dignity as he moved to sit at her side, his hands clasped round his drawn-up knees.

'I ask you to trust me.' He spoke clearly, softly. 'Love without trust is no love at all. I do not know the name of the man who fathered me. He has played no part in my life, it has never mattered to me. Just for that short time I believed it was Neil O'Hagon, I saw no reason not to believe. Then Rosie told my why she'd lied, she laughed –'

'I don't want to hear! It's no use. It's over. It's got to be over.' She pulled herself to her feet, standing up she wouldn't feel so vulnerable. There was panic in her voice, by contrast his had been unemotional. Yet when he reached to touch her, to stop her moving away, she knew his hand wasn't steady.

'Two days ago you were as sure of the future as I was, as I am still. It is written in the stars. You felt it too, from that first day in the lane. Were we strangers? No. You know I speak the truth.'

She wanted just to listen to his voice, the way he spoke his words. "Kate-ee". Never again would she hear it.

'It's like Mom said, we were drawn to each other, special because we had the same genes. Anyway,' in her misery she had to hit out and hurt him, 'if you were so sure the tale about my father being your father was all lies, why didn't you even mention it to me? Because it might have made me see you differently, that was why. You thought I wouldn't have gone to bed with you –'

She blundered into the accusation, hurting him, hurting herself. With one quick, graceful movement he was on his feet, his hands on her shoulders.

'If you think that, then go. Go now. Love demands trust. Did I not say so to you. Katie, if you cannot trust me then go. Get in that car and leave me. I have no need of you.'

Now who was turning the knife?

The scudding clouds again cleared the moon, the night was suddenly brighter. For a second or two they stood facing each other, his words hung between them. One movement and they could have overcome the torment that tore at them; together they could have faced anything, in trust they could have sought out the truth. But like statues they stared in horror. Then she turned away. Even then, did she think he'd follow her as she ran towards the car?

"How could he? He knows there's no way forward. Damn my father! And that Rosie woman. Damn, damn, damn them. Is he coming?" Once in the car she looked into the driver's mirror, it seemed impossible that he'd let her go. But he was still standing as she'd left him.

The moon disappeared behind another cloud. Katie started the engine. "Kate-ee" came the echo in the silence of the night.

Katie hadn't cried for years as she did tonight driving back to the Manor. It was late, she hardly passed another car on the road – and hardly noticed those few there were. She'd never known there could be such aching misery as this, the future was nothing . . . nothing. As the first hot tears rolled down her cheeks she moaned, loudly, finding some sort of strange comfort in the sound. She needed to wail, to cry out, she wanted to beat her breast and moan. Yet part of her seemed to stand outside, surprised that she could behave like it.

A mile or so from Newton Dingley she stopped the car. She was drained of emotion, she was empty. There was nothing . . . darkness . . . desolation. The conscious effort she made to pull her immediate thoughts into shape took all her will power.

Then in the unpredictable way memories have of springing to mind she found herself picturing a rag doll Kate had sent for her birthday once. She'd called it Wump. It had gone with her through childhood, it had grown limp and shapeless. Slumped in her seat she likened herself to poor, used Wump. "It's just she's had a lot of loving", wasn't that how Lottie had explained the doll's droopy state? Tonight Katie shied from the echo of the words. 'Too much loving,' aloud she said it, 'but love is good, love is clean . . . even animals don't behave like we did.' Her voice rose again, her head flopped forward onto her arms on the steering wheel. 'Even tonight when I knew it was wrong it didn't stop me. I hate myself, I do, I do. I do, God, I hate myself, honest I do. But I wanted him, I want him always. Even tonight,

54

knowing, when I realised what he was doing to me I was glad – I wanted it –' alone in the darkness she drew strength from the strident rasp of her own voice.

And out of that strength came at least a superficial reason. She had to go home. She even tried to smooth her rumpled hair, she blew her nose and rubbed her face dry with the backs of her hands. She had to get back to the privacy of her own room. She had to forget. Think of tomorrow when the family came. Think of Grandam and her birthday. Think of her parents and how excited Mom must be, her first night back at Bullington after all these years.

It was long after midnight. She decided to leave the car half way down the drive so that no one would hear her creeping in. She switched off the engine then got out and pushed the door closed quietly. At night every sound carried. That's why she walked on the grass verge as she rounded the bend and came within sight of the Manor.

Lights from almost every window threw long golden rays across the lawns. At the bottom of the front steps was a car she recognised.

Chapter Four

When Katie had crept out earlier in the evening she'd made sure the window facing onto the kitchen garden had been left unbolted. Now, at the sight of Dr. Holsworthy's car, her plans for a silent re-entry were forgotten. Only something serious could have brought him here at this time of night. Grandam!

Out from the shadows of the trees, across the wide forecourt and up the stone steps to the front entrance she sped. Upstairs and down the lights were on. The thought sprang to her mind that in less than twenty four hours it would be the birthday, the reason for the family to be congregating. *This* was how Bullington Manor would expect to look then, on the evening on the day Lavinia had so looked forward to – light and laughter, the Mathesons come together to celebrate. Only for a second did Katie's imagination jump that way. The sound of sober voices in the drawing room brought reality alive. Two at a time she leapt up the stairs.

'Miss Katie!' Hawkins' urgent whisper arrested her. He was crossing the hall, bearing down on the closed door of the drawing room with a laden tray in his hands. He'd been with the family since the master's days, he'd allow no one else to serve them at an hour like this. 'Miss Katie, Jenny went to your room to rouse you –' He didn't actually put it into words that he realised she'd just come home. 'It was all over very suddenly. She didn't even know . . .'

'All over? You mean – Grandam – all over . . .?' Grandam's life ending – and where had *she* been? Somewhere out there on the downs, lying on the rough ground making love to her brother! Glorying in his nearness even while she fought him off – while Grandam's spirit had been released from the prison of her worn out body, where had her own spirit been? She hated herself that now, even now, Dylan could still intrude, her mind couldn't be free of him. She'd forsaken Grandam at the moment when she'd made her

56

journey into whatever was waiting beyond the veil, not just forsaken her by not being at her side but by having no place for her in her mind. No place for anyone but herself and Dylan, shame for herself for what she'd unwittingly done and revulsion for both of them for tonight's part.

Hawkins saw most things that went on at Bullington Manor – and kept his own counsel. Often enough Miss Katie was out late and, he had no doubt, with that dark skinned young Romeo she seemed so set on. He could put two and two together and add it to four better than most but, seeing her tears now, he proved himself less than a mathematician. How could he guess it wasn't pure loss that crumpled her face and reddened her eyelids? Indeed there was nothing "pure" in the emotion that tore at Katie. Grief, shame, loss, self-disgust, anguish – and the knowledge of a black void, the nothingness of a future that tonight she couldn't bear to think about.

When she joined the others in the drawing room no one referred to her blotchy face, they had other things on their minds.

Lottie had noticed Katie's absence when the alarm had been raised, she'd guessed where she must have gone. Now she took her hand, by the pressure of her fingers meaning to convey her understanding. How could she know that her action only added to Katie's self abasement?

Ramsey watched them.

Kate Bradley had noticed Katie's absence too and, like Lottie, she'd guessed the excuse of a headache must have been a means to escape. Sitting in her favourite fireside chair she saw Lottie's movement. There was no fire on this summer evening and the sight of the empty grate, like the sight of her mother's empty chair, made the ever-ready tears flow fast. Always she'd been able to come home to Bullington to find peace, to renew her strength. But no more. "As if losing Mother weren't enough – now there's all this extra misery, and all because of that hateful O'Hagon man! It's Lottie's fault. If Lottie had listened to me, if she'd ever cared for anyone but herself, she wouldn't have gone chasing off across the world with that – that *animal*! But did she care? Never. And now, her first evening here – look at the trouble. If she'd sat downstairs with me like I wanted, like I deserved after all the time I've been without a daughter to talk to, then Mother wouldn't have got so agitated, so over excited. She must have heard what we were saying, she must have understood. She must have partly blamed herself. She's had Neil O'Hagon's bastard son here to the house, probably encouraged it! Oh dear, what would she say? Ah, but she couldn't say anything. That's what killed her I dare say, hearing it all and not being able to speak, being helpless.

When Lottie brought that man home I knew it meant trouble. Now, all these years on, there's Mother dead, poor little Katie with a broken heart, Lottie looking like a ghost. And today should have been such a happy time. Never look forward to anything . . ." Kate's frequent outbursts of tears were seldom noisy but often prolonged. Tonight she sat in her chair, sobbing silently, there was no sign of her tears running dry.

Rupert stood helplessly by, watching her.

So both Ramsey and Rupert were outside the close family circle, both of them were onlookers. Yet, although he remained in the background, no one would have doubted that Ramsey was capable of taking control, there was a strength in his soft Canadian voice, a sureness in his manner. Not so with Rupert Bradley, "the ninny", "Drupert", call him what they would. Yet the two men had something else in common, each of them loved his wife above all else. Now Rupert stood by the side of Kate's chair, his helpless and perplexed gaze resting on her; if only she would ask for some sort of help, if there might be some services he could perform to ease her wretchedness. Yet his very nearness irritated her; she could never forgive him that he might have her family's tolerance, but never its respect.

Hester Marks and Nigel were talking to the doctor. They had both noticed Katie's appearance when she came in, but neither of them suspected that she hadn't been upstairs nursing her headache until now. Hester had the ability to listen to Dr. Holsworthy even while her thoughts went their own way. "It seems Katie inherited more than the name from Kate. Nothing worse than a woman who melts into tears. Enough to make Mother ashamed – and she used to speak so well of the girl too. Tomorrow the Marks contingent will be here, at least they know how to conduct themselves! One blessing, Bullington will be in good hands with Nigel. He'll cope with all the arrangements. A good man, he's nobody's fool." And as if by contrast she threw a glance at Rupert just as he let his hand flutter tentatively to touch Kate's shoulder, then withdrew it before it could bring any reaction.

The small village of Newton Dingley had grown up around Bullington Manor. It had been Egbert Matheson who had built the church; there were few freehold properties, the cottages, the village shop and three smallholdings all paid rent to the estate. As a young woman Lavinia had been loved as warm-hearted, caring and beautiful; as a middle aged widow that affection had taken on a new respect. For years now she'd been elderly, but still she was regarded with affection and pride. It was the local branch of the Women's Institute who had first put about the suggestion of a flower festival in the church to mark the occasion of her 95th birthday. The idea had grown, from every garden the best blooms had been cut in readiness in the early hours of that morning when Lavinia's "tribe" was due to arrive at the Manor. Ovens were already hot and cakes being baked for the children's tea party that was to be held on the village green or, if the great day were wet, in the marquees that yesterday had been erected in readiness for the tenants' supper. The people of Newton Dingley were determined to show Lavinia Matheson their affection by marking the occasion with a celebration that would be remembered. There were some who'd known Lottie Bradley as a child, they'd pinned their hopes on her coming, believing that seeing her might break into the old lady's consciousness. For so long she'd planned this family gathering; there was no hope of her being brought downstairs, but how cruel if she weren't even able to appreciate them all being with her.

So Newton Dingley had made its preparations. A month ago a meeting had been held in the Church Hall, duties had been allocated. Nigel Matheson had overseen the positioning of the marquee, last night the menfolk had erected the trestle tables and this morning their wives were assembled armed with white sheets to cover them. Conversation buzzed, there hadn't been a party like this since the Victory Tea in 1945.

But before the morning was half gone word had spread. There was to be no birthday.

By mid-day Hester's family had arrived. It was twenty years since Lottie had seen her cousin Alistair, whilst his wife Claudia was no more than a figure on the occasional photograph, sent to show the progress of their family, andthe name on the annual Christmas card. Lottie had always been nearer to Luke, the younger brother who'd made a life for himself in New Zealand. Even so it was good to be with Alistair, she wanted her people to know Ramsey. Seeing Alistair's three children she thought of home, she wished they'd brought their own young sons and Ginnie, the cripple daughter of Ramsey's first marriage, with them.

The Marks children had been looking forward to coming to Bullington, every generation always looked forward to it. Then, this morning their parents had told them the news. It was their first experience of death, they were uncertain what to expect. That Lavinia had died was something they could accept without any real grief, after all none of their friends could boast a great-grandmother, it seemed quite natural that they should lose theirs. What made them uncomfortable was the atmosphere in the house.

'Shall we go and play tennis? Would that be alright, Daddy? Or can't we?' It was Tessa, the eldest who asked. Her two brothers stood in line with her but said nothing. They went down in stages, Tessa was thirteen, Billy eleven and Hugh nine. Their birthdays fell within a week of each other as if they had been planned with regimental exactitude.

'Play tennis?' It was Kate who echoed the words. 'With poor darling Mother not even laid to rest! Alistair you can't mean to allow them to. Oh dear, children have no feelings.' And, evidence of her own feelings, her mouth trembled ominously.

'If Grandma could answer for herself, she'd say that's what she'd had the courts marked out for,' was Lottie's opinion. 'We always used to have tournaments, do you remember Alistair. Grandma always said she loved to hear us. And I bet she wants to hear these three. Go on, Alistair, say they can.'

At his nod of dismissal the three children escaped thankfully, seeing the way Aunt Kate was digging for her wisp of a handkerchief. They walked sedately enough across the hall, then down the corridor to the games room. It was here that the tennis racquets were kept, the croquet set, two or three cricket bats that had belonged to Mathesons in previous years, darts and a dart board, a very old fashioned pair of skating boots, a netball net left here more recently . . . one of the things they loved about coming to Bullington was the store in the games room. Once there they sighed with relief.

'Whew!' Hugh hadn't learnt to hide his feelings as well as the elder two. 'Did you two see? Old Aunt Kate, she was off again!'

'D'you know what I think?' Clearly Tessa was about to give him the benefit of her wisdom. 'It's because she's such a weary willy that poor old Uncle Drupert's like he is.'

'If ever I have a wife – and I shouldn't think for a moment I ever will 'cos who'd want to get stuck with some silly girl,' Hugh was busy taking the racquet from its press, 'but, just supposing, then if she behaved like old Aunt Kate d'you know what I'd do? I'd give her the same as we used to get if we whined when we were little, I'd slap her hand with a ruler and send her to her goom till she pulled herself together.'

'Good man,' Billy gave his behind a playful whack with his racquet. 'See what fine fellows it made of us lot! Race you to the court.'

Watching from the drawing room window as they sped towards the court, Lottie could feel the spirit of those fun-filled summer holidays of her childhood still alive. Wasn't that what Grandma would want? Until these last few months she'd lived every moment with a zest that age could never take from her personality. Letters hadn't told of the batle she'd gought to keep her stiff joints moving; they'd shown her still as the same understanding, positive person who'd always held

60

such a special place in her grand-daughter's heart. Even when news had come of her illness, Lottie had believed that *she* could be the one to break through the barrier.

Turning away fromt he window she looked at the sombre faces. It was as if they'd put on a mantle of dolefulness. How Grandma would have hated it! Katie looked as though she hadn't slept for a week. If Lottie hadn't loved her so dearly she might have seen her as almost plain this morning, pale and washed out. Ah, but she had more pain in her heart than the loss of 'Grandam' as she called her.

Katie felt her mother watching her. Tomorrow would have been the birthday, the day Grandam had made such plans for. Giving herself a mental shake she, too, took in the scene here in the drawing room. Hester's spectacles, which she normally wore on a gold chain around her neck, were sitting half way down her nose as, ignoring the others, she sorted letters from the bureau; to escape Rupert's hand Kate had stood up, she fidgeted with china ornaments on the mantelpiece, picking them up, putting them down, not really seeing them at all; Rupert, a worried frown on his face, stood by ready to pick up the pieces (whether of Katie's shattered spirit or of broken china); Claudia, Alistair's wife, was glancing at old photographs Hester had found in the bureau drawer; Alistair looking through a folder containing household receipts; only Ramsey was out, probably in the stables or on his own exploring the grounds of the estate.

Nigel was determined to cope with the funeral arrangements on his own, and now he joined them from the study where he'd been making telephone calls. It was something in the sight of him that recalled to Katie an evening around Easter time. Nigel had been home on vacation. In the afternoon they'd taken Grandam for a drive. No, it was wrong to say they'd *taken* her, Nigel might have driven the car but Grandam had entered into the spirit of the outing, her enthusiasm for all she saw as fresh as the promise of spring.

'See over there,' she'd pointed. 'The first pussy willow coming into bud. Spring again! Soon be summer.' Then she'd chuckled as if she knew something they didn't know. 'I've been making plans. It's time Bullington had a party.'

'While I'm here, Grandam?'

'I'll keep you here until then, I'm not letting you run away before my birthday party.'

That had been the first they'd heard of what she had already started to arrange. That evening she shared her secret with them.

'Open my bureau, Nigel. That's it, now bring me that large brown envelope. It's all in here. See – the caterers have been booked, I've arranged for a marquee, we'll have it near the southern boundary, within easy access of the south gate. I've never been ninety five before.' She'd sounded as excited as she must have done seventy four years ago when she'd come of age! 'The family, the tenants, all the village people, I want all of us to enjoy the fun. We'll have fireworks – rockets so high they'll keep them awake up there in heaven. Eh? How's that for a party? Eh?' How her eyes had shone. Thinking back to that evening, Katie could almost hear her voice. Did Nigel remember it too, she wondered.

Alistair was opening that large, familiar envelope.

'The marquee's already up, it's too late to do anything about that, but we'll have to stop the caterers,' he said as he sifted through the papers.

'No! Don't! Don't cancel any of it!' Katie's voice was urgent, she *had* somehow to make them understand. 'Grandam arranged it all herself, all of us being here, the village people too. She did it without saying a word. She was so excited.'

It was too much for Kate, folding herself back into her chair she gave way to another flood of tears.

'You don't realise what you're suggesting, you're upset, Katie,' Rupert's hand fluttered from his wife's direction to his grand-daughter's. 'It's not possible. It wouldn't be right. Think how it would be seen – imagine what people would say in the village if we were to carry on as if nothing had changed.'

'Damn what they say in the village. Grandam wanted it to happen. She even saw Mr. Jenkins – the caretaker of the Church Hall – about getting the fireworks. She did it months ago. Fireworks that went right up to heaven, that's what she wanted.'

There was silence, broken only a watery snort from Kate.

'Grandma lived for almost ninety five years,' Lottie spoke quietly, 'don't you think we might look on it as a thanksgiving for all that she was to us.'

'How can you suggest anything so wicked!' Anger even overcame Kate's snivelling. 'As if we can celebrate anything with Mother gone, Mother lying cold and lifeless! And you propose we all gather round her dining table and have a party.'

Katie sat on the arm of the chair, putting her arm around her namesake's shoulders. 'Grandam organised things all her life, you know she did, Mom's always told me. And this was the very last thing. Of course it won't be like a party, but her family will be together for her special day just like she wanted. It would be dreadful for us to scrap all she planned. Remember her telling us about it, Nigel? Let it go ahead. Let the children have their tea party, and the local folk come together for supper in the grounds of the Manor. She would be

62

so pleased. And I bet she'll be watching out for those fireworks. Rockets they'd hear in heaven, that's what she said.'

Hester's spectacles slipped off the end of her nose as she raised her eyes to the ceiling in despair.

Yet no one could put the idea aside. It was as if old Lavinia were keeping her eye on them, making sure they did her bidding. It became important to Katie. In some confused way that she didn't attempt to analyse it was as if making her views over-ride theirs helped her regain her grip on life's tiller. And if it didn't quite do that, at least it filled some of the emptiness in her heart. Here was something that she could do for Grandam.

She was the youngest amongst them, her opinions counted for no more than Alistair's children's might have, had they voiced them. Yet, from Hester to Nigel, they found themselves taking her suggestion seriously. 'Disgraceful', 'wicked', 'heartless', 'in bad taste', 'enough to keep the gossips busy for months to come', all these things were said and more besides (especially by Kate and echoed by Rupert), yet the arguments put up to oppose her suggestion lost their force. Katie was winning – or was it Lavinia?

Ronnie and Millicent Bradley with their sons John and Cliff were due to arrive in time for tea, then the 'tribe' would be complete.

Not many people could weep as copiously as Kate then banish the evidence as effectively. Upstairs in her room she rinsed her face in cold water, then pinched her cheeks to bring colour to them. Was it really so wicked, she excused herself as she peered close to the mirror, to want to look her best? It wasn't that she didn't grieve, of course she did. But it would be silly to pretend that Mother could have been part of the festivities, lying up there in a world of her own. If only she could have hung on just that little bit longer, then they could all have enjoyed the pleasure of being together without this niggling feeling of guilt. Reaching for her hair brush Kate sighed. Now there was no way they could all have the jolly time she'd been so looking forward to. Wasn't it always the way! Never look forward to anything. If you let yourself anticipate something good, then you may be sure some dreadful stroke of fate will knock the stuffing out of you. Not that it used everyone as unkindly. Look at Hester. Had she shed a single tear about poor, dear Mother? It would take a lot to knock Hester off her perch, but then think of the comfortable life she'd always led, a fine home, no shortage of money and, now that Alistair was out of the army and had made himself responsible for the running of Claygate Hall, Hester must be snug in the Dower House with a good housekeeper and a maid to look after her. Conscience did nudge Kate with the reminder that Hester had been left a widow when she was in her twenties, but after all these years it was easy enough to gloss over such a distant upset. No, life had been good to Hester. Even now she could be with her son and his wife every day if she chose; she was part of the children's world. Not like *her* with a daughter who'd deserted her to live in Canada; a grand-daughter who would soon be gone and who'd spent nearly all her holiday here at Bullington; since that dreadful war had taken her darling Michael, only one son left to her, Ronnie, and he living too far from Brimley for her to see except on special occasions. Well, today he was coming and no one could grudge her trying to make herself pretty. From her wardrobe she took the new dress she'd bought especially to wear when he arrived. It was a soft shade of violet, she knew it flattered her. Hester was in black . . . just for a moment Kate hesitated, holding the dress at arm's length and admiring it. Black flattered Hester, she often wore it. Kate slipped the new dress over her head. It had been wildly extravagant, she'd noticed Rupert's surprised expression when the account had come from Madame Nobelle's salon. He hadn't passed any comment, she'd waited, she'd half hoped he would have objected so that she could have had the chance of making him realise what it must be like for her having to look at the price tage before she even tried on a new dress. It had never been like that for Hester, nor for Mother, nor for any of them – just for *her*. Then she put all thought of Rupert from her mind and concentrated on her face. Despite the pinching, her cheeks looked wan. Opening her cosmetics bag, she set to work, a smile touching the corners of her pretty mouth. She may have been the one who'd missed out on life's luxuries, but nature had been kind to her.

A touch of rouge, a hint of lipstick, even a suspicion of eye shadow – not sufficient for anyone to notice and yet enough to enhance the blue of her eyes. Her reflection smiled back at her. Ronnie could arrive as soom as he liked now, she was ready.

Looking out of her window she could see Katie and Ramsey coming across the grass that sloped away towards the lake. The child had looked very washed out this morning. How much of it was because of Mother and how much could be laid at the door of that wretched redskin? That's probably what they were talking about out there, away from the house where no one could hear. Yes, there was Lottie going out to join them. And wouldn't you think she'd feel some sort of shame? Not that it was her fault that Neil O'Hagon had given some slut of an Indian woman his brat when he was hardly more than a child himself. Lottie's crime had been in thinking she was in love with him, in persisting in going her own pig headed way and

64

forcing their hand into consenting to their marriage by giving herself to him like some common whore so that they had no choice. Again Kate slumped on the edge of the bed, her hands between her knees. If only she could do something to help Katie forget. At nineteen one can love so wholeheartedly, one can be scarred by the hurt . . . and who knew better than she did? Through her open window whe heard Nigel's voice. She'd had such hopes for Katie and Nigel. Mother had seen how well they got along too. Before her illness they'd talked about it – never actually putting their hopes into words, but both of them understanding what lay below the surface. Now Mother was gone . . . the one person she'd always been able to turn to . . . the one person who had known her as well as she knew herself . . . who made her feel protected, secure, just as she had as a child.

'Are you coming down, dear? They'll be here soon I should think.' She'd been so wrapped up in her own thoughts that she hadn't heard Rupert come in.

'I was dressing.' Then, as if she defied criticism: 'There's no point in wearing mourning, not today with Ronnie coming. Anyway, it's depressing for the children. I'd looked forward so much to today.'

'You look very pretty. Lottie and Katie are in their ordinary things too.'

'She wasn't *their* mother. They can't feel it like I do.'

'Of course not. Poor Kate.' He rested his hand on her shoulder. 'You aren't any less sad because you wear a pretty frock. I know that.'

She gave him one of her rare smiles. Moments like this didn't happen often, but when his beloved Kate looked at him like that Rupert's sky held no clouds.

The moment was short lived. For it was just then that they heard the car coming up the drive. Ronnie was here.

The subject of the village supper was raised again at dinner that evening. Lottie threw the ball into the court, siding firmly with those in favour. Now that there had been a few hours for thought she was backed by Alistair, Claudia, Ronnie and, less definitely, by Hester; the team against her were Kate, Rupert and Millicent. Having made the original suggestion Katie didn't enter into the discussion and neither did Ramsey. They were all so busy airing their own opinions that no one seemed to notice that Nigel had said nothing.

'Excuse me, Miss Katie,' Hawkins moved with his usual silent tread to stand by her shoulder, 'there's a telephone call for you. The gentleman said it's important.'

'Who is it, Hawkins? Did he say?' She marvelled at the calm of her voice.

'He didn't give a name, Miss Katie.'

'If it's important, then I'd better come. Will you excuse me from the table a moment.'

Surely none of them could guess at the butterfly wings that were beating in her chest.

'Hello, Katie O'Hagon speaking.' She might have been answering a call from a stranger for all the warmth in her tone. The sound of Dylan's voice shattered her poise.

'Katie, I only heard when I checked back in at The Bell just now. Katie I am sorry. For you – and for Lottie.'

'I'll give her your message.' She tried hard to sound sure of herself. But she wasn't. And neither was he; she could tell it from those clear, separate syllables.

'You are listening with your ears only. Katie, please, hear me with your heart. I told you the truth last night. Rosie gave me her word.'

'Please – not again. I've talked to Dad too –'

'But how can he know anything but what was said in the court-room? Lottie heard it too, I heard it and I believed. But it was not the truth. Rosie wished to hurt Lottie for being Neil's wife; she wished to place me in a home with a future. I explained this to you. It suited her plans to lie to the Court.'

'And you bet it suited some plan to tell you the next tale too! Leave me alone, Dylan. Please. Forget we ever met. If you want to remember me, then let it be when we were children, like brother and –' Her voice faded on a croak.

'I will remember all of it. And so will you. Never think you can wipe out a single moment of it. I leave on Friday. Come with me Katie. Give me your trust. I beg you, forget everything except that we belong together.'

'It's not possible. You know it isn't. Anyway, Friday is going to be Grandam's funeral . . .' This time she couldn't disguise her tears. She was ashamed that she let him think they were just for Lavinia.

'I'll wait until –' he started to say. All he heard was the dialling tone. Katie had gone.

It was Rupert who typed the message on a single sheet of paper then with the precision that was natural to him backed it with cardboard. But the words were Nigel's and it was Nigel who supervised young Bill Huffkin, the garden boy, who fixed it to the main gate on the southern boundary of Bullington Manor.

'I know that sadness at the death of my great-grandmother, Lavinia Matheson, is shared by the whole of the village. Before her last illness she personally put all the arrangement in hand for

66

the celebration of her 95th birthday. Her family intend that her wishes shall be carried out. As a mark of respect to her I ask that whatever plans have been made for the children's tea party shall go ahead unchanged. At 8 p.m. supper will be served in the marquee. I ask you all to try to attend, to look on it as a tribute to her memory and a mark of the love and respect we all had for her. At 10 p.m. will come the finale, to be carried out exactly as she wished: a display of fireworks. Let this be Newton Dingley's farewell to a great lady.

Nigel Matheson'

There were those in the village of the same opinion as Kate, who felt there was something almost indecent in saying farewell to Lavinia with a shell burst of rockets.

As for Rupert, he might have made a neat two-fingered job of the notice to be erected on the gate but his heart wasn't in it. He knew just the sort of evening tomorrow would bring, how upset Kate would be when she heard the whistle of the rockets as they soared into the night sky. The sooner the whole thing was over and they were back in Brimley the better pleased he'd be. At the best of times he'd not been comfortable staying at the Manor. The family never changed, generation followed generation but nothing altered, they spent their time riding, playing tennis or badminton, visiting tenants, shooting in season, punting on the canal, each to his own; to all of them Bullington was "home", they did as they pleased. Meal times he particularly disliked. Matheson voices, all so sure of themselves, with supreme confidence in their own opinions. Every change society had known in the last forty five years had gone through the Matheson mealtime mill, as one government had followed another, as war had given way to peace, as Hitler had risen and fallen and once again war had given way to yet another peace, so opinions had been aired, decisions approved, decisions condemned. Not that Kate had ever been a political animal, sweet, gentle Kate. Yet even she, born a Matheson, seemed to glow in the vigour of their discussions. But not Rupert. Right from the start he'd been in awe of the beautiful woman who'd become his mother-in-law, just as he had of the conviction her family had of their own infallibility. Through all the years he'd never uttered a word in disagreement with her, indeed he'd seldom expressed an opinion. Now she was gone, the last tie with Kate's girlhood broken. He wanted nothing more than to get the next few days over and to go home.

With surprising sensitivity the village children managed to enjoy the tea party without letting it turn into a springboard for wild games. Mr Jenkins, the caretaker from the Church Hall, had promised to

67

supervise the entertainment and his talents surprised everyone. They made a team game of "telegraphs", he whispered a message into the ear of the child at the head of the trestle table while Eva Downs from the dairy whispered the same words to the one sitting at the foot. Then from mouth to ear, amidst stifled giggles, the "telegram" passed down each side of the table. 'Can't come. School started' became 'The car's come. School's started' and won the prize of a toffee each for the children on the left side of the table. 'Cartoon's cool star. Ted' won far more giggles, so a toffee apiece was agreed for the children on the right too. Then, after two games involving paper and pencil, all designed to occupy minds rather than voices, Mr. Jenkins brought the proceedings to a close with a display of card tricks. It wasn't the party they'd expected, no Cowboys and Indians in the copse, no races with cheers for the winners. But today was different, even the smallest children were aware that today was the birthday of the old lady from the big house – except that she'd 'gone and died just afore it'. The knowledge gave the afternoon an aura of mystique. Had Lavinia still been living none of them would have given her a thought; but she wasn't an ordinary living person any longer, the more imaginative amongst them even wondered whether she was up there in the sky looking down on them. No wonder they behaved themselves!

In the marquee the lamps were lit. From outside, shapes of people standing near the canvas sides could be seen silhouetted against the golden glow. Keeping in the shadows Katie went past, then out through the main southern gate to the road.

"I'm a fool, I ought to have more pride! I've told him to leave me alone – and I meant it – but I *have* to see him, just once more, to wipe out the beastliness –" By now he would have had time to think, he'd see the flaws in Rosie's story. If there really had been some other man, then she would have told him who it was. He'd been just a child, he'd accepted without question. It wouldn't have mattered to him who the unknown man was, whether it was Neil O'Hagon ("as of course it was, he must realise now") or someone else? He'd never known what it meant to have a father.

She'd have to play the scene as it came. She pictured herself in his room at The Bell (no, she wouldn't let herself think of those other times they'd been there together . . .), she on one side of the room, Dylan on the other. She had no idea what she meant to say to him, only that their final parting mustn't be full of bitterness. So where would that leave them? Friends? Brother and sister? No, no, don't follow that train, it led to shame, to sickening disgust.

68

'I'm not expected,' she greeted the landlord of The Bell. 'I only want to see him for a moment, to say goodbye. I'll go up and surprise him.'

''Fraid you won't, Miss. Mr. Kitashee checked out last night. Got the late train up to London.'

'But his car's in the yard.' For one moment she believed he'd left word that he didn't want to see her. 'I wanted to say goodbye.'

'Like I say, he's went last night. Very sudden it was. Asked me to fix for the garage to collect the car, but they don't seem in any great rush, he'd paid the hire on it for some days yet it seems. I'm sorry, Miss, about the sad news from the Manor. She was a grand lady. I dare say Mr. Kitashee didn't like to barge in on the family to tell you he was off so quick.'

Katie nodded. She even smiled her thanks and said she would have liked to have wished him a safe journey, but she expected he'd managed to get an earlier flight. Then she turned back to the door, leaving the landlord alone in the bar for tonight his customers were packed into the marquee.

Outside in the yard there was just one car – Dylan's. So it was all over, he was really gone. She'd not hear that familiar roar as he came up the drive of the Manor, nor listen for the over-revving of the engine, the squeal of the brakes when he brought it to a sudden halt at the foot of the front steps. Even as she thought it she heard another screech, the first rocket soaring into the night sky, ". . . high enough to keep them awake up there in heaven. And is it? Do you know Grandam? Can you see it all? We did it all just like you planned . . . and do you know about me? About Dylan? He's gone, Grandam. I can still tell you things, you still understand. But not him. He's gone. It's over. There's nothing. I know it was wrong, letting him love me, wanting him to love me. When I think of it I feel sort of withered up, unclean – but it wasn't like that. He said we belonged just to each other – yet all the time he must have known Rosie would have told him any old lies that suited her. Grandam, I don't know what I'm going to do. It's all just blank, empty. How can you fall in love with a brother? Can you? All the time in my mind I see just him – but it's no good – predestined, that's what he said, predestined that we should be together. . . ." So went her thoughts as she made her way home, the silence of the night rent by the whistle of the rockets. This time she didn't go to the southern entrance, but up Corder Lane to the east gate. This was where they'd met so often for their morning rides, this was where they'd met the very first time of all. Now it was just an empty lane, the familiar squeak of the wrought iron gate a small isolated sound in the night.

And above the sky was empty. The fireworks were over.

It was to have been a floral festival to celebrate ninety five years of life. The keenest of the assistant flower arrangers in the Women's Institute had each been allocated a window in Newton Dingley church, whilst the three stalwarts who vied with each other taking change of the pedestal in the chancel throughout the year were responsible for the lectern, the pulpit and the font. The same flowers, the same gentle rivalry between the cottagers as they compared contributions; only the occasion was different.

Today Kate let Rupert hold her arm, she was even glad of his unfailing nearness.

Walking behind them Lottie twined her fingers round Ramsey's. So many memories: Christmases here with the family, summer Sunday mornings when the sun cast its light through the stained glass windows just as it did today; and that other time when she'd walked up the aisle on her father's arm, Neil waiting for her at the chancel step. She remembered looking at her grandmother sitting in the front pew and, even then, all those years ago, dreading the day when she would no longer be here with them. Lottie breathed the heavy scent of the hundreds of flowers, a sign of the affection of the tenants and villagers; she pictured Lavinia as she'd been at the end of her long life; and unexpectedly she knew a deep peace, for her grandmother and for herself here with Ramsey. So many of the family had come today, just as they had when she'd married Neil. All of them further along the road of life just as she was, a road that for Lavinia had reached its goal.

And behind them Katie walked with Nigel.

The children had been left at home with instructions that they must play quietly in the house or else help Jenny prepare a packed lunch, for after the service was over Katie was going to take them for a picnic in the field by the canal. Today the Manor would be no place for them, Mr. Hickstead was joining the family for lunch and for the reading of the Will.

'I know you're not a child, dear,' Kate had told her, 'but someone has to keep an eye on the younger ones. And Nigel, of course, will have to stay behind. Well, Bullington will be in good hands. Oh but Katie you don't know how stripped I feel. All my life I've had my own room at the Manor, just as Hester has. Not that she's had the same feeling about it, her home has been Claygate Hall. But for me, home, my real home, will always be here. Now it'll be Nigel's. He'll marry, some other woman will be mistress, someone who never knew Mother . . .'

'Granny, Nigel will always welcome you here, you know he will.'

'Yes. I shall visit I dare say – if I can bear to.'

The young picnickers were glad to escape from the house. Today there was an echoing silence about the place, and they felt uncomfortably out of place in their summer shorts when everyone else looked unfamiliar in black.

Once back from church Katie changed into a cotton dress. She had no sense of disloyalty to Lavinia as she hurried to join the others, somehow she was sure that Grandam would have approved the expedition. It would have been far more to her liking that the sombre gathering in the morning room.

John and Cliff, Ronnie's sons, carried the two handled hamper, Katie and Tessa the fishing rods, Billy and Hugh a cricket bat and ball; it seemed they were prepared for anything. But how hard it was to listen to Tessa, to smile and answer, as they went out of the east gate, down the lane and across the main road to pass Redmans on the way to the canal. Where was he today? Somewhere high in the air, the miles between them growing, out of her world, out of her life . .

It was a relief to hear the chatter of the children. In trying to forget that which hurt too much to think about she threw herself into her first game of cricket, hunted without much success for the first barely ripe blackberries.

It was early evening by the time they made for home, all of them grubby and dishevelled, the food eaten, the ball lost and the only fish they'd caught put back to live another day.

'Katie!' Changed into her new lilac dress Kate called to her from the head of the steps, 'Katie, I've been watching for you. I can't believe it! Only this morning I said to you how I dreaded things changing – my room not being mine anymore – some other woman one day being mistress – you remember what I said – you know how I felt. Katie, I never dreamt this was what Mother had in her mind? I can't believe it!'

Chapter Five

Mid-sentence Alistair stopped speaking and turned an unsmiling countenance on Katie and her grandmother.

'They're back!' Kate announced. 'The children have gone to put the things away in the games room. But here's Katie.'

Katie took in the scene: they were all there, all except Nigel. Did she imagine it or was there hostility in the look they turned on Kate as she ushered her into the room? It was something to do with Grandam's Will. Where was Nigel? 'I never dreamt this was what Mother had in her mind . . .' It must be that Bullington was to belong to Granny. But how unkind of them to take the news like this! They were her family, they ought to be glad for her. She must feel so hurt.

Yet outside she'd looked excited, relieved . . .

'Mr. Hickstead had to go.' It was Lottie who broke the silence.

'That's why I stayed out, Mom. I thought you'd rather have us out of the way till he'd gone. Where's Nigel? Is everything – I mean – Nigel . . .?' Her question trailed away unasked. Bullington meant everything to Nigel, the family all knew it.

'Here, Katie,' Ramsey put an arm around her shoulder, 'there's a copy of the Will here. I guess you'd best sit down and read it for yourself.'

She felt she was intruding. Yet how strange. All the time she'd been here with Grandam she'd never once been made to feel an outsider, not like this.

'I don't need to, Dad. That's why I went out. But what about Nigel?' Nigel had never doubted that he'd inherit Bullington Manor; even the family who now appeared hostile had accepted that he was Grandam's heir. Her mind was tugged two ways: pity for him and anger that they should be so unfair to her grandmother. There wasn't a single one looking at her with pleasure, not a single one looking at her at all for that matter, they must be purposely ignoring her. It was hateful of them, didn't they understand that Granny could never be happy unless everyone else was happy for her? Knowing how hurt she must be Katie took her grandmother's hand in hers and felt the answering grip of her fingers.

'Do you want me to read it, Granny?'

'You needn't read it all,' Ramsay was saying, 'not right now. But this part, just here.' Opening the document his finger pointed.

'I bequeath Bullington Manor, with all its contents inside and out, except where stated in previous bequests in this my last Will and Testament, to my beloved great-grand-daughter Katrine O'Hagon of Higley Creek, Alberta, Canada, in the certain knowledge that she will have the courage to do what she knows is right.'

Katie read the words. Words, just words. Giving herself a mental shake she read again, surely she must have misunderstood. But she hadn't. Her first intelligent thought was her grandmother's bedroom: that was what she'd meant, she wouldn't have to give up the room that had always been hers!

'But Nigel . . .?'

'You may well ask! Mother must have taken leave of her senses. The boy was brought up to look on himself as the natural master of Bullington. The Will must be contested. Mother was a very old woman, she'd grown senile –'

'That's a wicked thing to say. Oh, not because of the Will. But to say Grandam didn't know what she was doing is a beastly way to talk about her. There was nothing she missed – even whem you thought she was dozing she was listening all the time, she used to open her eyes and join in.'

And into her memory came a picture so clear it took all her own will power to concentrate on the family here in the drawing room. The dinner table, Grandam at the head, Nigel at the foot and she and Dylan sitting opposite each other: Grandam, her head flopped forward, eyes closed and her hands still holding her knife and fork as they rested by her plate; Dylan's voice – she needed to remember, she clung to the bitter sweetness of every smallest incident, despising herself that even now, knowing all that she did, yet still he was there, constantly, at the front of her mind – '. . . give me a horse any time.' And Grandam proving that even if her body had grown tired, her mind had followed all they'd said as she'd told him: 'Then I will. Any time you care to exercise one.'

How dared Aunt Hester suggest she'd been senile!

'Of course it has to be contested. What can happen to the estate if it's left like this. You couldn't be expected to know the sort of fortune it takes to run a place like this. Nigel has her money – or the bulk of it

73

– and he has the knowledge of what's needed here. He's been reared to it. Even you, Lottie, must agree that Mother wasn't thinking clearly. This is the Matheson family home, it has been for two and a quarter centuries. You marry some wild cowboy, send his off-spring here to wheedle her way –'

'I guess you better take that back, Hester. Take it back and offer an apology for it.' Ramsey spoke quietly. The silence that followed was full of tension. Who would be the first to break it?

With the dignity that never failed her, Hester turned to Lottie.

'We're overwrought. I apologise, Lottie. It's not your fault, it's not even Katie's fault. But it's wrong. Bullington Manor should go to a Matheson, a male, then to his sons. That's the way it has always been. If Mother had had her full reason she'd not have drawn up this last will.'

Kate stood with her eyes closed, her fingers pressed to her temples. As long as Lottie could remember this had been the way all family arguments had ended.

'My poor head!' She rocked, somehow giving the impression that her world wasn't standing still. 'I can't take anymore. Haven't I suffered enough? What could Hester know about losing a daughter to a man like that?' Then, opening eyes full of pain, she turned to her sister. 'You wouldn't understand, you never had a daughter. One son, a son who came safely through the war, a son who is there with you still, his children part of your life. But what about me?' She didn't attempt to stop the tears. 'Michael, my darling Michael, never coming home from the war; Lottie forsaking me; Ronnie I see so seldom I'm a stranger to his children. Don't you think Mother might have thought of all that when she did this? Make Bullington Katie's and she'll stay in England. That's why she did it. Don't any of you see? She did it for me.'

'You seem to be overlooking the fact that Katie hasn't the means to run a place like Bullington.' As Kate's control was lost, so Hester's grip on hers tightened.

Over Katie's head the wrangling went on. Her eyes were riveted to the document spread out before her. Hardly realising she did it she reached out, moving the palms of her hand on the smooth walnut wood of the bureau. Hers! Grandam had wanted all this to be hers! The day she'd met Dylan, the day he'd come to dinner here for the first time, hadn't that been the morning that Mr Hickstead had come to see Grandam and then had stayed to lunch? That must have been when she'd signed the new Will. It had been during that same night – or early in the morning – that she'd had the stroke. But Nigel loved Bullington, it was his whole world. She let her eyes wander to the oil painting above the fireplace: a beautiful young woman, Lavinia Matheson, bride of only a few months, probably not much older than she was herself. Had Grandam recognised something of that girl bride's spirit in her, was that why she'd done it? 'She'll have the courage to do what she knows is right.' But what was right? To bow out and pass it to Nigel? No, it couldn't be that simple or what was the point of it? She looked at the carved ceiling. Such an elegant room – gracious, warm, full of the character of the woman who had been mistress for more than three-quarters of a century. Now the reins had been passed to *her*, the girl who'd bowled her first cricket ball this afternoon with the children as if she were one of them, the girl who'd lain under the stars with her own brother, her mind telling her to reject him, her heart telling her to believe his words: 'You belong to me, I belong to you.' Every minute they'd spent together she'd been conscious of the rightness. But it hadn't been, it had been wrong, unnatural, wicked . . . 'In the certain knowledge that she'll have the courage to do what is right.' The printed words seared into her mind.

'I'm going for a walk.' Let them think what they liked, she just wanted to get away.

'Shall I come with you, dear?' Kate suggested hopefully, wiping away her tears.

'No Granny. You don't mind, do you?'

'I expect you want to talk to Nigel. He went off too. You'll find him out there somewhere.' Kate sounded brighter by the second.

She didn't find him; but then she didn't actually look for him. Instead she went to the seat by the lake. The ducks waddled to within a foot or two of her, waiting hopefully for the offering she usually brought. When nothing was forthcoming they soon turned away, like a lot of gossiping housewives who found the grocer's shop shut before closing time. Katie found herself smiling as she watched them. She even imagined how Grandam would have chuckled to hear their quacking.

There must have been something about the peace and privacy of this lakeside bench, it had always been the "thinking place". Just for a moment she wondered that this hadn't been where Nigel had retreated to, but she as glad he hadn't. She wasn't ready yet to share his disappointments, her mind was too full. That Bullington should have been entrusted to her must have a reason, fate must have used Grandam as a channel. Was this to be her home, this the place where she'd make her life? But home was Alberta. There the very air was different, not soft and gentle like it was here. Back home when it rained it stormed; you never had days of gentle damp, moisture so fine it was hardly more than mist, raindrops that caressed your face.

Back home the sun was pure gold. Was there ever such sun as ripened the waving corn? Not that Higley Creek was real prairieland, but its corn grew just as high as it did further east. Home. The boys, Paul and Nick. And Ginnie. She and Ginnie never thought of themselves as step-sisters. Even as children Ginnie's five years seniority hadn't come between them and as time had gone on it had counted even less. Now would they all grow apart from each other? Since she was small England had been the magic place at the foot of her rainbow. In fact, she supposed it must have started when she'd been four years old, when Grandam had come to Higley Creek with Granny and Grandad, their visit timed so that they were there for Lottie's wedding to Ramsey. Had she always known deep down in her subconscious that this was where she belonged? But how could she belong here when she and Dylan were put in this world just for each other? Stop it! Don't even think of him. Don't think of how you expected these days to be, the plans you made for when the family met him, just a few wonderful days with all of you together before you flew back to Canada with him. 'I'll take you back with me,' he'd said. Now he was gone. He was thousands of miles away in that land that had always been home to her – to both of them.

And into her mind came other thoughts. Because the days had been so different from her expectations the dates had gone unnoticed. Only now did she realise. Emotional shock can upset the system. Yes, that must be what had happened. The excitement of Mom coming, then all that dreadful business about Dylan, losing Grandam. She'd been upset, the cycle of her days had been knocked off balance. She was only a few days late. Of course she was all right, until this moment she'd not given it a thought. It was probably because her lifestyle had been changed, she'd not even been riding for days. In the morning she'd go for a good gallop. She'd chase across the Common, take a few jumps. Like we used to . . . oh, Dylan, how could any of it have been wrong?

She got up from the "thinking seat". Yes, that's what she'd do if nature hadn't sorted itself out by the morning, she'd give it a helping hand. Not that she was worried . . .

It was at dinner that evening that Hawkins brought the message.

With a small cough and a self-consciousness that showed he heard more of what went on than he was told, he announced:

'Excuse me, Miss Katie, I have taken a message from Mr Nigel. He says he is staying with friends for a few days and sends his apologies for leaving without warning.'

'Did he say where, Hawkins?'

'No, Madam,' the word hung in the air, 'simply that he'd been invited to stay a day or two with a friend.'

The next day Lavinia's "tribe" began to break up. The Marks went back to Claygate Hall; Ronnie, Millicent and their two boys were waved on their homeward journey to Yorkshire.

'It's time we got back to Brimley, my dear. We've already been here longer than we anticipated.' There was a wistfulness in Rupert's expression. Even as he voiced the suggestion he knew he had no hope.

'But everything's changed. We planned to take Lottie and Ramsey back with us – and Katie, too. Now Katie's place is here and Lottie will want to stay with her. I don't see why we have to deprive ourselves of the few short weeks we might all be together. Unless, of course, you're desperate to get back. If so you must just leave me behind. It's not much to ask, Rupert, a few weeks with my daughter after all the years I've been alone.'

Rupert didn't press the point. In truth the prospect of staying on at Bullington Manor was far more pleasant now there were no Mathesons in it.

Nearly a week went by. Katie spent hours in the saddle. Sometimes during the day Lottie and Ramsey rode with her, but early each morning her only companion was memory as she went towards the Common. She galloped on the crest of the open downs, she turned towards the trees that fringed the eastern boundary, followed the woodland tracks that had become so familiar to her and to Dylan too. Now he'd gone, probably she'd never see him again. And wasn't that the best thing, for both of them? What would he feel now if he knew why it was she put such physical effort into these morning rides, if he knew the truth that with the passing of each day became more certain?

She felt she was playing a dual role. The early light of morning found her re-living those hours with him, sometimes she even indulged in recalling the unquestioning faith she'd had in the future. But not for long could she hold back the fear, first no more than a suspicion, then a cold fact from which there was no escape. And so the second role took over: back at Bullington she could almost pretend the nightmare that haunted her wasn't real. Bullington, the trust Grandam had shown in her; she kept her thoughts and sights just on that, like a blinkered horse her vision was narrow.

It was ten days since her parting with Dylan, exactly a week since Lavinia's funeral. Lottie and Ramsey had gone to Wantage, Rupert

77

had dropped off to sleep reading the cricket scores in the newspaper in the shade of the sycamore tree, Kate was in the rose garden cutting off the dead blooms.

'Do you want any help, Granny? How far down do I have to cut them?'

'Oh, Katie, how nice! I didn't hear you coming. No, I'm only playing. Why don't you cut some for the hall? *Your* roses! I hope Mother knows how happy she's made me in what she's done. And you, Katie, hasn't it made you happy too? It's pointed out the path for your future. You've not talked to me – about Dylan?'

'Please, Granny, I don't want to talk, there's no point. You know what happened, I heard what you called him – Neil O'Hagon's bastard. Isn't that enough! There's nothing to say.'

'We can't say anything that will change the situation, of course we can't. It's just that I want you to feel you can talk to me, I shall always understand.'

Katie nodded, she forced her face into a smile. Understand? How could any of them understand?

'I was just about your age, you know, when I fell in love. It was during the Great War. Bullington Manor was a Military Hospital and Matthew was a doctor. We were to be married. On the wedding day I was dressed for the church, Mother had already left the house. Then a message came – it was Rupert who brought it. My bridegroom wasn't coming! He'd jilted me for your Aunt Eva! There, I've said it, told you. I've never even told your mother – although it wouldn't surprise me if Eva had, she and Lottie were always thick as thieves.'

'Jilted you! Then, Granny, if he was that sort, you were better off without him. For Aunt Eva? But she never had a husband.'

'He was posted to France, they were to marry when he got leave. He was killed.'

'How awful. But Granny, think how much better things worked out for you. If you'd married him – and he couldn't have been good enough for you if he would treat you like that, right at the last moment – you'd have been a widow in no time. Anyway, you married Grandad, he must have been much nicer. You wouldn't have had him – nor Mom and the others – nor me.'

'The hurts we receive at nineteen make scars that last for life. Katie, try and see it as a blessing that you've learnt the truth. Supposing we'd none of us known who his father was, supposing that even against everyone's wishes you'd married him? Imagine the heartbreak if you'd had children.'

'Granny, that's a beastly way to talk! Because he has Indian blood in him, you mean? He's proud of it, and so am I.'

'Because he's got O'Hagon blood in him, that's what I mean!'

'I know it would be wrong, I know it's – it's – against nature. But I don't see what difference it would make to our children who their father was.'

Katie tried to sound calm, curious, nothing more. Yet the fear of what she would be told was a physical thing, something that tingled in her arms and legs, made her mouth suddenly dry.

'Haven't you heard stories of brothers and sisters who – who – well, you know what I'm saying.' Of the two Kate was the more tongue-tied. 'I remember reading about a brother and sister who lived as if they were man and wife. At the time of course no one knew that they weren't just an ordinary married couple. Then she had a child. Oh, don't let's spoil our afternoon imagining anything so dreadful.'

'Why was it dreadful?'

'Quite abnormal. I read about it when the case came up. They were accused of murdering it. Oh, it's too horrible to contemplate. Who could wonder at it if they had? Poor little soul was dreadfully misformed, had no sign of any dawning intelligence. Then, of course, the whole dreadful sorry story came out. I read it in the local paper a few years back; they'd rented a cottage not far from Brimley. Both of them were given long prison sentences, of course. Let's forget it, it's too beastly. Just let's be thankful that the truth was known about that wretched Kitashee woman and Neil O'Hagon. And, Katie, look at Bullington and be thankful again, dear. It's almost as if Mother knew that in giving you all she had to give, she was showing you the way to a new beginning. Cut a nice big bunch of roses, Katie, then we'll go into the conservatory and arrange them together. I love doing the flowers, don't you?'

Katie did as she said. But the story of the brother and sister with the abnormal child was at the front of her mind all the time, whether she was arranging the roses, listening to Lottie's account of the day she and Ramsey had had in Wantage and walking on the downs, eating dinner, watching the evening news on television . . . What could she do?

She'd never ridden as hard in her life as she did next morning; then on the edge of the woods she climbed into the high branches of an old oak tree, swung by her arms and then jumped to the ground, risking a broken leg and hoping to give nature the jolt it needed. But she did neither.

Sixteen days and Lottie and Ramsey were due to fly back to Canada. Katie's parents and grandparents had gone to bed. The night was airless, hot and sticky, the hours stretched ahead when she'd lie alone with nowhere to hide from the torment of her imaginings. To put off the moment, she went outside, sniffing the scents of summer, welcoming the darkness that wrapped itself around her. Down the stone steps, across the semi-circle of gravel that fronted the Manor, then on to the grass. The silence of her footsteps seemed to protect her. Here she was alone, safe. But what a foolish way to think! Safe! As if silence and darkness could change anything. What if she told Mom? No, that would be crazy. There may be no need to tell anyone.

Grandam, you trusted me, and just look what a mess I've made of everything. If some magic spirit could give me one wish, then it would be that Neil O'Hagon hadn't been my dad. Then none of this would matter. And Grandam, that's just one more thing that makes me into a real heel. Even Bullington, even the faith you had in me, I'd turn my back on it all. Can you forgive me? Can you understand? I know it can never happen, but I can't pretend. If a magic spirit could make miracles, that would be what I'd ask. Then I'd go and find Dylan. That's what would be right. Yet you put your trust in me to do what I knew to be right – what? What is it you want me to do?

In the dark she'd followed that well-trodden way down across the sloping lawns, the way the Mathesons had taken for generations when they wanted to commune with their souls. By the time she reached the lake her eyes had grown accustomed to the night. Without hesitation she walked towards her seat.

But someone was there before her!

Why should she be frightened? She told herself it must be one of the gardeners, or maybe Jo Dibbens, the stableman. Yet she was sure it wasn't. Now she welcomed her noiseless tread; she'd retreat before whoever it was knew she was there.

'The Lady of the Manor!'

Her fright melted at the sound of his voice, words that were meant to wound yet all she heard was his own hurt.

'Nigel! You went away without even seeing me. I felt dreadful – I feel dreadful. I never expected –'

'That makes two of us. And there's no point in my pretending. We'd talked about it often enough. What a joke you must have thought it, eh! All the time I used to talk about my future being Bullington, and while I was away you were here with her, wheedling your way into favour.'

'That's not true! That's a hateful way to talk. Aunt Hester says you ought to contest the will, she says Grandam didn't know what she was doing.'

Just for a second there was silence. Even the leaves were still.

'There was nothing wrong with Grandma's mind. I'm surprised you can repeat a suggestion like that. You don't believe it, Katie?'

'No, of course I don't. I was just telling you what the family are saying.'

Again they fell silent. There was so much that neither of them understood. And for Katie, it wasn't even as simple as that. Her overriding feeling for Nigel was pity. And that in itself was new. Previously it had been comradeship, carefree friendship.

'Kitashee's gone, I suppose? It wouldn't have worked, Katie. I'm not blind, I could see the way you were heading. I'm glad he had the sense to realise there was no future in it.'

'I would have gone with him, I meant to. Nigel, I didn't know until Mom came – Dylan and I have the same father.'

'Good God! Didn't he know either?'

'Doesn't matter. It's done with – he's gone. Granny seems to think Bullington is a sort of pointer to me towards the future.'

Another silence, but when he spoke he took up the conversation.

'If you have a pointer then, Katie, I envy you. I don't seem to see where to go. I just don't see.'

'Go? But this is your home. It always has been your home.'

It was too dark to see his face. It surprised her when she felt her hand taken in his, raised to be held against his cheek, then gently kissed.

'Bless you, Katie.'

It was too dark for him to see her face either, but he must have felt her draw away, move a little further along the bench.

Lottie was determined to visit Brimley.

'There's much more for you to do here, dear. Your days are so precious. Stay and enjoy them at Bullington.' That was her mother's opinion.

But Rupert was delighted. A visit to the Manor always sapped what little self-esteem he had and Lottie could have bestowed no greater accolade on him than her insistence that Ramsey must see the home and haunts of her childhood. So two days later the four of them departed. They planned to be away for a week, then to spend the last part of their stay with Katie.

Watching the car disappear round the bend in the drive she felt strangely alone. The great house was full of silence. It must have been in her imagination that each footstep seemed to echo on the marble floor of the hall. She put out a hand to touch the carved stone fireplace; she raised her eyes to the high domed ceiling. Hers. Never in the days since Lavinia's funeral had the truth borne home to her as it did now that the family had gone. Everything here was hers, not just to possess but to be responsible for. From generation to generation it had been cared for. It had given stability and security to the family and in return it had been loved. Generation to generation . . . Katie shivered. As if to escape her own thoughts she turned back to the August sunshine.

There was no running away from the truth. She had to face it squarely, add up her assets. If things had been different, if Neil O'Hagon had played no part in their lives, then she and Dylan would have been here together. For a moment she indulged in fantasy. She imagined them both at Bullington with the child she was so sure she was expecting. Then she gave herself a mental shake. This wasn't adding up her assets, carving a future. Then another thought: even with Dylan gone, then she would gladly have their child. Let people say what they liked! It was the outcome of love. She and Dylan had been put on this earth for each other, hadn't he told her so? For answer came the silent reminder that even while he'd said it, he *must* have known that Rosie Kitashee couldn't be believed. And worst of all was that other fear, that terror that blotted everything else from her mind: her grandmother's warning that a child produced by a brother and sister would be a monster, a freak of nature!

By now she'd walked some way from the house. Looking back at it she seemed to see it anew, the simple line of its Georgian architecture unchanged in a changing world. Just as she'd felt herself to be one with that regiment who'd trodden the Roman road for two thousand years, now she felt the stirring of a new emotion, something she hardly understood. Was it pride? Certainly not in herself, but in this edifice that had been the family's sanctuary for more than two centuries. So, was it humility? No, not even that, for if Lavinia had seen her as the next link in the chain, then she'd move heaven and hell rather than fail. Was it for Lavinia, for the Matheson "tribe", or even because all through her childhood far away at home in Alberta Lottie's stories of Bullington had fired her imagination? No, what she felt wasn't as simple as that. It was something between herself and the gracious building, between herself and the soft, green countryside.

Was this what Nigel felt? Forcibly she turned away from thoughts of him. She told herself that he had an Upper Second in History from Oxford, and most of Grandam's fortune. If right now he was taking stock of his own assets, he must surely realise his future was anything but bleak.

She'd wandered away from the house, instinct taking her to the sloping parkland. Now, squaring her shoulders, she walked back at a brisk pace.

In the morning room she rang the bell, and almost immediately, as if he'd been standing by ready to be of service, Hawkins appeared.

'You rang, Miss Kat – you rang, Madam?'

'Yes. Hawkins, I want you to rustle up all the staff. Everyone, if you can. I'll wait in here. Get them into the hall and tell me when you're ready. Will you do that for me?'

'Certainly, Madam.' She heard the query in his tone, and for a second she was tempted to let him carry her message. But Bullington hadn't been handed to her for her to shirk her duties, so she picked up the morning paper, pretending she hadn't recognised the question.

After he'd left her alone some of her confidence melted. If she were honest with them, she'd tell them how scared she was of the task that had been given her. But she figured that that kind of honesty might as well be called "weakness". For three-quarters of a century Bullington had had a mistress who'd never shirked what she saw as her duty. Katie's chin was high – even though she did grit her teeth tightly.

Minutes went by, messages were taken to the estate office, to the stables, to the potting shed, to the kitchen garden; Mrs Moggs, the housekeeper, put on a fresh apron and carried out her own inspection on her staff before they finally presented themselves.

In the hall Katie faced them. Her task wasn't made easier by the sound of a door closing upstairs. Nigel! He was her friend, yet she wished he were somewhere else. The thought that he might come down the stairs and listen to what she was saying chased her planned speech from her mind.

'Listen,' she plunged in, 'I guess you all know about Grandam's – my great-grandmother's – Will. You know that she has entrusted Bullington Manor to my care. I guess it came as a surprise to all of us. But if she had faith that I could follow in her shoes, then I'm going to see that I don't let her down. And I know I can depend on all of you to back me. Since her illness everything has gone on smoothly. I mean, meals, housekeeping, the gardens, all that kind of thing. I want to learn, but it would be presumptuous of me to reckon that I could start off right now doing all the things she used to do. Like I said, the wheels have been turning smoothly in the house, thanks to Hawkins and Mrs Moggs, and for the present I'd like it to go on that same way.'

The smile she turned on the housekeeper would have melted a harder heart than Mrs Moggs'. It held trust, hope, even gratitude. 'Right now I've not acquainted myself too well with how things go on on the estate,' that same look was turned in Frank Fulford's direction, 'but I do want to learn. Mostly what I wanted to say was how glad I am to have all of you here. I'm new and strange to these kind of responsibilities – but I'll learn. Right now we're all looking back, of course we are, she was a great model to live up to. But the future will be good too. Won't it?' Was she encouraging them or seeking reassurance?

'I'm sure I speak for everyone, Madam, when I tell you you have our complete support.' Hawkins spoke with a dignity she envied.

Only Frank Fulford, the estate manager, failed to join the chorus of assent, but in her relief that this, her first duty as mistress of the house, had passed of well, Katie didn't notice his silence.

'I heard your homily. Guess it was spoken with simple honesty, guess you'll have them eating out of your hand, guess they'll see the wheel jus' keep right on a-turnin' with no help from li'l ol' you.' Nigel's voice surprised her as she escaped once again into the gardens. His words were sarcastic, even spiteful, but there was a teasing note in his voice that took away the sting.

'Beast!' She laughed, pretending she felt no hurt.

'On the contrary, I think you struck just the right note.'

Together they started across the lawn to the parkland that sloped towards the lake.

'You know what I believe Grandma had in mind when she concocted that crazy Will? You the house, me the money? The house can't exist without money, and I can't think of my existence away from here.' He didn't look at her as he spoke.

'Nigel, I'm truly sorry you feel that way. You'll get yourself sorted out, same as I will. I was thinking about you just a while back – you've got your degree, Grandam must have had a heap of money . . .'

'The money and the house shouldn't be parted.'

'So what are you telling me? That you mean to contest her Will, to pretend you think she's lost her reason?' During the months she'd been here she'd grown to love Bullington; but only now did she realise just how much the trust that had been put in her mattered. If Nigel wanted a fight, then she'd give it to him.

'Grandma was sane, we both know that. Until you met Kitashee, you and I were together a lot. We got along well, didn't we? She saw better than most of us what went on around her. What she had in mind was that we'd make a match of it. Don't you see? To you she said something about having the courage to do what you knew was the right thing – and to me that the money would lead me to what I wanted.'

'But why didn't she just leave things as they were? The estate and the money all yours.'

In the easy way he so often had, Nigel took her hand as they walked.

'She wanted you to know you were important to her, I suppose. But she meant us to unite the two, estate and wealth. Katie, the

84

money she left to you can't run this place for more than a year. What are you suggesting she meant? That you'd have the courage to put it on the market, let some rich industrialist buy Bullington? It was built by a Matheson. If we marry, when we have a son he'll be a Matheson, the natural heir to the place.'

'Shut up. I don't want to talk about it.'

'Honestly, Katie, I'm sorry that swine treated you like he did. He was older than you. You can't tell me he was ignorant of who he was.'

'Shut up, can't you? I don't want to talk about it,' she repeated.

'All right. There's no panic. But think about it, Katie. You may have looked on me as family, but we're not that closely related. Until Kitashee turned up we were heading down the path Grandma wanted. Just now you may not be in the mood to hear me say I want to marry you, but it's true. I was well on the way towards telling you so before this brother of yours turned up and Grandma was taken ill. Can't we pick up the pieces, Katie? That way Bullington will be safe. If you're not in love with me, then can't you do it for her?'

'It's not possible. Don't say anything more. Please.'

'All right. Just this. Think about it, think about the future. If the Manor has been put into your trust, then you have a duty to see it run properly.'

She pulled away from him. This time he let her go. Only the smile that teased the corners of his mouth as he watched her gave any hint that he thought the point scored had been his.

He went on to the estate office where he spent an hour or so with Frank Fulford. It was as he walked back towards the house for lunch that he noticed her, and at what he saw he broke into a brisk run towards the tree house where every generation of Mathesons had played. Bit by bit the rotting wood had been replaced more than once through the years, but to every child of the family the tree that housed it was a friend.

'What the devil are you doing? What's happened to the ladder?'

She didn't answer. Instead, hanging from a high branch, she swung herself backwards and forwards then, just before he reached her, and with her eyes tight closed, she jumped.

'Katie, you ass! Are you all right? There's nothing the matter with the rope-ladder, what in the world did you do that for? Are you all right?'

She'd landed on her feet, then from her squatting position fell forward to lie on the ground. Instinct for survival had prevented the damage she'd intended.

'Don't want to be all right.' She turned her head away from him. 'That's why I did it.'

85

'I don't understand.' Nigel knelt by her side. 'Here, let me help you up. Sure you're not hurt?'

In his voice she heard genuine concern. It brought home to her how desperately alone she was with a worry that grew worse with each passing day. He was her friend; he was of her own generation; he would understand.

So she told him. Listening to herself, she was aware of her expressionless tone. Sentence followed sentence. He was silent, he didn't attempt to interrupt her.

'Now you see what I was doing. I've taken jumps, I've tried all I know.'

'And he went off and left you?' Somehow Katie wished he'd not said it, not spoken at all. It was easier to talk while he listened quietly. 'How long have you known?'

'I didn't think about it until the night of Grandam's funeral. Perhaps I'll be OK. Next time round, perhaps I'll be OK.'

'Does it work like that?' Nigel looked doubtful.

'It's just got to. Granny told me about what happens when a brother and sister have a child. She said she read –'

'You mean you told Aunt Kate?'

'No, of course not. She was trying to say all the right things about Dylan and me finishing, saying how awful it would have been if we'd married without knowing.'

She'd struggled to a sitting position by now, while he was still kneeling near to her. Neither spoke for a while and she was glad. She'd shared her secret, the weight of it was lessened, Nigel was her friend. Even now that she'd taken from him what he wanted more than anything in the world, she was certain he was her friend.

'We'll work it out together, Katie,' he said at last. 'Your people are coming back in a week's time. I'll arrange for a special licence. We'll be married quietly in the village church while they're still here.'

'I can't. I've told you how I am. I can't marry you when I'm going to have someone else's child!'

'No one will know it's not mine. There's a chance that you'll reject it if there's something dreadfully wrong – isn't that so? Perhaps nature will put things right. From what Aunt Kate says the baby won't be normal. With animals those are the ones that often don't come to anything. Let's cross our bridges when we have to.'

Things seemed to be rushing ahead out of control. How could she marry him, she wasn't in love with him? He was her friend, he was a Matheson, his world was Bullington. And into her mind came the echo of another voice, the syllables clear and precise: 'Just as surely as the sun and the moon have their place in the firmament, so we have ours here on the earth – together.'

'I'm not in love with you, Nigel'. Oh, but how could she be when that other voice was never out of her head?

'I'll see about the licence this afternoon. Then I'll go and talk with the vicar.' She might not have spoken for all the notice he took.

'But . . .' She looked at him and beyond him, up the slope to where the great house crowned the summit. Another memory, this time the printed word: ". . . in the certain knowledge that she will have the courage to do what she knows is right." Was this right? To become Nigel's wife? And when news got around that she was pregnant, to let the baby be looked on as his?

For a long time she didn't answer, but let her gaze linger on the Manor. There it stood, solid, permanent, unchanging. What were any of them but pawns in the game of life? Twenty years, fifty years or even a hundred years on, there it would stand; more pages written in Matheson history; more babies conceived and born under its roof; more children to make their own memories, games in the tree house, tournaments on the tennis courts, rosettes to be won at the gymkhana, boats to be sailed on the lake. The young would grow old, their names be added to those already in Newton Dingley cemetery . . . Matheson . . . Matheson. Katie gave herself a mental shake. She wasn't a Matheson, she was an O'Hagon from Alberta.

Then her glance moved away from the gracious old house to rest on Nigel.

Chapter Six

Of them all, Nigel was the most at ease.

'I wish you'd wait a while, Katie.' Lottie looked anxiously at the young couple. 'It's because we're only here for such a little while more that you feel you have to arrange everything in such a rush.'

'How'd it be for us to promise to come back again next spring?' Ramsey stood by her side, his hand on her shoulder. 'What you're planning to go into is the biggest step of your lives.'

'That's a great idea.' Lottie clutched at the idea with relief. Mightn't she have known he would come up with the right answer! 'I'll buy a big hat, play the bride's mom's part up to the hilt.'

'Mom, please don't try and stop us. Nigel's been moving heaven and earth to get things fixed so it can be before you go back. It's crazy to suggest we wait. Grandam wanted it for us, why else do you figure she said what she did in her Will?'

Ramsey's blue eyes half closed as he looked at her. At her? Into her? ". . . have the courage to do what she knows to be right." Courage? Was that the way to go into marriage?

Lottie's fears weren't as simple. Katie never mentioned Dylan, but the hurt must be there. To marry one man in order to forget another? How could that lead to anything but misery?

If Nigel was the most at ease, then Kate Bradley was the most delighted.

'Oh, hush, Lottie, don't spoil it for them – for all of us.' With her arms outstretched she moved to embrace Katie. 'It's what I've prayed for. Yes, truly I have. And Mother must have done too. I know just how she felt when she saw how well you two got along. Just think, dear Bullington will go on just as it always has, only better because Katie will be here too.'

And willingly she let herself be enfolded in her grandmother's embrace, let herself be enveloped in the assurance that what she was doing was right. Bullington Manor had been given into her care, but more than that, it was a shield between her and all that she had to free herself of. To love one man and marry another, could that possibly be a road that would lead to contentment? It had to be. No road could take her to Dylan. Nigel was her friend; he was her confidant; he said he'd seen this as their future even when he'd believed the Manor would be his, before Dylan had come to Redmans. So if anything could help her to forget it was to let herself sink into the happiness that radiated from her grandmother – and from her grandfather too as he clasped Nigel's hand.

Lottie knew she'd lost the battle. Katie was under-age; she could easily have forbidden such a hasty wedding. She said as much to her mother later.

'Oh, yes, you've the authority. But you wouldn't be so stupid.'

'Mother, she's dong it on the rebound. You know as well as I do where her heart is.'

'With that by-blow of Neil O'Hagon's? It was no more than a young girl's infatuation. And the sooner she gets on with living, the sooner she'll pick up the pieces. If all those years ago something had got in the way of your being able to tie yourself to Neil O'Hagon, then you'd have turned to Barrie Miles. You remember Barrie? He'd have picked up the pieces just as keenly as Nigel is now. And a good deal happier your life would have been for it.'

'I wouldn't change my life. And I wasn't blind to the way you used to push me and Barrie together. He was a dear, and a really good friend. But that's not what marriage is built on, surely you can see that?'

Kate bit her lip.

'Marriage is built on – on – endurance, on putting away your dreams, on making do. I ought to know!'

'Oh, Mum!' Lottie even laughed indignantly as she answered. So she might have spoken to a rebellious child. 'Dad eats out of your hand, he always has.'

Kate shrugged. 'You wouldn't understand, you never have understood. But for once listen to me, Lottie, and try and see the wisdom of Katie and Nigel letting their plans go ahead now while everything is new. With Mother gone this is the right time for change. Think of the responsibility poor Katie would have here on her own. Not that Nigel would let that happen. Even if you insist on her waiting until the spring, I'm sure he'd want to take over the running of the estate. But let them go into it all together, right from the start. Nigel will make a splendid master here. Mother had such faith in him. Anyway, if it's the Canadian boyfriend she's hankering after, the sooner she puts someone else in his place the sooner she'll get him out of her system. She's young. A wild infatuation for a few summer weeks, that's all it was. She's had no experience of men and what marriage means – in bed – you know what I mean. Once they're married she'll forget all that other nonsense, it'll fade into nothing once she belongs to Nigel. And he's a good boy, Mother thought so well of him. Another year or so, perhaps you'll be coming over again for a christening, a new Matheson. Think of that. Think of the joy it will bring me to have her here.' Then, with a smile that lit her eyes: 'I fancy you'll be visiting more often in the future – and, as for me, there just aren't the words to say what it will mean to have a share in their lives.'

Lottie made no more objection.

In answer to the bell, Hawkins came into the drawing room.

'Ah, Hawkins.' Nigel turned to him with a smile. 'We have cause for celebration. I want you to bring champagne.' Then, with his arm around Katie's shoulder, 'Miss Katie is to be my wife. Carry the glad tidings down to the staff, and open a bottle or two downstairs to drink to our future.'

'May I say, Sir, how delighted I am. And to you, Miss Katie – Madam. I know I speak for everyone below stairs when I say what pleasure the news will give.'

Dabbing at her eyes, Kate's happiness overspilled.

'Of course,' she explained, 'it will have to be a very quiet wedding. Just family and I dare say one or two friends of Mr Nigel's. So soon after poor Mother – well, it has to be quiet. Next Friday week, Hawkins, before Miss Lottie goes away from home again.'

Across the room Lottie's brown eyes sent a silent laughing message to Ramsey. Miss Lottie goes away from home, indeed!

'I'll convey the message to Mrs Moggs. She'll be overjoyed if I may say so, Sir, to be catering for the occasion.'

'Thank you, Hawkins. I'll come down and speak to the staff later, bring Miss Katie down,' Nigel dismissed him.

She felt the doors of her cage close. She told herself she was being over sensitive. She and Nigel would work together. There would be hurdles but they'd take them together. He'd already proved that to her. She was no longer alone to face the nightmare begotten by her grandmother's story of the couple who'd lived near Brimley. A freak of nature, a misformed monster. 'They were accused of murdering it, but who could blame them if they had?' Perhaps Nigel was right and nature wouldn't let it happen. But if it did, if she bore a child who was all she feared it was bound to be, then he would share the tragedy. So why did she suddenly feel trapped? Maybe people always did when

90

they were committed to a set course, maybe he felt the same himself. She turned to look at him, hoping for a conspiratorial smile, something that would unite them. But Nigel didn't notice.

The wedding photograph would date, future generations of Mathesons would see something of their family history in the pictures of the couple. Less than a month after Lavinia's death there was no traditional white wedding, no morning suits, bridesmaids and page boys; this bride of the 1960s was a girl of her time. Certainly she abandoned her normal above-the-knee skirt. For the wedding the full hem-line of her ice-blue silk dress was mid-calf, her golden-brown curls topped by a small flowery hat. She needed no attendant, for she had neither veil nor bouquet. Instead she carried a small prayer book that had belonged to Lavinia. It was a reminder to her of the trust that had been placed in her.

Walking up the aisle, her arm through Ramsey's, Lavinia's spirit seemed very close to Katie. It helped to give her the courage she needed for this step in the dark. In the dark? She tried to push the thought from her mind. How could it be that when she and Nigel got along so well? They had no secrets from each other . . . they were friends . . . so why couldn't she see through this dreadful fog ahead of her? Perhaps it was like this for every bride. She held her chin a little higher, she smiled into the mid-distance as heads turned to look at her.

Help me, help me! What am I doing? A life, a whole life, all that I am, all that's before me. Memories crowded in on her. "Kate-ee" . . .

From her place in the front pew Lottie watched them walk down the aisle. The moment brought alive so much that was buried in the recesses of her mind. Memory can leapfrog. The years between melted and she was the bride, her hand on Rupert's arm. How clearly she remembered the feeling of certainty as she'd seen Neil waiting for her; here in the midst of her family she'd been so sure that all was well lost just so long as she was with him. Now, in one short flash, she felt it all again. She could re-live it without any hurt left by what had followed. Her gaze moved from Katie to Ramsey. She wanted to reach out to him, to tell him what it was she'd just discovered; because the girl she'd been all those years ago had loved Neil, the woman she was today was all the richer, had a fuller and deeper appreciation. But what of Katie? Today she must be at the forefront of all their thoughts, this was her day. What sort of a future would she have with Nigel? How strange life was. Here was Katie, marrying the very sort of man who so long ago the family would have wanted for *her*, while her heart had belonged just to Neil. And Katie's heart? Since those first days she'd refused to talk about Dylan. He'd gone, that's all she would say. And on the rebound she was tying her life to Nigel's. How could it bring happiness? Yet better with Nigel there to fill the void than the emptiness without him. They both loved Bullington. That surely would give them a basis to build on?

And Kate's thoughts, as she dabbed at those every ready tears? She too had her memories, but the years had done nothing to help her look at the past without bitterness. Was Katie doing just what she'd done herself, marrying on the rebound, committing her life to one man while her heart belonged to another? Oh, but how could she compare? Even if he hadn't been the son of that hateful man there could have been no chance of happiness for Katie with him. How glad Mother would be today if she could see these two young people joining their lives together – and how thankful *she* was too. With Lottie back in Canada and dear Mother gone, she would be all the family the young people had (well, Rupert too, she added grudgingly), and when there were babies she'd be more than just a grandmother, she'd be everything rolled into one. The tears spilled silently, tears of happiness too great to be contained. She wanted to believe that Fate was trying to make up to her for some of the disappointments.

The "tribe" hadn't expected to be back in Newton Dingley again so soon, but none of them failed, they all made the journey.

The honeymooners were the first to depart. By dusk they'd all gone, Bullington Manor was quiet. Early the next morning Lottie and Ramsey would be aboard their plane, going home to Higley Creek.

Below stairs there was a festive mood amongst the staff. Lunchtime had been for the family; this evening was their own. There'd be no jangle of a bell to disturb their meal.

'Port, Mr Hawkins?' Joyce Luckley, head parlourmaid, beamed her approval as he came back from the cellar carrying two bottles of 1937 vintage. But then the hapless Joyce beamed her approval at everything he did.

'Indeed, yes, Joyce.' Could Hawkins be as impervious to such open hero worship as he appeared? 'The master left instructions that I was to take what we needed, this is no ordinary day. A bottle of Sauternes with our meal and a good port to drink the health of the happy couple.'

Mrs Moggs threw a frosty glare at Joyce. Ridiculous! A woman well into middle age making sheep's eyes the way she did! Couldn't have been anything to look at even twenty years ago. Did she have any idea what a laughing stock she made of herself? But men were such fools – give 'em a bit of flattery and they puffed up, full of their own importance. If the kitchen's views were to be voiced, then it was *her* place to give an opinion, not some jumped-up, middle-aged parlourmaid.

But before Mrs Moggs could think of anything cutting enough to bring her down to size, Joyce rushed on:

'Mrs Matheson would have been pleased with today, Mr Hawkins.' She voiced aloud what she knew to be his own view. 'We've always looked to Mr Nigel as the young master, that's the way the mistress meant us to think of him. I'm right, aren't I?' The gaze was fixed on Hawkins went far beyond his due as head of the staff below stairs.

'Quite right, Joyce,' came the dignified answer.

'Times change,' Mrs Moggs cut in. But there was no stopping Joyce, her large teeth flashing in a smile at Harold Hawkins' affirmation of her opinion.

'We know the mistress became fond of young Miss Katie. Of course she did. Having her for company brought a breath of springtime to those long empty days when Mr Nigel was away. It would have been a lonely thing for him to come back from that university to a great empty house now the old lady has been taken. He needs a partner.' One quick look at the butler to make sure she hadn't overstepped her mark, then she lowered her eyelids demurely, her over-large teeth gripping her bottom lip like a vice.

Mrs Moggs could contain herself no longer. Her face was red from the heat of the oven as she lifted out the baron of beef to baste; upstairs and down alike, she believed in the importance of good sustenance and, as Harold Hawkins said, today was no ordinary day.

'Young Miss Katie? Did my ears hear aright? Don't any of you forget that it's she who's the mistress here. If she sees fit to take Mr Nigel for her husband, that's her business.'

Joyce couldn't let an opportunity like that pass.

'It takes a man to run an estate like this.' Then, getting bolder, for the hierarchy of the kitchen was strong and, with the one exception of Harold Hawkins Mrs Moggs reigned supreme: 'Why, Mrs Moggs, you can't argue that I'm wrong.'

'I see nothing to argue about. Facts are facts. Call him the young master till we're blue in the face, but Bullington Manor was left to Katie O'Hagon. She's mistress here.'

Harold Hawkins looked at her over the top of his spectacles. He couldn't think what was happening to some women these days – and Gertrude Moggs had always been something of a rebel! However the property had been left, Miss Katie and Mr Nigel were man and wife.

And what sort of a marriage would it be if he weren't master of the house?

'I'll not have a word spoken against the master, not in my kitchens,' he warned. Then, hitting below the belt: 'I know the way a lot of women are clamouring about equality. I'd have expected at your time of life, Gertrude, you would have seen enough to have more sense.'

'Don't reckon sense is something that grows with the years,' she retorted with a meaningful glance.

From Effie, only fifteen and not blessed with her full quota of intelligence, came the makings of a giggle, cut off before it developed by a threatening look from Mrs Moggs.

It was old Clara Hitchens, one-time under nursemaid, loved by generations of Mathesons and who for years now had been responsible for little else than the household linens in this house that had been home to her for sixty years, who brought peace back before it had been quite lost.

'Well, my dears,' to her there was no hierarchy amongst the staff, or, if there was, then she was outside it, 'there's one thing we can all be sure about. If our own dear Mrs Matheson knows about the knot that's been tied today – and I don't doubt it for one minute – then she'll be lying peacefully there in the cemetery. She loved them both. So we'll raise our glasses and wish them long life and happiness. Ah, and babies to fill the house. Children to play in the gardens, laughter and fun up there in the nursery again. When I first came here, Miss Kate – Kate Bradley, I mean – she was a delicate wee mite. As lovely as an angel. That's what we want here at Bullington, children to put our sights on tomorrow.'

To Katie everything was new. She'd holidayed in the West Country, she'd visited various tourist spots in the Home Counties, she'd been to London (no, not that, blot out the memory of that visit that had altered her life, remember just the Changing of the Guard, the National Gallery, the steamer trip with her grandparents), she'd been to Stratford, watched the swans on the Avon, many times she'd driven to Oxford – but in her sixteen months in England she'd never been in the direction Nigel took her now.

He had made the arrangements for their honeymoon, told no one his plans.

'Say! Won't you look at that! Up there on the hilltop. Nigel, what is that place?'

'Ludlow Castle. At least, that's what it was. It's a ruin these days – yet what a position! It's where the sons of Edward the Fourth and Elizabeth Woodville were raised – the princes who ended their days in the Tower of London. But maybe you've never heard of it –'

'Oh, but I have. We learnt lots of English history back home in school in Radley. I just lapped it up, anything I could find out. But actually seeing it, that's –' She shrugged, lost for the right word.

'If you like to delve into history you'll find plenty of evidence of it around here.' Then he added, laughing: 'And if you're prepared to mix legend into the cocktail there's a place in this county called Whittington. That's where the legendary Dick is reputed to have hailed from.'

Her eyes were like stars. She seemed frightened to blink in case she missed anything as they drove on towards Wales.

'It's different here. Open, wild. You feel it's been like this for always, nothing could change it. I wish you'd tell me where we're going.'

'If I did it wouldn't mean anything to you. But it's in North Wales. We've still got a couple of hours' drive ahead of us. We'll stop soon and have dinner, shall we?' He wasn't actually asking.

'Let's not waste daylight inside some place eating – I want to see everything. Just look at those hills.'

'You're in border country, Katie. If hills could speak, these would have their own story to tell.'

She felt her roots reach deeper into the soil of her ancestors; it seemed fitting that her ancestors and his were one. This was the Nigel who'd been her friend since first she'd come to Bullington. Only the unfamiliar feeling of that gold band around her finger reminded her that this was no ordinary holiday. She looked down at her hand. Grandam's wedding ring, and now she was wearing it. It was a symbol of something more than her vows to Nigel, it signified the responsibility that had been entrusted to her and the old lady's faith that she wouldn't fall.

Already dusk hid the distances from them, swathing the outlines in mystery. Gradually their world grew smaller as darkness fell, until finally there was nothing but the confines of the car and two beams of light on the road ahead.

As soon as they stepped inside the hotel she realised that Nigel was known here. He was greeted by name as he went to the small reception desk, and by the porter who carried their cases to their room on the first floor.

'I know dinner is officially over, but if something could be found for us we'd be grateful. Here in our room might be rather nice. We didn't stop to eat on the way and we're starving.' And Katie knew no one would refuse him. His smile was so friendly, his request as natural as if he were making it to a doting elderly aunt.

'Leave it with me, Mr Matheson,' came the reply, as the porter extended a gate-leg table and set two chairs by it. He'd been born and bred in the district. Except for four years in the army he'd been nowhere else. Even in those few words there was such variety of tone. No wonder Katie was fascinated.

The room wasn't opulent, but it was certainly enormous. At one end was a double bed, the mahogany of the head and foot boards polished to a mirror brilliance; the same wood and the same shine for the wardrobe and dressing table. At the other end of the room was a sofa, a writing desk and the gateleg table where they were to eat their supper. And somewhere about the centre of the room was a fireplace with a marble surround, gleaming brass fender and two easy chairs close by. While between and around, there was space, empty space.

'Hey, I just don't believe it!' Katie looked around her as the door closed on the friendly porter. 'You could hold a dance in this place! And what's through those doors, do you suppose? You must have been here before, Nigel, they all know you.'

'I love these parts of Wales. I come rock climbing. This is where I usually stay.. There may be smarter hotels, but this one makes no pretence of changing its habits. I like it. Through those doors? I imagine a bathroom and a dressing room.'

He imagined right. The bathroom, too, was huge and in the centre of it, raised on a plinth, was The Bath. Even in her mind, Katie gave it capital letters.

'Whew! Sort of Louis XIV. Won't you look at those legs? It's big enough for all the family to tub together!' As soon as she'd said it she wished she'd kept her thought to herself. But Nigel let the idea pass.

It wasn't in Katie's nature to feel sorry for herself. And anyway, she told herself, if she'd made a mess of things, whose fault was it but her own? She'd been naive, she'd trusted, she'd let herself hurtle into love – stop it, don't think about it. You got yourself into a hell of a mess and you're lucky that Nigel is sharing it with you. These were some of the thoughts that chased themselves around in her head as, supper over, she lay alone in the bath made for at least two. Nigel was downstairs in the small bar. By the time he came back she was already in bed.

'I'll take my things in here,' he told her, opening the door to the adjoining dressing room. His tone was friendly, Second Cousin Nigel. Lying there she could hear him moving about, heard the click of the door as he went through to the oversize bathroom.

Help me to be all I should be, help me to be generous. I know he deserves it. Katrine Matheson – that's me. That used to be Granny's name. She said she married on the rebound. Did she suffer marriage?

96

Is that what makes her so sorry for herself? But she ought not to be. Grandad's a great old guy, and he dotes on her. Ah, maybe that's where it's different for Nigel and me. Does he just suffer me for the sake of the Manor?

It was easier to try and believe that he'd been heading towards asking her to marry him before – before –

She was almost glad to have her thoughts interrupted by Nigel's return. He took off his dressing gown and, clad in dark blue silk pyjamas, climbed into the large bed by her side.

'Katie Matheson. My wife.' She felt her hand taken in his as they lay, side by side, a foot or so apart.

She knew what must be ahead. She'd vowed to be fair, to be generous, to make this a beginning that somehow would lead them to a good marriage. But she was surprised by his sudden movement, his left hand reaching to switch off the bedside lamp, his right pulling hers to press it against the column that escaped the confines of the silk. Never had there been any passion in her friendship with Nigel. Even over these last days as they'd planned the wedding, his only kisses had been affectionate pecks – on her forehead, her cheek, or more often on her hand. Now he pushed her hand against him; what she felt seemed to bear no connection to anything that had been part of their relationship.

'Damn, Kitashee, damn him!'

'Please, Nigel, no.' With all her strength she meant to make a success of this step she'd taken. To hear Dylan's name knocked her off course. She clenched her teeth, shut her eyes tight. Nigel . . . Dylan . . . one man was all men. It had to be. Under her hand she felt his passion mounting. Her own determination to keep her side of the bargain became the only thing that mattered.

Nigel didn't speak as he turned towards her. With a sound half sigh and half moan he moved on to her. She guided him. Her husband. As long as they lived they would be partners. Tonight was important, she mustn't fail him – with tunnel vision she wouldn't look outside the path they must make together. She arched her back. Like a young animal she moved under him. One man – all men. Was she running from her own memories as with steady rhythm her body performed its loveless ritual? Be fair, be generous, for his sake, for your own sake and because of the promises you've made. Make this a new beginning. Only when his mouth found hers did she momentarily recoil. 'Kate-ee, we belong to each other, we always will.' The present was blotted out by the past. Nigel's passion found its release; she gripped him close; she felt numb.

He knew so many people, and everywhere he was popular. Had her own upbringing been different she might have been surprised to find his friends so representative of a cross-section of the local community: the mountain rescue team; the doctor; the minister from the chapel; a barrister from London who had a "retreat" amongst the hills; the butcher who spent his weekends leading parties of walkers; a museum curator; a sheep farmer. To everyone he introduced his wife with the same possessive pride. It ought to have given her confidence in their future. So why didn't it?

'I see there's a riding stable down the road,' she said at breakfast one morning. 'How about we rent a pair of mounts and go off into the hills? I'd like that.' She suggested it, sure that he'd fall in with the plan.

'You do that, Katie. I thought I'd go climbing and I did wonder how you'd manage to fill your time. They take rides out every day from the stable, you'll find some company.'

It seemed to her an odd way to spend a honeymoon, especially when she found that most of the riders were capable of no more than walking their horses, each one following the other in an obedient line. Riding? It was like comparing a trip on a river steamer with a battle against the elements under sail in a storm at sea. She said something along those lines to Nigel at dinner that night.

'What were you expecting? Cowboys and Indians?' His voice teased, but there was something mocking in his eyes. The conversation died, there was nowhere for it to go?

He spent most of his time rock climbing, while she walked the hills alone with her thoughts. During the first days neither of them made any reference to the coming baby, and he didn't ask her when was the "next time around" she'd been pinning her hopes on.

Today had been different. He'd taken her for her first lesson in fly fishing. All their old camaraderie had been there. Her casts had improved as she'd practised, but even if they hadn't the day would have been fun. By the side of the clear, fast-flowing river they'd eaten the packed lunch the hotel had put up for them. The sun shone, the sky was high, it was one of those perfect days of late summer. There might have been no yesterday to throw a shadow, no tomorrow to shy away from. Such had always been her happier times with Nigel.

In the evening he was ready to go downstairs before her.

'I'll have a drink while you titivate. Come and get me in the bar when you're ready,' he told her. 'There's no hurry.'

'O.K. I'm still scrubbing away the smell of fish.'

'Ho, ho,' he gave an exaggerated guffaw, 'hark at the woman! Fish, she says. Nearest you came to a fish was taking one off my hook.'

'Well, river then,' she laughed. 'Fishing tackle. As for that flukey catch you made, no bigger than a sardine, I wonder it didn't choke itself to death on the fly! As well we weren't relying on getting our supper.'

'It was a good day, Katie. Maybe we'll go again tomorrow, eh? See you down in the bar.'

Her optimistic nature had been given a boost today. She dressed for dinner with care – care in her appearance and care not to let her mind wander from safe tracks. Gwynedd House Hotel had only twelve bedrooms – all of them large and, as with Katie and Nigel's, one or two of them enormous. In time to come someone with an eye to business would probably move in, take away the existing character, divide the rooms, add en suite showers to conserve space. But until now it remained as it had been when Lavinia had first brought Nigel here as a boy. Never more than two dozen guests, usually less. As Katie passed the open double doors leading to the dining room on her way to the small bar she could see that most of the tables were full. Nigel must be waiting for her on his own.

To her surprise there was a young man with him, both of them standing at the bar with their backs to the doorway. As she came near she heard enough to know they were friends.

'. . . so we were prepared for it to happen,' Nigel was saying.

'You're still at the Manor?' They both understood the meaning behind his question. So too did Katie.

'Naturally. Of course I am. Bullington is a full-time job.' Nigel became aware that she had joined them. 'Ah, here she is. My brand new wife. Katie, an old mate of mine. We were together at school, then at Oxford – Brian Wadmore. He's come here for some climbing. You'll let me off the hook tomorrow, won't you? He and I shinned up our first rock together, isn't that so, Brian?'

It wasn't that she was disappointed about tomorrow, nor was it that she resented company, Katie told herself as the waiter set a third place at their table. Brian Wadmore was just the sort of friend she would have expected Nigel to have: good-humoured and fun-loving. Yet as the meal progressed her good spirits took a nose dive.

'I'm lucky,' Nigel said, with the confidence that comes from authority. 'I've a good estate manager. He takes care of the home farm, shooting permits in the high woods, re-stocking the birds, all that sort of thing. Fortunately he and I get along well. My grandmother had had to leave a good deal of the responsibility to him over recent years, but now that I'm home he understands that I mean things to be different.'

Instead of answering Nigel, Brian winked wickedly at Katie.

'He's been planning his campaign since he was in the Third Form. I fancy you've married yourself into quite a task, taking on a house like Bullington. Might scare a lot of girls.'

'Bullington couldn't possibly scare me, I guess it cast its spell on me right from the first. Anyway –'

'She'd been there visiting for best part of a year.' Did she imagine it or did Nigel interrupt her purposely? 'The house runs along smoothly. My grandmother had been out of action for some months. Katie won't have to concern herself with anything except enjoying herself.'

If there was an undercurrent Brian didn't notice it.

The men turned the conversation to their plans for tomorrow's climb. Katie excused herself, saying she had letters to write.

It was true, she meant to write to Lottie and Ramsey. After her day by the river she'd looked forward to penning the sort of letter she knew they'd like. Now, though, the words wouldn't flow. Her attempt found itself in the wastepaper basket before she'd completed the first page. The truth would be easier to accept if she'd face it squarely. And the truth was that Nigel had married her for one reason – Bullington. And was that so dreadful? Had her own reasons been any more altruistic? Responsibility for Bullington had been put into her hands. Courage? But how could it be courageous to step aside and let Nigel rule supreme? That's the way it would have been if Grandam had made him her heir as he'd expected, as they'd all expected. And if she had, then Katie was sure of one thing: Nigel wouldn't have asked her to be his wife knowing what had been between her and Dylan. Her thoughts went round and round, covering the same ground, getting nowhere, yet plummeting lower.

She decided to go to bed. She could be asleep when Nigel came up.

'Fancy bumping into old Brian like that!' Disregarding the fact that not only Katie but most of the other guests were already in bed, Nigel burst into the bedroom, letting the door slip out of his grasp to close with a slam. 'What an evening!' He laughed at the memory of it. 'You should have seen his face when I told him I was here on my honeymoon.' The word seemed to bring him up short, change his mood and his expression as if a light had gone out. 'Not very bride-like, lying there with the blankets around your shoulders.'

She only half opened her eyes. She didn't want to see the uncharac-teristic way he was pulling off his clothes, throwing them into an untidy heap on the sofa until he stood naked in the harsh glare of the overhead light.

'D'you know what I told myself when we got married? I wasn't going to touch you until that bastard's brat was got rid of.'

100

'Shut up!' She pulled the blankets tighter. 'You've been hours down there drinking – well, you needn't think you can come back here and talk to me like that.' Then, hitting where it hurt hardest: 'I know just why you married me, Nigel Matheson. It was because you wanted to lord it over Bullington Manor. But you'd better not forget – Bullington Manor belongs to *me*.'

'I'll tell you why I married you. I married you so that you wouldn't shame the family by producing some illegitimate half breed.' He pulled the covers off her. 'I married you so that when you miscarried that would be the end of the affair. There'd be no gossip, no stigma on the family name.'

'Family name? My name was O'Hagon.'

'Yes. Yours and his too! Might be all right the second month around, that's what you told me. Yet even after the pounding I've been giving you –'

'Don't talk like that. Nigel, it's no good us going on like this. We've got to make things work, we've got to try.'

She was unprepared for his next move. She cried out as he lunged on her, the flat of both his hands on her stomach, all his weight, all his force, on her.

'Perhaps this'll do it.' Again and again he bore down on her, sweat breaking on his brow in the effort.

'You're hurting . . .' She tried to speak.

'You won't lose the brat without it hurting, for Christ's sake! But this I swear – if I'm taking you back to Bullington as my wife, then what that swine Kitashee left behind has to go.'

She felt sick. What a moment to remember the hours they'd spent by the river! Beneath the pain she knew his behaviour was the outcome of too much to drink. She could retaliate, answer one verbal blow with another. But this was no ordinary rage. In his nakedness his rising passion was obvious. The more he abused her body the more excited he became. As he bent close she turned her head away, loathing the smell of drink on his breath.

'You're breathing on me. It's beastly,' she panted.

'Is that what you used to say with him? Out there under hedges somewhere? Is that where he used to lay you? "Don't breathe on me", was that it? What was he like? Did you encourage him too, like you did me?' Ever more heavily he bore down on her stomach. 'I wasn't going to touch you, you hear me? Not till you were clean. It was *you* – Delilah. Did he teach you?' One last enormous pulverizing movement. Tonight his strength seemed super-human. In a swift, unexpected movement he pulled her so that her legs hung over the side of the bed. She knew what his next move would be. His behaviour was uncontrolled. In this state it must be over quickly.

But she was wrong. In his mind was one predominating need – to get rid of the child Dylan Kitashee had given her. His own desire was a tool to be used for that purpose, just as his hands and his weight had been.

'Nigel, you're hurting me. Not like that. Please.' She tried to wriggle free, but his hands gripped her thighs. He didn't look at her but stared into the mid-distance above her head. His movements didn't flag, neither did he lose control. He was like a robot, tireless, inhuman. She felt empty of all emotion, even her anger had died.

Then cunning got the upper hand. She knew she held the trump card. "Delilah" he'd called her. Until then she'd been dormant, rigid. No actress could have played a part more convincingly than she did now; with arms, legs, mouth, hands, she led him to the point where he was beyond holding back.

It was over. All that violence was stilled. Silently she pulled herself away from him as he crouched on his knees by the bedside.

'I thought I wouldn't care,' he mumbled, looking directly at her for the first time. 'I thought I could bluff it out, pretend the brat was mine. But I can't. You've got to get right. Whatever sort of animal that swine's planted in you, then it's got no place at Bullington.'

She lay very still, her hand on her bruised stomach. In that moment she hated him.

'That's for me to say. Bullington Manor is mine.'

Chapter Seven

Only once did they refer to that dreadful night, and even then instinct, fear of raking over ashes that all too easily could burst into flames, held them back, kept their voices low, put a barrier of politeness between them.

It was the next morning. For hours Katie had lain awake. The first hint of dawn had glowed in the sky before finally sleep had overcome her tormented mind. Now it was Nigel coming back from the adjoining dressing room that woke her.

'Hi.' Her normal morning greeting, but today it was no more than an expressionless mumble. Last night's scene crowded in on her returning consciousness. She didn't want to open her eyes to face the hours ahead.

'Katie, about last night –'

'Just leave it!'

'That's what I want to say. We have to forget it. I'm not sure how clearly I even remember some of it. Got a hell of a head this morning, that much I do know.'

She nodded, glad to latch on to any excuse for the scene that was so vivid in her mind.

'Guess you were pretty well tight. Leave it, I said.'

'I behaved badly. I'm sorry. Let's pretend none of it happened, forget the things we said.'

For a second he thought she wasn't going to answer.

Then her movement was sudden as she sat up. What was the use of pretending? Running away from the truth could never be an answer to anything. She was wide awake now. Determination was in the tilt of her chin.

'I don't want to talk about it, I've said so. But if we say we shall forget, then we're not being honest. Sure, we'll push it under the surface, we'll take care we don't dig where it's buried.'

'We'll bury it deeper. We have to set our sights on the future, Katie – five years, ten, twenty. Another generation of Mathesons at Bullington – ours. We've got a hurdle to surmount, somehow we'll get it behind us. Nothing can alter the solid foundation we're building on to. It's been there for centuries.'

He looked at her so earnestly. She was touched with – what? – even after last night could it be affection? Sympathy, affection, whatever it was, it immediately gave way to realism. They were bound to each other, they'd both gone into this commitment with their eyes open.

'Like I said,' she answered, 'we'll throw a veil over last night. I guess every marriage has to be worked at and I shan't be afraid of working at ours. You play fair with me and I will with you. We both know where we stand. Five, ten, twenty years . . . oh, yes, we'll have something worked out – or something will have worked itself out. You'd better go on down to breakfast if you and Brian are going climbing. I'll come when I'm ready.'

'I was wondering – would you rather we went fishing again? I could explain to Brian that you were disappointed. Would it help put last night out of the way if we picked up from the day we had together fishing? I'll do that if you like. I could climb tomorrow instead.'

She shook her head.

'No, you arranged it with Brian. Anyway, I don't think I feel much like it.'

'Don't you feel well? You mean –' He didn't even try to disguise the note of hope.

'I didn't say that. I said I didn't feel like us going fishing.' Neither did she attempt to put any warmth into her quiet voice.

'All right, I was rough with you! Damn it, Katie, it was for your sake as well as mine! We've got to try anything we can.'

'There, you see. Already last night's back with us. Let it rest, can't you? Go and have your breakfast. I'll see you this evening.'

When he'd gone she lay still, her eyes closed, her hands on her flat stomach. She felt bruised, tender. She expected his hands to have left marks. When, a few minutes later, she pulled off her nightgown and stood naked in front of the wardrobe mirror, she was surprised that there would be no outward sign of what he'd done. She stretched to her full height, her hands towards the ceiling. Nothing had changed in her slender form. But ought she to expect that it would so soon? She hadn't quite reached that 'second time around'. It was too soon to look for physical signs.

Supposing she and Dylan had been free to love each other? Now she was to have his child . . . their child. She slumped to sit on the edge of the rumpled bed, indulging in her day dream, letting her mind wander where it would. If only that were true, then all that nonsense Nigel had talked about a slur on the family name, none of that would count for anything; even on her own she could have faced it. She would be looking forward now to a normal, healthy baby, something of Dylan. She had no clear picture of the young Indian boy who'd been like a god to her as she'd left babyhood behind. Even though so many ghosts had teased her memory over these summer months, yet still all she was sure of was the sensation of idolising him, the wonder she'd felt in being with him; now in her imagination father and child merged into one, she pictured herself with a son like the hero of her own early years. Her mouth softened.

Just as suddenly as it had come, so the vision vanished. Nakedness stripped her of all pretence. From the wardrobe mirror the girl looked back at her, a picture of unmasked hopelessness. The pale skin of her body showed no marks, the scars were in her heart and soul. She shivered. 'For your sake as well as mine' – that's what Nigel had said. And he had a right to say it. She'd pledged her life to his: five years, ten, twenty, thirty. "A hurdle we have to overcome." He'd said that too. How could it be a hurdle when it was the outcome of what she and Dylan had felt for each other? Yet could he truly not have seen that Rosie couldn't be believed? Another echo: "When I go home I shall take you with me", and her reply: "I know. Of course I shall come with you." She'd been so sure. Now he'd gone, gone out of her life. What she was left with was nothing more than "a hurdle to overcome". The girl in the mirror sat with her hands hanging limply between her parted knees. For a moment her mouth was pulled down at the corners, her face about to pucker and the tears fall.

Katie held her lips immobile, she took a deep breath and raised her chin ridiculously high as though that would help her keep control. Then she stood up and opened the wardrobe door; the mirror image was gone. A hot bath and some clothes, then a good breakfast, that's what she needed.

In trying to cover the traces of that one dreadful night they were always careful not to speak one wrong word, not to say anything that might ignite the still warm embers. They treated each other with exaggerated politeness. Granted Nigel spent a good deal of time rock climbing while Katie took the car and explored on her own, but that suited them both. The days went by. No mention was made of the "hurdle" or their own inability to remove it.

Nigel didn't refer again to his pre-marital resolution not to touch her. They were both determined to make a success of their union. They were young, they were healthy, living in close and intimate contact; neither of them put into words what they believed, that to end each day making love must be the way to dim the reality of what had happened. Each time they came together, surely it must bury the memory a little deeper, put it more safely out of reach? But even the act of love was performed with restraint. There was an aloofness between them.

Then Katie made a discovery: it was as Nigel was working his way towards his goal that a driving need in her put everything from her mind except the certainty that somewhere, almost within her grasp if only she could reach out to it, her spirit would find Dylan's. Instinct kept her face turned away from Nigel's. If he were to kiss her the spell would break. She had to reach Dylan, she had to, had to . . .

After Nigel's even breathing told her that he slept, she lay in the dark, her eyes wide open. When she felt a tear roll down her cheek she tasted the saltiness. Yet she was more at peace than she'd been for weeks. She'd found the way to Dylan. It was her secret; no one would ever know. So why was she crying? She turned and buried her face in the pillow.

'Welcome home, Sir.' Hawkins threw open the great door as they came up the steps. 'And madam. I'll have your luggage carried up to your room.'

'It's all ready to be used? They've got it finished?'

'Oh, yes, Sir. And made a beautiful job of it too. The paintwork has been dry for some time, long enough to have lost the smell. We've had the windows wide open, given the room a good airing, but I'm afraid the newness still lingers in the air from the carpeting, and from the fabrics. It was yesterday before Derry and Lowden's men finally finished. Miss Anstey was here to see everything was as you'd agreed.'

Katie looked from one to the other, mystified.

'Good,' Nigel approved. 'Never mind the newness, it'll soon go. Get the luggage sorted out, will you, Hawkins, and have some tea sent to the drawing room.'

Katie let herself be ushered away. She waited until the door was closed. Then she turned to Nigel with a puzzled frown.

'What paint? What carpet? Who's Miss Anstey?'

'I've had the master bedroom re-decorated – re-fashioned, you might say.' He smiled at the expression. 'Before we went away Derry and Lowden sent Miss Anstey to see what was needed – she's their senior interior designer. I fancy it was the day the rest of you were in London shopping for wedding finery. Naturally that will be our room.'

106

'Grandam's bedroom? You mean, you've had it changed?' Deep down she must have been angry, but her first conscious reaction was disbelief that anything so radical could have happened to the house. Lavinia's character had been embodied in that room.

'Don't look like that, Katie,' he laughed. 'When our great-grandfather brought Grandma here as a bride you don't suppose they moved into it the way the previous generation had wanted it. It's always been the master bedroom. You'll like what I've had done. I don't expect I'd be much use at interior design, but this Anstey woman seemed to know just what was needed. Let's have tea first, give them time to get our things unpacked, then we'll go and take stock.'

'But you've got no right . . .'

The smile vanished. 'Of course I have the right. I'm your husband. Any work I authorise will be paid for from Grandma's money. Don't you think that was why she left it to me? And plenty of work will have to be done in a place like this, you've no conception of what's needed to keep it in repair. You say I've no right – are you throwing it in my face again that the Manor is yours? You'd better realise that it would soon fall into disrepair without the money I'll be able to put into it, money I shall gladly put into it.'

'It's not just who it belongs to. We ought to have talked about what had to be done. That room was Grandam's.'

'And she would have been delighted to know that the next Mrs Matheson to be taken to it would be you. Katie, it's only right that I bring you to a new beginning. The home goes on, generation by generation. But each one makes its own mark. I wanted to make mine. I intend to make it. I doubt if that room can ever have looked as good as they'll have made it now. I could tell Miss Anstey had a real flair. Good, here's tea. Thank you, Effie.'

'You can pour your own tea. I don't want any. I'm going to see what's happening upstairs. I'd like to know where they're hanging my clothes at least!' She heard the pout in her voice and knew she was being childish. Driving back to Bullington she'd looked forward to the familiar feeling of security, the permanence of the house she'd grown to love. One room had been changed, that was all. She was over-reacting.

Effie may not have been the brightest in the kitchen but she was sensitive to atmosphere, Katie knew that word would be carried downstairs that "the master's lovely surprise" hadn't been well received, and she knew too that the girl was watching her as she walked with exaggerated and uncharacteristic composure up the curving stairs to the first floor gallery.

107

When she came to the room that had been Lavinia's she halted, the porcelain handle on the door familiar to her touch. Logic told her that it couldn't be kept unchanged, like a shrine to the past; logic told her that if she and Nigel were to forge their own link in the chain that was Bullington, then like every generation before them this should be their room. So why was she frightened of seeing it altered? She turned the handle and pushed the door wide. Her first impression was of space, light. The large, beautifully proportioned room was quite lovely. It might have graced the pages of one of the more expensive glossy magazines. It meant no more to her than a room in a strange hotel. To come in here had always been to be warmed by Grandam's personality. Now there was nothing but the cold perfection of the décor.

The sound of footsteps told her that Nigel was coming up to find her.

'I say, this is incredible! It's hardly recognisable, so uncluttered. It looks twice the size . . . full of light.'

Katie moved towards the window that all day had been wide open. The pale lilac of the new curtains was shot with silver. The material glistened in the sunlight. She felt like a visitor, an outsider. Then she leant out, her hands on the sill. New paint couldn't alter the familiar feeling of the wood, new wall coverings and fabrics couldn't mar the spirit of the old house. The tall elms that lined the drive, the sloping lawns that led to the lake that from here was out of sight, the sound of voices from the kitchen garden, the soft scent of the air, no, nothing could detract from the things that made Bullington what it was. All this was here. Just as for years it had been Grandam's, so now it was hers. Her momentary, unspoken fear left her.

'. . . glad I gave her a free hand?' She didn't hear the whole of Nigel's question, but she could guess what it must have been.

'Am I glad? Oh, she's done a good job if what you wanted was that she should kill off every trace that anyone's ever lived here. Was that the idea? To give us a new canvas to paint our own picture on? But, no, I'm not glad. O.K. If this is the room we're expected to use, then I guess like you say everyone has to make their own mark. But when there's a mark to be made, I mean to have a hand in it. That's the way I am. And I get the feeling that that's why Grandam wanted me to be the one to follow her here at Bullington.'

Nigel lit a cigarette, concentrating on what he was doing, rather than looking at her.

'Come on, Katie old thing, don't let's argue as soon as we get home. You know that whatever I do here is for the good of the place. And if it makes you feel better about not being consulted, think of it as my wedding present to you, something I wanted to surprise you with.'

'Well, give yourself full marks, you sure did that!' She even tried to smile. He was right, they mustn't argue the moment they arrived home. 'But one surprise is enough for any girl. If you have any other schemes, then I want to be in on them. O.K.?'

They went back downstairs. The matter of the re-decoration was closed, by unspoken mutual consent they knew it wouldn't be referred to again. It was too near the dangerous ground they skated around so carefully.

'Life's not all honeymoon.' How often it's said when the first shocks hit the new foundations, testing to see whether they're built on sand or solid rock. In Katie and Nigel's case life progressed on much the same lines as those three weeks in Wales. His days were full, he spent more time with Frank Fulford than he did in the house. As for Katie, her life seemed to be in limbo. To look ahead was impossible. With every passing week she was more certain that whatever cruel trick nature meant to play, her body was too healthy to miscarry. Yet it was a subject that neither of them cared to broach.

In October, six weeks after the wedding, she wrote her news to Lottie.

'How do you like the idea of being a grandmother, Mom? I know it's pretty soon, but it looks like that's the way things are. I'm feeling so well I can't believe it's true, not a twitch of anything. Still, I'm not complaining. Just hope I keep right on the way I've started.'

Then one to Brimley, the only difference the word 'great-grandmother'. There, it was done! Seeing the words in her own handwriting made the whole thing definite, shut the door on any chance of escape.

'Letters?' Nigel came into the bedroom as she sealed the second envelope. 'What are you hiding yourself away up here for? You'd be much more comfortable downstairs, there's a fire in the morning room.'

'I've been writing home – and to Granny and Grandad – telling them.'

He dug in his pocket for his cigarette case.

'Couldn't it have waited a bit longer? Just in case . . .'

She shook her head.

'We're half way through October. I've got to take it from, oh, I don't know, July somewhere. I'm so well, I've never felt better.'

'Christ!' He bit his bottom lip, tapping the cigarette on his gold case. 'What about the brat, though? You may be well, but the brat can't be, you've said so yourself.'

109

She shook her head. She'd never felt so without hope.

'Telling them makes it all final. They'll be so excited.' They both heard the croak in her voice.

'Don't go on about it, you'll only get upset,' he tried to stop her.

But she had to talk about it, she had to say the things she couldn't keep to herself any longer.

'Bet by tomorrow Granny'll be in Brimley buying wool. And Mom – Mom and Dad – they'll brag to everyone. They'll probably plan to come visiting again next spring. Maybe bring Ginnie and the boys. They'll want to see the baby . . . my baby.' She couldn't hold her face steady. No matter how hard she clamped her back teeth together, her mouth twisted in an ugly line. 'What'll it be like? I'm so frightened . . . my poor baby.'

'Hey, come on, Katie, we'll sort it all out. Didn't I promise you? You're not on your own. Damn nuisance anyone has to know, except us, though. What if we cleared off somewhere for a few months – didn't post the letters – didn't tell anyone? Came back when it was over.'

'It won't be over!' All these weeks she'd kept a steely control on herself. Now it was lost. There had been one other time when she'd cried like this: the night she'd last seen Dylan, the night she'd turned her back on him. If only she'd stayed, if only Dylan were the one to share whatever lay ahead. They would have faced this together. Their poor baby . . .

'All right.' Nigel's voice was firm, he was trying to encourage her. 'We'll stay here and see it through. We'll pretend everything is perfectly normal. When the kid's born it'll be premature – hell, we weren't married until September! However bad things are, Katie, we're more fortunate than an ordinary working family would be. It'll probably turn out stillborn – I've seen it happen in the animal world, like I told you. Don't cry like that, Katie. If Fate does the dirty and it turns out like you think, I can afford to have it taken somewhere to be looked after.'

'All their knitting . . .' She had to find an excuse for her tears. 'It's not just us. The whole family will be upset.'

'It'll soon pass. A few months and it'll be behind us. Go and wash your face. I'll take the letters and put them to be posted. You'd better stay out of sight for a while. I'll tell them downstairs that you're not feeling well and I don't want you to be disturbed.'

Left alone Katie did as he said. Cold water brought colour to her cheeks and helped to bring a mood of realism. It was no use crying for the moon. "The moon and the stars have their place in the firmament, just as we have ours on the earth." Yes, of course they had: his

110

somewhere in the forests of British Columbia, hers here near the edge of the downs, in a land where for two thousand years men have lived and left their mark. We're insignificant, each of us just one life amongst millions in that long pageant of time. That's what she must keep telling herself. She mustn't imagine Mom, mustn't picture how proud she'd be as she carried the news to the folk they knew back home; neither dare she let her thoughts go down that other path that led to where she might be now if she'd not left Dylan . . . Dylan standing there alone on that old Roman road. That's what she must hang on to, the century after century of lives that had been lived and forgotten, each of them someone, each of them loving, crying, laughing, grieving. She wasn't alone, no one was ever alone, just like all those others who'd trod that stony track she had her part to play, she had to make something of the short span of time that was hers.

Even as she gave rein to her thoughts she knew the role she'd set for herself. She *had* to act it out, and realised that Nigel would need to put up a pretence too. Sending off those letters had taken them to the next stage. Mr and Mrs Matheson of Bullington Manor were looking forward to welcoming an heir. Help me, help me, she pleaded silently, her gaze fixed unseeingly on the great sweep of lawns, I don't know if I can do it. I've got to prepare all the things a baby wants, I've got to show all the pleasure that any girl would – and for nothing, for something that won't be a proper whole person.

'I don't know if I can do it,' she whispered. Her knees felt weak, perhaps from that spate of tears. It was a relief to slip to the floor, to kneel on the thick carpet and bury her head against the velvet-cushioned chair. 'Why couldn't you have taken it away from me? I tried so hard. All right, I'm a rotten weak coward, but it's not fair. We didn't know – I didn't know. Oh, but I did . . . that last time I knew. Is that why you're punishing me? I don't care what you do to me, make me ill as you like, but please, please, can't you understand. It would be like a living proof of something hateful between me and Dylan. There wasn't, there wasn't. Haven't I been punished enough?

'We had such a lovely Christmas with darling Katie and Nigel,' Kate wrote to Lottie. 'She's looking really glowing, as pretty as a picture. I had a talk with her, tried to make her see that it was time she gave up riding. But she just laughed. Said she's never felt better. I do think it's not quite the thing to see the way she swings herself into the saddle. Not that I'd ever criticise anything she did, you know that. Just as long as she doesn't take any risks. This baby is important, to all of us and to Bullington.

'Nigel is very solicitous of her.' She didn't go into any details, just the one sentence. It stemmed from the fact that she'd noticed he was using his old bedroom again. She would have liked that kind of privacy, but Rupert had never suggested such a thing.

She tried to make her voice casual when she remarked to Katie: 'What a wise move, dear. You won't always feel you want him by your side in these next months, no matter how dear he is to you.'

The actress in Katie rose to the occasion.

'Maybe, Granny.' She even managed to inject a hint of regret into her voice. 'Nigel's as anxious as a mother hen,' she added with an indulgent laugh. This game she played was her protection; she stood outside herself, watching her own performance. For a second she wondered what her grandmother would say if she knew that Nigel had moved out at the first visible sign of her pregnancy, revolted by the constant reminder.

Kate and Rupert went back to Brimley content that all was more than well with the young couple.

Katie had had such resolutions about the running of the estate. She'd meant to learn about the stocking of the pheasants, the letting of the shoot, about the milk yields, about the stock that went to market and the prices the animals made. She'd already understood the rotation of crops, and been interested in how much was fetched for a ton of wheat. For as long as she could remember the price of corn had been the fabric of life at Higley Creek. How often now she'd stand and gaze over the wide farm gate that divided Tilley Meadow, where the annual gymkhana was held, from the arable land of the Home Farm. It was a link with home. If she shut her eyes she could picture the great expanse. This time of year in Alberta it would be an endless sea of snow, the white merging into the grey horizon. The snow would go, the yearly cycle would start, seed be sown, the first hint of green shoots, the strong tall growth, then a golden carpet, rippling and waving in the winds that tore across the prairie. A link with home? Sometimes the very difference in this gentle countryside made Higley Creek a world apart.

The growing of corn was something that had been bred in her, but she'd meant to learn about the other things that went on on the estate.

To start with Nigel had always had some plausible reason why it wouldn't be a good time for her to spend an hour or two with Frank Fulford, or why the stockman wouldn't be free to talk to her. She could have been more persistent, but she'd been sensitive enough to his manner to realise how jealously he guarded his position on the estate. For the present she'd let it rest. She honestly intended that they should run well together in harness, that they should each keep the bargain they'd made. Later, when her mind and body were her own again, she'd spend more time outside.

112

She believed the staff were her friends. One winter evening half watching on television a gangster film that neither of them would have gone to see at a cinema, she let her thoughts wander then spoke them aloud, the film forgotten.

'You know, I really believe Mrs Moggs quite likes having me here. They're all of them my friends, I'm sure they are. Don't you think that's great, Nigel? After all, they might have resented me. They didn't know me even like they do the rest of Grandam's tribe who live nearer.'

'Friends?' He chuckled at the idea. 'Hark to the voice of Canadian sorority!'

'And so I should think,' she bridled. 'Why not?'

'Why not? A friend is someone you can confide in, talk to as an equal, knowing they see things from the same angle. I suppose that's why not.'

'Then I guess I haven't any friends.' The retort was the first that came into her head. It wasn't until she heard herself speak the words that she realised just how true they were.

From Hawkins down to Effie, from Jo Dibbens who looked after the horses and had a soft spot for Katie down to Bill Huffkin the under-gardener, all of them were touched with a kind of possessive pride at the thought of a new Matheson.

'Seen Mrs Matheson around lately?' Bill said as he took aim at the dartboard at the Barley Mow. 'Had you noticed? We're going to have a youngster up at the house.'

'That's quick work, Bill.'

'Why not? They got plenty of money, she don't have to go working to earn enough for a fridge or a washer before she can think of having kids. Their sort can get ahead and have a family without a care. Not that I grudge her. I dare say it's because she's from over there in Canada, brought up different, you know what I mean, but there's no stuck up nonsense with the missus, never was.'

And that same evening, while the public bar of the Barley Mow buzzed with the news, Clara Hitchens was in Mrs Moggs' sitting room keeping the housekeeper company and busily checking the minute stitching of the christening gown that had been handed down through the years.

So too from Brimley to Higley Creek, Ramsey's wheat growing station on the edge of the Albertan prairie, the coming baby was at the forefront of their minds. In Brimley Kate looked on it as a blessing, the most certain way of putting paid to any lingering thoughts of the young Canadian. She ought to have known better.

113

She'd had three children, and loved them devotedly, yet they'd brought her no closer to Rupert and she'd hung on to her girlish dreams of "what might have been" even when in truth time had dimmed her memories.

At Higley Creek the coming of a baby stirred so many memories. Where had all the years melted away to? Lottie marvelled, remembering so clearly the toddler Katie had been when they'd come to make a new life with Neil's people. From there it was only a short jump to the memory of Dylan, left at the house each day while his mother helped with the round-up, Dylan with Katie invariably following in his wake, Dylan with Katie on the saddle in front of him, Dylan being questioned at Neil's inquest, trying not to cry as he had to repeat what he'd heard. Now Katie was married and mistress of the family home. That would be her life. Lottie had been uneasy about the hasty marriage, yet reason had told her that when one road is closed, then the best thing one can do is look for another. 'When life knocks you down, them jump right back up. Don't give yourself time to think, fix yourself a goal and work at it.' That's what Eva, her father's sister, had said to her when she'd been just a child. Because it was Eva who'd said it more than because she'd understood at the time what it could mean to have life knock you down, the words had stayed with her, had helped her when, years later, the chocks had been knocked from under her. Katie had certainly jumped right back up; the goal she'd fixed her sights on had to be that she'd make a success of the responsibility Lavinia had put on her. And surely there was no one better able to share that goal with her than Nigel? If a voice told Lottie that that wasn't a good enough reason for marriage, she answered back that Katie had her eyes wide open, she'd work at the partnership and so happiness would come. That there was to be a baby so soon must be good, it would bind them together. Perhaps it would be a son, a new heir for Bullington, a hold on the future.

Last week the sun almost beguiled them into thinking summer had arrived months before its time. Last week it had still been March. Now they were into April, outside on the forecourt frost was leaving a patterned film of ice on the roof of Dr Holsworthy's car and for hours the gas fire had been burning in the master bedroom. Down in the kitchen condensation trickled down the window panes from the steaming kettles that Mrs Moggs insisted mustn't go off the boil in case they were needed.

The door of the study was closed. In there Nigel tried to keep his mind on the monthly accounts Frank Fulford had brought to him earlier in the day. Anything rather than imagine the outcome of what was going on upstairs. Occasionally he heard footsteps on the stairs, the nurse coming down, probably Joyce or Effie carrying up whatever was needed. He didn't want to know.

At the Barley Mow Bill Huffkin passed the word: 'Looks like the mistress has run into trouble. They've got the nurse in and I see the doctor's car come up the drive when I was knocking off to go home.'

'Can't be having it already. Blimey, that'll be one for the books, Bill? When was it they were married?'

'If that's the way of it,' the faithful Bill answered, 'then that's O.K. But, no, you can't tell me that. No time ago she was galloping about each morning, she'd never have done that if she'd been that far gone.'

Bullington Manor held its breath and waited.

There had been plenty of coming and going up and down the stairs, yet this time was different Nigel knew. He opened the study door and came out to meet the doctor.

'Can you hear him?' The elderly man beamed, raising his own head to listen to the new-born yells. 'That's your son, my dear boy.' He held out his hand. 'Congratulations. You've a fine son, Nigel.'

He let his hand be shaken. Play acting had become second nature to him over these last months.

'Everything in order?' He heard the cheerful note in his voice. No one could guess how he hoped for a change in the elderly doctor's expression.

'Give them a quarter of an hour, let them settle Katie and clean the boy up, then you can see for yourself just how much in order he is. Come on, old fellow, it's all over. You've had a long wait.' He'd seen it before, the way a man could stay calm all through the hours of waiting, then in relief go to pieces. Not that he'd expected it of Nigel. He'd known him since he was a small boy, had visited Bullington socially many times in the old lady's day. Now he put a fatherly arm around Nigel's shoulder. 'I think you could do with a drink, my boy. How about offering me something? Let's wait together until the nurse says you can go up.'

Only for that second did Nigel almost forget the role he had to play. A whisky with Dr Holsworthy, concentrating on listening to the older man reminiscing about the days when Lavinia had held sway here, talking about his own plans for the estate, and his usual assurance returned. By the time the nurse came down to tell him his wife and son were ready for a visit he took the stairs two at a time, the model of a proud young father.

'I'll give you just three minutes.' The nurse's concern was for mother and baby, fathers were no more than a necessary nuisance. She looked at her watch as she spoke.

115

'They say I can come and see you.' He stood just inside the door. 'They say – the baby – he – they say he looks fine.'

'He's beautiful. He's all wrapped up, you can't see much of him.' She held the tiny bundle against her as she lay back on a pile of pillows. 'But I've seen him. He's perfect.' She didn't hide the tears that brimmed over. 'All the worrying . . . I nearly went crazy. And all the time, he was just perfect.'

'Yes, Holsworthy said he couldn't see anything wrong. But, Katie, you can't tell by looking. You mustn't let yourself get attached to him. It'd be asking to get hurt. We can't know how he's going to develop. The important thing is that you're O.K. The nurse is well trained, we'll have to see how the child goes. She can stay as long as necessary. Appearances aren't everything. How long before she could suspect if, for instance, he couldn't hear or see? For your own sake, Katie, you must play it like we planned. Just be grateful that at least he looks normal.'

How would you know? You've not even looked. But she didn't voice her thought. She didn't want him to look. She wanted him to go away and leave her with the miracle she held in her arms.

Chapter Eight

Named Christopher Ramsey, this newest member of the Matheson tribe performed exactly as was expected of a perfect baby. That's not to say there weren't days when he screamed – and nights too – but in that he was no different from any other. For months Katie hadn't been free of the grip of fear. Now with each day her confidence grew, and with each day she fell more surely under his spell.

Nurse Kinsey was still with them. Nigel had asked her to stay on for a few weeks. 'I'd be much happier to know you are here to keep an eye on my wife. If I suggest she needs rest, she'll tell me I don't know anything about these things,' he'd said with that open smile that won all hearts. 'If you're here I needn't worry, I can be sure she'll behave herself.' He gave no hint as to what he really meant: the infant might look normal, but how could they be sure that his mind wouldn't remain as empty as the unfocused gaze of a baby? The nurse agreed to stay for an extra six weeks or so, until a nursery nurse was engaged for Christopher, and moved into the nursery quarters where she took charge of him. But Katie would never be one of those mothers who put aside just half an hour a day for her children. To her her son was pure joy. Already after less than a month the nightmare she'd lived under for so long was almost gone.

Then something drove away the final shadow.

He was nearly five weeks old when he took her by surprise and threw his first proper smile at her. She was sitting with her knees together to make a firm base, holding his little body cradled in her hands so that he was facing her. What nonsense she talked to him she hardly knew and he certainly didn't, but he must have understood her message. Quite unexpectedly his mouth opened, his tongue poked between the parted lips, trembling with his dawning intelligence, and then he smiled.

'My little kitten! Kit – that's what you'll be. Not Christopher, no, nor Chris, not Christo, but Kit. Kit . . . Kit . . . Kit.' The more she said it, the wider he beamed, until his frame was shaken by a huge hiccough.

Thank you, oh, *thank you*. More than that, more than all words. He knows me, he can see, he can understand. Now nothing matters. *Thank you.*

Her relief and happiness was almost more than she could bear, she wanted to shout it aloud. But there was no one she could tell, least of all Nigel.

Kit was a beautiful baby. His hair was very dark, but it wasn't the kind of thick mop that would probably rub off to be replaced with something much lighter; it was silky and fine, lying close to his tiny head in a circle around his crown.

'Going to have a wave in his hair, you see if I'm not right,' Mrs Moggs predicted as she peered into the pram while Katie stood proudly by. 'What a little dark nut. Perhaps he'll lighten to Miss Lottie's colour, like a ripe chestnut. Funny things, genes, Miss Katie,' the old name jumped out so naturally, 'I recall a day when Mr Nigel was but a wee thing, come with his parents to stay. They often did that – second home to him it always was, even as a tiny mite. The mistress talked to me out here in the kitchen garden, stood just about where we are – now isn't that strange? – she said to me that the little fellow was the spitting image of her eldest, Mr Jonathan that would have been, him who got killed out there in France in that dreadful Great War. Now what would have been the relationship there? Great-uncle wouldn't it be? And him dead and gone must be twenty-five years before the child was born. Yet he was the spitting image. I think that was why she always thought so much of him as a boy, always looked to him to –' She pulled herself up short, suddenly aware that she'd done an awful lot of talking.

From the pram the object of their admiration yawned as he woke, then opened his light blue eyes.

'No chance of his eyes being anything but blue, with you and the master for parents.'

No, there was no chance that his eyes would be anything but blue. Like his black hair, he'd inherited the colour of his eyes from Dylan. His complexion was less dark, but nothing like either of his fair-skinned "parents". It must set the family casting about in their minds for some bygone Matheson who could have contributed genes for a child so swarthy.

Harold Hawkins liked to think he was nobody's fool. All very well for Mrs Moggs to accept what she was told the innocent way she did, but then down in the kitchen she didn't see the comings and goings upstairs. Probably she'd never clapped eyes on the Red Indian-looking fellow who'd been hanging around Miss Katie all the summer. If the girl had hood-winked the young master into picking up the pieces of the mess she'd made, then she ought to be ashamed of herself. Hawkins said nothing – but he knew just where his loyalty lay. Joyce Luckley had been pretty sure where Katie used to disappear to most evenings and she'd seen enough of Dylan to put two and two together and be certain she'd added it right. Not that she voiced her suspicions. Any criticism of the family would have been firmly stamped on by Hawkins. But she managed by a slight pursing of her lips, a flare of her nostrils, to let him know she condemned what she saw as an injustice against the master of the house. And if it ingratiated her in her own hero's eyes, that was a bonus point scored.

At last confident that the Manor wouldn't need the services of a nurse, Katie wasted no time. The very day after Kit's smile had lifted the last shadow she wrote out an advertisement. She would send it to a national newspaper and to the weekly magazine aimed at childcare. As soon as she could find someone she considered worthy to take care of Kit, the starchy Nurse Kinsey could go.

Satisfied with the wording of her advertisement she addressed the envelopes and decided to walk to the village herself rather than leave them in the hall to be collected for posting. What's more, she'd take Kit, give him his first view of a world beyond the grounds of the Manor. So far his days had been spent either in the nursery or cocooned in a shawl, hands anchored to his sides so there was no chance of his scratching himself, lying in his pram within the confines of the sheltering walls of the kitchen garden. Today the buds of May were heralding a promise of summer, the air was full of birdsong; today he would launch himself on Newton Dingley. The grounds of the Manor or the buzz of interest his appearance would bring to the village street, it was all one to him. Katie was excited enough for both of them.

It seemed fitting that for his début he should go out through the east gate into Corder Lane. In all these last months she'd not once gone that way. Only now that the nightmare was over could she look back on it honestly, admit to the shame she'd felt, her certainty that the child she carried in her womb had been sent as a permanent witness to the sin she'd committed against nature.

She was free. Today the clear sky, the signs all around her that another spring had come, wiped away her self-abasement. She wanted to shout and sing. It was as if she'd been to confessional, had been absolved. Dylan was gone, but that couldn't take away the pure joy in her heart. Katie's faith in some Deity greater than man was a simple one, and unquestioningly she took Kit's perfection as a sign that because she'd not known it was wrong to let herself love Dylan, then she'd been pardoned for the sin she'd done. Willingly she went a step further and let herself believe that Kit had been given to her in recompense. If this omnipotent Deity had been as fair as that with her, then it was up to her to keep her side of the bargain. She was married to Nigel and her intentions hadn't wavered. She'd be a loyal partner to him.

The way to the east gate took her through the stable yard, and where could be more fitting? That Jo should be grooming Black Knight was carrying stage management to the extreme!

"morning, Ma'am. Brought the boy to see the horses? Can't start 'em too young,' he chuckled, nodding his head in the direction of the pram. 'Or have you come to say your goodbyes to our old friend here?'

'Goodbyes? Who's going somewhere?'

'Black Knight, here. I'm just giving him his last bit of titivation. Always been a favourite of mine, has the Knight. Didn't you know the sale was today? I have to check him in at Reading market by one o'clock.'

'But why?'

Jo probably had his own ideas but, like Hawkins, loyalty silenced him.

'Can see the Knight now,' he reminisced with an impish gleam in his eye, 'the way he flew over those jumps back at Gymkhana day last year. A sight I won't forget in a hurry. No more will anyone else who saw it, if you ask me.'

'Jo, do you know where my husband is? Well, never mind, I'll speak to him later. This is most important: I don't want you to take Black Knight to Reading. He belongs here.'

Jo bit his lip. 'Perhaps you'll find the master down at the office with Mr Fulford. Best you have a word with him, Ma'am. Gave me the instruction, clear as a pikestaff.' He mixed his metaphors in his agitation. 'Best you ask him to come and see me, Ma'am. If you can't get hold o' him – well, like I said, he told me plain, get Black Knight to Reading before one o'clock.'

'I'll see if he's in the office. I'll tell him that I want Black Knight kept.'

'Yes, but . . . look, Ma'am, I got to be on the road in half an hour. What if I don't hear no more?'

'Then, Jo, Black Knight stays.' She hadn't meant to say it, but there was no other way. 'He's my horse. He stays here.'

That seemed to settle it. Jo returned to the grooming, unhappy that he had to serve two masters but taking solace from the fact the best horse in his stable wasn't to be lost.

Katie didn't change her route. On the way home would be soon enough to call at the estate office, so she went on her way to the village. This was turning out to be quite a Red Letter Day.

Right from the start Lavinia's great-granddaughter from Canada had been popular in the village.

'It's to do with the way she's been reared,' had been Polly Dawkins' opinion, given freely as she weighed out the vegetables in her husband's shop. 'Jack's as good as his master there on the other side of the Atlantic. And quite right too. Mind you, Miss Lottie was a sweet-natured child. She probably got some of it from her.'

Not all the inhabitants of Newton Dingley had Polly's opportunities for airing their views, but regarding Katie they were all of a like mind. Her easy friendliness and ready smile had endeared her to them even when they'd thought she was here just for a brief visit.

That her baby's first outing should be to the village seemed fitting. No wonder her progress was slow. 'Just a quick peek out of the front window' brought a cluster of people around the pram; doors opened and one after another the women came, drawn to the sight of a new baby, especially a baby that belonged to Newton Dingley as this one did.

'My word, but what a little darkie!'

'He'll lose that black hair, you see if he doesn't. You know how fair my Ted is, you'd never believe he was born with a great mop of hair. Black as the ace of spades it was. Lost the lot by the time he was three months, a proper baldie then till I got to think he'd never get any hair . . .' No one listened.

'Look at those little ears. Did you ever see shells so perfect?'

'Everyone was that worried, Mrs Matheson, when we heard you'd gone into labour before your time. But you've nothing to be anxious about now, not with this beauty.'

'Like your side of the family, I expect? Your father's people, I mean. Not got the Matheson look.'

Katie didn't need to answer, no one would have been listening even if she had; they were all much too engrossed in out-doing each other in their praise of Kit. It wasn't until she'd left them and gone well out of ear-shot that the first silent glances were exchanged. Friends and neighbours of long standing, they were well able to read each other's thoughts.

'Well, what do you think?' Again it was Polly who voiced what was in their minds. 'A fine baby for a prem, if you ask me.'

121

'Very dark. Swarthy dark. Like you were just saying, Gwen, he might lose his hair. But swarthy dark.'

'Umph,' came the chorus and again, 'Umph.'

'If that baby was born early, then my name's not Gwendoline Meldrum.'

'Well, they weren't the first to get wed in a rush. It's not for us to stand in judgement.'

'Umph . . .' And a long silence before Polly, the clear chorus master mused: 'Wonder what became of that dark chap. Up to the time the old lady died, he and young Mrs Matheson – Katie O'Hagon as she was then – they were thick as thieves. He seemed to disappear right off the scene.'

'Sets you wondering, I'm blowed if it doesn't.'

'Well, one thing's certain. If what you're suggesting is right, either she's pulled the wool over Mr Nigel's eyes up there at the Manor, or else he knows she was dropped in the cart and wanted her that much he'd take her at any price.' The woman who spoke preferred romance to scandal. The nearest she ever came to it was her weekly magazine and anything she borrowed from the lending library that set its books out in the Church Hall each Friday evening. 'My guess would be that that foreign-looking rascal let her down. She's not the sort to deceive a nice young man like Mr Nigel. But perhaps the wee mite takes after someone in the family we've never seen – one of old Mr Bradley's people, for instance. He's her grandfather, after all. Whatever the story is, one thing's certain: if Mr Nigel cares as much about her as he must do, then that must more than make up for any wrong she's had done to her. Doesn't it show, though, having money doesn't give you an easy road to happiness.'

By this time the object of their interest had reached the end of the village street and rounded the bend out of view.

The last word, like the first, went to Polly.

'Friendly enough girl, always has been. And the old lady was very overseen in her, we all know what the upshot of that was. Friendly or no, what we've seen this morning has opened our eyes. Oh, well, the more you know of any family, the more you see there isn't one without a skeleton or two tucked away in the cupboard. Like you say, Hilda, money doesn't buy an easy road to happiness.'

Walking home Katie hummed to herself, remembering the excitement Kit's appearance had caused and knowing nothing of the remarks that had followed her retreating figure. If she'd thought this a Red Letter Day before, her trip to the village had confirmed it.

She found the estate office locked. Back at the Manor a message from Nigel was waiting for her. He'd telephoned from Reading. He'd not be home until evening.

Cards on the table, she and Nigel faced each other.

They'd eaten their dinner in unbroken silence while Hawkins hovered. It wasn't until the dessert was served and he had withdrawn that Nigel challenged her.

'How dare you make me look a fool before Jo Dibbens – and Frank too!'

'Why did you tell him to take Black Knight to the sale?' She met his eyes defiantly. 'And without even mentioning it to me!'

'Why did I? For the same reason as you over-ruled my order.' He pushed his plate away from him, his food untouched. 'I want *nothing* in this house that reminds me of that man.'

For a moment her blood seemed to run cold. If he'd planned to get rid of Black Knight behind her back, had he some scheme for Kit's future? No, she was being fanciful. He hadn't the authority so much as to send a horse to market, what power could he possibly have over Kit? Even so it was fear that put cold mistrust in the look she cast on him.

She knew he was angry – and that in itself was unusual. She tried to put herself in his position and was fair-minded enough to feel a sneaking sympathy for him. Of course he resented his orders being rescinded. But it was his own fault, he shouldn't have tried to go behind her back.

'By coincidence,' he was saying, 'Frank had to go to Reading today. Nothing to do with the horse sale at the Cattle Market. I decided at the last minute to go with him, get his business finished then go on to see how the sale went. Damn it, Katie, what sort of a fool do you think it made me look? I told the auctioneer I had a horse, Black Knight, coming up for sale. What time was he expected to be brought into the ring? "Seems to be some mistake, sir," and the way he said it made me a liar, "Lot 23 has been withdrawn." Not even that the damned horse hadn't arrived! At least then it would have appeared there'd been a breakdown on the way. But no, Jo Dibbens had telephoned the auctioneer and said he'd been given instructions not to sell. And there was I, the owner . . .'

'The owner? Nigel, you'd no business to arrange to sell Black Knight, and well you know it. You knew I wouldn't have let him go, that's why you didn't mention it.'

He pulled his plate towards him and started to eat, staring at the food as though its appearance fascinated him. When he spoke again his voice was over polite.

'You certainly know how to turn the knife. In the study you'll find the monthly accounts for the farm. You'd like to check through what's been used, I'm sure. The feeds, the fertilizers. I really must remember not to overstep my position again.'

123

'Please, Nigel, you're not being fair –'

'Oh, yes, and I didn't mention it, I'm afraid, but I've asked for a quotation for some re-pointing that's necessary on the north face of the Manor. Your Manor. That's on the desk too, you'll see it there.'

'You're behaving like some kid.' She hoped her voice wouldn't give away just how alone she suddenly felt.

'On the contrary. I'm behaving like the person who will meet the endless bills for maintaining your Manor.'

Like a child, she pouted. 'I've got money.'

'Invest it wisely and you've enough to pay the wages for the inside staff. Well, that's an exaggeration, but you could put something towards it. Why don't you eat your dessert? Your friends downstairs will be upset if you leave it.'

She wished she were a child, then she could cry. The rhubarb crumble tasted like sawdust, the cream clogged her teeth. She wanted to tell him that they'd made a huge mistake, they'd married for all the wrong reasons, they had no future. But she couldn't. She was frightened to speak.

'Look, Katie, we're just being bloody silly, both of us.' As suddenly as his anger flared, now he sounded like the Nigel she knew. She nodded her head, still not sure enough to trust her voice. 'All right, I went over the top wanting to get rid of Black Knight. And if I'd sold him, what then? I'll tell you. It would have driven the wedge between us deeper. And that's not what we want, is it?'

She shook her head.

'I'm sorry too. I was rude and horrid.' As she spoke her voice became steadier. 'I want us to be friends. More than anything, that's what I want for us. We always were. We had lots of good times. Now suddenly we're guarded, wary. Nigel, can't we start again?'

That night she sat in bed in the room he'd had refurbished. The light was on, she was alone. When she heard the soft tap on the door and saw the handle move she knew this was his answer.

Throughout Katie's childhood she'd never questioned her assumption that life would be good. Why should she question it? She'd known nothing different. When for her eighteenth birthday she'd been sent her airline ticket for a holiday with her mother's family in England, the trip she'd always dreamed of making, she'd accepted it with gratitude, with excitement, with wonder even – but not with surprise that out of the blue the way should be made so easy for her. Her naturally optimistic nature had never envisaged a hurdle that couldn't be overcome. That was the root of her friendship with Alice Piper.

124

Like so much more in Newton Dingley, Wyche Cottage belonged to the Matheson estate. The tenant, Alice Piper, had gone there as a bride in 1902 and when, some ten years ago, her husband had died she'd not considered moving out. Why should she? Wyche Cottage had been her home for fifty years. Usually one of the boys from the village would give her garden its winter dig for a few shillings, then with all the determination of her independent nature she would plant out her vegetables in the right season. When keeping the small front lawn neat had become a problem she'd paid the boy and had it taken away; she'd made a deal with him on the price and let him cut the turf carefully so that he could trade it in on another job. She might be old, but Alice prided herself that she was as canny as the next. Then she'd ordered fruit bushes, gooseberry and currant, planted them and heeled them firmly in. If folk thought it strange to see fruit bushes in the front garden, then let them enjoy having something to gossip about. For herself, she was well pleased; she and her hoe could manage to keep the weeds away.

Katie had become a regular visitor to the cottage. She liked the old lady's honest approach to life, liked the way she battled with the adversity of advancing years, liked her spirit of independence.

The first time they'd talked had been only a week or two after Katie's arrival at the Manor. Walking into the village she'd seen the old lady hoeing between the fruit bushes in her front garden. To stop and speak had been the natural thing to do. And that had been the start.

A week or so later Katie had called at the cottage. She'd been surprised how disappointed she'd been when there had been no reply to her ring. She was almost out of the gate when Alice's voice called to her.

'That silly bell couldn't have rung.' Her look had discouraged Katie from replying that she'd clearly heard it herself, but Alice was no fool.

She's not going to say she heard it, Alice realised. Making allowances because I'm not up to the mark. That was worse than acknowledging the truth.

She'd ushered Katie into the small front room before she said in a hushed voice as though she'd been about to divulge a state secret: 'I don't hear the way I used to. I saw you opening the gate to go. Didn't hear the silly bell. Don't you go telling anyone this, I don't want my little problems chattered around the village. I might get a knocker put on the door, see if that gets through to me better. But that's just between you and me, Miss Katie.'

'Cross my heart, I'll not tell. But couldn't you get some sort of a hearing aid?'

'That I never will! I am as I am. If the good Lord says my ears have come to the end of their usefulness, then that's the way it's got to be and I'll manage best I can. Only reason I told you about not always catching the sound of that front bell is that I was going to say, don't you bother to wait for me to come and open up to you. The door's always on the latch and I'm always about the place. Just you come straight through and find me.'

'Can I really? I'd like that. Grandam said I was to bring you some dahlias. A sign that summer's well on its way, she said. I don't know much about the flowers you grow in England. Shall I put them in water for you?'

'Bless the child, I'll get a vase for you. T'isn't that I'm not able to put a few flowers in a drop of water, but I'll enjoy having them arranged real nice for me. If I can find a good piece of writing paper I'll put my thanks down for you to carry to the house to Mrs Matheson. Fancy her thinking to send me lovely blooms like that.'

'Don't do that, Mrs Piper. I'll tell Grandam you wanted to write to her but I said no, I wanted us to have time for talking.'

The old lady had made a pretence of needing to be persuaded, but Katie had had her first suspicion that Alice Piper's eyesight had come as near the end of its usefulness as her hearing.

'If I don't write, you promise you'll tell her that I wanted to. Tell her I say thank you. Yes, dahlias are a sign that summer's had its first flush. Still, there's no flower with more colour. Just look at them, so bold and bright. That's the way with your great-grandmother. And I try to make it my way too. Summer's over for her and for me, we're in the autumn of our allotted time, no doubt about that, but jigger me, there's no need for us to lose what bit of brightness the good Lord saw fit to give us. But enough of my chatter. Back the other day you when you stopped at the gate for a word you were telling me about your home out there in Canada. The edge of the prairies. Fancy, to think you've come all that way. I've read about places, you know. Now I want to hear some more, about – something Creek, didn't you call it? Those young brothers, you promised to bring me a picture . . .'

That had been two years ago. Katie and the old lady had formed a relationship that spanned their differing ages and backgrounds. For half that time Katie had been mistress of Bullington, for almost as long she'd been married to Nigel, but to the old lady she was still Miss Katie, and she still let herself in to Wyche Cottage sure of her welcome.

'I've been watching out for you for a day or two.' Now Alice scurried down the path to the front gate as she spied Katie riding back towards the Manor. 'Miss Katie, can you just climb down off that

126

horse and come inside? I won't keep you. I just want you to see something.' She was clearly agitated.

Swinging herself to the ground Katie looked around for somewhere to tether Cleo, finally hooking the rein over the low gate post and hoping the horse would get the message.

'What's happened, Mrs Piper? Is it something needs attending to in the cottage?'

'Something wants attending to in young Billy's brainbox, that's nearer the mark.'

'Billy? Your grandson?'

'Here, just you read this. Time I went to them, indeed! He's a dear boy, I wouldn't want you to misunderstand me. But to live with them!' Like a Jack-in-the-Box whose spring had snapped, Alice's legs folded under her and she slumped on to a chair, her body sagging. Scanning the letter Katie saw the situation. It was generous and kindly meant. But it broke her heart to see her friend with the fight gone out of her. Her family saw her as old and frail – so old and frail she'd suddenly become.

'They all came to see me last week, Wednesday it must have been. Billy and young Tess, his wife, and the three children. I baked a cake, got in a few little extras . . .' her wrinkled face crumpled '. . . it was the bread, that's what set all this going. Tess went to cut the bread and butter. There was mould on the loaf, and I'd not seen it.' She wept. 'Don't expect it would have harmed us.' She swallowed her tears and forced the old fighting spirit back into her voice. 'Still, I felt ashamed. I gave their lad Kevin the money to run along to Mrs Briggs and fetch in another. Thought that would be the end of it. "Time you came to us, Gran," that's what Tess said, but I never thought to take her meaning seriously. Of course I didn't. Miss Katie, I think the world of Billy and his little family, but how could I live like they do? That beastly thing they call the telly . . . every evening it's on, hour after hour. The noise of it goes on till you feel you want to throw something at the silly grinning faces on it. I had a week with them back last summer, you remember. Tess works in some café most evenings, Billy sees the children off to bed. But the noise! They can't make me go, can they, Miss Katie? You see what he says there at the end, something about getting in touch with the estate office and arranging everything so I'd not have anything to bother with. But they can't do it! They can't, can they? Oh dear . . . I've lived too long, that's the trouble. All my usefulness is gone. Why don't the Lord let me hand in my ticket and be done with it?'

'Don't let me hear you talk that way! I guess you and me are two of a kind, we don't care to have things taken out of our own hands.'

127

Alice nodded, wiping her eyes and putting paid to her tears with one last sniff.

'But they *are* family.' Katie knelt by her side, her arm around the bent shoulder. 'They want you to go there because they care about you.'

'You make me sound ungrateful. I'm not.'

'You don't want to give up your things? Well, perhaps there would be room for you to take some of them.'

'Things! Bits of wood, bits of brass. Oh, Miss Katie, it's not the things. They're all young, all busy living. And what would I be? Just the old lady whose life's behind her.'

'Billy's probably older than I am. Yet you and I talk, proper talk, like two people who are friends. Couldn't it be like that with Billy and Tess?'

Alice shook her head. 'You and me, we clicked right from the word go. You're the lady from the Manor, I'm just me. But it's never made a jot of difference. Like you say, we talk proper talk. That's why I had to see you. Miss Katie, promise me you won't let them make me go?'

Katie promised.

As the summer progressed Kit added to the repertoire of his talents with each day. For all the interest Nigel took in him there might have been no baby in the nursery and, in a way, Katie was glad. Kit belonged to her, he was part of the secret she carried in her heart. Uncomfortably lodged at the back of her mind was the knowledge that the present situation couldn't last for ever. Babies grow to be boys. She pictured Ramsey with her younger brothers back at Higley Creek, the companionship between them. That's what Kit would need. But that's ages away, time will sort things out, she told herself.

It was an afternoon in August. Katie had taken Kit to the lake. Lying on his stomach on a rug, he gurgled with excitement as the ducks waddled close, gobbling up the pieces of crust she threw to them.

Across the parkland she could see Nigel talking to Frank Fulford, and as they parted company, she waved to him. To her surprise, he started towards her.

'Haven't any bread in your pocket, have you? This greedy lot have just finished what we brought them.' Purposely she said 'we' not 'I', defying him to ignore Kit.

'Where's the nursemaid? Isn't it *her* job to keep an eye on the baby?' Nigel dropped to the grass by her side, not quite looking at Kit.

'The nursemaid! The baby! What am I? The woman? Her name is Meg, his is Kit.'

'You sound very edgy. What's up?'

'Nothing *was* wrong, we were having a lovely time.'

'You mean until I came? I took it from your wave you wanted company.'

These days they didn't quarrel; but then, neither did they have conversations with this little olive-skinned creature chortling his contribution.

'Of course I was glad you came over to us. Nigel, you never even look at him. All those awful things we thought might be wrong with him . . . sometimes I think you're sorry – no, I can't say it, it's like tempting fate even to remember what we expected.' She put out her hand and touched Kit's tiny foot, to be answered by a turn of his head in her direction and a gleeful squeak. 'Just look at him, can't you? None of it was his fault.'

'No, of course it wasn't. Youngsters his size aren't much in my line, Katie.'

But she knew it was an excuse for something he couldn't help in himself.

'By the way, for some reason this letter got mixed up with the estate things. Frank just handed it to me.' He frowned as he looked at the stamp. 'Canada. Not your people's writing.'

Do hearts really miss a beat? She'd heard the expression but until this moment had never known the true meaning. Then, just as quickly, the illusion was gone and the hope with it.

'Sort of. It is from one of my people. That's Aunt Eva's handwriting – Mom's aunt really, Grandad's sister. You remember I told you about her? She's retired from work now, she used to be a nurse in Calgary.'

Nigel's face lost its guarded look. Sitting on the grass he drew up his knees and clasped his hands around them. He and Katie looked directly at each other, something they didn't always manage to do. He smiled; she smiled back. Then she tore open the envelope.

'Hey, hear what she says! I just told you she's retired from being a nurse – well, she's coming over to England for a while. Isn't that just great!' Great enough to bring home to her how much she missed the familiar Canadian voices, the easy bridging of social strata that was in such contrast to life here. Not that she behaved in any way differently here from how she had been at home. Her way was accepted because she came from Canada; some people might have liked the informal way she treated them, others successfully covered their embarrassment, she never knew which.

'She knows she'll be very welcome to stay at the Manor, Katie. But I expect she'll want to be with your grandparents.'

129

'Maybe. But of course she'll come here. Aunt Eva's a very special sort of aunt – Mom used to call her her "lookalike aunt". Of course she's older than Mom, and as a kid that's all I could see, just that they were different generations. But they *are* alike. The same dark chestnut, not quite auburn hair; the kind that never goes colourless like ours will one day – that's what mostly happens to fair people, isn't it? It doesn't even turn a proper good white. Then they've got the same eyes, brown and warm-looking, the sort of eyes that give away all their secrets. Gosh, though, won't you just imagine! Aunt Eva coming!'

'Perhaps a visitor is what the house needs.'

It was an acknowledgement that for all their determined friendliness, something was missing.

Almost out of Katie's span of recollection there was a time when she and Lottie had lived with Eva in Calgary. She knew now, of course, what had led up to it. Her father's affair with Rosie, Dylan's mother, the fight when somehow Donald, Neil's simple-minded uncle, had taken up a knife in his defence and in the confusion killed him. Even if all the sordid details hadn't come to light at the Inquest, Lottie couldn't have stayed on at Kilton Down once Neil was dead. There had been nothing there for her without him.

Katie's memories were no more than momentary impressions: sitting on her mother's bed watching her pile clothes into a suitcase; a frightened feeling in her tummy when she'd recognised the hate in Old Pop's eyes as he'd looked at them, then the way he'd turned away and spat on to the logs that burned in the grate; curling up on her mother's knee in a car – that must have been when they'd been on their way to Calgary – knowing a new, warm, safe feeling, liking the sound of someone's voice. The someone had been Aunt Eva. Most of the things they'd done in Calgary were long forgotten. She knew they'd been there some months, could remember a playschool where she and Lottie had gone each day; only since had she realised that she'd gone there to play, Lottie to work. She could recall another car journey and this time her excitement. They'd been going to stay at Higley Creek with her friend Ginnie. At just four years old she'd had no conception of anyone else's emotions, had known nothing of the growing love between her mother and Ramsey.

But Aunt Eva, that's where her thoughts were today. Aunt Eva who was so special, the only relative they'd had. Usually during each summer she'd come to Higley to stay for part of her vacation. At least once a year Lottie would take a shopping trip to Calgary. It had been Eva who'd suggested that the girls should come too, so the annual expedition would set out in the car that had been adapted to take

130

Ginnie's wheelchair. Ramsey and the boys had never come, the Calgary trip had been strictly "girls only". Looking back on it now Katie could see what an influence Eva had had in building Ginnie's ever-growing confidence.

'Did you hear that, little man?' Katie swooped Kit into her arms and held him high above her head, to be rewarded by a tug on a small fistful of hair. 'Aunt Eva coming to Bullington! A week or two indeed! She's not getting away that soon.'

Kit chuckled with delight. From his airborne position he cast a gummy beam on both of them.

But Nigel's gaze was fixed obstinately ahead.

'I've been talking to Frank about old Mrs Piper,' he said with exaggerated casualness. 'I know what you said about her. I know you promised her you'd see she stayed in her cottage. But, hang it, Katie, she's not fit to run a home. Just because she's had.all those bits and pieces of furniture all her life, it's crazy to encourage her to make a god of them. And that's what it boils down to. It's as if life revolves around the few things she's gathered into her nest. The old girl's jolly lucky to have a grandson prepared to take her in.'

'That's a beastly thing to say. Did you think of Grandam that way? No, of course you didn't. And I should think not too! But, Nigel, Alice Piper's treasures aren't the trappings of her home. They're her freedom, her independence. I know Billy means to be kind, but what sort of a life would it be for her? No one to share her memories, no one with time to listen to her, no peace. She's an old lady, frightened of being caught up on the treadmill of their modern, rushabout lives. Of course she must stay where she is. Anyhow, what's brought this up? Has Billy written to the estate office again?'

'No. Frank made an excuse to go and check over the cottage, see if there was any maintenance that ought to be carried out. She didn't even hear the door. When he finally made himself heard by banging on the window she reached for her poker, thought he was an intruder. She's known him for years. If she can't see well enough to recognise anyone at that distance she has no business to be on her own. He said there was quite an air of neglect, even cobwebs in the corners – and she'd never been that sort of a woman. It's further evidence if any were needed. I told him to write to this nephew of hers. The kindest thing would be to tell her we need a cottage for someone coming to work on the estate. That way we don't actually have to put it into words that she's not a fit tenant.'

'You told Frank Fulford to write to Billy?' Her eyes blazed. 'Nigel Matheson, how dare you? There's nothing wrong with Mrs Piper except that she likes to live her own way and at her own pace. You

131

knew I'd promised her! Well, I don't care what sort of a fool it makes you feel, you can go back to your damned Frank Fulford and tell him the letter isn't to go. She's my friend!'

'Oh, Katie, for heaven's sake!'

'She's my friend, and she was Grandam's friend too. I don't care what you tell your precious Frank Fulford – say that you've had second thoughts, say you can see it's a wicked, hateful way to treat an old lady. Or tell him the truth – that I won't have her turned out. Who the hell do you think you are?'

He got up and walked to the edge of the lake, standing with his back to her.

'You might ask yourself that,' he said after a while. 'Who the hell do *you* think you are? I'll tell you: you're the wife of Nigel Matheson. Yes. Me.' He turned to face her, tapping his chest with his finger. 'All my life I've learnt how to care for this estate. If our marriage is to have a ghost of a chance, then there can only be one master.'

Kit started to grizzle, then to scream.

'Nigel, she's a very old lady. It would break her heart.'

The look he threw at her said as clearly as any words that he thought her a sentimental idiot. He turned and left her, gong in the direction of the estate office.

Katie thought that would be the end of the matter. She thought she understood exactly Alice's need to have her own things around her, to live at her own pace and to find her own peace. So when she next visited Wyche Cottage she was surprised to be told: 'Dr Holsworthy paid me a visit this morning.' Today Alice was very cheerful. Katie was surprised when she went on: 'I got the feeling – although he didn't admit to it – that young Billy had asked him to look me over. I told him, I'm as fit as any other at my age and a good deal fitter than most.' She chuckled at the point she'd scored. 'Couldn't argue with that, now could he?'

'Did he talk to you about Billy's suggestion? Is that why you thought he'd been asked to come?'

'He didn't ask. No, it was me. I told him all about it. A good man is the doctor. Always ready to listen. I told him I didn't want to be a burden in the young ones' house, not even a burden they were all fighting to pick up. I told him I couldn't live the way they do. Dear children they all are – I told him that too. But you just listen to this, Miss Katie! He's put my name up for a place in what he called the "twilight home". Run by the council – not a charity, you understand. I believe they take most of your pension, give you back enough to buy your postage stamps and get your hair done when the girl comes round.'

'But, Mrs Piper, you don't want to move from here. I told you, you've no need to worry.'

'Oh, I'd go off to this twilight place, of course I would. Don't you understand? It's run by the council, it's my right to have a place. Just for the present they haven't the room for me.' She laughed. 'Got to wait my turn. When someone moves off upstairs,' and with something not far from a wink she pointed skywards, 'then Alice Piper's name is on the list. I'll be able to write and tell Billy that. That'll quieten his conscience. He's a good boy. Not many grandsons would bother – nor their wives neither. Ah, but this twilight home, this is paid for by my rates and taxes, it's no more than my due.' Her rates were paid by the estate, she'd never been in a position to pay any income tax, but neither of those things altered the fact that she could move to a council home and keep her independence intact.

It was a conversation that Katie was long to remember. On that afternoon she could have no idea how big a part Alice's words were to play in her own life.

Chapter Nine

Soon Eva would be here. For all Katie's determination that her future was at Bullington, her anticipation of Eva's coming told her just how much she missed the sights and sounds of home.

There had been a weekend in early summer when the contingent from Claygate Hall had come to see the new heir; there had been occasions when Kate and Rupert had motored over to surprise them, for still having her own bedroom at the Manor gave Kate the freedom of an open invitation. But to have Eva here would be different. She was a link with Katie's own folk.

Everything was turning out well, Katie told herself. Yet, if that were true, would she even have considered it, would she have needed to reassure herself?

It was the first week in September. She and Alice Piper were picking the blackberries from the hedge at the bottom of the garden of Wyche Cottage. Or rather, Katie was picking them while Alice, not admitting that her failing sight wasn't up to letting her help gather the fruit, was hooking the brambles into reach with the handle of her walking stick. Alice was enjoying herself, out here in the warm sunshine in her own garden, with Katie for company. Peering close into her young friend's face as Katie brought a handful of berries to add to the basin, a moment's worry shadowed the perfection of the afternoon.

'You look peaky,' she said in her forthright fashion.

'Peaky! Now that's no way to make a girl feel her best.' Katie bantered.

'Not telling you the truth won't do anything for your looks. I dare say you're a mite homesick once in a while, is that it? Want to show that baby of yours to your family. But you've lost your bloom. You look as though you could do with a tonic.'

'Honestly, I'm fine, Mrs Piper. Anyway, if it's a tonic I'm needing, then next week I get the best one possible. Aunt Eva will be here!

She's Mom's aunt, really. She's always been special. I shall bring her to see you, you two'll get along great. I can just picture you together.'

But it wasn't to be.

It was arranged that Eva should spend two days at Brimley, then Rupert and Kate would bring her to Bullington.

Late in the morning of the day they were to arrive, Rupert telephoned.

'Katie, my dear, can you send a car to meet your aunt from the train. It's due at the Halt at 2.27.'

'But I thought you were all coming. Is something wrong with the car?' She tried to instil a tone of regret into her voice. She felt guilty that she should be so glad she was to have Eva to herself. There were a million things she wanted to hear about home and she knew the pained silence they would get from Kate as they talked of Canada.

'No, no, the car's perfectly in order. Even when I realised she'd be making the visit without us, I intended to drive her to the Manor myself. Not to stay, you understand, just to save her the train journey. Two changes make it a tedious business. But in the end I felt it would have been unkind to leave your grandmother.'

'Leave her? But I was expecting all of you.'

'You know the punishment she's subjected to with her headaches – it's been the same as long as I've known her. Any excitement, any tension, and she suffers. I'm afraid the last two days have been quite an ordeal for her. I've been taking Eva out as much as I could, trying to keep the house quiet. Poor Kate! Hardly touched her food. She tried so bravely to keep going. The tension – you've no idea. This morning she couldn't keep up the charade a moment longer. Broke down and wept, like a disappointed child.' Never a note of criticism for his wonderful Kate. 'She said she'd be better once we were gone, once the noise of all the chatter was over. I really didn't intend to put Eva on the train. But Kate was so upset at not being well enough to come with us, you know how she loves to see you and Kit. I admit I was thankful when Eva insisted on making the journey by rail.'

'So she's on her way now, Grandad? We'd have come to Brimley to collect her. You ought to have phoned instead of taking her to the station.'

She could clearly hear his sigh.

'To be honest, my dear, the best thing was just to get her out of the house and on her way. All the excitement of your seeing each other – and poor Kate feeling so wretched – no, it would never have done for you to come to Brimley. Kate's slept for the last couple of hours. It's always the same when Eva comes – not that she very often does, and

135

perhaps that's as well. I wish it were different, I wish they could accept each other as friends.' Which was the nearest he'd ever come to referring to the story Kate had confided about her broken romance and the part Eva had played in it.

'Tell Granny I'll expect you both to join us when she feels better.'

So it was that at five past two Katie was sitting on the solitary bench of the wooden platform at Bickley Halt, about three miles from Newton Dingley. She was much too early, but once she was actually here, waiting, it felt like Eva's visit had begun. Just imagine, in only a few minutes she'd hear that voice of home! At the first sight of the train snaking into view she leapt up from the seat. Oh, but how silly, she'd never been so shaky, her legs had no strength, things were far away . . . none of it real . . . dim . . . dimmer. Sit down, quickly, sit down and shut your eyes tightly just for a second. It's just the excitement. The train's coming . . . hold on . . . just hold on . . .

'Hey, honey, it's all right, take it steady.'

That was Eva talking. Through the clearing mists Katie recognised her. She realised she was still sitting slumped on the railway bench, her aunt next to her with a firm arm around her shoulders.

'What a way to greet you,' she gasped. 'I didn't even see you get off the train.'

'Just sit quiet for a minute, get your breath back, eh? We've got all the time in the world. The train's gone, there's no one here but you and me.'

'Aunt Eva! Oh, but it's good to have you come. I don't know what happened to me. I'm better now, truly. Guess I got too excited. I didn't waste time eating lunch. I figured when we got home we'd have a real English tea.'

'That sounds like a good idea.' Nothing in Eva's warm smile suggested what was going through her mind. She'd never seen Katie look so wan. Could skipping lunch do this to a healthy young girl? A good job she'd come visiting. No use pressing now, best to take it gently.

'I'll load my cases into the trunk. Then, if you'd rather, I'll drive. Unless you're sure you're O.K.'

'Quite sure, honestly. I can't think what happened, I've never done anything so stupid. I just felt everything slipping out of reach. It was the excitement, seeing the train coming . . . I'm fine now. Anyway,' she laughed, 'traffic goes on the wrong side of the road here. Remember?'

'Oh, I remember right enough. I was an English lass, have you forgotten? Bickley Halt. I might have jumped right back in time.'

She didn't elaborate. Katie felt she was talking more to herself. And as they started off towards home Eva looked around, missing nothing, wishing she had an extra pair of eyes in the back of her head. 'But doesn't it just telescope the years, bring back times long past? I was here before. Did you know that, Katie. I mean, I've lived at the Manor.'

136

'I know. Granny told me about it.'

'You mean about Matt?'

Katie nodded, keeping her eyes on the road ahead. 'Yes. She told me how he walked out on her on her wedding day – because of you. And about what happened to him. People's lives are so full of things we don't guess at, aren't they? Happiness . . . tragedy . . . things they keep tucked away where no one can see.'

'I guess so. I'm glad she talked about it. It's not a healthy thing to do, hug your unhappiness to you.'

They drove in silence. Eva thought the conversation was over until Katie said: 'It was because of Dylan – that's why she told me. I think she believed I was doing what you said, hugging my unhappiness to me. She thought that if I realised she'd lost someone she cared about too, then I might talk to her. But I couldn't, Aunt Eva. How could she have understood Dylan? She hated him without ever seeing him simply because he was Neil O'Hagon's son. I guess you know what I'm talking about? Mom must have told you?'

Eva nodded. 'Yes, she did. She was blaming herself that she'd never explained to you about who he was. But why should she have? It was all years ago. There's no point in raking over dead ashes. How was she to know you'd meet up, and in England of all places? But, Katie, you've pulled through it and got back on course again? Nigel, Bullington and now little Kit, life's tried to make up to you?'

They were almost back into Newton Dingley. The narrow road was empty. All Katie had to do was to answer: 'Sure, life's fine.' Yet she found herself pulling the car off the road into a farm gateway and switching off the engine. She'd known how much she'd looked forward to having Eva to talk to, but she'd not planned to say what she found herself saying now. Quite positively, though, she knew there was no other way. She had to confide in someone; that someone had to be Eva.

'Life has made it up to me, it's given me Kit. Aunt Eva, Kit's not Nigel's son, he's Dylan's. I've never told anyone, I don't know why I'm telling you now. Mom knew Dylan and I meant to marry, but not about the months we'd had. She would never have suspected it somehow, I know she wouldn't. Back home, I'd not had a serious boyfriend even. All right, you can tell me that what I did was wicked, unnatural because he was my brother. But wouldn't you think some sort of instinct would have stopped me falling in love with my brother – my half-brother? Kit's mine, Aunt Eva, he's all I have left of that time. Even Mom doesn't know that. No one except Nigel, and now you.'

'Nigel? You mean he married you knowing it?'

137

Katie nodded.

'He must love you one heck of a lot. Not that that could have made it any easier for you.' She covered Katie's hand with hers, her long fingers as strong and capable now as they had been half a lifetime ago.

'He doesn't love Kit. He never even looks at him.' Katie didn't attempt to switch the engine on. Eva waited, not prompting her. She was sure there was more to come. 'He and I were friends, we got along well right from the start, had a lot of good times together. Looking back now, I can see how pleased Grandam was that we spent so much time together. Then I met Dylan. That was the day before she was first ill. You've no idea how much I wanted to tell her about him and me. But she never knew. You know about her Will – me the estate, Nigel the money? Well, that's not quite accurate, but more or less. I couldn't afford to keep the estate going without him – and he'd lose Bullington without me. She must have believed that would make sure we stayed together.'

'And it's working out, Katie?'

'It's got to work out, hasn't it? We both knew what we were doing. We shall see to it that it does work out.'

'And what about Kit? You've told me, but you say no one else knows?'

'Oh no, no one knows. Aunt Hester and all her lot have been down to pay their respects and look him over; Granny and Grandad come often. No, no one suspects he's not Nigel's. Aunt Eva, sometimes I look at him and I can't believe anything so wonderful can have happened to me. He's mine. Nothing can ever change that. When I was with Dylan I was sure that it was right for us to be together, I didn't dream I'd find out the things I did. But no one can spring anything on me about Kit – I know it all. Christopher Matheson of Bullington. Well, if that's what he's to be, then that's fine. But to me he's just Kit. He's mine. Nothing can take him away from me.'

Eva could see all manner of black clouds on the horizon, but this wasn't the time to bring them to Katie's notice.

'I'm glad you felt you could tell me, Katie.'

'And I'm glad I did. It feels good that you know it all.' She switched on the engine and started slowly forward. 'There's just one thing I never can work out. In Grandam's Will – I'll tell you the exact words: ". . . to my beloved great-grand-daughter Katrine O'Hagon of Higley Creek, Alberta, Canada," and this is the important bit, "in the certain knowledge that she will have the courage to do what she knows is right." If she was so happy to see Nigel and me getting along well and that's what she wanted, why should she think it would take courage for me to marry him? I've wondered an awful lot about it. It did take courage. But Grandam couldn't have guessed at that, she never knew about Dylan. I'd give a lot to know just what she had in her mind.'

'Maybe she thought you'd need courage to decide to make a life away from Canada.'

'Maybe.' But Katie said it without conviction.

The moment of confidence was over, by now they were in Newton Dingley. Coming towards Wyche Cottage she slowed the car half hoping her old friend would be in the front garden. But today there was no sign of life, only a group of woman gossiping on the opposite side of the road.

Coming to Bullington Manor brought back to Eva memories that had been dormant for years. She'd never seen the house as it was now, filled with beautiful furniture, family portraits lining the walls of the dining hall, treasures collected together by generations of Mathesons. But the great marble-floored hall, the sweep of the stairway that curved to the first-floor gallery, the carved ceilings, nothing could change these. Indeed seeing each room again, it was easy to discount the furniture that made the Manor a home, in her mind's eye to see again the iron bedsteads, the rows of wheelchairs. And upstairs when Katie took her into the nursery to see Kit, how the years rolled away; she was back in the dormitory she'd shared with five other nurses.

That first hour was crowded. There was Kit to be admired, there was a brief tour of the main rooms on the first floor. The large, airy bedroom that Nigel had had re-furbished for his bride was beautiful, yet clearly in her memory she recalled it as one of the main wards. It had housed sixteen beds with ease. Most of the others had had no more than four, some of them less. It seemed a strange twist of fate that had decided Katie to put her into the room that used to be Matt's.

'I think you'll be O.K. in her, Aunt Eva. Through that door you've got your own bathroom. And if you stand on this side of the window and crane your neck –'

'I know! I'll just be able to see the lake. I remember.' Oh, yes, she remembered, that and so much more that had been kept suppressed for more than half a lifetime.

'I keep forgetting. I guess you worked in most of the rooms. How many beds did you get in each?'

'Usually three or four. Don't forget, the men were mostly convalescing. Those in the three wards needed more nursing. One of the wards was what is now your room, and then downstairs there were two more. I never saw them as anything else, so I don't know what you use them for now.'

Katie was more than simply interested – she was strangely excited. From the day she'd first seen the Manor she'd felt drawn to it; over the weeks, months and now years, the spell it held her under had tightened its grip. As she'd grown familiar with each room, each secret corner of the gardens, she'd believed she knew all there was to know. Now suddenly she saw it afresh. It was like discovering that a trusted friend had a secret life.

Downstairs again she led Eva through the main rooms.

'You'll remember it as something quite different, but this is the dining hall. Normally we don't use it, we'd be lost in here.'

Eva nodded. 'Yes, this was another ward. There were none of the portraits on the walls. They must have been stored somewhere for safe keeping. Then there was another room, it must have been just as vast. What would that be? It looked towards the rose garden, I remember.'

'The music room. I'll show you. I suppose ages ago families used music rooms – large families, everyone performing on something while guests had to sit and try and look as though they were enjoying themselves.' Katie giggled. 'Dear Grandam, she was much more practical. It was she who started the annual music evening here. Mom told me about it. She could remember it from when she was a child so it must be quite an institution by now. The Claremont Trio are coming this year. An evening of music and a buffet supper.'

'Hey, honey, the Claremont Trio are top rate. I heard them in Calgary. Them and supper! That must cost an arm and a leg!'

'Oh, Grandam was too practical for that! Tickets are quite expensive, the evening covers its own costs. The first year I was here for it I remember her saying that it was Bullington's night. A silent music room was like an unused fiddle, that's what she said. And she loved to see people here.' Katie smiled at the memory of Lavinia's: "The manor needs to be appreciated." Then, with a chuckle that robbed her of her years, "Of course it does. Don't we all?"

As they came out of the music room they found Nigel returned; introductions brought them back to the present, hospital wards and music rooms seemed to be forgotten. Nigel was at his most charming. Nothing pleased him more than to welcome guests to Bullington.

It wasn't until after dinner that he was called away to take a telephone call from Frank Fulford.

'Nice guy you've married, Katie. Easy to get along with.'

'Sure, we'll make out O.K. Whoever he'd married would have come second in his life. The Manor is his first love.'

Eva laughed. 'Good thing he married you then, or he'd have to have got his act sorted out. There would have been no Manor for him.'

140

'Nor for me either, for long. I just haven't that sort of money. I told you, Aunt Eva.'

'Yes, it's quite something, not the sort of family home to run on a shoestring.'

Nigel came back, a worried frown on his face.

'Trouble?' Katie asked.

'Not directly. Frank phoned in to tell me about the cattle sale at Oxford Market. But – yes, there is trouble. Your old friend Mrs Piper, Katie. You wouldn't have it that I was right. I told you she wasn't fit to live on her own. Frank's had her grandson on the 'phone again.'

'Nigel, we agreed. You promised Frank Fulford wouldn't even suggest to her that she ought to give up Wyche Cottage. It may not be long before the doctor gets her taken into this twilight home, as she calls it. That's where she wants to go. I won't have –'

'It's too late for you to say what you won't have. She tipped a pan of boiling water over herself.'

'Aunt Eva, come with me! You're a nurse. We must go and see her.' Already Katie was on her feet.

'Too late for that,' Nigel told her. 'Fortunately someone was passing, heard her cry out. A good thing the front door wasn't locked. It must only just have happened. Whoever it was who went in to her rushed down to Percy Dawkins' shop to phone for an ambulance. But Mrs Piper was unconscious by the time it arrived, and dead on arrival at the hospital.'

'Oh, no . . .'

'Oh, yes, I'm afraid. Polly Dawkins went in the ambulance with her. It was she who told the hospital about Billy – the next of kin. The hospital contacted him, of course. He's been on the phone to Frank. You can imagine what he says. If we'd done as he wanted, got the old girl out so that she had to go to him, then she wouldn't have been messing about trying to look after herself. It was plain lunacy. Her sight had nearly gone, she couldn't hear . . .'

Katie looked helplessly at Eva.

'I promised her she could stay there. There's a council home she wanted to go to, the doctor put her name down. That way she felt she kept her independence. She *couldn't* have lived with her grandson and his family. She loved them dearly, they meant to be kind, but she wouldn't have been part of all the noise and bustle of their home. How could she?'

'Maybe you ought to be glad it's over for her. She went out in her own way. There are things more important than sheer length of life,' Eva answered.

141

Katie nodded, her blue eyes swimming.

Nigel was frankly puzzled. It seemed to him so clear that if the old lady had been fortunate enough to have family ready to give her a home, then that way she would have been safe. But, even so, he didn't like to see Katie looking so sad.

'Honestly, I am sorry, Katie. You were really fond of her, weren't you? Perhaps if I'd had a word with Holsworthy, or with the council people, I might have got them to take her. As her landlord I ought to have kept a better eye on her.'

'It wasn't an eye on her she needed,' Katie answered with spirit, 'it was a home where she would be looked after without feeling herself beholden to anyone. Not even me. There was no one around her who shared her memories. I loved to listen to her, but that couldn't have been the same as talking to people who knew without having things spelt out to them. She had a brother who was killed in the Boer War. Just imagine – she went to London and waited in the crowd for hours to watch Queen Victoria's funeral procession. She told me about it – how all the men stood with their hats in their hands, and people bowed their heads as the cortège went by. That was one of her special memories.'

And as Katie said it, there flashed into her mind her own London: the white-painted brick wall of a cellar where they'd danced, the wild beat of the rhythm, a hotel bedroom . . .

'Lots of things, she talked to me about. I loved to listen, but none of it was part of any sort of life I'd known. It must have been so lonely for her.'

On their own Nigel might have managed to say something to comfort her, but as it was he did the next best thing he could and poured them each a drink. After he'd passed Katie hers he touched her shoulder for a second, in a silent message. And just as briefly she raised a hand and covered his. Alice Piper had been the reason for more than one argument between them, yet now it was she who brought them close to a new understanding. She and the echo of something Eva had said earlier: "He must love you one heck of a lot." Katie had to believe it was the truth, she had to build on it.

Two things persuaded Eva that an early night was called for. One was that she wanted to indulge in memories.

Eva Bradley, you're sixty-seven years old, not some dewy-eyed youngster, she chided herself. Then answered: So what if I am? Just think back to how it used to be, let the me of those days struggle out of the wrappings. She may be a stranger to the me of today, but she won't be a stranger to Matt, to the way things were. Maybe she won't be such a stranger to me either once I find her again.

142

That was one thing that decided her on an early escape to her room. The second was harder to define. It had to do with the way Katie had talked about her marriage, the will both of them had brought to it that it should be a success. Something in the atmosphere told her that this evening was important.

'I know it's early and I can hardly blame the short trip from Brimley for making me ready for bed, but I'm going to ask you two to forgive me. Maybe it's just that I need longer for beauty sleep than you two young ones. Tell me, do either of you ride in the morning? If so, can you count me in?'

'That's great!' Katie beamed. Then to Nigel: 'Back at Higley when Aunt Eva visited, she and Mom and me always rode early. Then home to a huge dish of bacon, eggs, waffles and maple syrup. There's no breakfast like it.'

'Riding on an empty stomach isn't my idea of a start to the day, Katie knows that,' he said.

Eva couldn't know the subject pushed them towards thin ice. This evening they skirted safely around the edge, both of them conscious of the harmony between them and determined nothing should crack it.

Left alone they watched a television programme about a mountain rescue team. By Katie's side on the settee Nigel reached to take her hand, she twined her fingers round his. The scenes on the screen turned her mind back to a year ago, to their honeymoon. She wanted to say to him that – that what? That she loved him? Yes, of course she did. That she was in love with him? If only she knew how to ignite the spark that would turn her affection for him into what she longed for. Perhaps in her determination to make a good marriage she was trying too hard. And Dylan? Where did he fit in? More dangerous ground, more thin ice. Dylan was her brother; if she met him again, then he would be her friend. Any anger she'd had that he'd been fool enough to believe Rosie's lies had faded. She tried not to think of him at all, but there were moments, like this, when memories haunted her. She yearned for a love like she'd known with him, the fusing of their spirit, the excitement of being together, the sense of belonging.

Nigel was her husband. He was her friend. Perhaps that was the best rock to build on. And he was her lover, she told herself. In making love surely they had moments when they reached towards the true union she longed for? "He must love you one heck of a lot." Again she clutched at Eva's words. Dylan . . . no, she wouldn't let herself remember. Instead she moved closer to Nigel, carried their linked hands to rest on her leg. Without looking at him she knew that the screen had lost his attention. She leant against him, turning ever

143

so slightly so that when she crossed her knees her foot was against his leg. She wanted to be near him. This evening they'd both felt that moment of sympathy. Dear Alice Piper, it had been Nigel's awareness of her sadness for her old friend that had brought them close.

By her side his gaze was on the television screen, but his concentration was lost. As if he'd followed her own wayward thoughts, he whispered: 'It's nearly a year, Katie. We're doing well, you and me, aren't we?'

'Of course we are.' She couldn't stop herself adding: 'All three of us.' She'd said to Eva that Kit was hers, and so he was. Even so, he would follow all the Matheson traditions, grow up to be part of Bullington. They were a family.

How much were either of them watching the mountain rescue team bring a climber back to safety? The frosty scene turned remote. For September the night was unusually warm.

'Let's go up, shall we?' For a rock climber he was remarkably willing to switch off the set.

'Yes,' Katie whispered. Just the one word, but her eyes must surely have told him so much more.

They both knew that evening would culminate in the physical satisfaction of making love. But more than that. She told herself that tonight would be different, tonight they'd find the deeper union she longed for. Nigel was her husband, Bullington was her world, they'd build a wonderful future. Of course they would, she had to believe it.

A year ago her body had craved Nigel's love because in it she had found the way to reach out towards Dylan. Her eyes tightly closed, it had been *his* body she'd gripped to her, *his* name she'd longed to cry out as her passion found its ultimate release. At the first visible sign of her pregnancy Nigel had moved back to his own room, she'd felt his revulsion. She'd been alone and lonely. Driven by a need stronger even than her own shame she'd found her own way to Dylan. She may have tried to thrust him out of her mind, but in that moment when control was lost, as she'd clenched her teeth to stifle her cry, always he'd been close, always he'd been with her. 'Kate-ee'. Then from the heights she had plummeted to the depths. To want him was a sin, so the secret of what she'd done had been a sin, the loneliness of the dark nights even emptier.

With Kit's birth had come another change. It was as if her love was transferred to him. After that, when Nigel took up his old role she gave herself to him with no ghosts of the past to come between them. Her mind was prepared to accept him as a friend, her body needed his love.

144

He was still in the dressing room, she could hear him moving about. Turning off the lights she pulled back the lilac curtains and leant out of the open window. Her thin negligee hung open, the night air was cool on her naked body. There was a hint of autumn in the scent of the garden. Her excitement was a physical thing. It gripped her throat, her knees, even her fingers. It reached beyond the next hour into a future whose shape was unknown. In a moment Nigel would come and stand by her side. By the light of the waning moon he'd see her nakedness. She knew with certainty that tonight was important. Because of where the next moments would take them? Yes, that too. But it was something more, something bigger than either of them, and she didn't know what. A bat flew out of th darkness, circled in front of the open window, then disappeared as suddenly as it had come. In her present mood she saw it as a symbol of freedom, and from there her thoughts moved to Alice, her brave spirit released, no fear now of losing the one precious thing she still had, her independence. Then from Alice to Eva, and again that nudge of excitement that under the surface of her mind was something waiting to be discovered.

With a start she realised that Nigel had crossed the dark room to her side.

'Don't get cold,' he said softly.

'I'm warm. Smell the night, Nigel.' Her voice was no more than a whisper, to speak aloud might break the spell. 'Summer's over, it's almost fall.'

'Almost autumn.' She heard the teasing note. Side by side they leant out, listening to the silence of the night.

She laughed softly. 'Autumn or fall, everything's so beautiful. Gentle . . . still . . .'

'So are you beautiful.' Moving back inside the room he turned her towards him, pushing her negligee from her shoulders to slip silently to the carpet.

Freedom had been in her thoughts as she'd looked out on the night. And it was still spurring her now – freedom to use her sexuality, greedy for every physical gratification, for her, for him. The final act of love was violent and quick, and as it always did, left her wide awake and him drifting straight into sleep. She wished he would stay awake. Wasn't this the time they ought to be able to talk to each other, heart to heart? But from his deep, even breathing she knew that if she were able to wake him, his mind would be out of reach.

So with her eyes wide open she gazed at the dark ceiling. If it could talk what would it tell her of all those other Matheson husbands and wives who'd made love in this room? For more than two centuries the

145

family had been perpetuated here. There were other eras though, when this had been one of the main wards of a hospital, for instance, and after that all the years Grandam had been alone, alone and growing old. Poor Alice. Katie's mind was wandering now as her eyelids started to close. To be frightened of becoming a burden in her grandson's house. Grandam had been surrounded by beauty, by security . . . Katie's eyelids were shut. There had been something almost within her grasp as she'd looked into the dark night. But before she could recognise it sleep had closed her mind.

Eva was a good-looking woman. Why was it Lottie called her her "lookalike aunt"? She was taller, her hands and feet long and slender. The rich chestnut colour of their hair and eyes were the most obvious resemblances, yet there was something more fundamental than outward appearance. Being with Eva always gave Katie the same warm, happy feeling that radiated from Lottie. In her pale cream jodhpurs and rust-coloured polo-necked sweater she might have passed for far less than her sixty-seven years. On closer inspection her face looked "lived-in"; experiences both sad and happy had written their lines on it. No sagging jowl or double chin, but then there was no spare flesh on Eva. When she'd been younger she'd worn her hair in a coil in the nape of her neck; nowadays she pulled it higher, anchored it to the crown of her head. She sat her horse well.

Each morning she and Katie cantered over the Common, she on Cleo and Katie on the more temperamental Black Knight. It was during her second week that she was ready first, waiting in the hall when Katie and Nigel came down the stairs.

'*You* try telling her she ought not to go. She won't listen to me,' Nigel said without so much as a 'good morning'.

'Not go? Why? Is something the matter?' Not for the first time Eva thought how washed out Katie looked.

'No. I'm quite all right now, I keep telling him so. The fresh air and a gallop is all I need.'

Nigel shrugged. 'Well, if you must. Aunt Eva, keep an eye on her, won't you? I thought she was going to pass out.'

'Oh, Nigel, don't fuss. I jumped out of bed too fast, I expect, felt a bit swimmy. I'm perfectly O.K. now. Don't eat all the breakfast. We shall come home starving hungry.' She forced a laughing note into her voice, determined to forget that moment when the world had rocked and grown foggy before her.

He found Eva's promise far more reassuring. 'Don't worry, I'll see she behaves.'

As always they rode towards the Common. There was never anyone about at this time of day, and even later there wouldn't be more than a few locals hunting for blackberries. The open countryside, the wide panorama spread out before them, made confidences easy.

'How often have you felt like that, Katie?'

'I was only a bit woozy. It's nothing.'

'Wooziness is never nothing. But most likely it's nothing to be alarmed about. How old is Kit?'

'Five months. But having him didn't pull me down one bit. I know some people say they take time to pick themselves up after a baby, but I didn't. I was fine all the time he was coming and afterwards too. Nothing to it!'

'It doesn't follow you'll be as frisky next time round. Is that what it is? Have you missed?'

'No. Of course I haven't. Of course it's not. How could I be having another baby? You know I'm still partly nursing Kit. No period or anything. I can't get pregnant. Granny told me.'

Eva laughed.

'Oh, Katie, no girl should believe all their grannies tell them. It's my bet that if you have your doctor examine you, you'll find Kit isn't to be an only child for long.'

'You mean that's why I seem to be firing on one cylinder most of the time? I don't feel ill, Aunt Eva. Not really bad, I mean. I get hungry, then when I see the food I don't want it. That sort of thing.'

'When we get home, you telephone your doctor.'

Eva was relieved to think that this might be the solution. Katie had always been a happy child, full of vitality; it had bothered her to see her so wan, almost plain, her light brown hair with no sheen. It might be just that it was time she stopped nursing Kit.

They said no more about it as they cantered sedately homeward. It was only when the horses were handed back to Jo and they were leaving the stable yard that Eva put her arm around Katie's shoulder and said with a grin: 'Bet you ten cents.'

Dr Holsworthy arrived later that morning. By lunchtime he'd gone and at the side of her plate Eva found a ten cent piece, one of the few Canadian coins Katie hadn't changed at the bank at the beginning of her holiday three years ago. It was a neat way of breaking her news, news that Nigel had already been told; Katie was expecting a second child. As far as the doctor could say at this stage she was about three months pregnant. For a man who had a five-month-old son sleeping in the autumn sunshine of the rose garden, he was remarkably elated!

On the day of her arrival Eva had seen black clouds on the horizon. Storm clouds that darkened and gathered speed as the wind whipped up, bringing them this way.

147

Chapter Ten

It was all so long ago. Matthew Harkin, the handsome young Irish doctor, had been serving in the Army at Bullington Manor when he had fallen for the young daughter of the house. And no wonder. Even now, after all these years, Kate was a delightful-looking woman; at eighteen she had been exquisite and as gentle as she was lovely. That the family had always cosseted and protected her was something she'd taken as natural. Her father had given permission for she and Matthew to become engaged, on the understanding that marriage must wait until the war ended, or until she came of age. She'd asked for no more. Sometimes Matt's impatience had frightened her. Proudly she'd worn the sapphire engagement ring; contentedly she'd dreamed of being his wife. For Kate, that had been the happiest period of her life. For more than a year the engagement had continued, she shying away like a frightened fawn from any of Matt's advances that would have carried it a stage further. When Eva Bradley had been sent to work at the hospital, it hadn't entered Kate's head that he might have a change of heart.

It was the news that he was to be sent overseas that had persuaded her father to agree to bring forward the wedding. By that time Kate had been nearly twenty, and surely the happiest girl in the world? Or so she'd believed. Wedding gifts had flooded in despite wartime austerity, the great day had come, the guests arrived. It was when she was dressed ready to be taken to the church that Eva's brother Rupert had brought the news – Matt had jilted Kate because of Eva. The medical staff had been welcomed into the East Wing of the Manor; Lavinia had revelled in the life they brought to the place. Rupert hadn't been one of them, he'd been an officer in the Army Pay Corps and stationed only a few miles away. That he was Eva's brother had been enough to make him a welcome visitor. So for months he'd known Kate; he'd fallen under her spell from the first. With Matt gone Rupert had been there, ready to give comfort, his open adoration balm to her wounded spirit.

Six months later, still awaiting his leave from France so that he and Eva could marry, Matthew had been killed. When life knocks you down you have to jump right back up, set your eyes on a goal and work for it. That had been Eva's dictum. All that Matt had left her had been their unborn child. And fate had stripped her even of that – a son, stillborn. Perhaps she had been running away from the past when she'd set sail for Canada at the end of the First World War, but if she had she'd not realised it. She was a nurse, she was determined to be a good one. Canada was part of the brave new world, it looked to the future. And so too must she.

Married to the adoring Rupert, surrounded by suburban comfort if not riches, mother of three children, mistress of a middle-class detached house which boasted one living-in maid, a two-days-a-week gardener-cum-handyman, a tennis court on the back lawn, thirteen fruit trees known as 'the orchard', and the luxury of a motor car in the early nineteen-twenties, of the two surely it was Kate who'd had the good life? Yet disappointment had made a martyr of her, her changed life-style something that even now, after forty-five years, she resented. At heart she was still Kate Matheson, child of Bullington Manor. That her only daughter's childhood dream to go to Canada stemmed from Eva, that it became realty when Lottie married the loathsome Neil O'Hagon, that their grand-daughter should be brought up to look to Eva instead of to her so far away in England, all these things made it impossible for Kate Bradley to put the past behind her and come to terms with her sister-in-law.

Long ago it might be, yet for Kate it still cast its long shadow.

Eva's visit to the Manor was almost at the end of its second week when a letter from Rupert arrived addressed to Katie and Nigel, suggesting it might be better if he and Kate put off their visit until his sister had left for the Continent – all part of her planned visit to Europe. Katie knew the bare facts of what had happened; Eva tried to fill in the gaps so that she would understand.

'But it's crazy, Aunt Eva. It's all ages ago. Even the bit you said about you being the one to talk to Mom about Canada when she was just a kid. You could have said the same thing to other people and they wouldn't have got all fired up with enthusiasm. Canada is right for Mom. Sure, she must have missed her folk when she first went there, but she – oh, you know how it is for Mom. Canada – Alberta – it's right for her.'

'And you, Katie? You must miss your folk too. Maybe we all have a sort of spiritual home. Have you found yours here at Bullington?'

149

'I miss Mom and Dad and the others, of course I do. Sometimes I go over to the farm, look at those fields of corn and just – just yearn to see the vastness of Higley. I'd even like to struggle along in a dust storm, shutting my eyes against it, feeling it scratching my face. I'd like to be scorched by that great big sun. That's how homesick I sometimes get. But it's healthy, Aunt Eva, it's natural I feel like I do. But . . . my spiritual home, you say? Yes, I guess this is just about it. I believe Grandam knew.'

'When I've done my sightseeing, may I come back here, Katie? From France. I want to go there last. I'd like to come from there to the Manor.'

'Are you going to Matt's grave?' Katie felt it an intrusion to ask and yet she wanted Eva to know she'd followed the association.

'Silly, isn't it? Just a bit of French soil.' That's all she said as, sitting on the seat by the lake, they watched the ever-hopeful ducks lining up waiting for any morsel that might come their way. Katie imagined her thoughts were with that plot of French soil, so she was surprised that when Eva spoke again it was to say: 'So sad for them. For both of them. Once happiness turns to bitterness, it can't be handled.'

Katie wanted to reach out and touch that long, capable hand. Unhappiness had never soured Eva who had always had compassion.

'I guess poor Kate still looks on me as "the other woman", the one who spoilt her life.'

'If she does, then she ought to look a bit further.' Katie spoke with spirit. 'If Matt had loved her a quarter as much as Grandad does – and did then, I suppose – then none of it could have happened. But he didn't, he loved you. It's Grandad I feel sorry for. All right, she married him knowing she wasn't in love with him. But she could have played fair.'

'Maybe she thinks she has. And you'd never hear Rupert complaining. Poor mutt, he'd willingly lie down so that she could wipe her shoes on him. Anyway, now you understand why it is Kate doesn't want me here when she comes – here of all places. They were great times we had with Mr and Mrs Matheson, I can see it now. Usually there'd be four or five of us, depending on who was free. Mrs Matheson loved to have the house full.' She smiled at her memories. 'She was like a bright flame and we were a lot of moths drawn to her. Matt used to play the piano – and I remember Mr Matheson used to call me his "jolly chestnut". He was a dear. Kate was – if I say beautiful it doesn't do her justice, she was more than that, there was an ethereal quality about her. She never joined in the singing, she used to sit with her embroidery and, if he got the chance, Rupert used to join her on the settee. Oh, Katie, I wish you could have a peep back

150

through time and see Bullington Manor in those days. It's a wonderful home for a family, for generations of family, but at that time it was more than that. Its generous heart was big enough for everyone.'

'That must have been Grandam.'

'Maybe it was. Or maybe it just took her insight to realize its potential.'

Two days later the Bullington car drove Eva to Victoria where she caught the boat train to the Continent. The following week Kate and Rupert paid their expected visit.

On their first evening it was Nigel who said: 'Has Katie told you the news? No? Tell them, Katie.'

'It's not a secret. Of course I'll tell them. I'm only just getting used to the idea myself. I'm having another baby. Dr Holsworthy thinks it'll be about March.'

'Oh, my dear, no wonder you've been looking so washed out and colourless. I've been worried about you.'

Katie laughed. 'Well, you can pack your worries away, Granny, I'm fine.'

'Now promise me, Katie, you'll be sensible this time. You know how I said to you when Kit was coming that you ought not to be riding and doing the things you were. You got away with it once, you might not be so lucky a second time. See she behaves sensibly, Nigel. Remember, Kit was premature. That probably pulled your health down.'

'That's right,' Nigel agreed.

That was the way the seed was sown. In the weeks and months that followed Nigel watched her every move. He made himself the self-appointed protector of this new Matheson. Katie looked forward to Eva finishing her grand tour; he'd respected her knowledge, once she was back at the Manor he might give Katie the space to find her freedom.

About a week before Christmas she saw the large pile of holly outside the back door, holly that had been gathered from the estate and would be brought in to decorate the hall and family dining room. At Higley they'd never had holly. To her it represented an English Christmas, or more exactly a Bullington Christmas. At Higley the scent of the spruce tree had filled the house, just as it did at the Manor; tinsel had twinkled, illuminated by coloured electric light bulbs, coloured baubles had turned the house into a fairy grotto. But no holly and no mistletoe. She was disappointed now to see that the heap of greenery at the back door didn't include mistletoe.

'Bad year for it,' Bill Huffkin the garden boy told her, 'I been out hunting but there's hardly a sprig to be found.'

151

'But last year we had lots.'

'It's like that with mistletoe, Ma'am. Some Christmasses we get it easy as wink, others it's a real scrape round to get a bit to hang by the front door. Just as well too. Have it hanging inside the front door and you're fair play for all the callers.'

'To be kissed under the mistletoe?' She laughed. 'Is that so awful?'

'Mightn't be – but you ain't seen the sort o' callers we get coming at Christmastime! My mum has the whole lot of 'em for their dinner at our place – old aunts and their friends, those what got no family to go to, and those with families glad to shift 'em off on someone else.'

'I guess that's what Christmas is all about, Bill.'

'Ah, suppose you're right. Mum seems to get a kick out of having them. For me, I'd rather keep my sprig of mistletoe to put in my buttonhole, see if I can't put it to a bit better use.'

'Well, I'm off on a hunt for some. And if I find any, I promise you a bit for your buttonhole.'

Mistress of the Manor and gardener's boy laughed together.

'Reckon you won't be finding any, Ma'am. I kept my eyes peeled all through Abbots Wood. That's where I been getting it since I was a nipper. Ain't a sign this year.'

'Then I won't waste time going there. Kit and I'll drive out to Yatsham Hill. Bet you anything we'll bring some back from the woods up there. We can't have your aunts deprived of their annual kiss. Whatever I get, we'll share out.'

That was before ten o'clock, the frost turning the December morning into a winter wonderland. Whenever she expected to go to Yatsham Hill, Bill certainly didn't imagine it would be in weather like this. The ground was rock hard. If she found any mistletoe, her fingers would be frozen trying to cut it. So he went back to his equally cold job of gathering sprouts, smiling to himself at their friendly chat but not looking for it to lead to the Christmas buttonhole he'd find so useful at the Saturday jive in the Church Hall.

He didn't see her come out of side door into the yard that led to the coach houses where the cars were kept. Today it wasn't her own car she took – comfortable for two people with room in the boot for luggage. Instead she opened the end doors and climbed into the limousine that had carried Lavinia in regal comfort. Meg stood waiting with Kit in the carrycot and an extra blanket under her arm. With the car reversed into the yard she put her charge safely on the back seat, watched them drive away, then closed the coach house door and went back up to the warm nursery. And all the while the garden boy was prising the frozen sprouts from their thick stems.

'Young Bill!' He looked up at the sound of Terence Ridley's voice. Bottom of the ladder as he was, he was at everyone's beck and call, but this was the voice of real authority. Except for war service Terence had been gardener at Bullington all his working life and head gardener for as long as Bill could remember. Their first encounter had been some twelve years ago when Bill had headed a gang of lads from the village, creeping into the grounds of the Manor through the east gate to hunt for beech nuts. Terence had marched them off with threats of where a return visit might lead them. The incident had left its mark on the young lad. Even now he was far more in awe of the head gardener than he was of the master or mistress of the estate.

'Yes, Mr Ridley?' What had he done wrong?

'When Mrs Moggs has finished with you, just get yourself over to the glasshouses and give Harry a hand cleaning down and disinfecting. Time you learnt something about the care of the glasshouses.'

Fancy Terence the Terrible giving him an indoor job! Bill tore a few more sprouts from the frosty plants, took the basket to the kitchen then hurried in the direction of the glasshouses before anything broke his luck. So it was that he didn't hear the concern when Katie didn't return at lunch time. And no one thought to ask him if he could throw any light on her whereabouts.

By mid-afternoon Nigel had checked in the small end coach house where the sports car was housed; he'd enquired whether Katie had left any messages with Hawkins or any of the kitchen staff; he'd been to see Jo Dibbens to find out whether she'd been to the stables; he'd phoned the estate office to ask Frank if he'd seen her. There was one person in the house he never considered: Kit. Had he done so he might have spread his net wider much sooner than he did.

'I'm getting so worried.' He turned with a start at the sound of Meg's voice close by him as he stood at the top of the drive. 'Do you know when they'll be back, Mr Matheson? I didn't think they meant to be out as long as this. Kit must be starving.'

'They! You mean she's taken the pram?'

Meg could see that he knew no more than she did.

'No. She drove – in the big car. Because of having the carrycot, you see, she needed a large back seat. I can't think what can have happened. They went quite early, before half-past ten I should think. Suppose they've been in an accident?'

'If anything were wrong she would have managed to get a message home.' Nigel tried to sound reassuring.

'Yes, of course she would. Oh, but we say that – something must be wrong. By now poor Kit will be hysterical. He's hours late for his dinner and he won't understand.'

Damn Kit! It was Katie who mattered. Easy to say she'd get a message home, but suppose she'd been in an accident . . . she hadn't

153

just herself to consider, an accident could have hurt the baby. This silly twittering woman fussing about that bloody child being late for his dinner – what of Katie? What of the baby? Nigel took his pipe from his jacket pocket. He needed to grip the stem hard with his teeth, to draw in deep breaths as he held the flame to the tobacco in a show of calm.

'Leave it with me,' he said between smokey puffs. 'I shouldn't be surprised if she's taken him over to Brimley to her grandparents. She likes to surprise them sometimes. In the excitement they must have forgotten to telephone. I'll find out.'

Meg had met the doting Kate Bradley, she thought it unlikely she would have forgotten to send word to the nursery that Kit was being cared for. She watched Nigel go into the house and make for the study to put his call through, then went back into the yard by the coach house as if expecting that by some miracle the limousine would be there. Instead she found Bill pushing a wheelbarrow of empty pots to be stored in the shed. Usually she would have considered herself too superior to gossip with the garden boy, and anyway it was silly to think he might know something that even Mr Matheson didn't. The pictures in her mind of Kit, red in the face from hunger, wet and sore, drove her.

'We're worried in the house. Mrs Matheson and the baby have been out in the car since mid-morning. Not that you could know –'

'Blimey, you mean she went with frosty roads like we got today!'

Another minute and Meg rapped on the study door, opened it and charged in, interrupting Nigel's telephone call to Brimley.

'I know where she went,' she panted, 'Yatsham Woods. That lad who works in the garden knew all about it. Stupid boy!'

'What in the world for? Hold on just a moment, Aunt Kate, I've just been told she went to Yatsham Woods. Hold on while I hear.'

So he heard, even to Meg's final: 'She ought never to have taken that poor baby!'

'I'll drive straight out there,' Nigel told Kate. 'You're not to worry. As soon as I've collected her I'll find a telephone kiosk and ring you. I can't understand how she could do anything so irresponsible! . . . No, you mustn't imagine that. There's identification in the car, the police would have notified me . . . I must go, the light will be fading before I can get there.' He didn't wait for her answer, he'd known from her voice that nervous fright had already brought on the ever ready tears.

Yatsham Wood was on the road to Brimley, a few miles nearer there than it was Bullington Manor. There was no other way to get there. If the car had skidded surely he would see some sign of the accident? Tracks on the grass verge; even – and here his mouth felt dry with fear – the vehicle in the ditch. But there was nothing. Not so much as a small rift in the thin cloud had let the sun break through. Last night's frost was as white now as it had been this morning.

'Damn fool thing to do.' He talked to himself as he drove. 'Katie, Katie, why couldn't you have told me where you were going? God, as if I'd have let you do such a damn fool thing. But when do you ever tell me what you're doing? Never! You and that bastard brat. Don't let anything have happened to her . . . No, that's bloody daft, of course something's happened to her or she would be home. But please – the baby, our baby – and Katie. Perhaps she broke down? If I go to the police perhaps I'll find that they've been trying to get in touch – oh hell, but of course they haven't. There's nothing wrong with the telephone. Blast you, Katie, how can you do it to me? Looking after my child's your job. There's nothing I can do. Can't you use your sense, take extra care, just for these few months?'

His voice grew louder. He wanted to draw comfort from haranguing the absent Katie. Instead of comfort he felt ever more isolated in his helplessness. What did he expect to find at Yatsham Wood? The light would already be going. Suppose he got there and found no car . . . then what? Where could he look? Who could he ask? Perhaps she'd been taken ill, had a miscarriage. Oh, no, not that!

He turned off the road on to an uphill lane that led to the wood. Even at this distance he could see there was a car parked – no, look again, there were two cars. Oh God, someone must have followed her, perhaps she'd been raped, murdered . . . With temperatures below freezing his hands were sweating as he gripped the steering wheel.

Then he recognised the second car.

Over the stile, up the track that skirted the sloping meadow he ran, then through the 'kissing gate' that led to the wood. This must be the path they'd taken. For a second Nigel stood still and listened, half expecting to hear Rupert calling Katie's name. The silence must mean that he'd found her. Even with the leaves gone from the trees, the woodland path was already losing the afternoon light. The ground was uneven and rutted, frozen leaves crunched under his step. As he hurried forward the wood seemed still, the only sound his own footsteps. Then he heard a child cry and knew the frenzied screams came from Kit, somewhere much higher up into the wood.

'Katie!' Nigel yelled as loudly as he could, but how could he hope that she would hear him above the noise of the baby? 'Katie, I'm nearly with you.' He knew he was, Kit was guiding him.

'Thank God you've come,' Rupert greeted him. 'Somehow we'll have to get help. Katie can't walk.'

Joggling the screaming baby, Kate was whispering: 'See, here's Daddy come. Hush, baby, hush. Granny's got you nice and warm. Hush.'

Nigel paid no attention to her, he didn't look beyond Katie. Rupert was helping her struggle to her feet from the frozen ground. Involuntarily she cried out in pain as she moved her ankle even though she stood on only one foot. The other was swollen, ballooning above her tight shoe and right up to her calf. With both arms on her grandfather's shoulders she leant against him.

'You'll be all right now, Nigel's come to take you home. We'll both steady you. We won't let you fall if you can just hop on your good foot.' He spoke gently, his voice almost drowned in the roars of his great-grandson.

'What the hell were you doing lugging the carrycot right up here? Dear God, Katie, have you no sense at all!'

'She can't hop all that way,' Kate turned a withering glare on her husband. She'd just about caught the gist of his words. The sort of stupid suggestion he would make! Turning her back on him she told Katie: 'The last one you didn't go full term . . . Hush now. Hush, Kit, my sweetie. Just fancy, suggesting you hop all that way!'

'I was crawling,' Katie told them. 'We've come right from the top, me crawling, pulling Kit.'

'What the hell were you dong? You damned little fool!'

'Poor boy.' Rather than condemning him for his reaction, Kate excused him. He was overwrought, he must have been worried out of his mind. Secretly she thought his outburst romantic.

'Shut your bloody noise up, can't you?' Nigel turned on Kit. And this time Kate was less forgiving.

'He's wet and he's hungry, poor lamb.'

But Nigel didn't even hear her. All he saw was Katie, a lump the size of a walnut on her temple, a trickle of dried blood on her pale cheek, her swollen foot held off the ground, and her harsh breathing telling him that she was in more pain than she'd acknowledge.

'We came up for mistletoe,' she panted. 'Top of the wood, I've seen it growing.' Then with something that tried to be a smile she nodded her head in the direction of the carrycot where she'd tied her scarf around the treasure she'd gathered. 'It was Kit who worried me. It was nearly his dinner time. I was hurrying, carrying him in the cot. Ground's so uneven – and there was a hole – I didn't see it – felt myself falling. But I managed to hang on to the cot, he wasn't hurt.'

'Is he all you ever think about? That bloody man's brat! If you've hurt my child . . .' He stopped mid-sentence, hearing his words and realizing what he'd said. Just for a moment everything was still, not a rustle in the wood. Even Kit was staring at him, wide-eyed and silent.

156

It was Katie who spoke, not to him but to Kate and Rupert. Shock at his outburst had temporarily quietened Kit, and it had given her her voice back. Her words no longer tumbled out between breaths.

'It's true what he said. Not that I don't care about this new baby – I do. But about Kit. He's Dylan's son. He wasn't premature.'

'I don't believe it! Katie! Oh, dear heaven, that devil of a man Lottie married! Is there no end to the harm he does to this family?' And as always Kate's emotions found their release in tears – tears that were a cue to Kit.

Rupert looked helplessly from one to the other. As if the present predicament weren't bad enough, now there was all this extra upset. Poor Kate. Just when she was so happy to have Katie and the baby within an hour's ride, the past had to catch up with them again. How could she love Kit now? Every time she looked at him she would be reminded of the old hurts. With Kate leaning her weight against him he couldn't move. All he could do was hold out an arm in the direction of his weeping wife. But she didn't so much as look at him.

'I'll carry Katie to the car.' When Nigel had spoken, he'd wanted just to lash out at her, had not stopped to consider her grandparents. Now he spoke with a new calm.

'I'm too heavy. Who do you think you are? Tarzan?' Kate did her best to take the drama out of the situation, she even forced a laugh. 'If you and Grandad each let me put an arm on your shoulders, I can hop. I won't fall again if you're there.'

'I shall carry you.' He wasn't to be argued with. So Rupert took up the carrycot, still bearing its bunch of mistletoe. Kate walked ahead with Kit who'd fortunately cried himself into a state of collapse and was falling asleep with his head against her neck, and Nigel picked up Katie and followed. A short walk, a short rest, another short walk, another short rest. It was some time before they came out of the wood, to find the mist of a gloomy twilight hanging over the meadow.

'We're nearer Brimley than we are Bullington,' Nigel panted as he sat Katie on top of the kissing gate while he had a final rest. 'Can you take the child with you? I'll send the nurse to fetch him later. Can you find something he can eat, do you think?'

'He's Kit, not the child,' Katie hissed. 'And she's Meg, not the nurse.'

'Of course we can, my boy.' Rupert tactfully pretended not to have heard her. 'You can give him some porridge or something, I'm sure, can't you Kate? Now he's asleep it's better if she doesn't put him down, she can hold him going home.'

'Are you sure, Granny? If we take him from you he'll wake. Poor little boy . . .' Katie had come to her lowest ebb. More than anything

157

she wanted to hold Kit, to have him fix her with those light blue eyes. Poor little boy . . . who was there to love him? Only her. Nigel hated him. She'd always known he had no interest in him, but not until today had she seen just how much he hated him.

'Of course she's sure. We shall want to know what the doctor says about that ankle when the nurse – Meg – when she comes for Kit.'

'How could she? How could she let him do it to her?' Kate sniffed. 'I suppose we ought to have guessed. Look at him. Hair as dark as night. What Matheson ever looked like that? When Hester told me about the silly girl getting herself entangled with some undesirable, wouldn't you think I would have wondered how she could have a premature baby so unlike the rest of the family?' Still holding Kit against her, she managed to mop her eyes. 'Makes me feel quite sick. Yes, sick. In that hell Neil O'Hagon must have gone to, how he must be laughing! It would be degrading enough if the Kitashee man had been just someone she was infatuated with. But her own brother! How could she do such a dreadful thing!'

'She didn't know anything about that. It's him I blame. He was old enough to remember what had happened. We mustn't be too hard on Katie. Young people today don't look at things the same way as we used to, Kate my dear. You know, it might be quite nice, you and me having the little chap for the evening, eh?'

'It would have been,' she sniffed, 'it would have been like a dream come true. But you! You're as weak as water! "Nice to have the little chap." And what will we think every time we look at him? We'll think of Katie rolling in the fields with her lover! I can't forgive her!'

Rupert took his hand off the steering wheel and rested it on her knee. She didn't draw back, but then she probably didn't even notice. Her voice rasped as she said: 'I don't think I can even love him. It's not his fault, but I don't think I can love him.'

Katie thought back to her solitary nights when she'd been expecting Kit. This time, even tonight when she was patiently uncomfortable, Nigel didn't suggest she might be better alone. Half waking, he turned towards her. Without his realising it his foot knocked against her leg.

'Ouch!' she yelped.

'What? What's matter?' He woke with a start, then remembered. 'Sorry, did I hurt you?' Moving closer he put an arm around her. 'You're sure everything else is all right? It's just your ankle? The doctor was positive.'

'What a fusser you're turning out to be! Sure, I'm fine, just that my ankle is sprained.'

'I can't think what made you do such a crazy thing. To go on your own would have been stupid enough, but to carry that cot thing up that hill, in that freezing temperature, being so irresponsible with a baby . . .'

'I know when you got there he was screaming, but that was just that he was hungry.' She snuggled closer to him, she even forgot the pain in her foot in her sudden burst of happiness. He was concerned for Kit!

'You know damn' well the baby I'm talking about. Mine. Ours.'

She wouldn't let him guess at her disappointment. And, in truth, did she really care if he wasn't interested in Kit? No, a silent voice whispered, you don't want to share him, you don't want him to be given lukewarm affection. He's yours, you love him enough to make up for everything.

'How could the new baby have known it was cold? He was the only one of us who didn't feel it.'

'"He" – you said "he". Imagine if it is, Katie.' Nigel seemed unaware of her reactions; hope, disappointment, possessiveness, all of them were lost on him as he indulged in his own dreams. 'A son. Another generation of Matheson to carry on here.'

'I already have a son. Christopher Matheson, remember?'

'I'm not likely to forget. I've kept my word, Katie, he's well looked after. I won't cut back on his education, he'll have all the chances any of us had. But this one, if it's a son, will grow up to take over from me here at Bullington. I'll teach him all I know . . .' His voiced faded into silence. He must finally have sensed how her body stiffened. 'Katie?'

'How can we say what will happen to either of them or to Bullington? *Kit's* my eldest son. I may be having a daughter – perhaps there won't be any more children for us. We can't decide other people's futures.' She felt inexplicably lonely, isolated from him by generations of Mathesons. But that was stupid, she told herself, moving a few inches away from him. Wasn't she a Matheson every bit as much as he was himself. 'Grandam was my great-grandmother just as much as she was yours. Her son was your grandfather, her daughter is my grandmother. Does being a man mean you've better Matheson blood in your veins than I have? Course it doesn't. All it means is that I had a different surname.'

'Well, I changed all that. I made a proper Matheson of you.' He knew they travelled rocky ground, and tried to choose a safer path.

From the way he settled comfortably close to her again she knew he was satisfied that the last word had been his. "I made a proper Matheson of you." Sometimes she believed he'd honestly forgotten that the estate was hers. Anger at his attitude towards Kit gave her

159

the courage for what she knew she had to tell him. This must be the moment.

She struggled clumsily to sit bolt upright.

'What's the matter? You did hurt yourself, after all?' He reached to turn on the bedside lamp.

Then they were sitting side by side, the room flooded with light – and the moment had come to tell him. Unexpectedly, into her mind came the memory of Alice Piper who'd stood out so hard for her right to independence. How proud the old lady must be now if she knew that it had been she who had sown the first seed of change at the Manor.

'Never mind the next generation. It's not the future, it's now I want to talk about. Anyway, I told you I'm not hurt. But there's something else. Nothing to do with the baby, hardly to do with you or with me. It's about the Manor. I'm going to make its heart beat with life again.'

'I don't understand what you mean. The estate is well managed, every house is let, every acre farmed. From the way you speak, anyone would think I was letting the place run to seed.' His voice was guarded, she only could guess at the underlying anger.

'Of course you're not. It's the Manor I'm interested in, not the estate. Anyway, I imagine the tenancies bring in enough not to bleed us dry. But the Manor would, you've said so often enough.'

As he'd listened to her he'd taken stock of the situation, decided she should be humoured. So he put an arm around her shoulder and told her indulgently: 'I thought you just said maybe we'd not have any family after this one? Now you talk of bringing new life back into the house! You concentrate on the job in hand, see you give me the son I want, eh?'

'That's not up to me. Listen, Nigel, you won't like what I'm going to tell you, but – but – well, you're not going to be able to stop me doing what I believe is right. When Grandam left the Manor to me she said it would take courage to do what had to be done. She said that, knowing she hadn't left me the fortune it needs to run it.'

'But we've been all over that. I had the money, you the estate. She meant us to join forces.'

'Did she? A funny way of going about it. What if by the time she'd died you'd have been in love with some other girl – or maybe I'd have been back home in Canada and married? No. Courage to put Bullington back on its feet, courage to give it a purpose, that's what she meant. And that's exactly what I'm going to do.'

'And how do you suggest you perform this miracle?' She'd felt hostility beneath the surface. Now he took no pains to hide it. His voice was cold. He looked at her with something akin to dislike.

160

'Right now I'm not going into all the details. But listen, think of all the years Grandam was an old lady living here, all it gave to her. It's a beautiful old house, Nigel, it sits here in this lovely setting, hugging its peace to itself. And that's not right.'

'Good god, what are you suggesting? That you throw it open for hoardes of sightseers. An icecream kiosk in the drive perhaps? A café where they can get their sausages and chips!'

'During the First World War it was full of people. It served a purpose and came alive. And Grandam liked it that way.'

'Ah! So that's it. You've been listening to your Canadian aunt. She used to be one of the staff here, I believe.'

'She doesn't know yet what I've been planning. I was waiting until she got back to tell her. But now that you know, there's no point in keeping it secret. I'll write to her hotel in Paris.'

'Actually, I don't know. I don't know what the hell you're talking about.'

'Stop interrupting and I'll tell you. When people get old there are lots of them who can't keep their homes going.'

'Oh, dear God,' he breathed, 'so now you want to fill the Manor with a lot of Alice Pipers!'

'I said, shut up and listen. Mrs Piper was a courageous old lady. Just because she hadn't any money you don't need to take that tone when you talk about her. But that's not what I'm going to do. That couldn't be the answer to my having the Manor and not enough for its upkeep. No, old age comes to the rich as well as the poor. One thing they all have in common is that independence is precious to them. Here that's what they'd have – independence, care, companionship, tranquility – all the things that Grandam treasured.'

'Fill the house with wealthy Alice Pipers, is that it? And what, I wonder, do you intend to do with us, the family? Perhaps you'd like us to take one of the cottages?'

'Listen, Nigel, I know you're being nasty because you don't like things to be altered, but it won't spoil things here.' She hesitated, groping for the word she wanted. 'It'll enrich our lives.' He didn't answer. 'I wish you'd take that "bad smell" look off your face. If you'd think about it seriously you'd see what a good scheme it is. We shall go and live in the East Wing, the same as the family did when the house was used as a hospital. I've not had the builders here yet to give me estimates, but I know what we have to do internally will cost a lot of money.'

'Ah ha! Well that, my dear Katie, puts an end to your brainstorm. I'll not put a single penny into it, and the sooner you get used to the idea the better.'

'Oh, but I don't want you to. Don't you see? If you and I had already been doing different things with our lives when I'd inherited Bullington – if, like I said, you'd had a sweetheart –'

'If I had, I'd have ditched her, that I promise you. Bullington means more to me than . . .'

His words trailed into silence. Levelly they looked at each other. He couldn't have said more plainly that he'd married her for a hold on the estate.

'I guess we both had our reasons for what we did.' She was the first to speak. 'About the money: I've been to see Mr Hickstead and Mr Arkwright,' naming the solicitor and the bank manager, 'and I've been to the County Council offices. If the Council agrees that the place is suitable – and by the time the work is done they say there is no reason why there should be any problems – then the bank will let me have all the money I need. I shall hand the deeds of the estate over as security.'

'Hand over the deeds of Bullington! You'd do that! An outsider, a foreigner – that's what you are and always will be! Fit only for rolling under the stars with that Kitashee bugger. You, him, your damned illegitimate brat – what have any of you to do with the way we live here? Grandma was overseen in you. You wormed your way into her affection while I was away. Schemed then, just like you've been scheming now.'

With a lumbering movement she was out of bed, the pain that seared through her ankle matching her fury. Her eyes were bright with anger. She felt undignified, standing with one foot firmly on the ground, the other leg against the side of the bed to balance her. The last thing she expected was the effect of the outline of her enlarged breasts, her body swollen in pregnancy, under the fine silk of her nightgown would have on Nigel. By nature he wasn't a highly sexed man. For him lovemaking had been a satisfactory and companionable way of ending the day. Since he'd known about the baby he'd not touched her; all her advances had been ignored. Nothing must hurt his unborn child. Now he was driven by something beyond his control. Frustration from months of celibacy, fear that he was losing a world he'd thought impregnable, both these things, and added to them the images he conjured up of her with Dylan Kitashee. He was as agile as she was clumsy as he moved to stand in front of her.

'It's for me to say what you do . . . you're my wife! You do as I say . . . as I want.'

She found herself pushed back on to the bed with her nightdress dragged up to her shoulders. In a flash of memory she was back in the hotel bedroom in North Wales. She recalled the feeling of revulsion when he'd forced himself on her. But then she'd been slim, supple. Now her figure was heavy, her movements clumsy. She felt cumbersome, ugly. Her body ached for love, but not like this. There was no tenderness in his touch. Damn him, why couldn't he look at her with pride, gentleness? That she was a misshapen hulk had to do with him as well as her! Yet her anger was tinged with pity for him. She knew he was frightened by the changes she would make at the Manor. What she meant to do was right, not for a second did she waver, but the compassion she felt was akin to affection – at least it came close enough to it for her to want them to find their way back to the way things had been before this evening. They'd pledged their lives to each other, both of them determined to make it work. They were a marriage, they were a partnership, a family. She told herself that was why she reached to draw him to her. But it was more than that. Her body yearned for his touch, for the moment of union. A hungry longing consumed her, made her cry out eagerly as she guided him. In a second what she craved for would be hers . . .

'No! Christ! No!' Nigel gasped pulling back from her. She knew that he only just clung to his control.

'Yes . . .' They tottered on the edge of a precipice. Her legs wrapped themselves as far around him as nature would allow. 'Yes.' He couldn't do this to her. She panted as she arched her back, bringing herself closer to him. Instead she felt herself pulled to sit on the edge of the bed, with him standing upright between her legs. His hands were rough as he kneaded her breasts, pressing himself against them, between them, groaning, crying out. In seconds it was over. Weak and breathless he knelt, his shoulders bent. Her eyes were closed. She couldn't bear to look at him nor yet at herself.

'Did he do that too, your wild man of the forests?' he panted. If he hadn't said that, if even now he'd told her that he'd been frightened for the baby, that he'd wanted her so much that he hadn't been able to stop himself. But he didn't.

She wanted to cry. Only by keeping her voice small and cold could she hold back the tears.

'I'm going to take a bath. I wish you'd move into the other room. You find pregnant women distasteful. You told me so last time. You must remember.'

Struggling to his feet, he didn't quite look at her.

'How do you think you can climb in and out of the bath after what you did today to your ankle? In the morning you'll have to get that nurse to help you. Get into bed and let's get to sleep. There's plenty we've said and done tonight we'd be best to forget.'

In silence they lay down, he switched off the bedside light and they pulled the covers over their shoulders. He was soon breathing deeply,

163

but she suspected he wasn't really asleep. Certainly the child wasn't! Heaving herself to lie on her back, she cradled her hands around the moving mound.

Don't be a goof, she told herself, don't know what you've got to cry about.

Her teeth gripped the corners of her mouth. Hot tears trickled down her cheeks.

Chapter Eleven

Morning did nothing to restore an atmosphere of peace. The nocturnal scene could no more be pushed to the backs of their minds than the announcement of Katie's that had led up to it. She'd handled it badly, she told herself. She ought to have told him what she intended at some companionable daytime moment, she ought to have led him to feel involved, made him see that what she was doing was right. For it *was* right, she had no doubts.

At breakfast the silence was almost tangible. Once or twice she looked along the table at him. His expression told her nothing, yet now by daylight her old sympathy was stirring. Try and forget the way he'd behaved, just hang on to the fact that he did it because he was hurt and frightened. He hated things at the Manor to change.

'Before you go out anywhere, Nigel, come into the morning room. I'll show you the drawings. You'll see just how the bedrooms are to be altered so that each one has its own bathroom. I didn't tell you sooner because I knew you'd argue. But I'm right, I just know I am. Don't you ever get a feeling about something.'

'Katie, what you do with Bullington Manor is your own business. You've made that abundantly clear to me.' They'd quarrelled before, but she'd never seen him look at her with this cold contempt. The corners of his mouth that used to turn so readily into a smile were pulled down with distaste. 'You hold the trump card, there's nothing I can do. We made a pact. And why do you think I did that? I'll tell you why. To prevent you bringing disgrace on the family. Is this the way you keep your side of the bargain? Is it?'

'Yes, it is.' She envied him his frigid calm. It was anger that brought the sound of tears to her voice. He mustn't think he could make her cry! Her words hit at him, she needed to shock him into dropping his mask of calm: 'And if you weren't such a staid prick, living for yesterday with all your talk of generations of Mathesons, then you'd be glad that I mean to make the Manor of some living use. All those ancestors you're so blindly proud of – if they'd all sat on their butts and done nothing like you expect me to, where would the Manor be now? Probably sold to some industrialist without so much stuck-up pride!'

He got up from the table, carefully pushing his chair back, his gaze denying her the satisfaction of guessing his thoughts.

'You'll do as you like. You always have. But Bullington isn't some toy to amuse yourself with. You'll hand the deeds to the bank and then where will you be when you can't meet your repayments?' Just for a second the mask slipped, she saw the triumph. 'When they foreclose, whose money will repay the loan? Mine! Be sure of that!' Without waiting for a reply he was gone, leaving her alone at the table. Alone and frightened by the enormity of what she was going to do.

Returned from the Continent, Eva heard the plans.

'Have you honestly thought it through, Katie?'

'Sure I have, Aunt Eva.' She was disappointed. She'd been confident of Eva's support. 'I want to do this thing. But more than that – it's part of the deal with Grandam and the way she left things. I've figured it over and over in my mind, trying to make out why it was she split things like she did. Then I came to see that because she wanted Nigel and me both to have a share, there was no other way. If she'd left me her money and Nigel the Manor, he would have been stuck. He's dead against what I'm doing. But if he had the Manor and no capital, all that would happen would be it falling to ruins. I'm borrowing money against the property, so it has to work. I've staked all her trust on it working.'

'What you're planning will make a big difference to the way the family lives.'

'We shall hardly be deprived! Look at the size of the East Wing – compared with most houses it's enormous. And we shall still have the stables, the tennis courts, everything just the same. The people who come to be looked after at the Manor won't be using those. Anyway, my mind's made up. It's no good your trying to change it for me.' In her disappointment at Eva's cautionary tone, Katie sounded aggressive.

'I'm most certainly not trying to do that, Katie. I just want you to be sure that you aren't going to wreck things between you and Nigel.'

'Aunt Eva, I have to do this. I thought you'd understand. I know Grandam does. It's going to come alive here. Sure, it's great now, the family enjoy it, the folk who work here take a pride in it. But there's more to Bullington than that.'

166

Eva nodded. 'Oh, yes, you don't have to tell me that, I've seen it.' Her brown eyes smiled warmly at Katie's enthusiasm.

'And you can see I'm right? You think I can do it?'

'Set your sights on your goal and don't let anything stop you. Of course you can do it. You'll need to market it well. You'll need good staff, some of them trained nurses – you mustn't cut corners. The quality you give must be as high as the Manor deserves.'

'It will be. And the fees will match it.' Katie smiled, her confidence restored. 'Qualified staff . . . Aunt Eva, are you in a great rush to get back to Calgary?'

That was the first week in January, two days before work started.

Nigel's every instinct was to oppose what Katie was doing. Two things stopped him. He couldn't impose his will on her. The Manor was hers, and for him to tell the world – or even the family – that she was acting against his wishes would make him look a fool. The second thing that silenced him was the fact that she was carrying his child. Suppose they quarrelled and she did something rash? Suppose she miscarried? So he wrapped himself in a stony silence, held himself aloof from the changes that were planned to what had been his home for so long. But he didn't turn his back on the affairs of the estate. Katie had never interfered with what went on outside, and he had no intention of relinquishing his hold. She was inexperienced, knew nothing about business, what hope had she of succeeding with her hare-brained scheme? What she was doing must ultimately lead to his having possession of the Manor.

Nothing was cramped at Bullington. Luxury could be found at many homes for the elderly, coupled with nursing care and attention. But here there was something more, something indefinable in the spirit of the beautiful old home. It was as if the gracious lifestyle of other years still lived.

Katie's vitality seemed to increase with her girth.

'Just look at me!' she laughed to Eva. 'I lumber about like a baby elephant, but I feel livelier than I have for ages!'

'Must be having babies suits you.'

'I'm more than just ordinarily sort of pregnant – I'm giving birth to a whole new way of life.' She looked with satisfaction at the finishing touches they'd been putting to one of the recently transformed rooms. The adjoining bathroom was bright and modern, but the furniture that had been put in place had graced the Manor through generations of Mathesons.

It was Katie who organised the all important marketing. To live at Bullington Manor would be expensive, so she advertised in only the best monthly magazines. The brochure she designed was honest; with a house like this there was nothing to hide. It showed a picture of the music room where she intended to arrange regular recitals for the residents – and where at other times card tables would be set up; another of the formal dining hall where their meals would be served; a view of the house from the park, and of the parkland from the house; another of the lake. With pictures like that there was little that needed saying in words: just something about the caring staff and congenial company of other residents. She sent the brochures to various London clubs, ladies' and gentlemen's, to officers' clubs, and finally, when the work in the house was complete, she put a notice in *The Times*.

Sometimes she'd wake with a feeling of panic. Supposing no one came! A few more weeks and everything would be ready. What if the staff were engaged and there was no one to fill the rooms – and, more important, to pay the mortgage! The enormity of what she was doing was magnified in the stillness of the night. It was easy then to believe that she should have let things go on as they were, be a wife to Nigel and nothing more. But by morning her doubts always melted away, optimism took over again.

By mid-February she'd begun to look for the morning post with excitement, Each day brought enquiries. On the 7th March the first residents arrived: Hilary Goodchild, the widow of an Army friend of Alistair's, and Cedric Hardaker, a retired professor. Nigel had always been the perfect host at Bullington, but not now, not to people he looked on as intruders. For him they didn't exist. It was Eva who welcomed them to their new home, for on that day Katie had more pressing business on hand. In the East Wing her second son was making a slow and difficult entry into the world.

It must have been because her mind was taken up with the work going on in the Manor that she hadn't queried Kate and Rupert's non-appearance over those winter weeks. At Christmas her grandfather had telephoned to say that Kate had taken cold resulting from their trip to Yatsham Hill on such a dreadful day, it would be wiser for them to stay at home. After that, if Katie thought about it at all, she supposed they didn't visit Bullington because they knew the place was alive with workmen, or even because Eva was there. Whatever had happened between them it was years ago. To bear a grudge all this time was stupid. Worse – it was wicked. Eva was Katie's link with the past. It seemed natural that she should be a part of the future too.

Late on the evening of the 7th March Nigel telephoned Brimley. 'Hello,' came Rupert's voce.

'It's a boy! About half an hour ago. I've just seen him.'

'Wonderful news, splendid!' A boy! What problems would that cause? 'Is everything all right – with Katie and the boy?'

Kate, clad in her nightdress and dressing gown, hurried down from the bedroom and took the receiver before Nigel could answer.

'You've got a son! Oh, Nigel my dear, I'm so happy for you, so relieved. Tell me about him? Is he fair like the Mathesons?'

It seemed he was everything a Matheson heir should be. It was too much for her. She promised that she and Rupert would come the next day to see him.

'He is perfect,' Kate held the little creature almost reverently. 'What are you calling him?'

'Nigel wants Egbert. It seems a bit pompous for a wee mite. I guess I'll call him Bertie.'

'Egbert. The Matheson who built the Manor was an Egbert.' Then, with sudden spirit: 'He built it as a home for the Mathesons. This Egbert will give it back to the family. That must be what poor Nigel has in his mind. I can't believe it, Katie, filling our home with strangers. Doing it for money. It's – it's – degrading. I'm sure Nigel doesn't go along with your commercial greed. Perhaps I shouldn't upset you, not today when you're still weak from your ordeal. But, Katie, you can't imagine the tears I've shed. This is my home, it has always been my home.'

'Baloney, Granny! Your home's been in Brimley for getting on for fifty years. Anyway, I've not let anyone take your room, it's always there for you like you wanted.'

Kate seemed not to have heard. She went on: 'If you'd waited until you'd held this precious little bundle in your arms, you would have felt the dreadful thing you'd be doing to take away his heritage.'

'I held Kit in my arms – or had your forgotten? Listen Granny, please. Have you ever wanted to do something that was your very own? No, you don't have to answer me. But be fair in your own mind. Grandam must have known that I'd not be able to keep Bullington going unless it learnt to pay its way.'

'But Nigel can do that!'

'She wasn't to know that. How could she have known that by the time he inherited her money he wouldn't be married to someone else, same as I might have been back home in Canada.'

'This is your home, Katie.'

'Sure it is, and I'm not going to fail it. Have you met any of the folk who've come to live here?'

169

'No. I came straight to the East Wing. I suppose you've turned it upside down like it was when it was a hospital. Eva will have taken over. And you ask me whether I've been in there!'

'Granny, I know all about what happened. But that was ages ago. Grandad loved you even when you were engaged to Matt.'

'Matt! His name was Matthew! Even that she had to meddle with and alter.'

'Heck, Granny, what does it matter what he was called? I bet you he couldn't hold a candle to Grandad. Anyway, to keep harking back to before you were married is like saying you wish you'd never had Mom, or Uncle Ronnie –' and then, timidly, looking to see the effect of her words ' – or Michael.'

'That's a wicked thing to say to me.' And just as Katie had expected, she saw Kate's lips tremble on the edge of tears.

'Or me, Granny.' Then with a grin that salved Kate's hurt: 'Or even little Bertie, here. I guess there's plenty of things don't work out the way we plan, but when a door gets shut in our face and we feel trapped, then we have to make for the nearest window. We have to get out there somehow. The rest of life is waiting for us.'

Kate didn't answer. She seemed engrossed in examining Bertie's exquisite fingers.

'Bullington is my challenge, Granny. Can you understand that?'

'You said I should be fair in my mind. Yes, I can understand it. And I envy you that you've found something. I had nothing, no chance to be anything but a dutiful wife after all my dreams were stolen from me. I know you had an infatuation for Dylan Kitashee –'

'There's no point dragging Dylan into it. He didn't run out on me.'

'Oh, Katie, that's unkind. You're just trying to hurt me.'

'What I'm telling you is that I accepted there was no other way. You know about Kit, and I'm grateful for him. I'll always have something of Dylan.'

'Hush, Katie, don't talk like that. How must poor Nigel feel if he thinks you still hanker after someone else?'

'I didn't say that. I said I was grateful. Now we've got Bertie too. And Granny, you don't need to worry about Nigel and me. O.K., he doesn't like what I'm doing to the Manor. But I don't interfere with what goes on on the estate.' Then, her eyes dancing with sudden mischief: 'Wait just a while and he'll start to get to know some of the residents. So far there are only two. In a few days Lady Halborough is arriving, then Colonel Menzies. And Estelle d'Arc – you must remember her, the one-time ballerina? Oh, and all the others. I met them all when they came to look around. They're great. Honest, Granny, it's going to be a happy place, I promise you. Bullington has

170

plenty to give to them, of course it has, but they've got plenty to give to Bullington too. And I don't just mean the vast sum it'll cost them to live here.' She laughed. 'When Nigel dismounts from that high horse he's on and gets to know them, he'll suddenly be the charming host he always has been.'

Bertie's fingers had his great-grandmother's attention again.

'But it's so commercial, Katie.' Without changing her expression Kate managed to convey just by her voice how she disapproved. 'Commerce isn't for the Mathesons. My dear father was in banking, his father had been an Army –'

'Commerce not for the Mathesons?' Katie cut her short. 'Don't let Bertie hear you fib that way! Egbert Matheson built this place on the money he made growing tobacco in the southern states of America. Growing and exporting it. He married a girl whose father was an importer here in England. Oh, Granny, we've got our roots in commerce, we Mathesons. Like you say, maybe one day Kit or Bertie will decide to turn the Manor back into a family home, maybe they'll earn their living some other way. But that's for them to say. For myself, I mean to see that it gives its guests a feeling of peace, stability, endurance – I'm not clever with words, but can't you feel what it is I'm trying to say? People have lived here, been born here, died here, for more than two hundred years. Kind of makes me feel small.'

She wished she could explain how she'd felt showing the prospective guests around: they all facing the final chapters; she somewhere in the shaping of her life's story. Yet the spirit of Bullington reached out to each of them, past, present and future. 'It seemed kind of providential that yesterday Bertie was getting born just at the same time as the first of the guests was arriving.'

Once each month the music room came into its own. A quartet from Oxford, a trio from Reading, a pianist from music college, and occasionally a Chamber Ensemble of national repute. Always on these evenings, although Bullington provided the refreshments, it was the residents themselves who enjoyed playing host to the musicians. Summer and winter alike the musical evenings were part of the pattern, an opportunity for those who'd made their home at the Manor to invite guests of their own, sure they could entertain them with confidence there had been no lowering of their standards.

Katie had been right when she'd said the stables and the tennis courts would still belong to the family. But the study lawn had been mowed, rolled and pampered until it was like velvet. Only one person, Hilary Goodchild, had played bowls previously, but she was a persuasive lady and before the first July was over she had inveigled seven others to join her.

It was Katie who drove them to town to buy their woods.

'I wish you'd let yourself know them, Nigel. I had a great time yesterday with the Colonel, Madame d'Arc and Mr Lane. Today I'm taking Lady Halborough, Professor Hardaker, Mrs Tilley and Miss Routh. We'll all manage to squeeze in, Miss Routh is tiny.'

'You seem to be turning yourself into a chauffeur.'

'Don't be so stuffy! Anyway, I'm no such thing. Yesterday we had lots of fun. We stopped for tea at the Mermaid Tea Room. If you met them anywhere else you'd get on so well with them, I can't understand –'

He turned away before she saw the expression in his eyes. 'I'm not meeting them somewhere else, I'm faced with them here. Or I would be if I let you have your way. I'm afraid, Katie, you're wasting your breath.' He didn't wait for her reply. As far as he was concerned the matter was closed.

Watching from the window a few minutes later she saw him outside where, in the shade of a sycamore tree, two prams stood side by side. In them the two babies had been put for their morning sleep. He stopped by the side of one and leant to look under the canopy. This time she clearly saw his expression and her own softened as she watched him. The occupant must have been asleep. The other pram rocked with the movement of the older child. At fifteen months Kit had his own ideas about being expected to lie down when all around him things were happening. Katie saw him pull himself to sit up, impatient at the harness that strapped him. His arms were stretched towards Nigel, his mouth open in a wide smile of hope.

It was as if neither pram nor baby existed. When he was ignored Kit kicked his heels in fury, roaring his disappointment at Nigel's retreating figure. How could he treat an innocent baby like it? Easily. Just the same as he treated the residents of the Manor. Katie's eyes were misted with tears, tears of anger. It wasn't simply so that Bertie wouldn't be woken by the sudden noise that she hurried outside, wheeling Kit's pram to the kitchen garden where there was plenty of activity and always a friendly word to encourage his growing intelligence.

Crossing the forecourt towards the East Wing she was surprised to see Dr Holsworthy's car coming up the drive.

'Hi, Doctor. Is someone not well? They hadn't told me.' She and Jack Holsworthy were good friends.

'No, my dear. Just happened to be passing, thought I'd drop by and check with your aunt that all's well.'

172

'I'm sure it is, but they'll be pleased to see you.'

But did they all see him? she wondered five minutes later. His car was still parked at the foot of the front steps and inside it he and Eva sat smoking, talking, laughing.

That was in July. She noticed that most days the doctor "dropped by", always to be joined by Eva. When the weather changed his visits looked more formal. He mounted the steps and pulled the bell to be admitted.

Unlike the rest of the family, Eva didn't live in the East Wing. She had a room in the main part of the building where she could be on call if she was needed. Day or night there was always one trained nurse on the premises. But the residents weren't invalids. There was a hand-picked staff of attendants, but Katie considered that with these personality was more important than qualifications. Living in the main body of the Manor, Eva supervised the staff. She was the pivot on which the establishment turned. Or was she? If the residents had been asked, it was more than likely that they would have seen Katie as the driving force. Eva had her meals in the dining hall, she had her own sitting room – and Katie soon realised that she also had her own visitors, or at any rate one particular visitor. Most evenings the doctor's car would be at the head of the drive.

'Jack's taking a younger man into the practice,' Eva told her towards the end of September. 'For a while they'll work together. But he figures that by spring he'll retire.' Then with a smile that started in her conker brown eyes before her wide mouth joined in: 'Spring's a pretty good time of year to get married, don't you think?'

'Aunt Eva, that's wonderful. He's nice.'

'That's what I thought,' Eva twinkled. 'You know, I only meant to be over here for a month or so. Already I've been a year and now I'm talking of still being around in the spring.'

'That's Bullington for you! Then what will you do, you and Dr Holsworthy?'

'You'll have to get used to calling him Jack. Jack and Eva, eh? Drop the aunt bit.' She chuckled. 'I'm not trying to grow young again, but somehow I don't think Jack sees himself as uncle.'

'Wouldn't matter what I called you, you'll never be old. But you didn't tell me? What will you do, where will you live?'

'We're going to travel around for a while. Then we'll go back to Calgary. I still have my apartment, it'll be somewhere to hitch up while we decide where to settle.'

They'd visit Higley Creek; they'd be home for the colours of fall; they'd breathe the air that was so clear it seemed to sparkle. Home . . . the country rooted deeply in Katie's heart so that no matter how

173

long she was away nothing could take its place. Yet all her life, even as a little girl, her dream had been to come to England. And when she'd got here she'd loved it every bit as much as she'd expected. But home . . .

Through these last months she and Eva had laid their plans, watched them grow to fruition, even Dr Holsworthy and his daily visits had been part of it all. Perhaps it was the void their going would leave that Katie found so hard to accept.

It was a year now since Kate had made the excuse of having a cold so that she wouldn't have to face Katie and Kit at Christmas. Katie had always been precious to her; as a baby when during the war Brimley had been home to Lottie and her, all through her childhood when the regular flow of letters backwards and forwards across the Atlantic had forged a link. Two generations separated them, yet sometimes Kate had prided herself that she was nearer to her perfect and only grand-daughter than the child's own mother could ever be, certainly nearer than she had been to Lottie all those years ago. Lottie had been eager for life, thought only of herself. Time after time there had been arguments in the home simply because of her selfishness, then look how she'd got herself entangled with that hateful Neil O'Hagon. Little Katie, her own namesake, had been far more understanding. When she'd come from Canada for what they'd anticipated was to be a holiday she'd been happy at Brimley, they'd had a lovely time together.

Even now, a year on, it still hurt to remember that dreadful day in Yatsham Wood. The words she'd heard were indelibly written into her memory, there to torment her. She'd suddenly felt that she'd never known Katie at all. Had she gone away with Dylan Kitashee, stayed with him in some unfamiliar hotel? Or had she given herself to him under the stars? That he was Neil O'Hagon's son was the final degradation.

Kate had been holding Kit in her arms, comforting him. In seconds she'd been stripped of all the joy she'd had in loving him, she'd not wanted so much as to touch him. She'd wished she need never see him again, for each time those light blue eyes smiled at her would turn a knife in her heart. But Katie? What did she feel for Katie? And that was what had frightened her, that's why she'd taken the coward's way out and stayed away from Bullington. She'd been afraid of looking at her, frightened that she'd never love her like she used to, that always the thought of what she'd done would put a barrier between them.

Bertie changed all that. In him she found her path back. She narrowed her vision, didn't look beyond a Bullington peopled with

174

Katie, Nigel and Bertie. And when Katie telephoned to make sure her grandparents were coming for Bertie's first Christmas, nothing would have kept Kate away.

'Eva has her rooms in the main part of the house,' Katie told her, 'but she'll be with us when she can – and Dr Jack.'

Kate heard the unspoken message: there was to be a truce between them, the past must remain buried.

'Dr Jack?' As if she didn't know!

'Eva says to call him Jack. But I'm still one stage away from that.' There was a smile in Katie's voice. 'He's a dear, you'll like him. He and Eva are going to be a great pair.'

Even on the telephone Katie could be sure of the expression on her grandmother's face.

'It seems that Eva is adept at taking up with doctors at the Manor. You needn't tell me what Dr Holsworthy is like, Katie. You forget I'm no stranger to Bullington. He was Mother's doctor for many years. He must be getting too old to practise. Hardly a romantic, I'd have thought.'

'Oh, I don't know, Granny,' came the chuckling reply. 'Many a lady in the Manor puts that extra dab of perfume behind her ear when Dr Jack is due around. He's a bit like Eva, older in years than he is in spirit.'

'It seems you're very taken with him.'

'Sure I am. I'd not want Eva mating up with a guy I didn't think good enough. I shall miss them like anything when they go off home.'

'I dare say. But Canada is Eva's home, she made it so from choice,' came her grandmother's tight little voice.

Twenty-month-old Kit could sense the spirit of Christmas. If Nigel had sometimes stopped marvelling at the progress of his little brother then Katie might have taken a more balanced view. But someone had to love him, someone had to share the wonder of it with him. He was a slightly built child; even in his first stumbling steps Kit had never blundered. He had all the feline grace of his father's ancestors – and the looks of his handsome father.

Bertie was a Matheson through and through. But how could he fail to be? As Katie had said, except that she came from a female branch and so had a different surname, she was Matheson every bit as much as Nigel. There was nothing dainty about Bertie, nor yet graceful. He saw life as a very jolly affair, his rosy face beamed easily and his blue eyes smiled with merriment. He was easy to love. And one person who loved him devotedly was Kit.

At bath time in the nursery Kit would drag the nursing chair into position for Meg, he'd get Bertie's favourite duck from the box and put it in the water ready, he'd pass things, he'd fetch and carry. Meg encouraged it, just as she encouraged Bertie to respond to his elder brother. Meg knew of no undercurrents in the family, so for her there weren't any. During Bertie's first Christmas she gave little thought to the fact that Nigel and Kate (with Rupert occasionally throwing in the odd smile or cluck as expected of him) gave all their attention to Bertie, while Katie gave hers to Kit. Meg simply saw two small boys revelling in their family's adoration – and very right and proper too.

'At their ages it's quite ridiculous! Dr Holsworthy seems to have no family – and not surprisingly for a man who's never married. You'd hardly expect him to have parents.' It didn't suit Kate's pretty face to wear that frown.

'We only get married once, dear. I dare say they mean their vows just as sincerely as they would if they were some young couple. And of course Eva expects me to give her away, I'm her nearest relative.' Then, spying a new hat box on the chair, Rupert clutched at what he knew would cheer his Kate. 'A new hat for the occasion? Put it on for me to see.'

She didn't need persuading. The hat had called to her as she'd gone towards the fitting room in Madame Nobelle's salon, followed by a fitter carrying the wildly extravagant creation she'd chosen for the wedding. The hat would be the finishing touch, its smoky blue so exactly right for her dress, so flatteringly right for her eyes. When she heard the price she hesitated, but only for a second. For Eva's wedding no price was too high.

'It was rather a lot of money, Rupert. But it is for a very special occasion – with your being on parade.'

He smiled indulgently. It wasn't often that Katie looked at him so pleadingly. How much was "rather a lot"? He picked up the bill that was still in the box and, before he could stop himself, let out a whistle of surprise.

'You can't grudge me! Surely you can't grudge me a new hat!' Her eyes were full of hurt. Didn't he understand how important it was that she looked the loveliest woman there?

'Put it on your pretty head. Let me see how proud you're going to make me.'

Young or old, there wouldn't be another woman to touch her. It was for her sake that he was thankful she'd kept her looks, her figure as slim and trim as it had been at her own wedding, her skin as soft as a young girl's. For himself, he would have loved her just as whole-heartedly had her shoulders become bent or her waistline taken refuge behind a spare tyre.

176

'On some women it would have been a waste of good money. On you, Kate, it's a crowning glory. Very pretty, my dear.'

Under his praise the last of her frown vanished. And if it was her unconscious hope that Matthew (fancy calling him 'Matt' like something one wiped one's shoes on!) could look down on the scene in Newton Dingley church and compare her with the woman he'd jilted her for so long ago, then she didn't openly acknowledge it. Enough that everyone still saw her as beautiful, that the family didn't look on her as an object of pity as Rupert brought Eva up the aisle. For herself, she thought it quite unnecessary that the family should have been invited at all. Eva was an outsider, not one of them. But Katie had insisted, and even Nigel was preparing to play host to them in the East Wing.

The Mathesons rallied to the call. Eva was "Drupert's" sister, and he was Kate's husband; and more important, the wedding was from the Manor. Of them all it was only Katie who saw the future as emptier for her aunt's going.

No, perhaps that wasn't quite true. The residents in the Manor had all grown fond of her, they charged their batteries on her energy. They all attended the wedding, they all attended the reception and, afterwards, they all stood at the head of the steps with the family to wave the happy pair on their way. Doctor and Matron: Bullington Manor would be poorer without them.

Katie found herself enveloped in Eva's bearlike hug, she was kissed goodbye by her newly acquired great-uncle. Then as the clamour of farewells and good wishes went on she escaped, believing herself unnoticed, to wait by the main gate to watch them drive away.

Eva's going would bring down the final curtain. As long as she'd been here, home had seemed that much closer.

Jack Holsworthy pulled up as they came to the end of the drive.

'I had to be the last to see you off.' Determinedly Katie kept a smile on her face. 'Be happy. Have a wonderful time. They're all going to miss you – both of you.' Then the smile almost getting away: 'Me too. So am I. Say "Hi" to the folks for me when you get home. You will go to Higley, promise me.'

'Cross my heart.' Eva had wound down her window and now she reached to take Katie's hand. 'And I'll describe everything to them, just how the Manor is. And you know what a great pile of pictures I'm taking of you all.'

'Aunt Eva,' only that slip back into the old name told of Katie's momentary feeling of insecurity, 'I'm doing O.K., aren't I? It's going to work out, the way I'm, heading with the Manor?'

177

Jack Holsworthy leant across his passenger to reassure her: 'Katie, my dear, if she weren't sure of that, do you honestly think she would have let me steal her away?'

'I may have had the title "Matron", but it's you who make it home for them all,' Eva told her. 'Maybe because you're young enough to be grand-daughter to any of them. Then there's the boys – they love the boys. Makes them all feel like part of a big family, I guess. Oh, yes, Katie, you're doing fine, never you doubt it.'

Katie's smile was back in place. This time it was even reflected in her eyes. Another minute and the car was gone around the bend in the road and she was alone.

'We shall miss her. And you will too, my dear.' The Colonel came down the steps to meet Katie. There was no sign now of the "waving party", it seemed that the family had all gone back to the East Wing.

'You've enjoyed the day?' By way of answer Katie changed the subject. Eva had bolsted her confidence, but she wasn't ready to imagine the Manor without her.

'We all have. A wedding party was a treat we hadn't envisaged. Life's full of surprises.' Then another thought struck him. She knew it had from the expression in the blue eyes that looked over his half moon spectacles and missed nothing. A debonair man, tall, slender, these days with a stoop to his shoulders that couldn't disguise his military bearing. But it was the imp of fun in him that made Katie fond of him. She knew there were days when lesser men than the Colonel would have complained of the pain that was his legacy from a leg injury he'd sustained on the beaches of Dunkirk. But not he! A bad day only set his chin that little bit higher, defying any word of sympathy. Now he laughed mischievously, looking closely at Katie for her reaction. 'This new Matron, Miss Hardy. What say we try our hand at matchmaking? Miss Hardy and young Dr Wadham. I had my eye on them at the wedding. Nice-looking couple, what?' Dr Wadham had been in the practice since the beginning of the year. Wanting the residents of the Manor to feel confident in his hands before Dr Holsworthy disappeared from the scene, over the early weeks of the year his car had often been at the foot of the steps. On the other hand Miss Hardy had arrived only last week. 'Let's see what we can do, eh, m'dear? Let's have another wedding to celebrate?'

He was joking, as yet Miss Hardy was an unknown to all of them. But Katie could feel the scrutiny in those blue eyes as he watched for the effect of his suggestion. But why? She laughed with him, told him she hoped they'd keep Miss Hardy for a while first, then went back indoors to join in the post-mortem she guessed the residents were holding on the day's excitement. She could feel their welcome and remembered Eva's words. Did they look on her as a grand-daughter figure? Her eyes shone affectionately as she looked at her self-appointed family. She knew that in the East Wing the Matheson tribe was congregated, all of them from Claygate Hall, Ronnie, Millicent and their children down from Yorkshire, Kate, Rupert, and, of course, Nigel. Katie didn't rush back to join them. They were hardly likely to miss her and, in any case, her presence was much more necessary here where, as long as she was with them, they all still felt included in the celebrations.

Meanwhile in the drawing room of the East Wing the discussion had turned to the changes at the Manor.

When they'd first heard that Katie had handed the deeds of Bullington to the bank, the family had been horrified. But that was more than a year ago.

Now Nigel was reassuring them that: 'When the time comes for the bank to foreclose, you may be certain I shall pay off the debt. I shall always retain Bullington, it'll never got out of the family. Eva was part of the trouble. She egged Katie on. Now that she's gone the novelty will start to wear off. Katie hasn't the experience. The inmates will sense the difference, they'll not be so keen to shell out their monthly cheques.' He laughed, so sure of himself.

Only Alistair, with his own heritage deeply rooted in Claygate Hall, had views that differed.

'Inmates? They'd not care to be called that, my boy. By the way, I'm going in for bridge this evening. I promised Hilary – Mrs Goodchild, you know. If you ask me, they're extremely fond of Katie. I've been in there talking with them. Pity you don't, Nigel. As she says, each one of them makes Bullington the richer for being here.'

There was no humour in Nigel's laugh. 'Richer indeed!' He purposely misunderstood. 'But you just watch, it won't last. Without Eva, Katie'll tire of it. They'll get the message and move off.' Then, changing the subject: 'I'm going over to see Frank. The forestry people were coming today to inspect the elms down by the lake. This damned disease, it's everywhere. Won't be an elm tree in the country before long. What's it like at Claygate?'

'They've managed to treat those in the drive. But how successfully remains to be seen,' Alistair answered.

Nigel had asked the question but wasn't listening to the answer. 'Can't imagine the lake with the elms . . . Anyone walking across with me?'

There was no rush of enthusiasm. Only Rupert, glad of any chance to escape, looked enquiringly at Kate for permission to excuse himself.

She didn't even notice, she was much too busy putting her oar into what was already troubled water.

'I think it's dreadful.' And they knew she didn't mean the loss of the elms. 'I've said so right from the first. Bullington's our birthright. Katie's selling it for a handful of silver. A woman should abide by her husband's wishes.'

Following Nigel from the room, Rupert squared his shoulders. Just for a moment he felt ten foot tall before this array of self-opinionated in-laws.

An hour or so later it was Hester who saw them coming back across the park. They must have walked to the lake to see the evidence for themselves. On Nigel's shoulders he carried Bertie while Kit straggled behind, the distance between them growing as the adults outpaced him. The upward slope towards the house seemed to his small legs to grow steeper with every step he took and despite his shouts no one waited for him. By the time the other three reached the forecourt he'd given up the struggle and was kneeling on the ground some two hundred yards away, bent low so that his dark head was on the grass, his eyes tightly closed as if by shutting out the scene he'd get rid of this feeling of isolation. At not quite two years old his walk had been a marathon. Now he was alone, left behind. No wonder he cried.

'Rupert!' Hester opened the window and called in that manner that expects instant obedience. 'Look at Christopher! Go and fetch him.' Her order given, she turned back into the room. 'I can't understand Nigel. Bertie may be a fine baby, but –'

'He's a Matheson.' Kate came to the window, smiling at the sight of the bonny blond baby riding on his father's shoulders.

'We none of us choose how we look. He's fair. Most Mathesons are fair. I never was. But Christopher is a bright boy, a son he should be proud of. Today was typical. I've seen it each time I've been here. He's besotted with Bertie. It's not fair.'

But this time Kate didn't answer. Her gaze had gone beyond Nigel and Bertie, back down the slope to where Rupert was hurrying towards Kit. Her lips set in a hard line as she watched. Now Rupert picked him up, was lifting him high above his head to put him to ride on his shoulders.

Kit seemed to have forgotten his tears. He jogged up and down on his high seat, his mouth open in a smile of pleasure. Now what was Rupert doing? He'd stopped, was swaying, was bent nearly double.

'Nigel!' This time it was Kate who called, the sound of her cry bringing the others to the window to see what the trouble was. 'Nigel! Make him put the child down! Is he hurt? What's the matter?'

But it was too late for Nigel to make him put Kit down. The little boy had already fallen as Rupert collapsed to his knees with his arms held out before him.

With no thought for the exclusive gown, Kate knelt on the grass twisting her fingers together helplessly. It was silly to be so frightened. Rupert was never ill. Whatever was wrong with him, in a minute it would pass and he'd open his eyes. He was still breathing. Well, of course he was still breathing. Rupert was never ill. Later, when he felt better, he'd be upset to think he'd let anything frighten her so. Yes, look, his eyelids moved. Yes, he was looking at her. She bent closer.

'You fell,' she whispered as if that way he'd understand it was nothing to worry about. 'They say you're not to move until Dr Wadham gets back to look at you.'

'Kate . . . sorry . . . dear Kate . . .' he breathed, his hands clenched as the pain in his chest reached even to his fingertips.

Chapter Twelve

'Why me? Always it's me!' Harsh, dry sobs racked Kate, almost swallowing her words. Usually when she wept she managed to look sad but beautiful. Now, her mouth was open wide, her face contorted as she gasped for breath. Shock had robbed her of all control.

It was hardly more than two hours since they'd come back from the wedding reception. Now the doctor had signed the death certificate, Rupert's body was lying in the small, unused, north-facing bedroom and before the evening was over the undertakers would have carried him away. The young people had made themselves scarce, Tessa to help Meg with Kit and Bertie while Ronnie's boys, John and Cliff, were with Alistair's Hugh and Billy playing a subdued game of Monopoly in the den. Uncle Drupert hadn't been anyone's favourite, but at his sudden death they had all had a feeling of built for the times they'd laughed at him behind his back. In the drawing room they'd not liked to look at anyone, not even at each other. Kate's loud sobs had seemed to fill every corner of the room. They weren't keen on Monopoly but it offered an escape. Surprisingly, with the family all there, Nigel had found things to do elsewhere. The Bradley's belonged to Katie just as much as Eva had.

'Poor Kate, you mustn't cry so.' Hester knelt in front of her chafing her hands. 'We are all with you, Kate. You've got us. You're home, here at Bullington. Hush, Kate, try not to cry so. You'll give yourself a dreadful head.'

'That woman! All my life she's ruined everything for me. That damned, damned woman!' She couldn't know what she was saying. There had been no woman with Rupert, just little Kit in his arms as he'd panted up the slope trying to catch up with Nigel.

'Granny, he couldn't have known. Dr Wadham says he wouldn't have known a thing.' Katie sat on the arm of the chair, her arm around her grandmother's shaking shoulders.

Alistair brought a nip of brandy and held the glass to Kate's lips. "She'll turn the taps on . . ." came the echo of his less than sympathetic view of his aunt. Oh, but today he must feel pity for her. Rupert gone. Snuffed out like a candle.

'Granny, he'd be so miserable to hear you cry like that.'

'What wickedness have I done to deserve it?' Kate's voice was a high-pitched squeak, no more than that. 'Last time she took away all my hopes of happiness. And today, if it hadn't been for her . . .'

'Aunt Eva ought to be told.' Ronnie's mind was already turning to the arrangements that had to be made. Eva was his father's sister, she ought to be brought back for his funeral. 'I've no idea where they were making for. Heathrow perhaps? Southampton? Did Holsworthy give any clue at all? To you, Katie?'

'No! Not her! I don't want her here! I'll never see her, never!' The very idea of Eva's coming gave Kate's voice sudden clarity, put her in control of herself again. 'You can't do that to me, Ronnie. You don't know what my life's been because of her. Matthew, Lottie, Rupert – everything I've had she's taken away from me. If she'd stayed in Canada where she belonged I'd still have a husband. Oh, what shall I do? For nearly fifty years, he's been my whole world. You don't know, you couldn't understand.'

Just for a moment there was silence. No one could find an answer. This was certainly not the way she usually spoke of him. "Drupert" had been a willing doormat, worshipping her every move. But she?

'Now what is there for me? To go back to that house alone . . . a poor widow . . . no one to care if I'm well or ill, not even if I live or die. What does it matter to anyone?'

'Don't think about it yet, Granny. You have your place here. You always think of Bullington as your home.'

They couldn't be sure whether Kate even heard. The brandy seemed to have stopped her trembling. Moving free of Katie's hold she lay back, resting her head on the back of the chair, her eyes closed. Seconds ticked by. Perhaps she'd fall into an exhausted sleep.

'Everything . . . it's all been because of her.' She spoke quietly, as if she were talking to herself. 'Matthew, all my plans, all my dreams, she stripped them from me. I tried to be content with what little my unfair life gave me in exchange. But what was there? Nothing, not even memories. She stole him before I even had memories. Marriage – no joys – no colour – I'd hoped for so much. Was that a sin?' Katie put her hand on her grandmother's shoulder, she wanted to stop her; these rambling thoughts were her own, not to be shared. Kate went on, unchecked. 'But I had the children. Until *she* came back again. She cast a spell on Lottie. My little girl, but from that day all she thought of was going off to Canada to that woman. Well, she went. If it hadn't been for the power Eva had on her, Lottie wouldn't have looked twice at a low-down man like Neil O'Hagon. All of it Eva's doing.' With a sudden movement she sat up straight, her eyes wide open as she looked at the family gathered around her. 'She cast a shadow that was evil, evil and long enough to stretch down the years. The sins of the fathers – fathers, aunts – oh, you don't know the half of it! Because of her Lottie went to Canada, married a man who had already fathered a half-breed son –'

'Granny, you're upset.'

'Not today, Kate. There's trouble here enough today,' from Hester.

Kate wouldn't listen.

'Dylan Kitashee. It was you, Hester, who told me about him and Katie. All of it because Lottie had been so crazy to rush away to Canada. All of it lies at Eva's doorstep.'

Katie's heart seemed to be beating right to her ears. No longer did she try and stop her grandmother. It was like counting the seconds, waiting for a time bomb to explode. Every eye was on her.

'Neil O'Hagon's bastard son . . . he and Katie. We were all too blind to see. But it's true. Ask her. She can't deny it. Christopher Matheson!' She seemed to spit the name. 'Kit Kitashee! Neil O'Hagon's bastard grandson killed my husband. If we hadn't had to come here for that wretched wedding Rupert would have been with me still. Carrying a screaming child up the slope – it killed him. And while he lies there with the life gone from him, where is *she*? On her way to some foreign land for a honeymoon in the sunshine. Two men – I've lost both of them because of her.'

How could anyone produce so many tears? This time no one tried to find words of solace, they were much too busy picking up the pieces from the bomb she'd hurled at them.

All this time Hester had been kneeling by her chair. Now she stood up. Of course what Kate said was true! How could they all have been so blind? *She* of all of them ought to have seen, she'd known Katie had had a silly infatuation for the man. Ask Nigel, Kate had said. But surely he couldn't have known? Then amongst those pieces Hester was trying to fit together she found one more, one she believed must be the key to why Nigel had kept silent about what Katie had done.

'What she says is true, isn't it?' Standing very straight she addressed her question to Katie.

'Yes, it's true.' Katie's voice was steady. It surprised her how calm she could sound while her heart was banging like a bass drum. 'Dylan and I meant to be married. Till Mom came over we didn't know about my father's part.'

184

'It's disgraceful! Meant to be married! And you think that gave you the right? Then you deceived Nigel –'

'No, I didn't. We made a pact. We knew just what we were doing. You don't need to concern yourselves with Nigel and me.'

'But damn it all,' for once Alistair was thrown off balance, 'he's the elder son. He's heir to the Matheson home.'

The room was full of silence. It was Katie who broke it.

'Grandam did what she thought was best. I guess I'll do the same.' She spoke with a dignity she was far from feeling. How was it that here, in her own home, they made her feel she had no place? She remembered Rupert. She'd never felt closer to him than she did at this moment as the Mathesons stood in judgment.

'I think as the eldest member of the family it's up to me to take a lead on this,' Hester told them in a voice that said clearly it would tolerate no argument. 'Had Kate not been so unbalanced by the day's events we should have known nothing of Christopher's unfortunate ancestry.' How sordid she made it sound. Katie's eyes blazed angrily. Hester had passed judgment, now she meant to pass sentence. 'I intend that we ensure the truth stays within these four walls. Certainly not for Katie's sake, she deserves none of our consideration, nor for Christopher's, but for the good name of the family. For word of it to spread would be degrading, yes, degrading for every one of us. We all know Nigel well enough to be sure it would have been to prevent just such a slur on the family that he shouldered the burden.'

Then she turned to look coldly at Katie. 'There was another time we all stood firmly together as a family. Your grandmother will remember it. When your parents were married. Mother arranged the wedding from the Manor. There wasn't one of us who didn't recognize him for exactly what he was, but family pride kept us silent. Only by our outward acceptance did we stem the inevitable gossip such a match would have created. So much tragedy stems from that liaison. One thing for which we may be grateful: you seem to have inherited enough family feeling from your mother to realise Bullington could never pass to Christopher.'

Katie stood up from the arm of Kate's chair.

'I've inherited enough spunk from Grandam to make my own decision.'

Her words reminded them that that wasn't all she'd inherited from Lavinia.

It would have been easier for everyone if the party could have broken up that evening. But Kate wanted Rupert's funeral to be held at Newton Dingley ('When my turn comes I shall be laid to rest here too. There's nothing for me in Brimley. Bullington has always been my real home'), and the Mathesons put family duty high on their list of priorities so they intended to stay on until after that. In the intervening days Kate took up residence in her bedroom in the main building. She'd resented what Katie had done to the Manor, yet now she found comfort in the presence of so many visitors in her old home, all of them looking on her as a daughter of the house, all of them treating her with sympathy and gentleness in her bereaved state.

'I have just one son, Ronnie. He's all I have left in the world,' she told the Colonel. 'He's taking so much of the burden from my poor weak shoulders. I shall never go back to Brimley, I can't bear to walk inside my home again, not now. He's sorting things out for me, bringing one or two little treasures for me to keep, doing whatever has to be done. Life can be cruel when one's left so alone.'

But hadn't she a daughter? Young Mrs Mathesons' mother? He'd understood she was flying from Canada for her father's funeral. But the Colonel took his cue, he knew when sympathy was needed.

'That's something you will never be, rest assured of that. Here in your old home, with your grand-daughter and her children. And, I like to think, amongst those who are your friends – not least, myself.' He looked at her over those half moon spectacles, but this time there was no imp of mischief in his blue eyes.

Kate smiled sadly.

'You are kind. I believe it might be better if I tell Katie I will take my meals here, not with the family. One doesn't want to be a burden on the young.'

'I'm sure you could never be that. But, yes, stay here. Make a life of your own amongst friends.'

The next day Ronnie returned to Bullington, the back of his car piled with her "one or two little treasures". She'd not expected to be so moved by the sight of Rupert's leather document case, his papers filed just as precisely as he'd done everything in life: a copy of his Will, leaving everything that he had to her; his insurance policies; his saving certificates; his war bonds; his national savings certificates. Everything was left in order, everything clearly and neatly marked. She laid the tidy bundles on the bed. Order had always been his way. How often she'd felt she could scream when he'd folded the morning paper, corner to corner, edges straight. Now these few folders represented his life, all of his affairs sorted so that she'd have no problems.

Her mouth trembled. She felt humbled.

The treasures she'd asked for had mostly originated from Bullington, but it wasn't these that touched her so deeply there in the

186

privacy of her childhood bedroom. Photographs of her with the children, each one with the date on the back in Rupert's neat hand; one of him with Michael, their firstborn, taken in 1940 on his embarkation leave before he'd gone away from them for the last time; an envelope of newspaper cuttings marking stages of the children's progress – Ronnie winning the long jump, Michael made school captain, Lottie carrying away the gymkhana cup. He'd never told her that he'd saved all these things. The warm tears ran unchecked down her cheeks. She'd believed she'd known him, she'd believed she'd known all there was. What was this? An envelope, stuck down and folded. On the front in that same precise writing: '3rd June 1925. Today Kate had her hair refashioned, her beautifully gold tresses cut off. One curl that will never change.'

Black didn't suit Kate, but that evening when she joined the other residents in the dining hall the only relief was the double string of pearls.

Someone suggested she might join the nightly game of bridge.

'You're so kind.' She smiled sadly. 'My mind just wouldn't be there.' No need to tell them that she'd never mastered the game!

'Perhaps we might have some music?' This time it was Colonel Menzies. He spoke quietly, his invitation going no further than her.

'Music is such balm for a sad heart.' It came naturally to her to speak like it, what surprised her was how sincerely she meant what she said. Whenever anything had happened to upset her, always Rupert had been there. She'd taken him for granted, she'd used him as her whipping boy. Now that it was too late she realised just how much she'd depended on him. Later, when she was alone, she'd let her mind stretch out to meet his. She'd not been a good wife. Oh, but if Rupert could hear her say that he'd not agree. If there was one thing she was certain of, it was that she'd been everything he'd wanted. Later she'd indulge in her own thoughts and memories. But first she'd go to the music room with Colonel Menzies – he'd asked her to call him Maurice, already they were friends.

Some of the residents sat in the drawing room watching television, some concentrated on bridge, some went early to bed. In the music room Maurice played the piano, songs Kate knew and loved. What a sweet voice she had, a voce as gentle as everything else about her. He couldn't remember when he'd enjoyed an evening as much.

Katie missed Eva. They'd shared the day to day running of the home, both of them had cared about the welfare and happiness of the residents. Miss Hardy, the new Matron, was efficient enough but had no sense of fun. Added to which she made no secret of the fact that she found Bullington too quiet and the area dull. Flora Hardy was a town mouse, a country area like this couldn't hold her for long. She and Katie didn't even start off down the road to friendship. Both of them recognised it would have been useless.

But everyone has to have someone. Kate Bradley was much too interested in the shaping of her own life as the months went on; to talk about the home to Nigel would have been quite impossible. So it was that the highlight of Katie's morning came when she heard the sound of Tom Wadham's car coming up the drive. Even to herself she didn't put into words how much his visits meant; perhaps she was frightened to delve too deeply.

Spring gave way to summer, summer to what Katie still thought of as fall, then to winter, one year to the next. It was just over a year after Rupert's death before the Mathesons gathered again in the East Wing. All his life Colonel Menzies had been a confirmed bachelor. Then Kate had turned her lovely blue eyes on him, looked to him for protection, even asked his help in arranging her affairs. The Colonel was lost. And Kate had discovered something that had eluded her since her girlhood dreams: the love of a man who'd never be a doormat, who had the respect of everyone who knew him, who escorted her with pride but never with humility. All that and Bullington too! No wonder she blossomed; no wonder when she walked down the aisle of Newton Dingley church, Mrs Maurice Menzies, the village agreed that beauty wasn't just for the young. Surely there had never been a sweeter-looking bride?

On the sloping lawn were two small boys, chasing a ball, tumbling about like young puppies.

'Do they never quarrel?' laughed Dr Tom Wadham, watching them.

'I guess they have their off days.' Katie smiled. 'But not serious quarrels. Bertie more or less keeps up with Kit these days – what he lacks in agility he makes up for in determination.'

The young doctor had fallen into the habit of looking in at Bullington Manor after surgery each morning before he set off on his rounds. Of course, emergency calls threw the daily routine out. The attraction certainly wasn't Miss Hardy. She'd lasted only six months and had been replaced by kindly, middle-aged and rotund Nora Ridley. Katie wasn't sure what had made her decide to take Eva's day room for her own use. It was here she did her book work – and it was from here that she looked out to the lawns where the boys spent much of their time and the driveway where each morning Tom's car rounded the bend.

She'd watched for him this morning, waved to let him know she'd seen him, been waiting as he'd taken the front steps two at a time and come through the open front door.

'I thought maybe you'd had to go to an emergency. You're later than usual. You've time for coffee?' She rang the bell as she spoke.

'Sounds like a good idea. No, Katie, I've had a light morning. Only a handful of patients in surgery so I got off early on my round. Fact is, I'm driving over to Oxford to pick up some books I've ordered.' Then as Sylvia, one of the green-uniformed assistants, brought the coffee tray in: 'I'll take a look at Lady Halborough before I go, I've changed her tablets. I'll see if she had a better night's sleep.' There was something in his smile as the door closed on the girl's departing figure that drew Katie and him together. Lady Halborough's sleeping habits were a long-standing joke between them.

'Are you busy? Why don't you come with me? Look at the sunshine out there, Katie. Come on! Get your bonnet on. Let the Manor look after itself for a few hours.'

What harm could it possibly do? Kit and Bertie would be having their lunch with Meg; the Manor could certainly get along without missing her. Nigel had gone to Reading to a cattle sale with Frank Fulford. The sun cast a golden beam through the window tempting her.

Ten minutes later two little boys stopped turning somersaults long enough to wave goodbye as the open topped and unprofessional-looking car moved off.

She cast a sideways look at Tom. He didn't appear to be aware of her attention so she grew more confident and let her eyes rest on him that bit longer. She'd come to know him well in the eighteen months since he'd been caring for the residents, sufficiently well that she didn't consciously think of his appearance. Now she took stock. To start with she'd seen him as good-looking. And now, knowing him better? She tried to look on him as a stranger. His brown hair was nearer to dark than light, nearer to wavy than straight; his chin was firm; when he smiled, as he so often did, he had a dimple in his right cheek that gave him a look of boyishness; although he didn't turn her way, she knew that that ready smile would bring a light to his hazel eyes. Usually when he made his rounds he kept the soft roof of his car closed. Many of his patients regretted his youth, it would never do for him to arrive windswept on his calls. Today, though, discretion was thrown out of the window – or more accurately out of the open top. The wind blew Katie's light brown curls, it stood his shorter hair on end. Today they were young, they were free, it was summer and ahead of them were hours to be enjoyed.

It was as they crossed Magdalen Bridge that he looked at her curiously.

'Something wrong, Katie? Why so quiet?'

She shook her head. 'Just thoughts, memories. I think Oxford must be the most beautiful city in the world, don't you?'

'Then why so solemn?'

'I was remembering the very first time I came here. It was dawn, May Day at dawn. Nigel met me back up the road there. He watched out for me so that he could drive us in and park the car. The May Morning Hymn – and I was a visitor from overseas. It's like looking back to another life. I'll never forget a single second of it, Tom.'

He concentrated on negotiating the build-up of traffic.

'Were you in love with him then?'

'He was my friend. But sure thing I was in love – in love with England, with Oxford, with the mystery of yesterday and today all getting confused.' She laughed, embarrassed for a moment that she may have said more than he could understand. 'Don't forget I was living what I'd dreamed back home. For me, England was always the end of the rainbow, even when I was just a kid.'

'And now? Sometimes it's easier to hang on to perfection as long as dreams don't get mixed up with reality. I wouldn't mind betting that from this distance, your dreams are more often of the home you left behind.'

She shrugged. 'Not sure that I have dreams anymore. Only babes or fools let themselves believe in the never-never-land where the sun always shines.'

'Well, let's be grateful. It shines for us today. We'll make the most of every bit of it. I'll park here, the book shop is just around the corner. Are you wanting to be thoroughly "girlie" and look at the shops, or shall I collect my books and drive on out to the Trout for lunch?'

'I'm not in the least "girlie". Let's go straight to the pub and the river. I'd like that.'

Easy to say, yet while he was in the bookshop those memories wouldn't let her rest. How good it had been in those early days with Nigel. Before she'd known the magic of being with Dylan – no, she mustn't let her thoughts go down that road – before Grandam had died, before darling Kit had been born, before their relationship had been bruised by the hurts they inflicted on each other. Think back to that morning, the moment of closeness as they'd heard the clear voices lifted into the dawn, the fun at that scruffy place where they'd had such an enormous breakfast. She'd been on holiday, no more than that. And yet, hadn't they both felt even then, in their youthful

190

innocence of life, that their paths were entwined? So they were, so they always would be. But where was the sparkle now? If only they could find again the magic of that May morning. She squared her shoulders, resolved that somehow she'd help them both find the way back.

And with that resolution made, she was in the mood to enjoy whatever fun the day provided.

That was the first outing she had with Tom Wadham. By the time she arrived home her mid-day resolve had slipped to a comfortable place at the back of her mind.

'You're not the only one to have been out and about today.' Her eyes teased Nigel as she looked at him along the length of the dinner table. 'Guess where I've been?'

'Somewhere with some of your old cronies, I imagine.' He cast the first shadow.

'Then you imagine wrong. I've been with Tom Wadham. We went to Oxford. We had lunch at a pub, then we walked by the river.'

'What's he done with his patients?'

'Even doctors get *some* time off.' For a moment she wished she'd kept her day to herself. It had been fun, now he was spoiling it. Then her resolve got the upper hand. 'Remember the first time I went to Oxford, Nigel? I was thinking of it today. Remember the dawn, the singing?'

He'd avoided her eyes until then. Now he looked at her. At her? It seemed to her that he looked into her.

'Katie . . .' But whatever it was he'd been going to say remained unsaid. Like a curtain coming down, his expression changed, his face creased into that easy smile. 'Remember the transport cafe? Like the entrance of the Queen of Sheba when I led you in there!' He chuckled. Just for a moment they'd almost let they minds fuse. Then the moment was lost, there was nothing deeper between them than superficial chatter, occasional light banter. The evening wore on. They watched television, she wrote a letter to Lottie. The atmosphere was relaxed, undemanding. Often Nigel liked to read for half an hour in bed, then turn off the light and go to sleep. This wouldn't be one of those nights, she was sure of it. She let herself anticipate. Her day had been stimulating, she strained towards what she believed was ahead. When at about ten o'clock he picked up a paperback thriller she felt an ache of frustration.

Where was her pride that she could act like it? She sat close to him, she rested her head on his shoulder, she rubbed her foot against his leg. He read the first page . . . he turned to the next . . .

191

He looked at her quizzically, his eyes teasing. 'Just one chapter,' he laughed. He might have spoken that way to a child who'd begged a sweet.

'I'm going to bed. I'm not sitting here waiting for you.'

'Right you are.' Then with a playful smack on her bottom as she stood up, 'By the time you're ready, your lord and master will be there.'

She played games too. 'That'll be the day, when you're my lord and master, Nigel Matheson.' But with the door closed between them her smile was gone, the game was over.

Upstairs she got ready for bed. The night was warm. With the light off she stood in front of the open window of their room. Why should a few hours with another man do this to her? Was something wrong with her that she could be filled with such longing for – for what? She clenched her teeth. On one wall was a long mirror. Turning her head she could see the reflection of her naked pale body, standing in a shaft of moonlight. How bright the moon was tonight. It lit the heavens and dimmed the stars to insignificance.

'Kate-ee'.

All her longings took shape in the memory of his voice. Her warm hands caressed her breasts. Guiltily, yet eagerly, she watched the woman in the mirror, saw the hands move down, pressing against her flat stomach.

'Kate-ee.' Was it his voice she heard? Or her own suppressed, hungry moan? Oh, God, bring him near to me, let me find Dylan, forgive me if it's a sin, if it's a sin I can't help it. Only minutes ago she'd clenched her teeth, yearning for something, not even sure what it was she wanted.

Nigel's dressing room door clicked shut. Instantly Katie reached for her silk nightdress and pulled it over her head.

'Not in bed yet? Don't you want a light?'

'The moon's light enough. It's warm to get into bed.'

'Lovely night. Light as day out there in the park.'

Damn him, how could he talk so casually? 'Lovely night' – as though she were a passing acquaintance. Did he feel nothing of the aching need that consumed her? She leant against him, the satin of her nightdress smooth as she pressed close, moving gently, wanting reassurance that his need was as urgent as her own. Damn him, what did he come up here for, why couldn't he have left her on her own?

Obligingly he drew her towards him. He was man enough to be aroused by her quick breathing, by her nearness, by the message of her body moving against his. She sat on the edge of the bed and pulled him down towards her. Her heart was pounding, she could hear

192

something like a moan as she breathed, she could hear it but she didn't care.

'Kate-ee'.

Nigel wouldn't have been human if he'd not been excited. As he lowered himself over her she gripped him, she devoured him, almost at his first touch she cried out, within seconds her orgasm came.Her mind was filled with that other voice.

'Kate-ee. You are mine. Always you are mine.'

'Yes, yes,' Nigel heard her gasp, 'oh God, don't take him.'

Just as Dylan had been close to her, so her moment over he was gone. She felt tears on her cheek, tears of joy, of sadness and frustration, she didn't know. For Nigel it wasn't over yet. He was plodding on to the end of the track, with every movement thrusting her short-lived ecstasy further away.

Afterwards he made no mention of what it was she'd cried out. Probably he'd already forgotten.

Chapter Thirteen

Two small boys dressed in short grey trousers, maroon blazers with gold braiding, maroon school caps with gold triangular sections in the front. Kit was five and a half, Bertie four and a half when they started to attend Highworth House School. Kit was always ready to protect his young brother; Bertie, already as tall and more solidly built, wasn't likely to need protecting. Bertie was always ready to back his elder brother; he was Kit's willing slave.

'No school tomorrow. I'm riding at seven, you can come with me if you're ready,' Katie told them on a Friday evening.

'I thought I'd take Bertie fishing,' Nigel put in. 'How about that, Bertie? Time you learnt how to tie your tackle.'

'Yippee! What about Kit? Why can't he come with us, Dad? You've never given Kit a lesson yet.'

Kit looked from one to the other, then again to Katie.

'I think I'd like best to ride with Mum.'

Why was it Mum had wet eyes when she looked at him? He bit his lip, feeling uncertain.

'And I'd like best that you ride with me, Kit.' Her smile reassured him. He must have imagined those wet eyes.

Soon their Saturdays fell into a regular pattern. Always Nigel had something planned for himself and Bertie. Never for Kit.

'Why don't we take Kit, Dad?' Bertie said as they got their tackle ready for a day's fishing, this time with a boat on the Thames.

'Don't you like just you and me going? I thought we had a great time. Here hold this bait tin a minute. Careful you don't let the water spill.'

Both boys were used to talking to the residents at the Manor. Nigel wasn't at all keen on the idea that Bertie should look on it as a home for outsiders; but on the other hand, it wasn't right that Kit should be made much of in there and Bertie left out. So he sank his prejudices.

Both the boys had been trained to be polite and considerate to their visitors, but of the two it was Kit with his naturally gentle manner who was most popular. Except with Kate, or Grandma Menzies as they called her.

It was one day during the summer holidays after the boys had been at school for a year, that Tom Wadham arrived to find Katie playing cricket with them.

'Go on, swack it!' Bertie yelled.

Katie swacked, Kit chased the ball while she ran.

'One, two, three four,' Bertie was counting, jumping with excitement that she'd managed to send the ball so far that it was rolling away down the slope, 'five, six, seven, eight, nine, ten . . .'

'Hey, hey, what's this then?'

'Don't stop me,' Katie panted, enjoying herself every bit as much as the children, 'yesterday I got nineteen. I want to beat my record.'

'I can see I'll have to teach you the rudiments of cricket! Single runs, a four or a six if it's a boundary.'

She stopped. 'You mean six is all you can get for a great swack like that? Oh, say, that's not nearly so much fun as the way we do it. Here comes the ball! Quick, let me get back to the crease or I'll be out.'

'You play too, Dr Tom,' Bertie passed him the ball, 'then you can teach us the rules. I did ask Dad, but he seemed too busy to come out and play with us. We don't have cricket at this school, you see.'

'Is everyone O.K. at the house, Katie? No one in need of a doctor?'

'No, stay and play with us. Our need's greater than theirs.'

'I wish you meant it.' He said it quietly, not for the boys' ears.

'Right now I do mean it.' She pretended not to have recognised the serious undertone. What ought she to do? She knew she was playing with fire. It wasn't fair to Tom, he ought to find himself some nice young girl who was free. But if he did that, what about her? Each day he came, each day she watched for him. He'd never so much as kissed her, she might be imagining the way he looked at her. But she knew she wasn't. Be honest, she told herself, how would you feel if he really did find that nice young girl? All the colour in your days comes from Tom. Go a step further, ask yourself something else. What if Tom told you how he felt, what if he tried to break up your marriage, your home?

'Boundaries? How d'you mean, Dr Tom?' It was Kit who asked.

Tom knocked out his pipe and put it in his pocket, took off his jacket and rolled up his sleeves, and started to pace out the cricket field. Wide-eyed at the mysteries that were being unfolded the boys strode by his side, then rushed off to find sticks to mark the corners. Katie knew she was concentrating on watching them rather than face the question she'd asked herself. No, nothing would break her marriage. She told herself that if most of the time she and Nigel came no closer than travelling their parallel tracks, was that so different from what she'd find in most marriages once the first romance and excitement had worn off? At the back of her mind was the wonder of what she'd known with Dylan; just occasionally something touched a nerve and it sprang alive. Her conscious mind told her she had to forget, to hang on to the dreadful truth that he was her brother, that it was a sin to let her imagination bring alive what they'd shared.

'Can we play with four of us?' Bertie wanted to know. ''Course we're jolly glad you're going to play too. But we have Bowlie, Batty and Fieldie.'

'We could take turns,' Kit suggested.

'A real team has many more, eleven on each side.' Their mentor was coming back with them, a hand lightly on each small boy's shoulder. 'But with four we'll have – what is you call yourselves? – a Batty, a Bowlie and two Fieldies, one each side or the wicket.'

'Whack-o!' Bertie took his familiar three jumps of excitement. 'You be Batty, Dr Tom, we'll get you out quick as anything with two of us. Me and Kit'll be Fieldies. Here's the ball, you can bowl, Mum.'

Coming to sit under the sycamore tree, Kate and her Colonel stopped to watch.

'Well run, sir, well run,' Maurice chuckled. 'That boy moves like a gazelle.' Then raising his voice: 'Well stopped, young Kit. You'll play for England yet.'

Kate said nothing.

'The sound of summer, Katie. It takes me back to our garden at Brimley. Each year dear Rupert marked out the tennis court. Such happy days.' Kate's expression managed to convey contentment with the present even while her heart was touched with sadness for joys gone by.

Katie frowned. All this talk of happy days had a ring of hypocrisy. Even from the few months she'd lived with her grandparents at Brimley she'd formed a very different picture. Perhaps no one ever sees the past with accuracy. What was it really like at Higley Creek? Was her home as she remembered? One day she'd go visiting. Would she be disappointed, find that she'd remembered a picture more brightly coloured than the truth?

'Who is it playing? Surely Nigel isn't teaching Bertie tennis just yetawhile?'

'Tom and Nigel. It's Kit who has an eye for ball games, and the speed too,' came Katie's unsmiling answer.

'You can't grudge Nigel the pleasure he finds in being with Bertie. You give enough of your time to the other one. Hush, I see Maurice is coming.' She held her hand towards him, as if some magnetic force would draw him to her. For a second Katie thought of her grandfather. How touched he would have been if just once he might have been given such a welcome.

Across the sward of green they caught a glimpse of the two boys, their whoops and shouts showing that imagination was making a background for some game.

'Sounds like cowboys and Indians,' Maurice smiled as they flashed into view and out of it again.

'More than likely, I should think.' Kate looked down her aristocratic nose.

Katie was still seething under the jibe when out from the woodland area dashed Kit, running towards them at speed.

'Mum! Mum!' Then what sounded like: 'Quick! I killed him.'

Kit's face could never be white, but there was no vestige of pink in his cheeks, his skin looked sallow. His light blue eyes were side with terror. Katie didn't stop to ask questions. Leaving Maurice to fetch Nigel and Tom from the tennis court, she took Kit's hand and ran back across the park with him.

'What happened?' she panted.

'I shot him with my arrow. Mom, he fell straight down.' Kit answered in short bursts. His side was knotted with stitch but his pace didn't slacken. 'I shook him. Never opened his eyes. Mum . . . Mum . . .' He was crying now, sobs that caught in his throat as he gasped for breath. He was frightened. He felt sick. Back in the wood he'd left Bertie lying where he'd fallen. He'd hurt Bertie. Killed him. No, he couldn't have. Katie was running fast, pulling him forward. A sob turned into a hiccough.

Heavy footsteps behind told them Nigel and Tom were catching up with them.

'Young fool!' Nigel rasped. 'What the hell have you done?'

'Cowboys and Injuns,' Kit gulped. 'He can't be dead, Dad, can he? He can't be dead?'

'Christ! Where is he? Where the hell is he?'

''Long here. Just along here.' There was no sign of Bertie. 'Must be further.' Kit turned to Katie, snivelling helplessly. 'Thought it was just here.'

'Christ!' Nigel turned on him in fury. 'Can't you even get that right!'

'Down there. I see him.' Some of Katie's fear dropped away. What a relief it was to hear Tom's calm voce. He was a doctor. Bertie was hurt, but Tom would soon make him better.

197

'Think he's moved a bit, Mum.' Kit looked at her for reassurance but it was Nigel who answered.

'Shut up, you little fool. Look at him! How could he have moved!'

Bertie had a good colour, that was the first straw Katie clutched. Surely if he were seriously hurt – and she'd not let herself think further than that – he would be pale? Tom knelt by his side, took his wrist. The others watched him.

'O.K., Kit old chap, his pulse is strong.'

Kit buried his face in Katie's skirt. She held him close.

Next Tom eased one of Bertie's eyelids open. It was too much for a mischievous five year old, who began to shake with giggles.

'Bertie! You naughty boy! You frightened us all to death!' In her relief Katie's temper snapped. 'That was a hateful thing to do to Kit.'

'Wasn't!' Bertie couldn't see what all the fuss was about. 'Wasn't, was it, Kit? Was the game. His arrow hit me right here,' he pointed to his chest, 'so I dropped down dead. I was a cowboy, the injun got me.'

Kit started to laugh. Just as he'd cried a moment ago, now he screeched with laughter. He pulled away from Katie and started to perform a sort of wild war dance, picking up the bow and arrow that had been thrown to the ground. It was too much for Nigel. In these last minutes of confused relief Katie hadn't looked at him, but now she saw that his face was working, his colour high, his hands trembling.

'Stop that!' He brought his hand down on Kit, letting it land where it would.

'Steady, old chap.' Tom put a hand on his shoulder. 'It was just a kids' game. No harm done.'

'Give me those things! I'll teach you to aim arrows at people. Do as I say!' Nigel held a shaking hand towards Kit.

'Nigel, it was a game,' Katie tried to calm him.

'Did you hear me?' Nigel ignored her, not taking his eyes off Kit.

'No, I won't! They're mine. I won't give them to you. I hate you. I hate you.' Tears had given way to laughter. Now laughter was gone, Kit screamed, clutching his precious bow and arrow with both small hands. But he was powerless against Nigel. With one movement he tore them away, and with another snapped them in half across his knee.

Silence, except that by now Bertie was sniffling. He'd never seen his father angry, it made his tummy hurt to look at him. He bit his lip and tried not to cry, but he lost the battle and a warm tear rolled down his rosy face. Katie hardly noticed, her gaze was on Kit, his look of loss, of disbelief.

'Let's get home, shall we?' Tom lifted Bertie to his feet.

198

And that's where it might have ended but for Kit. With dignity that hardly matched his years he turned away, walking further into the wood.

'Damn the child!' But this time Nigel only muttered it. The breaking of the bow and arrow had released his tension, now Kit's behaviour was nothing more than an irritant. 'Come back here when you're told.'

Head up, Kit marched on.

Bertie gave a big sniff, wiped first his nose then his eyes with the back of his hand, then chased after his brother.

'You can have mine, Kit. When we get home I'll give you mine. I didn't think it would get you in a row.' His face crumpled as he remembered what a big joke he'd planned and how it had turned out. 'Was only for a joke I did it. Please, Kit, let's go home. Dad's cross, everyone's cross. Kit . . .'

Katie held out her hands to them. Willingly Bertie took one in his, and Kit only hesitated a fraction longer. Before they'd crossed the park to the house both hands had been dropped, the boys were trailing behind, heads together, whispering. Before them were Katie and Tom, and in the lead Nigel carrying the broken bow and arrow to be thrown into the stable yard bin.

'I lost my rag this afternoon, Kate. I behaved badly.'

Nigel switched off the television news that neither of them had been watching.

'Yes, you did.'

'I'm sorry. I can't say more than that.'

'It's not much use saying it to me. If you really want to put things right, then go and buy Kit a new bow and arrow, be man enough to give it to him yourself.' She watched him closely, waiting for his reaction. But she was disappointed, his expression told her nothing.

'I've never approved of them having bows and arrows. They're dangerous and uncivilized.'

'Nigel, how would you have reacted if it had been the other way round? If Kit had spoofed and Bertie had shot the arrow?'

'That's purely hypothetical. Katie, that arrow might have blinded the boy! And you ask me to buy the little fool another. "Here, boy, have another go, see if you can do better!" Is that what you expect me to do?'

Katie shook her head.

'There's no point in talking about it. They're two small boys. Can't you try and see them just as that? No wonder he says he hates you. What sort of a person do you expect him to grow up to be if every time he looks at you he sees such – such contempt. He's worth knowing, Nigel.'

'I give him a name and a home, that was the bargain. The only good thing that has come out of this sham of a marriage is Bertie, my son. for his sake all the rest is worthwhile – even what you've done to the Manor. One day it'll all be his, he'll put the score straight again.'

'Your memory is conveniently short sometimes. You may give him a name, but it's me who gives him a home. And thanks to the way I run the Manor I don't need to come to you for handouts – no, not even to pay for his education.' How hard it was to try and sound dignified when inside she was crying in misery. "A sham of a marriage" he called it. And so it was. What else could it be when it was rooted in something that caused so much hatred? 'Anyway,' she hit out, needing to hurt him in her wretchedness, 'if it's such a sham of a marriage, then it's time we were honest with ourselves. I'll sleep in the back room. Next time you decide it's time to perform your marital duties, you'll be unlucky.' It sounded coarse and she was glad.

He shrugged. 'Please yourself, can't imagine I shall lose any sleep. I can take it or leave it.' The look he cast on her was evidence of his disinterest. 'I'm not likely to come rattling at your door, you've usually made the running. Chuck me that paperback from the table if you can reach it, will you? I suppose these days you're getting all you need from your doctor friend?'

'How dare you say that to me!' The book hit the side of his head. 'Tom's my friend, I thought he was your friend too. I'm going to bed, there's no point in our talking.'

Again he shrugged.

Upstairs in the back bedroom she felt like a visitor in her own home. She moved about, touching an ornament here, straightening a picture there. What had happened to them? They'd never had a truly loving relationship, but except for a few bad times she's always felt they were friends. But no more. Not after the way he'd treated Kit. And another thing she vowed: never would she sleep with him again, she who "made the running".

The boys shared a room at the end of the corridor. She was lonely for the sight of someone she loved, someone who loved her. Tiptoeing, she passed Meg's room and went into theirs. Bertie was asleep, lying on his back, his arms flung out just as he'd slept as a baby. He'd kicked the covers off and very gently she pulled the sheet to cover him. Then she moved over to Kit's bed. Poor little boy, none of it was his fault. She knelt down and rested her head on the pillow by his. What was that? Something in bed with him. Lifting the sheet she peered in the dim light of the bedroom. Poor little boy . . . he must

200

have watched where Nigel had thrown his broken treasure. Poor little boy. Tears welled up in her, it was too late now for her to hold them back. She gathered the sleeping form closer, the broken bow and arrow still clasped in his hand.

Only later, alone in her room, did her mind go back to Nigel's accusation: '. . . these days you get all you need from your doctor friend.'

Staring at the dark ceiling, she'd never felt so alone.

The day of the cowboys and indians incident was a crossroads in their lives. The difference was far more than Katie moving to a room of her own, it had to do with the boys. Until then Bertie had never gone off for a jaunt with his father without his hopeful suggestion: 'Are you going to take Kit, too?' After that day he never asked again, neither did Kit watch and wait for the invitation that had never come. Bertie gravitated towards Nigel, Kit towards Katie; yet no shadow fell between the boys themselves.

'Look, Kit, I hooked both of these myself.' Coming home from a day's fishing at the trout lake, Bertie displayed his catch. 'Dad got three. But I kept mine separate so you could see.'

'They're fine fish, Bertie. What sort are they?'

'Brown trout. Dad told me. When we go to the canal I'll teach you how to do it. There aren't any trout there, Dad says, but I'll teach you how to do it. You flick your wrist, sort of like that. Makes the fly dance about on top of the water, then the silly old fish thinks it's something to eat and up it comes and takes the feather, hook and all.'

Kit picked up one of the fish, looking at it with admiration. Bertie felt almost a man.

'We're having them for supper. Let's take them to the kitchen and give them to Cook, make sure she knows which are mine. You can have one, which one do you choose?'

Seven years old, and already casting a fly better than many an adult. No wonder Nigel's eyes shone with pride as he watched them making for the kitchen garden on their way to see Cook. Bertie was no longer the same height as Kit. Now he was half an inch taller, his shoulders broader. Kit's black hair was like heavy silk, Bertie's blond locks coarser, in keeping with his physique.

'What did you do while we were out?' Bertie asked, really interested.

'Mum and I went riding this morning. She put up the jumps and we practised for the gymkhana. It's next Saturday, remember? You are going to ride in the gymkhana too, aren't you?'

'You bet.'

201

'We left the jumps out. We'll practise together tomorrow shall we?'

That Sunday morning practice was the reason that of the Matheson boys only Kit took part in the gymkhana. Watching the two of them together Nigel made his decision: he'd take Bertie away for the weekend. Seven was young to start climbing, but he'd see the lad didn't attempt anything dangerous. They'd have their first trip to Wales together, just the two of them. Bertie would get a hunger for the hills, would understand even at his tender age what it meant to conquer a challenge. And there were great advantages to his being young. He was light, he was supple, agile (and if at the thought Nigel's mind swung to Kit, he soon pulled it to order again), he knew no fear.

So Bertie wasn't there to see Kit's clear rounds, to watch the grace of his movements as he put his pony into the jumps. Had he been, he would have applauded as loudly as anyone, there was no jealousy in his love for his brother. Last winter when they'd ridden in the children's hunter trials, there hadn't been a rider who could handle a pony the way Kit could and Bertie had come home quite puffed up with pride to boast on his behalf. Today though when Kit rode away with the Junior Cup, Bertie was savouring his first hours amongst the craggy hills of Wales, already dreaming of the day when he could scale the sheer face of the tall rocks and know the world was his own.

In the way children do, they both accepted the division in the family even thought they didn't understand it. Kit wished Bertie had been at the gymkhana; he made mental notes of all that went on so that he could tell him after the weekend. And for Bertie, the only thing that marred the pure joy he was discovering was that Kit couldn't share it. But when he got home he'd tell him all about it – and later on, when they were older, they could come here together, he'd teach Kit. In his young mind it was all so simple.

Something in the way the child rode to the dais, the way he inclined his head as he took the cup, how it rolled the years away. There were other long memories as well as Katie's, but she didn't hear the whispers.

'Let's go and have tea in the tent, buy Kit the biggest cream cake they've got. You deserve it, Kit.' Tom had been with them all the afternoon, of course he had, he was such a regular caller at the Manor and at the East Wing, that he was almost part of the family. 'And you, Katie,' he said as they waited for Mrs White from the dairy to pour their tea from the urn, 'cream cakes, fruit cakes, we're spoilt for choice?'

'I know what Mrs Matheson'll like.' Rosy-faced Mrs White peered at them through a haze of steam. 'Eccles cakes. Got a few put by at the back here for my specials. Mrs Watkins' eccles. Not a body round here could hold a candle to Mrs Watkins when it comes to eccles. You too, doctor, how about an eccles for you?'

'Sounds like just the thing to round off a great afternoon. You miss all the fun, shut away in here, Mrs White.'

'Don't you believe it. I took a peak at this young gentleman here. Could out-ride John Wayne, I reckon. Regular cowboy.'

As well Kate had made the excuse that the day was too warm to come with them!

'Are you on call this evening, Tom?' Katie asked him as he carried their laden tray to a table.

'No. I was coming to that. How about if I take you out to dinner? You're at home on your own, I'm a poor lonely bachelor.'

'Sounds like fun.' If, hidden in the suggestion, was anything more than fun, she ignored it. 'But this evening belongs to Kit. I thought I'd have dinner early, let him stay up for it. He has to celebrate having got himself a silver cleaning job for a year. How about you joining us? Have our own party, eh, Kit?'

If it wasn't the evening Tom had had in mind, he gave the child no sign of it.

'Great idea. The way he rode today, I'd be surprised if he parts with that trophy after twelve months.'

Katie sent him a look of gratitude. Moments like this brought home to her what a lonely thing it was to love Kit like she did. Always she was on guard, watching out for the slights that came his way, ready to make up to him for the interest and pride that was showered on Bertie. It was sheer luxury to let herself indulge in this feeling of sharing, all three of them glad to be together.

The mood held. There was no childlike excitement from Kit that he was allowed to take his place at the dinner table, yet Katie didn't need telling that it was an evening he'd remember. At eight years old could he really have such a sense of occasion? Did she imagine the natural elegance in his manner, something that set him apart and brought back to her the ghosts of another evening? Grandam at the head of the table, Nigel at the foot, herself seated opposite Dylan – Dylan with the same movement of his head, the same eyes with their fringe of black lashes, their light blue accentuated by the dark rim of the iris, eyes that seemed to see into her soul . . .

Dinner was over and Kit gone to bed when Katie heard her grandmother's voice calling from the hallway.

'Katie? Is something wrong?'

'No, Granny, why should it be? We're here, in the drawing room.'

Kate took in the scene, not hiding her surprise.

'I knew Nigel was away, so I hadn't expected you to be entertaining.'

'We've been celebrating Kit's afternoon, Mrs Menzies.' Tom smiled at her disarmingly. 'You really should have seen him. No one else stood a chance.'

'How nice.' Her mouth smiled, her voice didn't.

If that's the game she wanted, then Katie could play it too and beat her at it.

'A pity he's gone to bed or you could have congratulated him yourself, Granny. I'll tell him in the morning that you came across and how pleased you are.'

'I won't disturb your little tête-à-tête. It's just that seeing the car outside for so long I began to imagine you were ill. And with Nigel away, I feel responsible.' Just for a moment Katie had knocked her off course, but now she was in charge again, the loving grandmother.

Katie could never stay cross with her for long. She put her arm around Kate's slim, straight shoulders and hugged her.

'Have you had a telephone call from Nigel? Have you heard how little Bertie got on?'

'No.' Katie was surprised at the suggestion. Nigel wouldn't consider reporting back, she was sure of that. 'He'll be fine with Nigel, you don't need to worry. But, if I do here, I'll slip across and tell you.'

There seemed nothing for Kate to wait for.

The shadows had lengthened into twilight. Upstairs Kit was asleep, his gleaming cup on the table by the side of his bed. Downstairs Katie had pushed the French door wide open, the glorious day was turning into a sultry night.

'Feels like a storm brewing.' She took a deep breath. There was no movement, just heavy, still air, full of the scent of summer.

'Is there, Katie? Is that what we're heading for – you, me, Nigel?' Tom came to stand behind her. 'How long can we go on like this Katie? No, don't turn away, look at me.'

'Tom, we're friends –'

'Friends! Can't we at least be honest? Of course we're friends. I've been here pretty well every day for six years! And for most of that time I must have been in love with you.'

'You make me ashamed. I've pretended I didn't know, yet I've clung to you. You ought to have some pretty young girl, someone fresh, someone without a family, without a past.'

'I ought to have you, just you.' He shut his eyes. 'What sort of a man am I to come here to Nigel's home, watching every move his wife makes, going home thinking of her? That's what I do, you know.'

The light was fading fast. They moved closer, talked more softly.

'You're married, you've got the boys. Tell me the truth, promise. Is what you and Nigel have right? I don't know, Katie. I watch you together, and you don't pull in different directions. Yet so often when I'm with you I feel that I' nearer to you than he could ever be. He's your husband, you've given him two sons. I must be crazy. Katie, say something.'

She said nothing. Her mind was in a turmoil. Yet why? What he said wasn't a surprise to her, even though she'd tried not to admit it. She'd tried to tell herself that what he felt was infatuation, one day he'd fall in love with some suitable girl; but she'd not followed that train of thought, it had been easier to accept his unspoken affection. Tonight must surely have brought them to the point of no return. So which way forward?

'Tell me he's the only man you want, tell me your marriage is complete and I'm just a fool with too much imagination. I'll clear right away, I promise you.'

'No.' Taken by surprise the one word escaped her.

'No?' With new confidence he turned her to face him, peering at her closely, trying to pierce the darkness and read the message in her eyes. There's a time for talking. This wasn't it.

As he pulled her into his arms, she raised her mouth to his. He loved her; he wanted her. Only now did she acknowledge how Nigel's "take it or leave it" attitude had wounded her; all this time Tom had been watching her, dreaming of being with her. In those first seconds she clung to him, she clung to his need of her, his desire for her. Like a bird who'd been caged and was suddenly free a wild abandon raced through her veins.

'No.' It was Tom who whispered it. 'No, Katie. We must stop this. We must talk. We must think ahead.'

The spell was broken. That wild bird was back in the cage, beating its wings against the bars.

They talked. As the wind unexpectedly gusted, rustling the leaves into a frenzy, and from far away came the faint rumble of thunder, she told him something of her marriage. Something, but not as much as she'd intended when she'd started speaking.

'Right from when I came to England, Nigel and I were good friends. Grandam could see we were. She was a great organiser, was Grandam.' She forced a laugh, the sound of it unnatural in her ears. Suddenly she knew that there were some things that could never be told. She wished she could have made him understand about Dylan. For Dylan and her to belong to each other had been right; memories of early childhood told her they must have known it even then. She

205

felt no shame for what had happened, only a bitter resentment towards her father. Then she thought of Kit, innocent, trusting Christopher Matheson, son of Bullington. It wasn't shame that silenced her, it was love. 'When Grandam died she left the house to me and the money to Nigel. I guess we did the wrong thing to let that drive us into getting wed. But we did. Maybe even then we might have hung on to some sort of a marriage, but for what I did to the Manor. He'll never forgive me for that.'

'And now? I'm not blind, I know something is missing between you. God, I never thought I'd try to come between a man and his wife. I come to his house as his friend, as your friend – all the time wanting to take you from him. It couldn't have happened, I swear it wouldn't have happened, if I'd seen you as a happy couple. Listen, Katie, I could take a practice somewhere away from here, we could make a new start. The boys will be off to prep school in a few weeks. What sort of life will you make then?'

The boys! Whatever was she dong letting herself listen to him?

'It's no use, Tom.'

'I could give you the sort of love you deserve – the sort of love you're starved of.'

'No. No, you couldn't. How can you know what it is I want? I don't even know myself. Only that I can't have it, I can never have it.'

He frowned, his mind floundering into first one avenue then another as he tried to find his way to what she was telling him. He prided himself he could size people up pretty well, he judged Nigel unlikely to be a passionate man. Katie was hungry for things outside his conventional capacity. Tom swallowed; he could feel the steady, heavy beat of a pulse in his neck; he was glad they'd not switched on the light, he welcomed the darkness that hid from her where his thoughts were carrying him.

'If a man and woman love each other, then there is nothing, *nothing* they can't have,' he whispered.

His reply had no bearing on what had been in her mind. For a second she was surprised at his words. Then she followed the way his thoughts had gone. In the kaleidoscope of her mind pictures converged: Dylan, Nigel, Kit, Dylan, Bertie, a Roman road, Dylan, Westminster Bridge, Kate-ee, Kit, Bertie. And of all, what was there left? Two little boys. And now Tom tempting her with a chance to live a full life.

'It's not that,' she mumbled. 'Nigel and I don't even sleep together, we haven't for ages. Tom, I can never run out on the boys. And if I could, then I reckon you wouldn't think much of me.'

For answer he drew her towards him. This time when the cage door opened the bird flew high, far horizons beckoned. She'd never leave

Bullington, she'd never leave the boys, but because she'd told him so she'd found her way to a new freedom. Tom loved her. When a man and woman love each other there is nothing they can't have. With Tom she'd find absolution for the sin of loving her own brother.

Her flesh was warm, his hand even warmer. They trembled on the brink. If reason whispered the dangers of where they were heading, they'd gone too far now to pull themselves back. In a minute they'd surrender, they both knew it and in the certainty they wanted to savour every minute. The night seemed to hold its breath.

A shrill ringing rent the silence – the telephone in the hallway at the foot of the stairs. As they pulled apart, there was a sound of hurrying footsteps as someone went to answer it. A quick tidying of clothes, smoothing of hair, switching on of the light, just in time for the knock on the door.

'It's the master for you, Madam. Telephoning from Wales, I believe.' Which Katie knew meant: 'Hurry up, it's long distance.'

'Coming, Jenny. I was outside in the garden,' she lied, hoping to account for her dishevelled appearance. Jenny didn't waste time looking at her, she wanted to get back to the television in the servants' hall.

'Nigel? Is everything all right?'

'Perfectly. That's what I wanted to tell you. The lad's asleep. Katie, you should have seen him, he's got no fear at all.' Such pride in his voice.

'You're not letting him do anything dangerous?'

'Now, would I?' Nigel laughed. 'I just wanted to say – oh, I don't know really, just that I was so damned proud of him. You would have been too. We may be a bit late home tomorrow evening. If the weather's good we don't want to set off too early. So don't worry about us. You know Bertie's fine with me.'

Listening to him, she smiled. It was impossible not to.

'Thanks for phoning, Nigel. Granny came over earlier to see if we'd heard anything. Tom was here.' Was here? Already she was lying. Guilt stabbed her and cast a shadow on what had gone before. 'We had a celebration dinner in Kit's honour so he stayed up for it. He won the Junior Cup.'

'Tom's come to keep you company? No wonder your grandmother came in to check.' But he said it without any real interest, he even laughed. She knew just how important climbing was to him, she knew that today had been something he'd looked forward to, she knew he felt ten foot tall with pride in his son. 'The way Bertie took to the rocks, you'd better get used to having weekends on your own. The pips will go in a second. Any message for him?'

'Just say I'm glad he enjoyed it all. And tell him about Kit –' But her words were drowned by the sound of the pips, then the operator telling Nigel his time was up. If he wanted longer he must insert more money.

He'd said all he wanted to say; a click, the dialling tone and he was gone.

Back in the drawing room the light was bright, the rumpled cushions on the settee the only evidence of the last hour. Tom was standing by the uncurtained French window, a tidy Tom whose feet had been as firmly brought back to earth as her own.

'That was Nigel,' Katie told him unnecessarily. 'He said Bertie had done splendidly, loved it all. I'm glad. If he'd hated heights or something like that it would have been awful.'

'Something else for them to share. Bertie will be a man's man, Katie.' She wasn't certain if, like her, he was filling the silence with words or whether he meant to imply that Bertie wouldn't need her if Nigel was there.

'I'd better slip across and tell Granny I've heard. Pour yourself a drink or something, Tom.'

'No, Katie. I think this is the moment when I should go home.' Very gently he took her hand in his, willing her to meet his gaze. 'I meant every word I said. The only midsummer madness was in rushing too fast. I can't stay in Newton Dingley, I can't come here every day just as if this evening hadn't happened.'

Her fingers gripped his.

'Children don't stay babies,' he went on, 'another month and they'll be away at school. Look how Bertie is enjoying seeing himself as a man already, and he's only seven. As for the Manor, there's nothing Nigel would like as well as to have it to himself without your "old codgers", as he calls them.'

She shook her head.

'Not tonight, Tom. I don't want to think of any of it.' Not of his going away, her days having no bright hour when he visited the Manor; not of her going with him – the idea was impossible. If she were free, if she were the young girl he ought to be planning to share his life with, if she'd never known that perfect sense of belonging, if she'd never been consumed by love for two little boys who depended on her, if . . . if . . .

He raised her hands, first one then the other, kissing each palm. Then, his hazel eyes lighting with the smile she knew so well, he gave her what was almost a wink, somehow putting their friendship back on an even keel. Then he left her.

The chime of the grandfather clock in the drawing room was soft, but that night she heard each hour. She got out of bed and watched the first light of dawn; she got back into bed shutting her eyes tightly, determined to find sleep that eluded her; she was too tired to relax, she was emotionally drained. As the clock struck the hour of six she gave up her battle and threw back the covers. A bath revived her a little, but her reflection did nothing to cheer her. She looked wan, her skin had no glow, her eyes were sunk in dark shadows, her hair had no lustre. Just one evening could never have done this to her. She studied her face closely, wondering how long the change had been creeping up on her unnoticed. As if by cruel comparison her gaze fell on a framed photograph on her dressing table. A family group just before she left Higley Creek. Eighteen years old, so full of confidence in what was ahead. Now she was twenty-nine – and what was waiting in the wings for her? She closed her eyes, she didn't want to think.

A rattle on her door handle and a loud whisper: 'Mum? You awake, Mum?'

She turned from the mirror, glad of the interruption.

'Come in, Kit. Couldn't you sleep either?' She smiled at the skinny little figure in his blue and white striped pyjamas and, had she but known it, in that smile she regained some of the old sparkle.

'I thought I heard you. Mum, are you up 'cos you're going for a ride? Can I come? Shall we go on the Common?'

The long night was over.

'Sounds like a good idea. Race you getting dressed.'

If she rode in the early morning it was alone, only later in the day did the boys saddle up their ponies. There was a new excitement in the race to get dressed, a new companionship as they let themselves out through the east door and hurried across the yard to the stables. She knew Kit felt it too. For both of them today was a milestone. Like yesterday had been for Nigel and Bertie.

But as they galloped across the Common she had no idea just what a milestone that Sunday was to be.

With fishing nets, jam jars and, to bring a purpose to the exercise, an illustrated book of pondlife, they were on their hands and knees by the lake. The ducks clustered around them, quacking and jostling, sure in their bird brains that somewhere there must be something for them in the visit, even if it were no more than a few crusts of bread.

'Look, Mum. I got him. Just look at this beauty!' Helplessly the newt gave itself up. But Kit was careful, he lowered it gently into the jar of water then held it to the light, examining every detail.

'He's the champ,' Katie agreed. 'Look, something jumped, out there in the middle.'

209

Kneeling on the bank they both watched, waiting for the next rings on the still water. What they saw made their eyes open wide with momentary surprise before they turned expectantly.

Bertie must be back, was Kit's first thought, that and admiration that the stone had been thrown with such skill that it bounced five times before disappearing to the grey depths.

Tom's come, was Katie's thought – and something of the same admiration for his prowess.

'It can't be,' she said, barely audibly.

'Kate-ee.' Dylan moved towards them, his footsteps silenced by the mossy grass around the lake. 'I went to Higley – Lottie will have told you.' He said it without preamble, obviously expecting her to follow his meaning. Still kneeling at the edge of the water she looked up at him. How could she have forgotten the way he stressed each syllable? Hearing it now she knew he was nervous, as uncertain as she was herself.

'No. She's never mentioned you in her letters.' Her hands reached towards him as she stood up. 'Dylan . . .' She couldn't think straight, couldn't go further than that she was seeing him. Suddenly, as if it were a dream, she could feel his hands gripping hers. Then her mind came alive again. Kit was scrambling to his feet. One look at his muddy knees and she was aware of the state of her own. As if it mattered! Dylan was here, here with her, here with Kit.

'You've come back to Redman's?' With an effort she took charge of her voice, making herself speak to him as though he were any other unexpected visitor. Then, without waiting for him to answer: 'Kit, this is an old friend from back home. I knew him when I was a wee thing.'

'Your eldest?' Dylan took the hand that Kit politely held in his direction. Dylan was here, he was speaking to Kit, touching Kit, smiling at Kit. Katie's mouth was dry. If she tried to speak she felt her tongue would be too stiff to move. So she nodded.

'Kate-ee.'

Kit looked from one to the other. What was he thinking? Katie put an arm around his shoulders.

'Yes, this is Kit. Bertie is not quite a year younger – he's away for the weekend with Nigel in Wales. You say you went to Higley Creek? I wonder why Mom didn't mention it to me?'

His slight shrug implied that he knew exactly why she hadn't mentioned it.

'We've been pond dipping,' Kit told him. 'This one is a newt. Do you know newts?'

Dylan took the jar and examined it admiringly. All of them concentrated their attention on the newt. A lake in the grounds of this ancestral home . . . a far cry from the wilderness where Dylan had learnt to fish and hunt.

This is your son . . . our son! Katie wanted to shout it aloud. Then another thought struck her. 'This is an old friend from home' – that's how she'd introduced him. Not: 'This is my half-brother.' A hysterical laugh rose in her. If that's what she'd called him, then one stage further and Kit would have been saying, 'Uncle Dylan'.

'I'm going to let him go,' Kit was announcing.

'Let's come and watch him swim free.' Moving back to the water Dylan had a hand on Kit's slight shoulder.

Anyone might have said the same thing. But he wasn't just anyone, he was Dylan. His words conjured up for Katie a picture of the open spaces, the wilderness of forest, the land of her childhood.

'You asked me if I was at Redman's,' he said when the newt had vanished into the murky waters and Kit straggled off with his net. 'Amongst other places. I'm only in England a few days. It was important I came – and Redman's offered me a reason. So she never mentioned my visit? Even Lottie.'

Kit was kneeling on the footbridge now, safely out of earshot and engrossed in dipping his net into the weeds in deeper water.

'If Mum didn't write about it, she must have thought it was kinder for me not to know. But she told you about me? That I married Nigel, that I have two sons.'

'How could you do it, Kate-ee? Not to tell me, to send me away without telling –'

'How could I tell you what I didn't know myself? Anyway there was nothing else for us to do. Please, Dylan, don't lets open all the old hurts.'

If only she could read his thoughts, but Dylan's expression was inscrutable as he said: 'You gave Nigel my son. If any man has a right to that child it must be me. Look at him. Look at me.'

'I do. Every time I look at him I see you. Gave him to Nigel, you say? So easy for you, off back to Canada, no idea of what was going on here. Nigel knew the whole story. He married me knowing I was pregnant with my brother's child?'

'If you'd had any faith in me you'd never have believed it. Did I not swear to you it wasn't the truth?'

'Rosie's word! Anyway, it's finished. It was years ago. We've all moved on, made different lives. Kit belongs here with me. Your part in it was over before it even started.' She hit back.

She stood some feet from him now, frightened to come close. Just for that one moment she'd felt the touch of his hand. If she moved near, would she be strong enough not to reach out to him? Just to

211

hold him, to feel his arms around her, the warmth of his breath . . . So she hit out at him, sheltering behind words that would wound.

'Yes, he's yours. He's yours and he's mine, Kate-ee. I am not your brother, I told you so and you would not believe me. Now I have come to know my father, my real father.' She opened her mouth but no words came. All these years, all the misery . . . things could have been so different. 'Had I been your brother, even so had I no right to my son? There was no sin in the love we felt.'

'I tell you, we've moved on. We were so young.'

'Young? You mean me to believe it was just a passing phase for you? That all the time you were in love with Nigel Matheson?' His voice mocked.

She couldn't lie, not about that. So instead she asked: 'What have the nine years brought for you, Dylan? A wife maybe? Children?'

Yet it was a shock when he replied: 'I am married, yes. To Shara. We have a daughter, Kamma. Your son is as dark as a raven; my daughter is blonde. Not golden hair as yours was, but so blonde it is almost without colour at all.'

'And Shara?'

'Yes, she is fair. Although she was born in the United States she has the colouring of her Scandinavian ancestors. We have been married for five years.'

'Is she with you? You must bring her to the Manor, Nigel and I would like to meet her.' She seemed to stand outside herself, listening to the casual friendliness of the invitation.

'She is not with me. I came alone to England. Shara is in Wyndhamslake.' He looked towards Kit, making sure he was too far away to hear and too busy with his net to be interested. 'Anyway, do you really think I would bring her here? Kate-ee, I must talk to you. Please. I have come just for that. There was no need for me to be the one to visit England, I used it as a chance to see you. All these years I've stayed away, purposely I've not returned. I am a coward, I could not bear to come here with you gone.'

'Gone? But I've always been here.'

'Have you forgotten? You were here with your great-grandmother, you were on holiday. I have talked with my father – I will tell you about that later – and as soon as I could I went to Higley Creek. What I expected I do not know. As you say, I am married. I could hardly have believed that you would not be. In any case, Lottie deserved to know the truth. She told me the rest – your marriage, your children. Why, Kate-ee, why? Even if the story had been true and we had shared the same father, we both had a right to our son.'

Fearfully she looked at Kit. She felt threatened.

'That's not true. I was a single girl. The baby was mine, no one else's but mine. You had no rights. You have no rights.'

He turned away, walking to the edge of the lake, silently watching Kit. She knew this time she'd hurt him. She couldn't help herself. A will greater than her own made her move to his side, almost timidly take his hand in hers, twining her fingers around his.

'Oh, Kate-ee.' His voice was tight, his jaw held rigid as he clung to self-control. 'What fools we've been.'

She nodded.

'It wasn't like you said,' she whispered. 'Just a passing phase. You know it wasn't.'

'I know. For you and for me. Tell me about Kit. Kitashee? Is that why you call him Kit?'

'His name's really Christopher. I expect people think of it just as an abbreviation of that. You like it?'

'Of course I do. Tell me about him.'

So she did. About the closeness between the two boys, about Kit's strengths and his weaknesses – but never a word to hint that Nigel treated him as though he didn't exist. She finished by bringing him up-to-date with: 'And yesterday was the gymkhana. Remember the gymkhana?'

'I even remember the dried sandwiches with curling corners and the steam from that hideous thing they poured tea out of. I remember the smell in the tent: warm grass, steam, canvas. You said that because you'd been there, absorbed it, you'd always have it as part of you. I did not understand, not at the time. Only later. That day, all our days, all our hours, they are part of me for ever.'

'Me, too,' she croaked.

'The gymkhana?' For both of them it was hard to talk, to keep their faces bright in case Kit looked their way. 'Did you ride?'

'Sure I did. I got a rosette. But Kit! Kit was the hero of the day. Dylan, *your* son rode away with the Junior Cup.'

Somehow that broke through the emotions that had threatened them. Her voice was full of pride, and it was reflected in his.

'Kit!' he shouted. 'Your mom has been telling me you won the Cup. Well done! May I have a go with that net? Why should you be having all the fun?'

Katie didn't follow him on the bridge. Instead she went to sit on Lavinia's "thinking seat". There were less trees around the lake than there had been in those days. All except one, the beautiful tall elms had had to be felled. On this side of the lake there was very little shade. The sun was hot. She closed her eyes and raised her face to it, thinking of what Dylan had said about the gymkhana tent. It was

213

true. Let me hold on to this, she pleaded silently. Always let it be there for me, this moment, the sound of their voices, Kit laughing, the water rippling as they pull up the net. Help me to take it into my memory . . . into my soul.

'Kate-ee.' She pulled herself back with a start. The sun had moved lower in the sky, the jam jar had been emptied back into the lake. She glanced at her watch. More than an hour had passed.

'We must go home.' She stood up. 'Dylan, will you come to see Nigel, have dinner with us?' It sounded formal. It was the invitation Kit would expect to hear.

'That's kind.' Dylan played his part. 'I'm here so briefly this time. May I ring you if I find it possible?'

They even shook hands. He ruffled Kit's hair and was rewarded by a smile that lit eyes that were a replica of his own. Then they parted, he towards the main gate and the village, they up the slope of the park to the house.

At the foot of the steps of the Manor was a soft top car.

'Dr Tom's here, Mum. Shall we go and tell him about our pond dipping?'

'In this muddy state?' She laughed. 'Best we go home and wash our knees.' She wasn't ready to face Tom, she wasn't ready to face anyone. To lock herself in the bathroom and hide in a tub of hot water was a coward's way out, but more than anything at this moment – more than anything possible at any rate – that's what she wanted. To be where no one could reach her, no one could disturb her thoughts as she dug into her mind to recall each word.

With Bertie sleeping in the other bed, Kit didn't even think of going to his mother's room to enquire if she was riding early on Monday morning. When Bertie and Nigel were away, Katie belonged just to him. Now they were a family again, each with their allotted role. In fact Kit didn't even wake to hear her creep down the stairs, her riding boots in her hand.

This morning Katie harnessed Black Knight and led him out of the stable. She usually rode Cleo, but not always. She felt she had a special responsibility for Black Knight. The years had sobered him, he wasn't as spirited as he had been, but if she wanted a hard gallop then he was her mount. Today though she took him for a different reason and as she put him into a canter along the track that led to the Common her heart was hammering. Fear that he wouldn't be there? Excitement in the certain knowledge that he would?

'I hoped you'd come,' she greeted him as he climbed down from the gate where he'd been waiting. 'We didn't say – but I expected you.'

'Of course. We have such a short time, I'll not waste any of it.'

'I should have brought Cleo,' she said, seeing he was in breeches and sweater. Always Katie wore jodhpurs, hacking jacket and, these days, a hard hat too, something she'd never used nine years ago when they ridden together. 'Here, you take Black Knight. You gallop him. I'll watch.'

'Indeed you won't. I will mount behind you. Move your feet from the stirrups. Hah!' As he settled towards the back of the saddle and drew her close against him. 'Kate-ee, the little girl I used to ride with so long ago.'

Black Knight started forward. No hard gallop this morning, just a steady canter. Katie leant back against Dylan. His arms gripped her like a vice even though his hands were light on the reins.

'Two mornings, three . . .? I ought to be so happy. I never expected to see you again, Dylan.'

He'd brought them to the copse at the edge of the Common. Now he dismounted and held up his arms to lift her down.

'Take that silly hat off.'

Willingly she did and with it seemed to dispel some of the shadows. She sat on the grass at the edge of the copse, her arms around her drawn up knees.

'Black Knight won't wander. Just let his reins hang down, he'll get the message. He's a wise chap. Dylan, tell me about you, about your father, Shara, Kamma? Tell me how the years have been for you. Yesterday we didn't get much further than Kit.'

'Who would want to go further than Kit? He is a very fine boy.' He lay down on the mossy grass at her side gazing into the high morning sky. 'Do you think Katie, my Kate-ee, that there is a god somewhere in that infinity who holds our destiny in his hand? We mortals make a mess, we snatch greedily, we let pride be our master. Then something like this happens. You and me. Remember that last evening? How you accused me of always knowing about your father, knowing and yet using you.'

'I don't want to remember it.'

'Yes, you must hear me. It was true that I knew what was said in court, it was true that Rosie told me afterwards it had been a lie, it was true too that I'd known Rosie always lie if it suited her to. I could no more believe one thing she said than another.'

'But that's dreadful! I was sure you were wrong to believe her, but I never doubted that you had. And all the time you . . .'

'Can't you trust me even now? I guess I grew up pretty close to nature. Animals live by their instinct. I never cared what Rosie said. No, nor who she said it to. I remember Neil O'Hagon. Often enough he came to the shack when I was supposed to be asleep on the couch. That man was nothing to me. If he'd been my father I would have felt something, surely I would? When you were a little kid I would have given my life if you'd needed me to – but I never felt a family bond with you. And later, when we met again, do you think it could have been like it was if we'd been brother and sister? Nature doesn't have brothers and sisters falling in love.'

'Oh, but Dylan, I've heard of cases –'

'Oh, sure, they've got together sometimes. Maybe they've been let down by nature, not been the same as normal folk.' The air was still, no movement stirred the leaves. Lying on his back he raised his arm, let his fingers gently touch her cheek. 'Nine years, my Kate-ee, nine long years. But nothing has changed. Not for me – and not for you.' He said it would certainty, reading into her heart as deeply as he could his own.

She covered his hand, then moved it to her mouth, not to much kissing his fingers as letting her lips graze them as she mumbled: 'If only we could go back those nine years, have a second chance.' Even as she said it a cold stab of fear prodded her. Whose lives was she bargaining with? Kit's, Bertie's, Kamma's? Too late to call back the words, she looked higher into the clear morning sky.

I didn't mean it. Please don't let anything awful happen to them, don't bargain with me – don't make things go wrong for them then give me Dylan to make up for it. I didn't mean it like that. We can't go back, I know we can't. And I have Kit, I have Bertie.

'The years only go one way, Kate-ee my darling. I loved you when were two, three, however old you were; when you were nineteen, twenty. Now we're nine years on, but nothing has altered. For us it never could.'

She nodded, understanding the truth of what he said. What else was there to say? What was between them was part of their very being. Nine years or ninety, it could make no difference. From out of nothing there flashed into her mind a picture of her gazing at herself in the bedroom mirror, the sense of loss that the bloom of first youth was lost. She smiled, remembering. Turning to lie on her side she studied Dylan: his skin had coarsened, his black hair was prematurely shot with grey. None of those things mattered. Moving closer to him she rested her head against his shoulder. His lips touched her forehead, she raised her head, his mouth covered hers. In the copse a blackbird sang its solitary hymn to the morning.

The Common was their own at this hour. But apart from that kiss they came no nearer than lying on their backs, side by side, fingers linked as they gazed at the outline of the leaves against the sky.

216

'Tell me about your father,' she prompted. 'How did you know who he was?'

'His name is Mick Finney – Irish, as if you can't guess. Rosie died a few months back. It was when she was very ill, she must have known she wasn't going to get better. She sent me a message, telling me where she was in hospital, saying she wanted to tell me things. Oh, I know what you say, but this time she had no reason to hide anything. Since she's died I've talked about it to Mick, I know her story was the truth. It seems he was married with sons when he got entangled with her. She found she was pregnant, she knew he'd never leave his wife – anyway I don't think she wanted him to, a permanent man would have had no place in Rosie's life. She didn't tell him that, though. She threatened to go to his wife with her story if he didn't pay her to keep quiet. It was just then that she met Neil, a boy of only fifteen and a useful tool, for if tales were ever carried to Mick's wife she could accuse Neil. For her the important thing was the little handouts that Mick would put her way.

'When she left Radley after Neil's inquest she went west to British Columbia knowing where she could find Mick. I joined up with her after I cleared off from Higley Creek, you know that. I told you ages ago how by that time I'd made my mind up to learn everything I could – not just to do better than my own folk, but to do better than the white kids in school. I got taken up by the head teacher at the school I went to. What I didn't know until I talked with Mick after Rosie died was that at the time I turned up she was after him for money; it says quite a bit for Rosie that when she realised he couldn't afford to do much for her, she agreed that he'd help me instead. I didn't know any of this, of course, only that I was to go to school.

'This head teacher was an Irishman. He and Mick were friends. I shouldn't think Mick told him who I was – although thinking about it, I figure he must have been blind if he hadn't guessed – but he worked hard with me. Most evenings I went back to the schoolhouse trying to catch up and then to get ahead. It was he who pushed me so I got a place at college. I knew all that, I knew that it was he who suggested I should go into the pulp industry – but I had no idea about Mick's part until Rosie came clean about the whole thing. He's in charge of a spruce plantation in the north of the Province. I'd come in contact with him in the course of business, we'd got along well. Of course all the time he knew I was his son.'

'And you see him still? You can be open about it now?' She was glad for Dylan. For a moment she remembered the little boy in a hospital bed, turning away so they wouldn't see he was crying. Her fingers tightened on his. Now he wasn't alone. But that was silly. Of course he wasn't alone. What about Shara waiting for him at home? What about Kamma?

Katie sat up and reached for her hard hat.

'I must go. Are you going to ride me back on Black Knight or is your time your own?'

'I'll walk. It would hardly do for you to be seen sharing your saddle with me.'

She led Black Knight to the trunk of a felled elm, then stood on it to use it for a mounting block, swinging easily into the saddle.

'Katie, I shan't be in Newton Dingley much during my visit. Here, this is a list of my engagements. Read it and tell me: when can we be together?'

She read his itinerary. Such a short time, most of it accounted for. As she folded the paper and passed it back to him she leant down from her high seat and whispered something. She had no sense of guilt.

Katie wanted to smile as she hurried across Trafalgar Square. Ahead of her an old woman was scattering food for the pigeons, to be rewarded by a flock of them descending like a crowd of bargain hunters at a jumble sale. From all directions they came, some running, some swooping from on high, rushing as if they hadn't had sight of food for a week. They gave Katie the excuse she wanted. She laughed openly. Into her mind jumped the memory of her childhood dreams, her picture books of London. For her, this had always been the very heart of the city. It was as if in her subconscious she'd always known that it would play a part in one of her life's important moments. Four o'clock, that was the hour they were to meet. She was five minutes early, but wanted to be waiting, to see him coming towards her.

Trafalgar Square, the foot of the steps of the National Gallery. The unoriginality of their choice of rendezvous pleased her. Over the years how many thousands of people had come together here? Now it was her turn, hers and Dylan's. In less than twenty-four hours she'd be home again, he'd be flying back to Vancouver. Yet her heart was bursting with such wild happiness. These few hours were their own, they were out of reach of all their responsibilities, they belonged just to each other. Today, tonight, couldn't be dimmed by thoughts of tomorrow – all the tomorrows. As she negotiated the traffic and came to the pavement by the National Gallery the future played no part in her thoughts. Dylan was there ahead of her, the present left no room to spare for anything but this.

He didn't kiss her. The grip of his hand on hers, the expression in his light blue eyes, told her all she wanted to know.

218

'I meant to be first. I wanted to watch for you.' Would he understand?

It seemed he did.

'That's why I was early. Looking across the square, then one way, then another, so many people, and in a minute I knew one of them would be you.'

So many people, all of them strangers, all of them suddenly so far removed that they might have been on another planet. She leant against him, she could feel the beat of his heart through his thin shirt.

'Have you booked us a room somewhere?' she asked unnecessarily.

'Of course. Somewhere suitably respectable. In Kensington. Later we'll walk through the park, but first of all, Kate-ee, I want to buy a large bag of peanuts and feed the London pigeons. Isn't that what all visitors from overseas are expected to do?'

It was a long time since Katie had been a visitor from overseas, yet suddenly that was what she was. More than a third of her life had been spent here in England, without her realising it she'd lost much of the accent of home. Yet, quite naturally, talking to Dylan hers was a voice of Canada just as surely as his. He'd only been to London once before and that time she'd shared with him too. Now she wanted to see it anew, her vision to be his.

From a street vendor he bought his bag of nuts.

'Take your picture, lady?' another one accosted them, his camera poised.

Even without a photograph they would have remembered those moments, but there it was in black and white, Dylan with as scruffy a bird as one could find even here walking down his arm to feed from his hand, Katie scattering her largesse around her feet. She shut her eyes tight, trying to record on her memory the sounds of the noisy city. In the still silence of Bullington she would re-kindle these seconds . . . no, she mustn't think ahead to that. She opened them again to find Dylan watching her. Tomorrow was forgotten.

'I have to buy a toothbrush,' she told him presently. 'I came up to London to deliver a brooch to Madame d'Arc's niece in Muswell Hill and to get some books the boys need for school. I'll phone a bit later and say I shan't be back tonight.'

'You will have to give a reason, tell a lie. Katie, it won't spoil anything?'

'It's for their sakes that I shall make up excuses. For myself I'm where I want to be, where I should be.'

And her conscience still slumbered peacefully when on the way to dinner she stopped to telephone Nigel.

'I took much longer than I expected getting to Muswell Hill, then I couldn't just rush away. Madame d'Arc's niece made me so welcome. I've really had a lovely time wandering around the shops – and I've got the books the boys had on their list for school. I didn't want to drive out of London in the rush. I thought I'd hang back till it quietened down. But now I just don't feel like a long drive with it getting darker, so I've found myself a room. Maybe I'll see if can get a seat for a theatre.'

'I say, I wish you'd said what you were doing. I'd have come up too. "Blithe Spirit" is at the Globe. Why don't you try that?'

'Maybe I will. Give my love to the boys. Say I'll be home tomorrow morning.'

They dined, they wined, they danced. Later they hailed a taxi to take them to Marble Arch car park where she'd left her car.

'Once in a world, a city like London,' Dylan murmured, her hand tightly in his. 'Won't you just listen to that chugging engine! London taxis, London voices, London pigeons.'

This afternoon he'd talked of them as visitors from overseas so, like him, that's what she'd been; now, just as suddenly, his words made a visitor of himself while the very things that set London apart for him had become part of her life. The shadow of tomorrow was falling on them.

All through the evening they'd looked ahead, happy with the moment but sure of where it was leading them. Now, lying close in his arms, the years between seemed to melt away. So many times she'd tried to reach him, her body the vehicle that must bring him close. Tonight he was real, he was flesh and blood, warm, needing her just as she needed him.

Sometimes during the night they talked softly, the honest talk that daylight would have made impossible. At home she had two sons, at home he had a daughter. In the years since they'd parted they'd both shaped their lives, laid down paths that they must travel separately.

'In the infinity of time and space, Kate-ee, your soul and mine are one. Wherever we are, the one truth we are sure of is that our essential beings can never be divided.'

If anyone else had said it, it would have sounded overblown. But not from Dylan. What he said was something to be accepted as unquestioningly as the great infinity of sky, the boundless oceans, the power of nature.

They fought against sleep. Only as dawn was colouring the sky was the battle lost. And afterwards Katie was glad, for if they hadn't slept, they couldn't have woken to find themselves lying close, their heads sharing the same pillow.

So soon the magic hours were over. He'd gone through the customs barrier at Heathrow and she was driving westwards along the motorway. Even the weather had broken. A steady rain was falling. By now his plane would have taken off, he would be looking down on a carpet of cloud, the clear blue sky above him. The drone of the traffic became for Katie the drone of an aircraft engine, the monotonous swish of the windscreen wiper the only other sound. Miles slipped by. It was the long hoot of a lorry horn that brought her back to reality. With instantaneous reaction she turned back into her own lane, her heart beating hard. At the next exit she left the motorway, preferring to travel on the old Great West Road. How magical it had sounded as she'd weaved her childhood dreams of England. She'd imagined into its name a link between where she was and the country she meant one day to come to, a country steeped in an antiquity she'd felt drawn to. And now? Today 'West' meant the places that were Dylan's, the forests, the mountains. The Great West Road. If only it were, if only
. . .

Guilt stabbed her. At home the boys would be waiting.

Chapter Fourteen

On arriving, the first person she saw was Madame d'Arc.

'Your husband told Mrs Menzies that you were staying in town overnight. I have been at the window waiting for your return.' She called from just inside the open front door, speaking as she always did in an indeterminate accent. Katie had often wondered whether it was real or assumed and, having met Stella Black, her brother's unmarried daughter from Muswell Hill, her suspicions were confirmed. Estelle d'Arc was as English as any of her companions. 'We were getting alarmed that you were taking so long to drive home.'

'It's the weather, Madame d'Arc. I hate the motorway in the rain. I didn't rush – not like most of the lorries did! They rattle along throwing up clouds of wet.'

'I am so sorry. And you did it just to please me. Come into my room –'

'I wish I had the time.' It was the sort of lie Katie permitted herself, 'but the boys will be waiting for me.'

'Katie dear, you're home!' Kate greeted her. 'And how was "Blithe Spirit"? Dear Nigel was quite envious. Such a shame you hadn't told him you might be staying overnight, he could have gone with you. These unexpected little treats must mean so much when you're young.' She managed to imply that such little treats had never come the way of her own youth.

'The traffic was so heavy, at first I thought I'd wait until the worst was over. But then it would have been dark before I got here and I'd really had quite a day.' How easy it was to lie. She was building such a clear picture of her trip, she could almost believe it herself! 'Anyway I didn't go to the Globe, I went to the Old Vic, saw "The Merchant of Venice".' No one could catch her out about that, she knew the play too well.

Professor Hardaker and Miss Routh were playing backgammon in the morning room. Hearing Katie's voice he called: 'Come in and speak to us, my dear, tell us how you fared in the wicked city.'

Already the Manor was closing in around her. Hearing her voice the residents were drawn to her like moths to a flame. She'd been away only twenty-four hours, but because she'd been to London, seen the lights of Piccadilly Circus, heard the roar of the traffic, been to the theatre and felt that hush of anticipation as the house lights were lowered, so in hearing about it their lives would be enriched; at second hand they could share it all, memories that had dimmed in their minds would be re-kindled.

'There was a little band of musicians in Oxford Street,' she started to tell them, this time truthfully, 'only a few players, but they made you want to dance.'

'I know! I know!' little Miss Routh interrupted. 'Dressed in red like bandsmen. One with a piano accordion, one with a trumpet, one with a saxophone.'

'That's it, and the fourth shaking a collecting box. "Here we go a-wandering",' she sang, '"amidst the leaves so green". You just had to walk in time to the music.'

Miss Routh's pinched face broke into a beam. 'I know them! I remember! Up and down the street they go. Wherever you are, there they seem to be. Fancy, they're still there!' Whether the jolly musicians who'd set Katie's toes tapping were the same as Miss Routh remembered seemed unlikely, but no one suggested it.

Did you do this . . . or that . . . go here . . . or there? Questions were fired at her. Held secret and safe in her heart was what really mattered of her few short hours. Where was Dylan now? Not even in Greenland yet, where the plane was to land for re-fuelling. Like a child saving a special treat until last she looked ahead to being on her own, to re-living every precious moment. But that was for later and because she was so sure of it she was prepared to wait; this half hour belonged to the Manor. Such a silly picture to spring to her mind: a sow with its huge litter, all jostling for place, all suckling from her as she lay sprawled on her side! But was it so silly? She laughed with her elderly friends, she painted pictures that were larger than life. Just like Dylan's plane that was to take on fuel in Greenland, so they took theirs from her. Watching them it was brought home to her that life, no matter how comfortable, needed a stimulant. Already her mind was busy.

'Tom,' she said to him when he called the next morning, 'I want to organise a theatre trip. Will you come too? We'll hire a coach, we'll book seats in the stalls, we could even take them out to dinner first.

223

As long as everything was organised there's no reason why those who'd enjoy it can't have an outing, is there? Will you help me?'

'Katie, for days you've been avoiding me, now you ask me this. I'll come anywhere you want me to, you know I will. But you? Have you thought? Since Saturday I've not seen you by yourself. I couldn't know what your thinking. About us?'

How could she tell him that since Sunday afternoon whatever she'd been thinking hadn't included him!

'Tom, we're friends. No more than friends. Please, let's just forget Saturday.'

'You're telling me your answer is no. You want to stay here, in a marriage that is no marriage, with two sons away at school, making a home for people who don't belong to you? Is that what you want your life to be?'

'You make it sound pointless and empty. But it isn't. Since Saturday I've done a lot of thinking. I've been completely honest with myself. Most of the time we're guided by things we get upset about: by hurt, by pride, by all the things that when it comes down to it don't matter. So I've taken my heart and looked deep into it and I've found a sort of peace.'

'Peace or an easy way out?'

'Peace, Tom. I can't explain. O.K., I know what you're thinking. Nigel and I haven't the sort of relationship we might dream of when we tie our life to someone else's, and you're right about the boys. For the next ten years they'll be away at school a lot of the time, and afterwards they'll be turning into men. Except for Granny, the folk who live at the Manor have no part in my past – but for all that they've come to be important to me, every one of them, just like I suspect I'm important to them. None of that sounds like the recipe for a full life, you think? No, on it's own it isn't. But, like I said, I dug deep into my heart and I found a sort of peace that I'd lose if I reneged on any of those things.'

'You're wrong. The girl you were on Saturday night couldn't talk so coldly.'

She put her hand on his arm. She wished so much she could have told him the whole truth instead of only part of it.

'Even the Saturday night me couldn't live with herself if she said anything different. So what hope of happiness could we have? None. Can't we put it away from us, Tom, pretend none of it was said.'

But he couldn't.

'A theatre trip, you say?' His voice businesslike. 'If you make sure Matron and both the nurses are in the party, I don't see why not. If I'm here, of course I'll come. You'll need to do a lot of arranging – a coach booked for the day, the restaurant you decide on must be suitable for their needs, the theatre management must be made aware that some have trouble with steps. You'll cope with everything, I'm sure. And as I say, if I'm still here, I'll gladly come along and help Matron.'

She couldn't blame him for the stance he was taking, yet she was disappointed in him, and relieved that she'd been thrown from that downhill slope where she'd hurtled so willingly on Saturday. Tom's words distanced him from her. But it didn't matter, it didn't touch the kernel of truth that dwarfed everything else into insignificance. Steadily the fine drops of rain ran down the window pane, a thick blanket of cloud hung between the wet earth and the bright, clear sky. But above the cloud it was there, as certain and unchanging as the truth that was part of her and part of Dylan.

Two small boys stood in the driveway and watched as she and Nigel got back into the car for the journey home.

'They look so young,' she whispered, as much to herself as to him.

'I remember the day my parents left me here. I was half excited, half sick with fright.'

Bertie stood his ground, his mouth set in a grimace he believed to be a smile. Between father and son a silent message passed. With the driver's window wound down Nigel put out his hand sending a jaunty thumbs up; and back it came from Bertie.

'Mum!' It was Kit, a year older, who called out. Just the one word. Then he too raised his chin, taking a lead from Bertie. There were other small boys here for the first time. One of them was sitting on the swing, his face crumpled as he cried.

'It's cruel! Look at them, they're just babies.'

By now the car was moving forward. Swivelling as far round in her seat as she could, she strained to watch through the rear window until the boys were lost to sight and the car turned out on to the road.

'I've tried to prepare Bertie. He's young, probably about the youngest there, but he's man enough.' Nigel meant to reassure her.

'They both are,' she answered defiantly. 'But it's a damn fool system anyway.'

'Tom Wadham is talking about gong into a practice down on the south coast,' Nigel told her.

'He told me this morning. We shall miss him – us and the people at the Manor. He probably needs to move to something bigger than Newton Dingley. From a career point of view it's a bit of a dead end for someone of his age.'

How easy it was to say it. Six months ago the very idea of Tom's going would have thrown her future into a fog of uncertainty. Even now she was sorry, she wished he'd change his mind and stay; but his departure had no power to upset her life. Then Tom was forgotten. Jenny brought the morning post and put the silver salver in front of Nigel.

'Ah! One from Bertie. Oh, and this looks like Kit. Here, you take that, I'll open Bertie's.'

Both boys wrote: 'Dear Mum and Dad', but only one letter would be read by both of them. Occasionally Nigel glanced at Kit's, there had been one that had even brought a comment that 'his writing has improved', but no interest that he'd been selected for the Football Junior XI nor that he'd come top in a test of Latin verbs. There was no one except Katie to care about him. She even imagined writing to Dylan, taking her letter to Redman's and asking them to forward it. But of course it was no more than a pipe dream. They had chosen their path, a path that must be even harder for him than for her, knowing that Kit was growing up in a background so different from his own.

It was a Sunday morning in winter. The boys were already into their second year at prep school. From the pulpit of Saint John's Church, Newton Dingley, the vicar was in full spate. What the Reverend Bernard Rogers lacked in inspiration he more than made up for in dogged determination, seemingly believing that if he hammered home his message, phrasing a sentence first one way then, as if to put emphasis on the point, re-phrasing it another, and often a third as well, his flock would be more sure in their progress along the straight way he set for them.

Katie and Nigel were sitting, as they did each week, in the front pew. She suspected that Nigel came with such regularity, reading the lesson every fourth week, to uphold the family tradition. And she? If that had anything to do with it at all, it was for the boys' sake more than her own, to give them an anchorage in life's stormy seas; partly that, partly because not to come would somehow be to fail Lavinia. It took a stout heart to submit to Matins at St John's each week. Reverend Rogers' chanting was out of tune, his sense of timing non-existent, his sermons never less than twenty minutes – by the end of which both preacher and congregation had lost sight of the text he expounded. But to come here was a duty she never shirked.

'How long this morning I wonder? Bet you fifty pence he waffles for more than twenty minutes,' Nigel whispered as they waited for the choir to troop in.

'You don't believe in taking risks!' she giggled. 'You know what Professor Hardaker says about him? If he hasn't struck oil in five minutes, then he ought to stop boring!'

'Fat chance.' Even the fact that the remarks had come from one of her "codgers" didn't take the smile of his face. In these last few months they'd come close to the friendship they used to have. Was it because the boys weren't there, his favouritism of Bertie a constant thorn in her side? Not for a moment did she wonder whether the better atmosphere at home had anything to do with her own mood.

In the choir stalls young Derrick Dawkins, grandson of Polly from the greengrocery shop, inched his cassock higher and under cover of his white surplice let his fingers feel for the bag of sweets in his pocket.

Polly heard the paper rustle. Any other boy and she wouldn't care. He wasn't any other boy, though, he was her Derrick – and sitting only a yard or so away from the Mathesons too! Their boys wouldn't disgrace them like this! Let him just wait till she got him outside! Still, from the look of her, young Mrs Matheson wasn't paying any more attention to him than she was to the vicar. Don't know what we'd do here of a Sunday if we didn't get a few come along from the Manor. That little old soul on the end of the pew – didn't someone say she was Miss Routh? – nodded right off she has. And who can blame her? Just look at Mrs Bradley – leastways her that was Mrs Bradley for all those years. Always a pleasure to see her there in the family pew. She won't see seventy again, but bless me if she isn't the prettiest woman in this church. Make quite a picture, she and the Colonel, fine-looking old chap 'cept for that gamey leg. I bet a pound to a penny that young Mrs Matheson isn't hearing a word the vicar says. She's away in a land of her own. Not like him, Mr Nigel. A credit, that's what he s. A real credit to all of us.

Since early childhood "the credit" had trained himself to keep his eyes on the preacher while his mind went about its business. This morning it was concentrating on the need for a new silo at the Home Farm, and the catalogues which Frank had given him yesterday. He'd studied them all, now he was weighing one against another, prices and capacity. While hardly blinking he kept his gaze fixed on the Reverend Rogers.

Kate's mind was on the plans she was making for a Christmas party – not for the family, or at least only if they came as guests, but for her friends at the Manor. It was such a pleasure to have money of her own after all the years at Brimley, knowing herself to be the poor one of the family. Selling the house had put her a nice little nest-egg in the bank and dear Maurice wouldn't dream of touching a penny of it. She smoothed the fine leather of the dove grey gloves that lay in her lap, gently stretching each finger. She examined her own soft hands, the delicate pink of her nail varnish. Tut, but look at the naughty boy in the choir, chewing hard on a toffee that seemed to be stuck to his teeth. Children these days had no idea of how to behave. No, that wasn't true. She'd sat next to dear Bertie here sometimes. He'd been straight as a little soldier. What was Katie staring at? Was there something on the ceiling? Cobwebs? Perhaps she was trying to count the thousands of specks of dust in the beam of sunlight that came in through that high window. Dear me, twenty-two minutes! Really, Nigel ought to speak to Reverend Rogers, point out to him that people have their ovens to see to on a Sunday morning.

Of them all it was only Katie who wasn't kicking against the monotonous drone of Reverend Rogers' voice. And that was because, for her, sermon time was her own to let her mind go where it would. Most people at least followed the vicar for the first two or three minutes; lately she'd tuned out before he'd told them the text he'd chosen to speak on. Much of the service washed over her, but in the drone of the congregational prayers, in the familiarity of the words, she found a special sort of peace. And when the vicar mounted the pulpit steps she cocooned herself in thoughts, memories, dreams, safe from interruption.

There were two high windows on the eastern side of the church, each casting its beam of light: one was of stained glass and set in the chancel wall, sending a streak of colour to come to rest on the back of the organist as if he were at the end of a rainbow; the other was in the nave, equally high but made of plain glass, its beam of light clear and bright and, at this time of year, its mid-morning ray resting on those in the front pew. From nowhere the expression 'the beauty of holiness' came to her mind. It had nothing to do with the service, nothing to do with the message the vicar was trying to drive home, nor even the rainbow of light shining through the stained glass. A smile played at the corners of her mouth. She held her head high, feeling the pale winter warmth of the sun. The beauty of holiness . . . was that any different from the wonders of Dylan's great god of the infinity of time and space, his great god of earth and sky . . . of lakes and flowing waters, virgin forest that stretched into the horizon as far as the eye could see and the only creatures that walked were wild animals, of ice and snow, rotting leaves on the ground, the sound of wind in the trees, of the boundless oceans or the eternity of the sky above them. All of it unchanging, everlasting. The beauty of holiness . . . the dawn chorus on a spring morning, the silver dew on gossamer spider webs, the sun glinting on the water of the lake at Bullington, the gentle warmth of the sun that touched her face.

228

What was it Mom had said to her all those years ago about loving Dylan? That even if Neil O'Hagon had played no part in it, still it would have been impossible. They were of different cultures. Oh, but Mom, you're wrong. None of that matters, don't you see, his beauty of holiness and mine are the same thing, neither of us is any more important than those specs of dust in the sunlight. It's knowing it that matters, knowing that we're just an atom in that great infinity.

Nigel dug his elbow into her side, whispering: 'You owe me fifty pence.' The congregation was stretching to stand up.

The boys had started prep school together, but when it came to the natural progression at thirteen, Kit followed the Matheson tradition a year before Bertie. At Highland House on the edge of Newton Dingley his olive skin had set him apart from the other children, to a lesser degree it had in the first years at prep school, but not any more. As a child Dylan had resolved that not only in spite of the native blood that ran in his veins – diluted as it had become after two mixed generations – but because of it, he would beat his pale-skinned rivals; Kit was aware of no such hurdle. He was Matheson major of Bullington Manor. At the end of the first term at prep school he was top of his form, a position he never lost in his five years there and one which he was to maintain when, like generations of Mathesons before him, he took his place at one of the country's foremost public schools. How proud the child Dylan would have been if, some thirty years or more ago, a Spirit of the Future could have given him a glimpse of his son carrying away not only sports day medals for running and pole vaulting but, at the Annual Prizegiving, bound volumes to take home for his bookshelf for his attainment in English Literature, French, Latin, and Science too. It seemed Kit had inherited more than his appearance from his father. With it had come the determination to concentrate the whole of his ability on what he meant to conquer.

Bertie was a year behind him, his place in form nearer the top than the bottom, but always comfortably sandwiched between those who did worse and those who did better, all of them his friends. Football – giving way when he was thirteen to rugby – cricket, rowing, anything that required strength and stamina, here Bertie flourished. He was never lazy, but for him there was so much more to life than book work. When Kit mounted the platform to collect his prizes, Bertie clapped louder than anyone, every bit as proud as if he'd won them himself. Each followed his own natural bent, yet the closeness between the two boys never changed.

And another thing that didn't alter was that when they came home on holiday Nigel gave all his attention to only one of them.

229

'It's just that it seems a bit rough on poor old Kit.' Bertie hated unfairness. Since he'd been small he'd tried again and again to persuade his father to let Kit join them when they went off on their frequent expeditions. 'This time I suppose it's a bit different – Kit never has come climbing with us so he's not had the experience. But Gran, the first day of the holidays when Dad and I were sailing, Kit handles the sails every bit as well as I do – he's learnt at school. But Dad made excuses not to take him.'

'I can understand how he feels,' Kate looked at Bertie affectionately. 'You and your father are two of a kind. He looks forward so much to your coming home for your holidays.' Such a dear boy, no wonder Nigel was proud of the way he was developing.

She and Maurice had had their chairs brought into a sheltered corner of the kitchen garden. It was a part of the grounds not frequented by the other residents, and a place full of memories of happy childhood days. She was always proud to bring Maurice here, a special place where he was entitled to come because his wife was a Matheson. It wasn't quite the end of March but the sun tried to tease them into believing it was May already. Shut your eyes and you could imagine the drone of bees. Seeing them out there Katie had come to join them, perching herself on an upturned wooden wheelbarrow.

Always on the defensive where Kit was concerned, she snapped: 'Kit doesn't need to go where he's not wanted. You won't find him hanging about not knowing what to do with himself because you and Nigel have gone off without him.'

Bertie looked even more puzzled.

'That wasn't what I meant about the three of us going together, Mum. It's just for the fun of . . .' His words faded into silence as Nigel joined them.

'Is Bertie telling you about the trip? We shall get away before first light, about five o'clock, make a stop somewhere on the road for breakfast. Have you checked the gear, Bertie?'

'Yes, Dad. Everything's ready to be loaded into the Land Rover.'

'We were just saying before you joined us, Nigel my boy, it's a shame you don't give more of your attention to Kit.' The Colonel feared no man's wrath, and it was time someone spoke up. 'Oh, I know he's a serious scholar, not the sort to have an idle mind. But, dash it, he's a sportsman too. Could outride anyone I know. I remember watching them when they were just scraps of lads – he could run like a hare. None of my business, I dare say, but you and he will inevitably be thrown together as the years catch up on you. Why can't you build towards it, let it come naturally?'

'Things are quite all right as they are,' Nigel answered, his words actually meaning: "Don't interfere in what's not your business."

But Colonel Menzies hadn't been awarded the Military Medal for running away from difficult situations. Kit was a fine young fellow, both the boys were. It must be because Nigel was so besotted with Bullington, saw Kit's interest in the place as a threat. Yes, especially his interest in anyone living in the Manor. That was something young Nigel couldn't abide. Stupid of him. Time didn't stand still for him any more than for anyone else. So, going straight to the heart of the matter, he looked Nigel in the eye and said: 'The boy is your heir. Dash it all, this estate is the common ground for you to build on.' Nigel's look might have silenced most people, but not Maurice. 'No good hiding from it, in the end you will hand on the reins. Get used to pulling together, man. If you're not careful you'll make an enemy of your own son.'

Katie could see how Nigel's colour heightened, how his mouth was working with an anger that was rare in him.

'Talking of Kit,' she tried to turn the subject away from dangerous ground, 'where is he? Why don't you go and find him, Bertie? If you're going off first thing in the morning, this afternoon might be a chance to take out the canoe.'

'Hand over the reins?' Nigel cut in as if she'd not spoken. 'To him? By Christ, that I never will! There's only one person who will become master here, and that's my own son.'

Colonel Menzies looked at them over the top of his spectacles, his blue eyes worried. Kate held her hand to her mouth, a hand that shook. Bertie couldn't understand. Of course Bullington would one day go to Dad's son, so what was he saying?

It was as if all movement was stilled. Then, breaking the silence, Katie stood up so suddenly that the wheelbarrow tipped.

'Bullington has two sons. Kit is the elder and it's time you remembered it.'

'You bitch!' Beads of perspiration stood out on Nigel's forehead. Full of hatred, his blue eyes stared just at her. For him there was no one there but the two of them, the fragile friendship they'd built so carefully shattered like a house of cards.

'Dad, you can't talk like that to Mum,' Bertie blurted. 'Please Dad, Mum, please don't row.' Bertie was fifteen, he hadn't cried for years, now he was ashamed at the way his voice croaked. He couldn't bear to see how they were looking at each other.

It was a long time since anyone had seen Kate "turn the taps on", but now she trembled as she wept. Maurice reached to take her hand, but uppermost in his mind was the way Nigel was speaking to Katie. Disgraceful to treat a woman like it! And what had he meant about handing on to 'his son'?

There was only one thing at the top of Katie's mind: Kit. He'd been brought up to believe himself a Matheson. Matheson major. He was confident, he was ambitious, he loved Bullington. He had to be protected. Yet even as she thought all those things another voice in her screamed out: "Tell him, let him know he is Dylan's son, let him remember him and be proud." Oh, but how little he had to remember, and how could he be proud to be told that all these years he'd been tolerated but not loved? Her eyes filled with tears. Not loved? She ached with love for him. It was a physical thing, her arms and legs were weak with love. Her firstborn son, hers and Dylan's, the boy she'd built her life around . . . but Nigel was talking, his voice harsh with hatred.

'I've kept my mouth shut. All these years the family have kept your shabby secret. I even imagined you were coming to your senses. It seems I was wrong. Well, I've come to the end. I watched you crawl your way into Grandma's affections and steal what should have been mine. I watched the way you threw yourself at that filthy scum. I've given a name to his bastard son – but by God in heaven he'll get nothing else from me. You've filled my home with strangers –' words that turned Kate's taps full on ' – now you tell me I should remember Kitashee's bastard is heir to Bullington! By Christ, I'll swing for him first.'

An outburst like this from a man whose moods were variable couldn't have unnerved them as this did. In the last few years Nigel and Katie's relationship had assumed a veneer which to a stranger might have given the impression of a happy marriage. And all this time he'd been eaten up with hatred – for her, and for Kit. It was as if his true feelings had been held in a strait-jacket. Now suddenly they'd burst free. One look at Bertie told her there was no turning back. She reached to take the boy's hand in hers, but Nigel was ahead of her. Somehow he was standing with an arm around Bertie's shoulders. His manner seemed to say it was the two of them against the world.

'It's O.K., Bertie.' Katie couldn't bear to see that lost look in his eyes. 'Maybe your father's right and it's time you were all told the truth. Kit's father was from back home. I'd known him when I was not much more than a baby, then he came to England and I met him again. He's a fine man. Kit wasn't the product of some sleazy affair like your father's trying to say.'

'If you're telling your sob story, then let's have the whole thing.' The sneer in Nigel's tone shocked her. How could they have lived together with so much bitterness and hatred hidden in his heart? 'This fine man who got you pregnant then cleared off and left you to disgrace the family . . . go on, tell them who he was. You won't?

232

Then let me! He was your brother, that's who he was. Your father's half-breed bastard son.'

'It's not true! I know that's what we thought, but it's not true. I should have believed him. I should have trusted him.'

Maurice pulled himself to his feet, reaching for Kate.

'Come, Kate my dear, I think we ought to go in.'

'I'm so ashamed,' she wept. 'To hear my family behave like it. All these years I've been frightened of the day the truth would come out – now, today, just when I believed nothing could spoil the feeling of spring being here again. I'm so ashamed.' Only Maurice listened to her, taking her arm and leading her towards the gate in the high brick wall. A stroll in the gardens would give her a chance to get over her tears before they came face to face with any of their friends.

'You mean Kit's not my proper brother?' Bertie blurted. 'You're just saying hateful things because you want to hurt each other. Stop it, can't you? Anyway,' he pulled away from Nigel and turned to glare at him as he shouted in a voice quite unlike his own, 'even if it's all true, it's not his fault. If you say rotten things about Kit I'm not going with you, not any more.'

It was hearing himself shouting at his father that destroyed all hope of his retaining control of himself. Now he was blubbering, his face contorted. 'Everything was fine. What did you have to mess it all up for? Both of you! You too, Mum. Why can't we be an ordinary, proper family like other people? But we never have been! Dad and me, you and Kit. Not like other families, never all four of us. I thought it was Dad's fault.' Once started he didn't seem able to stop. Now it was Katie he turned on. 'But it wasn't Dad's, it was yours. And what about Kit? You can't tell Kit! Bad enough for him to know Dad doesn't like him. You can't tell him he doesn't even belong.'

With an exclamation that might have been 'Bah!', Nigel turned and left them.

'One day I shall tell him.' Katie was amazed at how calm she felt. 'And when I do he'll be the richer for it, not the poorer.' How could he not be? Nigel had never been a father to him. To lose him and gain Dylan, even a Dylan who was no more than a spirit she would create for him, must make him the richer. 'One day I will. But not yet, and certainly not today. Now go and find your father, make up to him for what you said.'

The way she spoke seemed to Bertie to bring the curtain down on the horror of the last half hour. He didn't argue, and she was glad to see him go. Alone she walked to the lake, to the "thinking seat".

233

Back in the East Wing she found Nigel waiting for her. Now what could have changed his mood so abruptly? Could he have been doing some thinking too?

'Katie, I blew my top. I'm sorry. I wonder your grandmother hadn't already told the old boy, but she obviously hadn't. Well, I'm sure it's safe with him – and Bertie is scared to death of anything upsetting Kit so it won't go any further. Still, I ought to have kept my mouth shut, I've had practice enough.' She hardly listened. The afternoon's scene had brought home to her the need to sort out her affairs, something she couldn't put off any longer. 'It was old Maurice Menzies and his damn fool advice,' Nigel went on. 'There is a certain amount of sound sense in what he says though. Young Bertie ought to start spending more time learning about managing the estate. Bertie, who is *our* son, yours and mine.'

Katie raised her eyebrows, she said nothing. Opening the bureau she took out a thin file of papers. It seemed the matter was closed.

The boys raced their canoes on the canal. She heard them coming back early in the evening, first the two of them talking, then Nigel's voice with them.

'Mum.' At the sound of Kit's excited voice she looked up from her writing. 'Dad says this might be a good trip for me to join them on. I think it was his own idea, too. I know Bertie has sometimes suggested I go with them, but I don't think he did this time. He was as much taken by surprise as I was. It was Dad's own suggestion.' And as much as the actual trip, it was that that meant so much to Kit.

The anger she'd felt against Nigel in the kitchen garden was nothing compared to the rage that consumed her now. Kit didn't disguise his pride that Nigel had included him. It shone in his pale blue eyes and tore at her heart. She saw him again as a little boy, always left behind, always pretending not to care. Now one kind word from Nigel and all pretence was gone.

Bertie came into the room.

'What sort of a climb is it?' she wanted to know. 'Bertie, you've climbed for years. Kit's new to all of it.'

He laughed. He was still young enough for his outburst of crying to have left no mark. Once it was over it was forgotten.

'Kit'll be safe as houses. Cross my heart, you can trust me to see he doesn't do anything daft.'

Nigel was standing in the drawing-room doorway watching them.

'You want my word too before I'm allowed to take him? Then you have it, Katie. I promise I'll remember he's a beginner. I'll not let them go off alone. And you, Kit, put the woman out of her panic.' His smile encompassed both of them, but Katie only saw the effect of it on Kit, his thin face lighting with pleasure he couldn't hide. 'Promise her you'll not try anything without my authority.'

'Of course I won't, Mum. You'll be all right with all of us away all the weekend?'

'I'll be fine.' The look of gratitude she threw to Nigel said so much more.

She was awake early, heard the Land Rover leave. Breakfast on the way, then to book in at that same hotel. She let her mind travel with them. Would there be other climbers staying there, friends of Nigel's, men who'd watched Bertie grow and develop, men who knew the pride his father had in him? Throughout yesterday evening Nigel hadn't turned back from that new leaf he appeared set on turning. He'd included both the boys as he'd spread the familiar large-scale contour map on the table, even gone out of his way to describe to Kit some of the climbs Bertie already knew.

Take care of Kit. Make him have a wonderful time, she begged wordlessly. Perhaps this would be the beginning of something better. 'It was Dad's own idea . . .' More than anything that was what hurt her – to realise just how much Kit must have wanted Nigel's affection, as year after year he'd been left behind. Poor little boy . . . the Kit of today was sixteen, but in her memory was still the skinny child he'd been. Always he'd managed a smile for Bertie as he'd waved them goodbye. Not just climbing, but all the other things – things he could have done better than either of them. Was that why Nigel hadn't taken him? Was that why he'd chosen climbing now? Something Bertie was good at and Kit couldn't do?

In the evening Nigel phoned. They'd had a good day, had taken Kit to one or two easy climbs. She mustn't worry if he didn't call again. Just expect them back on Monday. This was Thursday evening. He sounded so cheerful, they must be enjoying being together. With a light heart she went over to the main building to tell Kate and Maurice about the call.

The weekend had loomed before her, hours to be got through until they returned. Until now she'd not realised that Nigel had the power to hurt Kit. Suddenly it was something she feared. But the phone call had lifted that feeling of foreboding. On Monday they'd be home, most of the Easter holiday still ahead of the boys. There would be other outings. If Nigel had harboured grudges over the years, he'd released them in that dreadful scene in the kitchen garden. Now they'd found a way forward.

In a euphoria of hope she sailed through the weekend. Saturday, Sunday, then Monday.

Last night she'd lain awake listening, half expecting them to come back early. According to the weather report she'd watched on television, winter conditions had returned to the Welsh hills. Nigel wouldn't have taken them far today. That they'd stayed on was obviously a sign that they were enjoying themselves. She even let herself imagine them in the hotel. She knew the side of Nigel that could be such fun to be with, and over these days that's how he would have been. So she'd pictured them as she lay, warm and comfortable, listening for the Land Rover yet glad they hadn't wanted to hurry home.

She was in her room at the Manor the next day when Kate put her head round the door.

'Are you busy, dear? I thought you might be watching the weather forecast. Right back to winter, and just look at that rain. I'll be glad to see Nigel home with Ber – with the boys.'

'They won't have got much climbing in today I shouldn't think. Switch it on, Granny, we'll see what they have to say.'

Kate pressed the button then lowered herself to sit on the settee, patting the cushion next to her invitingly.

'We're too early, the news isn't quite over,' she said as Katie joined her. Then, taking her hand: 'Katie, things are all cleared up again, are they, with you and dear Nigel? Maurice had no idea of the trouble his few words were going to make.'

'I think perhaps we have to thank him for this weekend, Granny. Nigel must have thought about what was said. None of it was Kit's fault. Nigel must see now how unjust he was being to blame him for –' But she got no further. Their attention was riveted to the screen.

'News has been received that the search is continuing for three climbers missing in North Wales, where some of the worst weather of the entire winter has been experienced in the last forty-eight hours. The missing persons have not been named but it is understood that although two were experienced climbers, the third was a novice. It is thought that he may have got into difficulties and the others made a rescue attempt.'

Chapter Fifteen

Katie stood up to switch off the set. It couldn't be! Please, please, no. Don't let it be them. There must have been dozens of climbers tempted out by last week's sunshine. Of course it wasn't them. Fear tugged at her. She felt she was choked by it. It must have dulled her senses for her not to hear the door open. The sound of Matron's voice so close behind her startled her.

'Mrs Matheson, a telephone call from Wales for you. It's in my office.'

It must be Nigel! They hadn't left for home yet. He must have just seen the news report and known she'd be worried. A surge of warmth for him chased all her fear away.

'How thoughtful of him,' she heard Kate say to Matron, 'he'll know how we'd panic if we'd heard that news bulletin.'

'Hello. Nigel?' Hardly a question, she was so confident of the voice that would answer.

'Is that Mrs Nigel Matheson?' The man spoke with the musical lilt of his native Wales. 'This is Inspector Griffiths here, Mrs Matheson. I am afraid I have some bad news. I wish I could make it easier for you, Mrs Matheson, but there is no way I –'

'I just heard the television news. You mean it was them, Nigel and the boys? Is that what you're saying?' No, no, please, let it be something else. Not that, please not that.

'The two boys have been brought back. Both of them were carrying identity.

'They're not hurt?' But if they weren't hurt they'd speak for themselves, it wouldn't have been left to the police to contact her.

'Have you a pencil handy, Mrs Matheson? Then I'll give you the number of the hospital where they have been taken.'

She wrote the numbers he told her, her mind leaping ahead: she'd get through to the hospital, they'd tell her there was nothing serious, all this was red tape. The Rescue Services would have to have gone through the channels of bureaucracy.

'And my husband? You haven't told me about my husband? Was he not hurt? Is he with the boys?'

'The message I have here is just about the two boys, Mrs Matheson. Now, you have that number written down. Will you read it back to me, let me be sure you have it?'

She knew from his voice that he was kind, caring. But hardly waiting to thank him she rang off, then put through her call to the hospital.

Frank Fulford drove fast.

'We'll be there before the light goes.'

'If anyone is safe on a mountain, then it's Nigel.'

'He'd never take foolish risks.'

'He knows how to protect himself against the cold.'

None of it added up to a conversation, no single sentence expected or received any answer. Yet each one was offered to boost confidence, to soothe nerves, like a shot from a medical syringe. And all the time, in both their minds, was the nagging fear. Why hadn't he been with the boys? And if he weren't hurt, why hadn't he contacted her himself?

There were only three patients waiting in Casualty. None of them was Nigel.

'My name's Matheson. You have my sons here. They were brought down from a climbing accident.'

The rosy young nurse nodded mutely.

'Can you take me to them?'

'They've been transferred from Casualty. But, Mrs Matheson, Sister said you were on your way. If you'll follow me, please, she'd like to speak to you.'

'Have you heard anything about my husband?' Katie was almost running to keep up with the young nurse, already trained in the fast pace characteristic of her calling. 'Surely he's not still on the mountains?'

'It's Mr Matheson Sister wants to speak to you about – before you go over to the Owen Lloyd Ward. This is her room.' A quick rap on the door before she ushered Katie in with a brief: 'Here's Mrs Matheson, Sister'. Then she disappeared even faster than she'd come.

'Mrs Matheson, do come and sit down.' There was nothing of the Welsh lilt in Sister MacGregor's voice. She was a daughter of

Edinburgh and it flashed into Katie's mind what a variety of speech one island could produce – the thought immediately followed by surprise that at a moment like this she could waste thought on anything so inconsequential.

'The nurse didn't tell me – has my husband been hurt too? And what about the boys? She said they've gone to a ward. Will they be able –'

'The boys were brought down first. Christopher,' she checked her papers to make sure she wasn't confusing them, 'yes, that's right, Christopher's injuries are slight. He'd slipped and given his head a nasty bump, knocked himself out. That and a night of below freezing temperatures are the extent of his injuries. Egbert, I'm afraid, is more serious. He is still unconscious. He had to be brought up from a ledge where he'd slipped. He is in the Intensive Care Unit.'

'Intensive Care? Bertie?'

A tap on the door and the rosy nurse entered bearing a tea tray. Sister held one hand poised, indicating her to wait.

'Did you travel alone, Mrs Matheson?'

'No. Someone is with me. He's in the corridor, waiting.'

'Would you rather he came in?'

'I don't mind. Yes, bring him in, he'll want to hear. You were telling me about Bertie?'

A nod in the nurse's direction and out she charged, within seconds ushering Frank into the office and shutting the door. Sister poured the tea and passed it to them.

'You must be needing this. Bertie, you call him? He hasn't yet regained consciousness. He is in Intensive Care, but you mustn't be frightened by the name. It means that he has constant attention, is being monitored and watched the whole time.'

'And their father?' It was Frank who prompted her.

'His injuries were very much worse.' An austere-looking woman with her long, thin face and large, bony hands, chapped from the cold of a long winter. Yet the expression she turned on Katie was gentle, compassionate. 'I am so sorry. There was nothing anyone could have done. The only comfort I can give you is that he must have died instantly. He'd have had no time to suffer.'

The hotel bedroom was unfamiliar. Even the decor in the dining room and bar had been modernised since she and Nigel had come here for their honeymoon seventeen years ago. For him the changes must have been gradual, not many weeks ever went by without he managed a trip to his beloved Wales; for her the stripped her of the false sense of security that had enabled her to persuade Frank she would be all right here on her own. Already he'd set out for Bullington. Nigel had been his friend. She knew what had happened had affected him deeply, was grateful that he was taking charge of the arrangements.

She slumped on the bed. There was nowhere now to hide from the pieces of the jig-saw that Kit had pushed her way as she'd leant over his bed. Already his memory was clear. Not that he was getting any comfort from the shadows that took shape. But Kit would be well, Kit wasn't lost. Yet even that relief was tinged with guilt. She sat hunched, her arms folded; she rocked backwards and forwards, hugging her misery. The room was full of silence, heavy with rebuke. This must be her punishment for loving Kit too well – loving him more than she had Bertie. But wasn't that the indictment she'd held against Nigel? That he'd loved just Bertie? Nigel . . .

Why did she sink to her knees by the bedside, hiding her head in the crook of her arm? To find him? To escape from her own shame that her marriage had been empty and so much of it had been her own fault? How much of his hatred had come from the hurt she'd inflicted? And yesterday on the mountainside, how much even of that could be laid at her door? Later she'd remember the things Kit had told her – not in a clear sequence of events but throwing out random sentences; thoughts spoken aloud, no more than that.

Look back to the days before Grandam died, before Dylan came, remember how good it had always been with Nigel. He'd been her friend, as a friend she'd loved him. If she'd honestly tried could she have made these seventeen years of marriage different? An echo of Bertie's voice: 'Dad and me, you and Kit. Why couldn't we have been like other families, the four of us?' Bertie crying in a way she'd never heard from him, ever as a little boy. The sound of it filled her heart, filled her head. Bertie? No, it was her own crying she heard. She seemed to drown in her own tears, wanted to drown in them.

Much later, the night porter downstairs was on duty when she picked up the telephone and asked him to give her an outside line. She wanted to make an international call.

At Higley Creek the phone rang. Katie waited.

'Come on, Mom. Please, Mom, be there.' She was thirty-seven years old, for nineteen of those years she'd lived in England. Yet never had she wanted Lottie more than she did at this moment. The bell continued to ring; no one answered.

That was late on Monday evening. By Wednesday morning Bertie's slim hold on life had strengthened. Broken bones would soon mend though he had no shortage of them – his right leg broken in two places, his right arm in one – his head wound would leave no lasting damage, neither would his long hours of unconsciousness trapped on a mountain ledge. So far, though, he wasn't ready to face the whole truth. It was easier to let him imagine that he and his father had both been hurt, only Kit had escaped. It might be Bertie who held the pieces of the puzzle that were still missing, but Katie couldn't ask him. Not yet, perhaps not ever. What would be the point? Whatever Nigel's part in it had been, what led up to it was of her making as much as his. If only she could speak to him just once more, both of them be honest – honesty without bitterness, could that be possible?

She tried to remember the disjointed sentences Kit had thrown at her. A lamb trapped on a ledge over the sheer side of the crag, its bleat so weak it was barely audible . . . the boys following Nigel, their world no more than a few yards they could see through the swirling mist as he led the way to the track that would take them down the steep slope . . . 'A chance to show your mettle, Kit,' and Nigel passing him the rope . . . then Bertie at the last second taking the rope from Kit, going in his place as Nigel shouted to stop him . . .

Then what? A knot that had slipped, a rope that had vanished over the edge and into the mists, Bertie's fall being broken by the rocky ledge where the lamb still bleated. But how many hundreds of times had Nigel prepared the rope to secure a climber? It must have been second nature to him. So how . . .? No, it was a mistake, it was an accident.

'Find your way down, get help. Christ, boy, don't just stand there.' More than once Kit repeated that. It was as if he blamed himself for failing them. Those must have been Nigel's last words. But what about his last thoughts? He must have looked down at Bertie lying there injured – perhaps he thought he'd been killed. She knew just how it was he'd attempted to climb down without a securing rope. Nigel's last minutes, his world crashed around him.

Kit told her something about following the track, then realising it was taking him along the ridge; about striking out from it in an attempt to get down. He shouted, he yelled, there was no one. Soon it was dark. Mist had given way to rain, then to hail. She knew Nigel always carried a survival kit, but that would have been with him.

It was on the Wednesday morning that Bertie's senses had returned enough for him to look beyond himself and the two by his bedside.

'Dad's not been to see me.' The words Katie had been frightened to hear. 'He's all right, Mum?'

'He had a fall too.'

'Poor old Dad. He's going to be O.K, though, Mum?'

Was this the moment? No, not yet. He'd been hurt enough.

'Now he knows you're going to be all right, then he will be too.'

241

And to prove that Bertie hadn't completely come back to them yet, he didn't question her.

Footsteps on the polished tiles of the corridor. Then a voice that cut right through Katie's defences.

'Katie, we came the first flight out, as soon as we had Mum's call. Ramsey's talking to the Sister.'

In the seconds that followed Bertie watched her reach out to her mother. In that fleeting expression as they came towards each other he knew the full extent of the tragedy. They wouldn't have come so suddenly from Canada just because he and his father had been hurt.

'Mum,' he rasped, 'you lied! You lied about Dad!'

It was Kit who told him the truth. Last weekend had snatched the remnants of childhood from them, but it hadn't torn them apart. Kit gripped Bertie's hands, he held his gaze with a directness that would make anything but the truth impossible, then he told him.

'You went down after the lamb. Remember? The rope slipped and you fell. Dad did just what we knew he would do, Bertie, he tried to get to you. He wasn't roped. He fell.'

Children can cry easily, cry and forget. Bertie's tears were a man's tears. They would leave a scar that would make him always remember the hopelessness of knowing Nigel was gone. His fingers clung to Kit's; but when Katie bent over him he turned his head away, he wouldn't meet her eyes.

The clan instinct was strong in the Mathesons, it always had been. But in any case the tragedy of Nigel's death would have moved even a less united family. All of them were at Bullington for his funeral.

The front pews were for the family. Behind them were staff, some of whom remembered him from a child. More tears than Kate Menzies' were shed in Newton Dingley church that day. It seemed all the village mourned him.

The undertaker opened the car door for Katie to alight outside the church; the pall bearers were already standing erect bearing their load ready to lead them in. Her gaze was fixed straight ahead. She tried to make her mind a blank. But, walking at her side, Kit held her elbow protectively. She swallowed the sob that rose in her throat. None of it was Kit's fault, her darling Kit. Oh, but what a mess she and Nigel had made. Seventeen years – they'd been friends once, today she could remember so many times when they'd been happy together. Now Nigel was gone. Bertie had been brought home in an ambulance and was being looked after by a resident nurse. All Nigel's hopes had come to this – a neatly dug trench in the churchyard, side by side with Grandam, and generations of Mathesons. If he could see

242

them now, what cruel irony for him that following the cortège she walked with Dylan's son.

Out of the sunshine and into the dim church. So many people from the village, tenants from the estate, shopkeepers, most of the men wearing black ties, most of the women wearing the black hats they kept for occasions like this. All of them part of Newton Dingley that for Nigel had been the core of his existence. Hundreds of Sunday mornings she'd sat here in this same pew by his side. Today Reverend Bernard Rogers would address his flock, extolling Nigel's virtues. 'How long this time, do you reckon?' She seemed to hear his voice. 'Bet you fifty pence he waffles for more than twenty minutes.' She bit hard on her lip. It wasn't fair. Grandam had lived to be ninety-five. Nigel hadn't even reached forty.

In the East Wing the family congregated. Ralph Hickstead had retired from the business. Today it was his son Roland who fidgeted with his briefcase, preparing to read the Will.

'Millicent and I will get on the road as soon as this is over,' Ronnie whispered to his sister. 'We've a long drive. When are we going to see you for some more cheerful occasion?'

'Who knows what's ahead?' Lottie answered. 'Who could have guessed at this? The children are getting off our hands now, what about making it your turn to travel? Come to Higley Creek. Ronnie, it would be lovely.'

Roland Hickstead cleared his throat. The family sat a little straighter. This wouldn't take long. A man with a wife and an estate with the upkeep of Bullington would have left a straightforward Will. Hardly moving their wrists they checked the time by their watches. As well as Ronnie, the contingent from Warwickshire had decided they could be on the road by three o'clock.

'If you're ready?' The young solicitor looked enquiringly at Katie. Again he cleared his throat. He too glanced at his watch. He'd have given a good deal to wave a magic wand and find he'd missed the next half hour. Then he started to read.

'. . . bequeath all my property of whatsoever kind, subject to the payment of my debts, funeral and testamentary expenses, to my sole beneficiary, my beloved son Egbert Nigel Matheson . . .' And yet again the young man cleared his throat, keeping his gaze fixed on the document before him.

His task done, there was nothing to keep him. Katie thanked him, offered him refreshment. But the only refreshment he wanted was fresh air. She walked with him to his car. There was nothing in her manner to hint at the turmoil of her mind.

243

Never until this moment had she faced what Kit's position was. He hadn't heard the reading of the Will. At sixteen it hadn't been considered necessary for him to be there. Katie turned away from the house. Instinct took her towards the lake. She could imagine what was being said indoors. It was fourteen years since Rupert had died, the day when Hester had decreed they should keep silent. Well, so they had. The young members of the "tribe" had grown up believing Kit to be Nigel's. Of them all, only Bertie knew the truth. But none of that mattered. Only one person mattered, and that was Kit. Until recently she'd not realised how much he'd wanted Nigel's love. How hurt he'd be when he heard: nothing for him, not a mention, not a word; everything for Bertie, just as it had been all their lives.

By now she'd reached the lake. Alone she sat on the "thinking seat".

'How could you do it?' she asked aloud. 'Nigel, couldn't you have trusted me? I'd not have used a penny of it. I'd have seen that one day Bertie had what was yours. Kit, my poor Kit.'

Had the time come to tell him the truth? Or should she let him go on believing? Perhaps she ought to tell him that she and Nigel had planned it this way: Kit to inherit from her and Bertie from Nigel. Yes, that sounded feasible. No one would have expected Nigel's life to end so soon.

But how could she deceive him? Hadn't he been hurt enough?

She must go and say goodbye to the uncles and aunts, thank them for coming, act as if she wasn't consumed with misery and self-accusation. Yes, that was the root of it. She'd been no better than Nigel. 'You and me – Mum and Kit,' came the echo of Bertie's voice, his wild crying telling them that he too had been hurt. And now what did he have? Nigel lost to him, all he had was her. 'You and me – Mum and Kit'. No wonder he wouldn't let himself look at her; when she went into his bedroom and saw him lying with his eyes closed it was the only way he had of escaping from her.

'It's all different, Mom. It's like a shadow between me and the boys. Between me and the Manor.'

'Shadows lift, Katie.'

They were walking together by the lake. It was three weeks since the warmth of the March afternoon had tempted Kate and Maurice to sit in the kitchen garden. Now the wind swirled last year's leaves along the ground and the daffodils that grew wild in the grass of the park danced to try and touch their trumpets to the ground. Tomorrow Lottie and Ramsey would be gone, just one more thing to add to the emptiness of the future.

'Not this one. If we'd had seventeen gloriously happy years, if now the emptiness was simply because I'd lost something we'd both valued, then I could – oh, I don't know, I suppose I could go through a period of sadness, look forward to being happy because I'd know that that's what he wanted for me.'

'And you think he wouldn't want you to be happy?'

They stopped walking and turned to look at each other. The years had been kind to Lottie, kinder than they would be to Katie. Her hair still had the same sheen, the deep rich chestnut hadn't faded. Katie had been fair; now her hair was as curly as ever it had been but no one would look twice at its colour. Lottie's warm brown eyes had lost nothing of their brightness, but then brown eyes never fade as blue ones do.

'It's not that,' she answered. 'Mom, every time I look at Bertie I hate myself. He and Nigel were such friends. That was the one good thing that came out of our marriage. And because he meant so much to Nigel I held back, I could never let myself love him like I should.'

'Nigel?'

'No, no. Bertie, of course. Poor little boy. The day before they went off to Wales, do you know what he said? He said we weren't like a proper family. Always it was him and Nigel, me and Kit.'

They started to walk again. Katie had never expected to talk like this. If her mother hadn't been going away tomorrow, perhaps even now she wouldn't have.

'It's now he needs your love, Katie.'

'Mom, I've made such a mess. And none of it need have happened. If I'd been worth a light I would have gone to Dylan right from the start, brother or no.'

Again Lottie stopped, pulling Katie's arm to hold her back.

'You can still say that? After all this time? No, Katie, it could never have worked. There's too much difference in your backgrounds. When he was a child Dylan came to live with us at Higley Creek. You were tiny, you wouldn't remember. He wouldn't settle. He was quiet, he went off to school – and that's something he'd never done before – but he was lost. In the end he went back to the settlement, to his own sort.'

'Mom, oh, Mom! Even you. His sort! Our sort! No wonder he didn't want to stay with us.'

Again they fell into step, neither wanting to dig any deeper. Tomorrow they would have parted. This might be the last chance they'd have to talk together, just the two of them; they needed to draw closer, not drive a wedge between them.

'You say you've made a mess, that you ought to have come home to Canada with Dylan no matter what? I stopped it. I told you Neil was his father. It's not true, Katie. Dylan came to see me, ages ago now. He'd met his real father –'

'I know.' In a few short sentences Katie told her mother the stark facts of those few days. 'Funny, isn't it? We were so sure we were doing the fair thing. We couldn't take our own happiness at the expense of other people. That's what we thought. How smug we must have felt! Forsaking each other so that no one else should be hurt. And all this time Bertie could feel it – always it was Nigel and him, Kit and me. And Nigel? I parted from Dylan, but not here.' She tapped her chest. 'I couldn't share my life with him so I involved myself more and more with what I was doing at the Manor, with that and with Kit.'

'Katie, it's no use blaming yourself for what's done and over. I guess there isn't a person alive who hasn't got things to feel guilty over. Looking back at my marriage to Neil, I'm sure I have – although if I had my time again, I'm honest enough to admit I'd act like I did then. But it's you not me we're talking about. Listen, Katie honey, if you'd not got wed to Nigel, what would his life have been? He'd have had to say goodbye to Bullington, and I always got the impression it was pretty much the centre of the universe as far as he was concerned. And another thing. If you'd not married him, then what about Bertie? I've only been back for short stays while the boys were young, but one thing I'd stake my last dollar on is that Bertie was the best thing that happened in Nigel's life. Whether or not he was ever in love with you is something that only you – or he – would know. But never say you made a mess, not so far as Nigel was concerned. Right, he hadn't expected the Manor to go to anyone but him –'

'And what did I do with it? I took away his home.'

'No, you didn't. You helped him to keep his hold on it. If anyone took it away from him it was Grandma. And she did it because she had the vision to know you could inject new life into it. Generation after generation, we've always taken Bullington for granted. A place to come to re-charge the batteries. Grandma was always the one to organise.' The way Lottie said it seemed to bring Lavinia close to them. '"Grandam" you called her. That's what she was too, a Grand Dame, no one quite like her. It was she who stood out against the family to support me when I married Neil.'

'But, Mom, look at the way it turned out! How can you pretend it was right?'

'Oh, there was plenty that wasn't easy, for him as well as me, Katie. Sometimes we touched the depths – but those other times, the heights more than made it all worthwhile. Grandma saw there was much more to Neil than the rough hobo Mum and Dad believed. And then there was you.'

'Grandam organised me, too, not just by making me responsible for the Manor, but by bringing me here in the first place. Remember my eighteenth birthday, Mom? The excitement when her letter came with that open ticket?'

Lottie remembered the excitement – and she remembered the ache of premonition when she'd watched Katie's plane take off, carrying her to the land she'd dreamed of.

'Anyway,' this time there was determination in Katie's voice, 'it's no use my mooning over what I've done wrong. There's no choice about the way the future has to be. I never would have fallen back on Nigel and his money, I made my mind up about that ages ago, but at least then I knew it was there. Now there's nothing. From his investments to the money in his wallet, his books, his cufflinks – even his toothbrush,' she added wildly, 'every single thing that was his is for Bertie.'

A sudden gust of wind caught them as they started back across the open parkland.

'There it stands,' as the house came into view, 'another page of its history written. In all its years I bet there hadn't been one of them who's cared more about Bullington than Nigel did. It's a sort of everlasting monument to all our successes, all our loves, all our failures and sadness. We'll write another chapter, but nothing will really change. Just look at it, Mom.'

Lottie was looking. By this time tomorrow she would have gone, but Bullington never failed her. Always she could draw on its strength: creeping out of the garden door at first light, a pocket full of crusts for the ducks; the warmth of the sun, the ping of balls on tennis racquets; the thrill of achievement on her first climb into the tree house; sitting next to her grandmother in the front pew of St John's; flying over the jumps as she practised for gymkhana . . . the spirit of childhood, the terror of losing it all as she'd said goodbye at the end of her final visit before setting off for Canada. But now she had no fears. Over the years she'd come back on the occasional holiday, to see Katie, to see the boys as they grew, to see her mother, the Colonel's Lady and loving every minute of it. Now she was safe in the certainty that if she never saw the lovely old house again, always it was part of her. And didn't it work both ways? Wasn't there something of her that would forever belong here?

'There's Mother watching us out of the window.' She waved, but didn't hurry. 'Katie, who knows what tomorrow has in store? For you, for me, for anyone. Look at Mum – I bet she never gets headaches these days. Poor Dad, how he put up with it I can't think! And Aunt Eva . . . she and Jack got off to a late start, they didn't have long together. It's not the length of a life, it's how fully it's lived that counts. Me, I've been doubly lucky. Ramsey and I have had thirty-three years.' She grinned, her face lighting up as it might have fifty years ago. 'And the best is still to come. For you, too, Katie. Pick up all the pieces left to you, work hard at making something of them – and suddenly you'll find yourself with a picture that is good.'

Listening to her Katie could almost believe. It was only later when she took each piece left to her and examined it that she was swamped by the hopelessness. Bertie: an invisible wall between them, a wall made of grief and loss he couldn't share, most of all with her; Kit, the elder son, always passed over for his younger brother, Nigel's Will making it impossible for him ever to forget; Dylan . . . what if her mother was right, it wasn't the length of time that counted but how fully one lived? But how long was one expected to live in yesterday? Misty memories of childhood, a few brief months, a golden summer when she'd been adult enough to know the joy of loving him yet adolescent enough to believe nothing could ever tear them apart; a few days, hardly more than a few hours, a confirmation of all that they were – and yet even that against a background of her life with Nigel. No, don't think of it, that was a piece of the puzzle that could have no slot in the picture she had to build.

The Manor: it had started as a challenge, a way of proving that she could be worthy of the trust Grandam had put in her. She'd never fallen back on the cushion of Nigel's money. She never would. It wasn't even there for her now, everything was held in trust for Bertie. Bullington Manor depended entirely on her, not just the house but the estate. So those were the pieces she had to pick up – collectively she had no chance to bring them together and make a picture. She'd take one at a time. She'd not be beaten.

That Thursday was a busy day. In the morning she'd left home early to drive Lottie and Ramsey to Heathrow. Then home again to collect Kit. He had to be back at school in time for the evening meal. Kit: his would be the first piece she'd take. Her heart told her his would be the easiest, even while her mind told her the prospect of what she had to make him understand held all the dangers of walking a minefield.

'We're early, Kit.' She was slowing the car as she said it. 'We have to talk.'

'Mum, you don't have to tell me. I know why it was Dad felt like he did.'

She braked to a stop. It even flashed through her mind that it was a good thing no one had been close behind them.

'Come on, Mum, we can't stop here, right outside someone's house. Come on.'

'It doesn't matter. Kit, I don't know where to start. I don't know if you're grown up enough to understand. Should I have told you before? Or perhaps even now it's too soon? Kit, please, don't hold back from me. If I'd told you sooner . . .'

'Mum, I know what it is. Grandpa talked to me.'

'Grandpa Menzies?' Oh God, what had he said? Memories of that afternoon in the kitchen garden sprang back to her.

'My proper grandfather. Well, that's what he feels like to me. Grandpa McFee.'

'Oh, Kit.' In her relief she felt her eyes burn with tears she blinked away. Dear, dear Dad, he who'd known Dylan, he who'd been as real a father to her as if she'd been his own.

'So you know about Dylan?'

'It was yesterday Grandpa told me. I've thought and thought about it. He came, didn't he? Dylan Kitashee. I remember. We were pond dipping, remember? Five jumps that stone made on the water.'

'Did Dad tell you all about Dylan? All right, I wasn't married to him so I suppose the world would say that what I did was wrong. But it wasn't. Nothing could have been wrong between Dylan and me. What else did Dad tell you?'

'That your father had had an affair with a half-breed Indian woman, this man Dylan's mother. That she'd sworn in Court that he was Dylan's father. That was why you and Dylan had to break up.'

'Are you man enough to understand? Oh, I hope so. You just have to be, Kit.'

And so she told him. At sixteen what would one make of it? She tried to look back and remember where her own understanding had been at that time, but she'd been secure at Higley Creek, a world away.

He didn't interrupt her. His expression was inscrutable, just as Dylan's would have been. She had no way of knowing what would come next. She came to the end of her story.

'I wish I could have understood when I was just a kid. Dad – Bertie's real dad, I mean – he was a good chap, he never hinted about any other man. If I'd known, especially after that weekend when my proper father turned up, I would have found it much easier to see Bertie always with Dad.'

'Kit, I've made such a mess of it all.'

'That you never have!' No Matheson could have sounded more truly English. 'Mum, listen to me. I'm proud to be who I am. From what Grandpa told me I have a right to be proud of my real father. And, Mum, I'm jolly proud of the way Dad behaved too. Of course he always made sure Bertie came first, I can understand that now. But

Mum, that last week, with all three of us – it was great. If we hadn't heard that wretched lamb . . . oh, things could have changed for us all. He was a good man, Mum.'

Katie had never felt so humbled as she did as she reached out to take Kit's hand in hers.

By the time Bertie went back to school at half term they had built a platform where they could meet. Under it they hid the things they weren't ready to face.

At the beginning of term she'd left Kit with a feeling of having drawn closer to him. He'd grown up, his mind had matured enough for him to have understanding. This time, leaving them both, watching Kit heave Bertie's trunk from the back of the Land Rover, she felt a sense of failure. Kit's hurts had been evenly spread throughout his childhood, and through them all she'd been there for him. Bertie's were new and sore; she'd failed to find any soothing balm. Driving home she was haunted by the empty look in his eyes as he'd submitted to her goodbye kiss.

Her own soothing balm came as she went in through the front door of the Manor.

'Good to see you home safely.' 'And how were the boys?' 'Takes me back a year or two. A pony and trap from the railway station in my day – during the Great War you know.' 'Miss Harding was feeling poorly, Matron sent for the doctor.' 'I see Huffkin has been rolling our bowling green. Summer nearly here again.'

The Manor closed around her. Here was the centrepiece of her puzzle, from it the picture must take shape.

It was two years after Nigel's death, the long summer holiday period. In fact Kit had finished school, and in October would start medical training. He had no doubts about the direction of his future. Bertie's sights wavered. From the army, to farming, to flying, to horticulture – each time it was something new. So often hearing him leapfrog from one thing to another Katie was aware that she was failing him; it wasn't a mother he needed, it was a father.

It was the first day of their holiday. They'd spent the morning with Frank Fulford. Bertie was with him still when Kit came upon Katie cutting flowers for the house.

'I left them to it,' he greeted her. 'Frank's nephew has just started at an agricultural college. He'd picked up some pamphlets to give Bertie.,'

'Frank's always been good to Bertie. But it would be so easy to push him the wrong way. He doesn't say much. He listens, lets himself be influenced – but he doesn't let one get a glimpse of what goes on deep down.'

Kit twirled a cut rose between his thumb and finger. He seemed to be weighing up his reply. And when he spoke it seemed to have no bearing on what had gone before.

'Remember Grandpa talked to me about my father, Mum?'

'Not the sort of thing I'd forget, Kit. What made you think of that?'

'Don't know, really. We'd been riding on the Common. We'd got off – I expect he'd engineered it 'specially although I didn't think of that at the time – we were sitting on a fallen tree trunk. When Dylan was a boy, that's what he talked about. By the time he got around to your meeting him again in England and all that part of it, I was ready to take in what he had to tell me. It's quite a thing to be told, you know, Mum. The way he did it there was no hurt, just a much better understanding of why things had been like they had. Of course I'd met Dylan, I must have been aware that there was something special, or why was it I never mentioned his visit, not even to Bertie? But it's only as time's gone on I've come to see that Grandpa looked at the whole thing through my eyes. Not many people could do that, could they, Mum? He's a great chap.'

Already the blades of her secateurs were positioned for the next bloom. Instead of cutting it she stood up straight, the flowers forgotten.

'Kit, what would I do without you!'

No one hearing them would have guessed the underlying meaning. But they didn't need to spell it out. What Bertie needed was a man to talk to him, to care about him and to understand.

Chapter Sixteen

When Katie had set out for England, Lottie and Ramsey had waved her off from Calgary. Now she insisted she wanted to be met at Radley, said it would be part of the excitement to finish the journey on the light aircraft used for short haul domestic flights. That was only half the truth. What she didn't say was that, for her, thoughts of Calgary were intermingled with thoughts of Eva; to see a sea of expectant faces in the Arrivals Lounge would bring home to her the loss that had never seemed quite real from so far away. Eva and Dr Jack had had ten happy years, they'd died within months of each other.

So in Calgary she and the boys checked through Customs and boarded a plane for Radley. Real flying, Bertie called it. What a country, hopping on an aeroplane like at home you would hop on a bus! There were only seventeen passengers: themselves, two women coming home from a day's shopping, one elderly man looking as though he belonged to a lumber camp, two not so elderly having all the appearance of cowboys, while the rest were in the uniform of commerce, dark suits, white shirt, briefcases. Bertie looked around him, then leant towards Kit with a grin.

'Howdy, partner!' Oh, boy! This was Canada.

When last Katie had seen Radley Airport it had possessed a single landing strip, a wood-built reception area and a control tower. But that was twenty years ago. As the plane circled to land she shouldn't have been surprised to see the concrete runways, the fleet of small planes standing near the modern passenger buildings. She remembered the few streets that made up Radley, the hospital which had been the town's pride. Looking down on it now she could see two lanes of traffic, people hurrying and scurrying like an army of ants. For a second she knew an unreasonable sense of loss. Then she forgot everything but that she'd brought the boys home. In only a minute or two now she'd be with Mom and Dad. Higley Creek would be like it always was.

Nothing could be as it had been twenty years before, not at Higley Creek, not anywhere. Imperceptibly changes come, children grow up, people grow old. When Lottie had married Ramsey, Higley had been home to him, to Ginnie, his crippled daughter, and to Marthe Kaparomy, the Hungarian housekeeper. With the march of time Lottie and Ramsey had added to the family. They'd had two sons, Paul and Nick. By the time eighteen-year-old Katie had left home to spend a holiday in England, Ginnie had been twenty-three. The gap of five years had melted to nothing between one so full of energy and one to whom every step of progress had been a battle. But Ginnie had never lacked fight, and she'd never given way to self-pity. It must have been a gift from nature, for she'd never had the advantages of attending classes as her contemporaries could. Ginnie was an artist. When Katie had left home Ginnie had been on the brink of her first romance. Her first romance? Perhaps her only romance. But that was something only she could know. The art master from the local school had been the object of her devotion. When he'd moved away she'd taken his rejection with the same courage she'd shown all her life.

So the years had gone by. It was nearly five years now since Marthe had died, but by then the family had shrunk to just Lottie and Ramsey. Ginnie had moved away to Victoria where her home was a ground-floor apartment, converted for her use, where she as making a living by her painting. Paul was a geologist in the oil fields of the Southern Atlantic; Nick was a journalist in Toronto.

'It's smaller than I remember, Dad,' Katie told Ramsey, standing outside the row of sheds that housed the implements and equipment.

'Twenty years at Bullington would dwarf most places, I guess.'

'Maybe. But the land, all that sea of wheat, that's just as splendid. Just goes on and on . . .' Her words trailed into silence as Bertie came to join them. 'Isn't that right, Bertie?' As if he knew what she'd been saying. 'Have you ever seen anything like that crop of wheat?'

'Coming from here, Gramp, whatever must you make of those pokey fields we've got at home?'

'Your farming is quite different, Bertie. How do you fancy riding out with me this afternoon? I figure on starting cutting most any day now.'

Katie felt as if a weight were being lifted from her.

She'd come to see the family; she'd come so that the boys could know something of the country of her childhood; she'd come so that Bertie

253

could be guided into finding the way he sought. Deep down in her subconscious she might even have pictured a chance encounter with Dylan, it might have been that that set her out towards the settlement where so many years ago he'd lived. But now it was changed. In the yards around the shacks were dumped broken washing machines, old oil drums, neglected toys, rusted vans. The glances that had come her way hadn't been friendly. "Dylan's sort," "our sort", came the echo of Lottie's words. But he wasn't like this! Were these the people whose battle he'd been fighting as he'd made his way in the hard commercial world? They were embittered, saw themselves as deprived. Perhaps they were. She could recall what he'd told her of his early days at Radley School. Dylan had been strong, he'd had the determination and the ability to overcome; not everyone had that sort of strength.

She was glad to put the settlement behind her and head for home.

'It was dreadful, Mom.' It was a statement, yet it was a question too. There were things she didn't understand. 'There was a sort of hopelessness about it.'

'I guess you can find areas like that in most cities. It's not just the settlements. It's nothing to do with colour or race even. But it's worse out at the settlement than it was when I first came here, that's true. Then they had their own way, but now they seem to be lost. Fancy your going out there, Katie.' And that was a statement and surely, just like Katie's, a question too.

'If Dylan hadn't gone west, if he'd grown up still living there, I bet you one thing – he'd not have been like it.'

'Remember the Trading Post in Radley? They still use their old scales in there, weights on one side, tray on the other. Things have to balance. I've often thought of those scales when I see the folk come to town from the settlement. None of us has stayed the same over these last years. Just look around the house and see what I mean. Look in the kitchen. I remember when Marthe used to take such a pride in the way she did things. But me? I guess I'm no great shakes in the domestic line, never was. A food processor to prepare the meals, a machine to wash up afterwards, microwave oven to defrost the things I stock up frozen. And I'm no different from most folk. We call it civilization. And the more electrical gadgets we bring into our homes and take for granted, the bigger the gap between us and the folk who can't keep up with it. It's like those scales. If one side goes up, then the other side has to go down.'

Katie didn't argue. She had a miserable feeling that her mother was right. But what had gone wrong? She remembered Marthe, the hours she spent so happily looking after the home. To her housekeeping

254

wasn't a chore, it was a craft, one she performed proudly. And those people who'd glared at her this afternoon, lolling in the doorways of their hovels, their litter strewn around them – how could Dylan hope to balance the scales?

The more she wondered, the nearer she came to accepting that deep down in her heart there had been another reason for her coming home. The boys ought to see more of her country, that was what she told herself. She'd take them across the Rockies, to the sun-drenched Okanagan of the south and the spruce forests of the north.

If Lottie realised the reason for the trip she didn't comment. She offered them the use of her car, went to Radley with Katie to buy maps.

Then the day before they were due to set out, Bertie surprised them by saying: 'Mum, would you mind awfully if I stayed here? We'll come again some day, won't we? I mean, I'll have other chances to go to British Columbia. Gramps starts cutting tomorrow. That's something I'd really hate to miss. You wouldn't mind leaving me here, would you?'

Katie's eyes met her mother's. Some sort of unspoken message passed between them. Katie told herself she was glad. Wasn't this the main reason she'd come home? So that Ramsey could talk with Bertie?

They motored westward, both of them exhilarated by the thrill of adventure. Higley Creek was given over entirely to wheat growing, yet it was barely on the fringe of the real prairie. Within a few miles they were on the cattle ranges; and on again, mile after mile, the character unchanging yet always that distant backdrop of mountains coming nearer. Then the foothills, the gravel road making Katie realise how vulnerable they were, a woman and an eighteen year old who'd just passed his driving test. They spent their first night near Crimson Lake, then off again. The spirit of pioneers burned bright in them, Katie's partly fostered by watching Kit's first sight of his land. For that's what it was. This must surely be where his soul belonged. Once they reached the principal highway they turned northwards towards Jasper for another overnight stop. She stopped often. Even to herself she didn't admit the force inside her that urged her on. The great mountain range was behind them, the country had changed again: hills, forests, lakes, the swirling water of the Fraser River cevouring tributaries high in the mountains. They saw elks, moose, brown bears. And all the while in the driver's mirror she tried to glimpse Kit's face, read his expression.

Then north again.

'Where are we making for, Mum? Anywhere special?'

Was this the moment when she had to admit to something that hadn't taken real shape even in her own mind? What had driven her on had been a vague feeling that this was Dylan's country, somewhere here he would be. Nothing more finite than that.

'We said we'd see the lumbering country. I've never been here, it's as new to me as it is to you.'

That's when she saw the sign that pointed the way to Wyndhamslake. Following it, she glanced into the driver's mirror to find Kit was watching her just as she had been him.

'Do you think we shall see him, Mum? Dylan Kitashee? Is that why we've come?'

Now there was nowhere to hide, she couldn't pretend any longer.

'Kit, I want us to see him. I want him to know what a good guy he has for a son. Do you remember when he turned up that afternoon? We played a sort of game, Dylan and me. I asked him to come to the Manor for dinner, I said how delighted Nigel would be; he said he had such a short time he didn't think he could. Both of us knew it was a game called convention we were playing. And that's how it's got to be here. The firm is called Timber Products of Wyndhamslake. We'll go there, visitors from England who happened to meet him when he was last at Redman's. That's all we are, Kit, all we can be. He has a family here, just like I had at home.'

'What else would we be, Mum? It's a far cry from Bullington. That's our home.'

Pulling in at a filling station, she asked the way to Timber Products.

'Not a name I know,' the lad at the pump told her. 'What is it? A pulp mill?'

'I guess it would be. You must know it, it's been going for years.'

The young lad shook his head, his jaw gathering momentum on his gum as he grinned.

'That's where it's got me beat. I only been in town here since Monday, came up from Quesnel. The pulp mill is out of town, about two miles, maybe three. Take the north route out,' then with what was almost a wink, 'and then follow your nose. That'll guide you in.'

She took the north route, and as they came out of town could see the vast building set on the hillside. Four tall chimneys belched forth a pale vapour that told them just what the boy from the filling station had meant. And further to the north again the land was dark with spruce, the wealth of the area. So this was where Dylan had made his life. Would he have had his tank filled by the boy she'd just talked to? Would these people driving along the highway be his friends?

'Nearly there, Kit.' She wanted to sing and shout, she felt young, free, unencumbered. It was as if her years had been stripped from her; a page was clean, waiting for her to write. She knew she was fantasising, but today she was entitled to. Here she was in Wyndhamslake, living a dream she'd carried at the back of her mind for more than half her life.

'Look, Mum, look what the place is called!'

There was a high wire fence around the plant, and over the double gate was a board bearing the words: 'Kitashee Pulp and Paper Company'. With her heart beating fast she drove in, parking near the fence, out of the way of the huge trucks. Then she saw something else. Her first impression had been of men working, manning the loading machinery. Now she looked closer and what she saw filled her with pride. "His sort," and "our sort". Hadn't this always been Dylan's crusade? The settlement back at Radley had shown her only half the picture.

'Well, here goes. Oh, Kit, couldn't you just burst with excitement!'

'Mum . . . he may not be pleased. He's obviously someone quite important out here. You and I may be an embarrassment to him.'

'It isn't like that. Honestly.'

Confidently she got out of the car. Less willingly he followed her, a worried frown on his face as he watched her. Supposing she was riding for a fall? They hadn't seen each other for years. Even then he'd been married. What man wants his past to breeze in on him? Just look at all these dozens of men working here, some of them from European stock, some ethnic Indians, but all of them Canadian. In front of all that lot how would Dylan Kitashee react? She was so sure, so patently confident. Just for a second Kit let his hand touch hers. But Katie didn't even notice.

'We've come to see Mr Kitashee. We're visiting from England. Will you tell him it's Katie and Kit Matheson?'

The receptionist was an attractive, olive-skinned girl, her black hair smooth and glossy. "Their sort" echoed Lottie's voice. Again Katie wished she could bring her mother to see what Dylan had done here.

'He's up north,' the girl answered. 'He won't be back today, nor tomorrow. I'll see if I can find out for you when he's expected, if you like.'

In her disappointment Katie couldn't see beyond the fact that he wasn't here.

Kit took over. 'Thank you. If you could tell us how long he's going to be away, perhaps we could fit in a visit before we leave the district.'

The olive-skinned girl turned a smile on him that spoke volumes. To Katie he might still be a boy; to the girl behind the desk he was a handsome young man already.

257

'There's someone here to see Mr Kitashee. Find out from Mr Finney when he's due back, will you?'

'Finney?' Katie interrupted. 'Mick Finney?'

'Sure. He'll be the one looking after things, he'll know.'

'Then will you ask him if he can spare me a few moments?'

Messages were passed. Yes, he'd see them. As soon as he was free he'd send for them. Minutes went by and with each one of them Katie felt more let down; this wasn't what she'd imagined as they'd driven out of town following their noses. It must have been a quarter of an hour before the call came. They were to be escorted up to his room. The young receptionist preceded them, with a flutter of her long lashes and a waggle of her hips clearly both for Kit's benefit, whisked them upwards in a lift and ushered them into a comfortable and airy office where behind a large desk sat an elderly man with the smile of a leprechaun and eyes of that strange pale blue, dark rims to the iris, eyes Katie had seen only on two other people – Dylan and Kit.

'Mr Finney, you won't know about us, but Dylan has talked to me about you.'

'Mick Finney not know? There's not so much I wouldn't be knowing about Dylan. First time he talked to me about you it wasn't Katie Matheson that you were. It was Katie O'Hagon.' And she fancied that the Irish ring to her name had been a point in her favour. He must have lived in Canada most of his adult life but his accent still clung to his roots; she suspected he wouldn't have it any other way. 'And this will be Kit.' He stood up as he spoke, reaching across the desk with his hand extended towards his grandson. A short man, hardly taller than Katie was herself, his face a map of lines which looked as though they'd been put there by laughter rather than cares, his wiry white hair thick and curly. Dylan's father. Except for the eyes there was nothing to hint at it.

'I kept you waiting a long time. It was the telephone. I couldn't get hold of him. He's already trucked out, seeing the timber that's being taken and looking into the planting. That's a lesson we've been learning – what you take you must put back. Yes, I wanted to tell him you and the boy were here. But once he heads out into the forests, there's not much hope of getting him to a telephone. I left a message he was wanted, but when he'll get it . . .' He shrugged and raised his eyebrows. 'I said to send a scout out to try and track him down.'

'Did you say I was here?'

'Sure an' I said to tell him friends from England, people by the name of Matheson.'

Katie looked quickly at Kit. Would he resent the suggestion that his real identity was to be hidden? As so often there was no way of reading his thoughts. Ignoring Mick, he pulled a chair forward for his mother.

'That's ol' Mick Finney given a pointer to his manners,' Mick chuckled. 'You sit yourself down too, my boy. It may be a while before that call comes through.'

Katie warmed towards the little old man – for she realised he must be past normal working age. She would like to have talked to him more freely, about himself, about all the things he'd done for the son he hadn't known. But there was something about Kit's manner that made it impossible. So rather lamely she muttered her thanks to him for trying to contact Dylan.

'I didn't think you would have heard anything about me,' she added, trying to fill the silence.

'There's nothing much about me that I haven't tried to explain to Dylan. And after that, talk came easy between us. There was a time when I thought of taking a trip out Radley way, tracking down this Katie O'Hagon girl. Good thing I didn't, eh? Wouldn't have found you there. That would have been getting on for fifteen years ago. Like I said, I thought of doing it. But I kept my mouth shut, same as I had all through the years. Maureen – she was my wife, God bless her dear soul – she had to be my first consideration. All those years I'd kept from her the way I'd behaved with Rosie Kitashee. So I held my tongue. Didn't tell Dylan, didn't go seeking out Katie O'Hagon. All that was when young Dylan was verging on getting himself wed to Shara. That's when he talked to me about how things had been between you. Just a young man's dream, I told myself. Better get him married to Shara. She was a good woman, someone who'd be a credit to him in the district.'

'Perhaps we shouldn't have come.' But how could she not have? 'A good woman, a credit to him in the district.' Had he found real happiness? How could he have? He'd been married to Shara long before she last saw him, before their short stolen interlude in London. Nothing had changed for them then, so how could it now? 'You see him all the time, you must know – is he happy?'

The shrill ringing of the telephone forestalled his answer.

'Told the girl no calls – that must be him. Hello there, 'tis me. Now listen to me, I got her sitting right across the desk from me now.' And with a sudden impish twinkle as he looked at Katie: 'Pretty a little lady as ever I saw . . . just steady though, son . . . oh, and while I think of it, Kamma called me up this morning. Her mother's got some talk to give this evening so Kamma's sleeping over at my place, thought I'd tell you . . . yes, yes, all right. Not so fast now, don't rush me. I'll take young Kit and show him around the plant.'

259

He got up and signalled for Katie to sit in his chair. 'Now then, Kit Matheson, I'll show you what we do with these trees. Living where you do, next door the plant in England, it's right you understand this end of the job. Away we go now. It's a bad line, very faint, your mother won't hear herself think with us chattering around her.'

The door closed behind them. She'd imagined the moment of seeing Dylan, had not thought beyond that for she'd been so sure that once she was with him the time between would count for nothing. With him . . . not sitting in a swivel chair, holding a cold telephone receiver, straining to hear him while the line cracked and echoed. And not with images of Shara and Kamma, part of the successful life he'd made without her, casting a shadow between her and the distant voice she waited to hear. With a hand that wasn't quite steady she pressed the receiver to her ear.

'Kate-ee.'

'You sound so clear. You sound so close. He said it was a bad line. He took Kit out so that I'd have a quiet room.'

'I came back from England yesterday. In Newton Dingley I heard about the accident, about Nigel. Katie, why didn't you tell me?'

'So many reasons.' She started to laugh. 'Newton Dingley? You've been to Newton Dingley while I was driving through your country, telling myself I was getting nearer to you with every mile.'

'*Our* country, Katie. I shall be in England more – either I shall or someone else from Wyndhamslake. You see, I'm taking over Redman's. That's why I was there.'

She wanted to shout it aloud, to tell the world what he'd done. Kitashee Pulp and Paper Company! And now Redman's. Into her mind flashed a picture. To her it was so clear, yet how could she expect it to have been important to him too?

'Dylan, I wish Grandam could know. Remember when you came to dinner? You talked about the industry and I remember how proud I was. You were *my* friend, you came from *my* country. I can see her now . . .'

'And I can too. Her eyes so bright, her spirit so strong. Then we thought she'd gone to sleep, but she hadn't. She opened her eyes wide and invited me to exercise one of the horses.' Neither of them mentioned Nigel, but he wasn't forgotten.

A few minutes more and she'd rung off. Her life had a whole new meaning. The shadows of Shara and Kamma had gone. Alone in the office she dug into her purse for her mirror. Inch by inch she examined her face. Of course she must have changed, she'd had nine years of living since they'd met; she'd lost a husband and faced all that his death had meant to her relationship with the boys; she'd worked

260

hard at the Manor, not just in "her" side of it but recently trying to learn something of the management of the estate too. All these things must have written the lines of living on her face. Yet the girl in the looking glass glowed with some inner happiness. Her eyes were bright, her mouth wanted to smile, her feet wanted to dance. This evening she would be with him. He was flying back, she was to be at the airstrip at five o'clock.

The shadow fell again. This evening . . . while they were together what about Shara, lecturing, giving an after dinner speech, however this highly respected woman would be spending her time? And Kamma? Even as the little leprechaun had spoken her name his eyes had lit up with pride. These were the people whose lives were woven with Dylan's. Next week . . . next year . . . no, don't think of it. This evening belonged to her. It had to be enough, just as it had been in that brief oasis they'd shared in London.

She meant to cream all she could into those hours until five o'clock, partly to hurry the time along and partly because she wanted to understand something about this great vapour-belching mill. When she joined Mick and Kit they'd been out in the yard, watched a huge logging truck being unloaded. But for her sake they started the round again. Logs that looked like entire tree trunks were being hauled from the truck, the grabber taking one at a time and passing each one on to the next stage. Automatically the machines took it through each process, stripped the bark, cut the wood into strips, then broke it down into chips, worked it until the fibres began to hold together. By the time they reached the chemical processing plant Katie was out of her depth. She only half listened to Mick's explanations of how they were removing the unwanted wood chemicals to leave pure cellulose fibres. He talked of logs being cooked in the digester in a chemical solution, he even went into details of the three major chemical processes, the type of end resulting paper depending on the process applied. Every now and again she made a vast effort to understand what he was talking about, but the only thing she was sure of was the strange smell – how long ago it seemed now that she'd followed her nose to find the plant – and, over and above everything else, the wild joy that soon Dylan would be here. She was inordinately proud of Kit who seemed to be taking it all in and asking intelligent questions. But for her there was only one thing that had any reality at all: she was to be at the airstrip at five o'clock.

She stood back from Kit and his newfound grandfather, watching them. For all that Kit had inherited Dylan's black hair and the Finney eyes, he was English through and through, his spirit as much Matheson as any of those who'd gone before him. And why not? Hadn't she Matheson genes as surely as Nigel or any of the others who'd been born to the name? Again her imagination carried her to the unknown airstrip. This time she saw herself standing with Kit as Dylan came towards them . . . For her those years she'd been Nigel's wife created no barrier; for her, Dylan had always been there. But could it be so straightforward for Kit? In a sudden clear flash of insight she put herself in his place, saw Dylan as the reason why Nigel had treated him as he had. Yet through it all Kit had loved Nigel, his admiration never wavered. So what now?

Mick led them back up to his office. His thoughts must have been on much the same track.

'You'll find the airstrip easy enough, Katie, just take the left turn from the gate here and it's on that road. No more than a mile. And how about you, Kit? Do you especially want to go with your mother? I thought you and me might drive on back to the house. With Kamma staying the night I've not the room to offer you both hospitality, but perhaps you and me could stop off at The Inn on the way home and fix you rooms for the night?' Katie felt that he made the offer to take Kit home against his better judgment. She was grateful to him.

'Dylan spoke about Shara and his daughter,' she told him, somehow feeling that would reassure him.

'Shara is a very busy lady. She's a member of the Council, and every day seems to be serving on some committee or other. She counsels couples on what they call "marriage enrichment".' Another look in Katie's direction to see how that news was received.

Marriage enrichment? Dylan's wife? Mick could hardly make it clearer to her that they'd succeeded in making a good marriage. And wasn't that exactly what she had meant to do herself? Yet today when Dylan had spoken . . . It's just the same. Nothing can divide us, he'd said.

'When Dylan's away – and he often is – Kamma sometimes comes along to keep me company. I keep a room just for her, so she knows she has a place that's her own. Her mother's a busy woman, out at meetings, giving talks, counselling. One of the advantages of getting old, you can please yourself. I'm here at the plant now because Dylan has been away in England, but usually I come and go. Maureen and I had two boys. Both of them spread their wings and flew these many years. Now I've lost Maureen too, Kamma is a real little bit o' heaven to me. See, this is her.' He opened his wallet and brought out a photo. 'Pretty as a picture.' Then, his light blue eyes fixed hard on Katie: 'She and I are good pals. But it's her dad she's closest to. Fathers are something special to a daughter. I daresay you remember it yourself.'

262

Katie nodded. The shadow fell again, dark and heavy. This time there was no ignoring it.

Could this really be happening? She and Kit in this noisy paper mill with Dylan's father, admiring a picture of Dylan's daughter? 'It's her Dad she's closest to'. His words filled her mind and brought with them ghosts of yesterday, of Nigel and Bertie, a bond that no one had a right to try and sever.

She smiled admiringly and handed the picture of the pretty child to Kit. His half-sister! Taking her by surprise another scene leaped to the front of her mind: she was standing at the top of the steps of the Manor. If she closed her eyes the sloping parkland before her had more reality that the sounds and smells of the mill, the lake just out of view, the gentle movements of life in the house behind her. What was she doing here? She ought to have left her memories intact. Marriage enrichment counselling! If Dylan had succeeded in making something of his life with Shara, then what right had she to come here disturbing what they'd built?

'She's very fair,' Kit passed the picture back. 'You don't have to worry about me, Mr Finney. I shall be quite all right waiting for Mother at the Inn.'

'I would be glad to take you home with me. It's a thing I've always been hoping for.'

Katie's fears melted. She'd been right to come. Five o'clock at the airstrip – she'd not think beyond that.

She saw him coming down the aircraft steps. She saw him and nothing else. As he hurried the short distance to the reception area she knew nothing had changed, not for her and not for him either.

'Kate-ee.' His hands gripped hers.

She didn't speak. Suddenly there was nothing to say, here in the leisurely bustle of the small airport.

'Your car or mine?' he asked. 'Guess we'd better take yours. I'll send out for mine tomorrow.' And only when they were inside it, she behind the steering wheel, did he tell her: 'When I heard about Nigel's accident I went to the Manor. So long, Kate-ee, why did you wait so long? Why didn't you come to me?' He raised her chin, looking hard at her. 'Nothing has changed. I am not asking you, I know it's the truth. So why did you wait so long?'

'I only came by chance.' She spoke fast, saying the first thing that came to mind. This was crazy. He had a wife, he had the same responsibilities now that he'd had nine years ago. 'I wanted the boys to see something of Canada. Bertie's at Higley Creek, only Kit drove across the Rockies with me.'

'Why, Kate-ee? Why did you wait?'

'You know why. You have a wife. You have a child. Just that when I saw the sign saying we were close to Wyndhamslake, I figured I would look you up.'

'And now tell me the truth. Nothing is changed, Katie. Not now, not ever.'

Some force beyond her control drew her towards him. He raised her mouth to his. Yesterday was forgotten, tomorrow had no meaning. She'd come home. Their world stretched no further than the stationary car, the next moments belonged just to them.

And just as emotion had consumed her, so just as suddenly she was wildly happy.

'You know what?' she laughed, nuzzling her face against his neck. 'Happiness does amazing things to your appetite. I'm famished.'

'Then we will eat. Not a romantic out-of-town rendezvous where men take their extra-marital ladies, but right there in downtown Wyndhamslake, where everyone can see us and envy me.'

Just for a second she had misgivings.

'Are you sure? What about Shara?'

'I am sure. I want everyone to see us together. I want to shout it aloud that this lovely woman belongs to Dylan Kitashee – yes, and he belongs to her. One day I knew it must happen. Did I not tell you half a lifetime ago that it was written in the stars?'

It was over dinner that he told her something about his marriage. Listening she could understand, for hadn't her own been built on foundations much the same? He and Shara shared the same house, yet their lives never touched. Business took Dylan away a good deal; Shara's interests were in the community, certainly not the home. It was only when he talked about Kamma that Katie saw his expression soften. She was ashamed of the jealousy that gripped her so unexpectedly. Into her mind there flooded memories of her own childhood, the warm, secure, loved feeling that had been part of her relationship with Ramsey. How could she grudge Kamma something so precious? Ah, but the centre of Ramsey's life had been Lottie. The only person Dylan had had to give his love to had been Kamma. Hadn't Mick warned her how close they were? Even if he hadn't, she would have known it from the way Dylan told her: 'It is right that Mick has taken Kit home. He and Kamma will get to know each other. And when we collect him you will meet her.'

She tried not to show her chagrin. She felt mean and guilty that she begrudged Kamma the part of him that could never be her own.

'Tonight I shall talk to Shara,' Dylan was saying, never suspecting the battle that was going on in Katie's mind. 'I shall ask her for a

264

divorce. We are not a proper partnership. It is many years since we have had a married life together.'

'It sounds so easy.' She bit her lip. Of course it was easy. Surely they'd always known that one day they would be together? He and Shara had no real marriage – of course it was easy, what was there to come between them and all they wanted? The restaurant was dimly lit, the candles on each table casting flickering shadows. Looking at Dylan, Katie forgot her jealousy, indeed forgot Kamma. If at that moment they could have forsaken everything just for each other, she would have done.

'Evening, Dylan,' someone passing their table greeted him. It was enough to remind her of his position here in Wyndhamslake. It was enough to make her see every obstacle that prevented their being together.

'It was my fault. I should have listened to you, come back to Canada with you right at the beginning, even if that awful story had been true.' All the 'might have beens' crowded in on her, making reality even harder to face. She sat a little straighter, her face resolutely hiding the tumult in her mind as she said: 'Mick tells me that Shara counsels people on their marriage problems. She must feel that what you have is good. Then I come here –'

'Katie, it is not like you say. She counsels people on all sorts of things – how to budget their housekeeping money and keep out of debt, how to raise their children, how to speak with confidence.'

'I don't understand.'

'No, Kate-ee my darling, you will never understand, because you could never be that sort of woman. Her days are filled with public work. Whether I am there or not will make no difference to her. I am not a poor man, she will be well provided for. She would not want your sympathy, she will not need it. There will be nothing of the cast-off wife about Shara, that I promise you. I will speak to her tonight. Now I will tell you about my plans for Redman's.'

'Redman's? Kitashee's, surely?'

'For many years it has traded as Redman's. In fact, when was the last Redman in the business? Long before our time. I think the name will stay. Enough that it is mine. There on the doorstep of Bullington, and it is mine.'

Later they called at Mick's house to collect Kit.

'Look.' With his arm around Katie's shoulder Dylan held her back so that they stood in the yard unseen by those indoors and looked at the scene through the undraped windows. The night was warm and the windows open wide, although the mosquito screen shut out some of the air and ensured they were unseen by those inside. Around the table they sat, Mick and his two grandchildren, playing poker. Until this evening Kit had never played, but Mick had taught Kamma as soon as she was able to count and to differentiate between the cards.

'Hi, folks,' Dylan called out as he ushered Katie into the room. 'Kit!' He held out his hand. Throughout the evening with Katie he'd not imagined what this moment would mean. He'd met Kit as a boy, had known that he'd been his own son; tonight was different, for now Kit knew it too.

Katie wanted to say something, anything, but her tongue didn't seem to want to move. Mick looked on, his light blue eyes unashamedly brimming with tears. What Kit's emotions were no one could say for hiding his feelings had been something he'd learnt young. So now he stood up from the card table and held out his hand to take Dylan's. He might have been being introduced to a stranger. They were all poised, like statues, uncertain of the next move. When it came it was from Kamma.

'Hello, Dad. You didn't stay away! I told Gramps that now you're going to be home, I'll come back with you.' Possessively, she went to Dylans' side, slipping her fingers through his.

'Kamma, this is Katie, Kit's mother, someone I have known for many years.'

'In fact, since I was three,' Katie laughed, trying to put them all at ease. At a glance she could see Kamma's adoration of Dylan. But, seeing the child, even recognising the way she was clinging to his hand, some of her resentment vanished. Kamma was tall for her twelve years, almost as tall as Katie herself. As straight and slim as a young boy, with the sure promise that one day she would be a beauty. Had there ever been hair such a silvery blonde? What broken down the barrier for Katie was the eyes, those strange eyes inherited from Mick, passed from Dylan to Kit, and to Kamma to.

They refused Mick's offer of a nightcap. There was something tense in the atmosphere, they all felt it even if they might not all have understood the reason. When they got outside to the car and Dylan opened the front passenger door, Katie told him: 'Kit and I will ride in the back. If you take the car on home with you, can you let me have it back tomorrow?'

'I'll return it myself.'

Settling into the front seat, Kamma looked from one to the other.

Next morning the sun shone clear and brilliant. Yesterday at the pulp mill Mick had suggested to Kit that he should take him to see the timber being cut. So this morning, even before they were away from the breakfast table, Mick had arrived and the two of them had set out for the North Garinco Station.

With Kit gone, Katie waited impatiently for Dylan. Had she been widowed from a happy and fulfilled marriage, then she might have mistrusted what he'd told her about himself and Shara. For a moment her imagination leapt to a scene where Nigel might have come to her asking for his freedom, telling her that he loved another woman. She tried to face the thought honestly. In truth perhaps the years between had misted her vision, but her memories were tender, her face relaxed into a half smile as she pictured him. Of course she would have done as he'd wanted. Of course Shara would do as Dylan wanted.

When her telephone rang she answered it eagerly.

'Room 405? Reception here. There's a visitor.'

Katie didn't wait.

'Yes, that's fine. Send him up.' She put down the receiver and opened her door, watching for him to appear from the elevator.

Only one person got out when it stopped at the fifth floor. A woman. Blonde, slim, groomed until she dazzled, not a hair out of place. There was no need for Katie to ask who she was. She'd never been more conscious that her own once fair hair was a faded mouse, her make-up had been applied in five minutes not twenty-five, her nails were unvarnished and her clothes last year's. One look from the elegant stranger told her that none of these things had gone unnoticed.

'You're Shara, aren't you? Come in. Kit's gone off with Mr Finney to see one of the lumber stations, I'm on my own.'

'And that's the way you're going to stay, too, Katie Matheson!' Shara followed her into the hotel room and closed the door. 'Dylan has asked me for a divorce. I expect you had it planned, the two of you. Well, forget it! I'm not a woman to change my mind. Presently I expect he'll come around here with some story that things were left up in the air, that he's not persuaded me yet to go to a lawyer, but once I've thought it through I'll do as he wants. Well, I won't! Not now. Not ever. That's what I told him last night. And it's final.'

Instinctively Katie had disliked Shara, yet the last words made her see her in a different light. Perhaps she had a deep rooted hatred of divorce, perhaps her religion didn't acknowledge it, perhaps the saw her world threatened? But before Katie could reply, the level voice went on.

'I'm not a woman to be frightened of the facts, so I'll tell you exactly why it is you'll be waving goodbye to your hopes. In this town I'm looked up to with respect; I have a stable marriage, I'm an authority on how to build a good relationship with a partner. I'm a person of some note around these parts. East side of town there's a training centre being built, did he tell you that? No, why should he? The Kitashee Foundation it's to be called – but I'm the Kitashee, not him. I've made a place for myself in this town. I'm a serving councillor, I'm a Justice of the Peace, I'm looked up to, a pillar of the community. And he has the effrontery to say he expects me to go to a lawyer and parade that my own marriage is no better than those couples who come to me for guidance! Wouldn't you think that he – even *he* – would have more sense?'

Any momentary sympathy Katie had felt had gone. Shara spoke unemotionally, her voice clipped, her accent a strange mixture of Europe and the New World, her tone expressionless. Katie had listened without interrupting. She was too angry to talk reasonably. This hard, cold woman was Dylan's wife! In a way she was too confused to analyse, Katie's anger was tinged with thankfulness. Here was someone it would be easy to fight.

'Have you ever cared whether Dylan is happy in this model marriage?'

'We make no demands on each other. If you're his mistress, that's O.K. by me. He can sleep with anyone he likes – as long as he doesn't do it in Wyndhamslake, and as long as it's not me. For myself, I've a busy and worthwhile life. I'm not having it tarnished by the sort of scandal folk in a town this size would love to get their tongues around.'

Katie didn't attempt to control the anger that tore at her. If Dylan's wife had been gentle, sensitive, caring, then she would have known herself beaten, she couldn't have fought that sort of woman. But this! She warmed to the challenge. 'I doubt if you care about anyone but yourself, with all that clap-trap about making yourself a pillar of society. It's all right by me if you won't give him his freedom. To be honest, I don't give a damn.' She moved in front of Shara, meeting her eyes defiantly. 'No, not a damn! A bit of paper with our names on, that's the only difference. Well, you can keep your good name – or lose it – I don't care. We've got our freedom, you've just given it to us!'

For a moment she thought Shara's feathers were ruffled, but if they were it was only temporarily. She soon sized up the situation and played her trump card.

'If you have no regard for me, a faithful wife for fifteen years, then what about Kamma? Do you think I'd let his lusting after some other woman take her father away from her? Do you?'

'He wouldn't give up Kamma. You wouldn't expect it of him. She adores him, I could see that last night.'

268

Anger had made Katie confident. But that confidence was stripped from her by Shara's threat. If she contested the divorce she could blacken Dylan's name, ensure that she was given custody. And what if they didn't bother about that "bit of paper" Katie had been so swift to scorn? If Dylan left his wife and daughter to live with another woman, would Shara be able to take Kamma from him?

Shara read the signs; she was winning. In a voice that reminded Katie of the marriage enrichment counselling role she played she went on: 'I dare say you're still in an emotional vacuum. You lost your husband, I believe. So many women feel that their life can't be complete without a man. Trust me, that's nonsense. These days there are so many things a woman can do –'

'Sure there are. And here's one of them!' Katie opened the door for Shara to leave. 'If you change your mind and divorce him, then great. If you don't, then still great. For twenty years we've waited – and if you'd loved him, if you'd been a proper wife to him, even now I'd have gone home like I expected to. If one of us has an emotional vacuum in her life, it's not me!'

Half way into the corridor Shara stopped. Her last remark was intended to plant seeds of doubt.

'In those twenty years, how many times have you been with him? Enough to know that he's a cold man, his only passion building his business, proving he's none the less able because he's of mixed race. And one thing more. If through you he loses Kamma, how do you think he'll see you then?'

Chapter Seventeen

Shara had scarcely had time to get downstairs in the lift when there was a knock at Katie's door. This time it *must* be him. She flung it wide open.

'Kamma! Your mother's just left. Were you looking for her?' But even as she asked it she knew it wasn't Shara the child had come to see. 'Come inside.'

'I waited downstairs till I saw her go.'

'Doesn't she know you're here?' But of course she didn't know it. One look at Kamma's pale face, the unhappiness in those strange blue eyes, made the question unnecessary.

'I told her I wanted to go to town, that's why I drove in with her.' Kamma was glad to hitch on to something normal to say. There was so much turmoil in her mind, she didn't know where to start. In fact, she was scared to start at all, frightened of tears that were threateningly near the surface.

'Is it about your father?' Katie wasn't any more sure of the ground than Kamma. But it was important that they were honest with each other. This was Dylan's daughter, someone he loved, someone who loved him.

'What did you have to come here for?' the child blurted out. It was rude, gauche. To Kamma it didn't even sound like her own voice. She mustn't cry. She mustn't let this woman see how screwed up she felt. 'Mom and Dad never have rows, I've never heard them shout or say beastly things to each other. Not till last night.' She held her jaw firm. 'I crept along the corridor and listened. Dad wants to go away – leave us. And all because of you!'

'Kamma, you don't understand. Have you talked with him?'

'No, I haven't. I heard it all. He wants Mom to give him a divorce. She said no, said she'd never divorce him. Anyhow, why should she? Why should you come here messing up our lives? Now you know that

270

she won't, you might as well go away and leave us be.' Her voice betrayed her. It broken on a high-pitched squeak.

Katie sat on the edge of the bed and drew Kamma down to her side. Still the child wouldn't look at her.

'You love your dad a lot, don't you?'

''Course I do.'

'I do too.'

'Not like I do. He's mine. You don't even see him. That's what I heard him tell Mom. You hadn't seen each other for years. Anyway, you've got the others – Kit, and Bertie, I think he called the other one. If you take Dad away, if you take him . . .' It was no use. The tears won.

'Kamma, we've talked about you loving your father. And him? Don't you know how much he loves you too?'

'No, he doesn't. If he did he wouldn't want to go away and leave us.'

'I shouldn't have come. Last time Dylan and I saw each other you were only three.'

'So it's all silly? I told you it was. If you go back home,' she turned to Katie, her brimming eyes holding a gleam of new hope, 'everything can be like it was before.'

Katie nodded.

'Yes, Kamma, like it was before. Like it's been for twice as long as that. There are some things neither time nor distance can alter.'

Kamma didn't know what she was talking about but there was a glimmer of light on her horizon.

'At school lots of the kids' parents get divorced. But it couldn't happen to mine. Why, don't you see, Mom understands about all that sort of thing. Just last term my friend Doreena's dad ran off with Philip Rackley's mother. Both of them are in my grade. Everyone was sorry for them – not just about losing their dad or mum, but because they hadn't mattered enough to stop it happening. I don't expect grown-ups understand what I mean.' She got up from the bed and went to stand at the window with her back to the room.

'How did you get along with Kit?' Katie snatched at anything that would lead them from the dead end they were heading for.

'He's nice. He's going to be a doctor, he said. He told me lots about his home. And about his father – Mr Matheson. He lost *his* father because of an accident, not because he ran out on him. So that way, he hasn't really sort of lost him at all.' It was a muddled way of expressing herself, and in Kit's case it was further from the truth than she could know, but Katie understood exactly what she was meaning.

Outside a car door slammed, the sound turning Kamma's attention to the parking bay.

'It's him! It's Dad! He mustn't know I've been. Promise you won't tell.' She grabbed Katie's hand, tugging at it as if to emphasise what she was saying. 'Please, please, don't mess everything up. Just tell him goodbye and go away. Please don't steal Dad.'

'Quickly, just one thing. If you could come with him, if you had to leave your mother –' Oh, but what a dreadful ultimatum to put to a child! She heard herself ask it with shame.

'That sort of thing doesn't happen. Mom never does things wrong. She teaches other people how they should be. If she and Dad split up, I'd have to go with her. I'd just die without Dad.'

Twelve years old, on the verge of adolescence, everything painted in black and white. Of course she wouldn't die! But watching her disappear down the stairs and waiting for Dylan to appear from the lift, Katie couldn't forget the fear in her eyes.

Kamma's words came back to Katie as she listened to Dylan. He'd been to his lawyer. The position was clear. If he left his wife for another woman he would have no right to take Kamma with him; if Shara divorced him for adultery there was no doubt that she would have custody.

She told him of Shara's visit. But not of Kamma's.

'Listening to Shara, I was so certain,' she told him. 'I could fight her but I couldn't really hurt her. At last we were free.'

They were standing facing each other. Dylan's hands plunged deep into his pockets as if that way he'd stop himself reaching out to her.

'I can't do it, Kate-ee. It would betray her. I cannot do it.'

'Shara?' What was he saying?

'No! No, of course not Shara. I told you, our lives don't touch. You said it yourself, nothing we do could wound Shara. Kamma is a child still. She could not understand.'

How quick that demon jealousy was to whisper in Katie's ear: "Kamma couldn't understand. But what about you? He'll betray you, that doesn't matter."

'Kate-ee.' He couldn't hold himself from her, but reached to take her by the shoulders. She was too quick. She stepped back out of reach. 'Kate-ee, my darling, now it is you I have hurt.'

She shook her head, her mouth trembling. 'I thought at last things would be right . . .' she mumbled, and found herself pulled towards him and held in a grasp that seemed to crush the breath from her.

'Kate-ee, my love. I'd give my life for you.' She knew from his wild words and from the break in his voice that for him, too, yesterday's glimpse of freedom only made today's shackles all the harder to bear.

272

'Don't do that.' She forced a laugh, her face buried against his shoulder. 'I don't want you to give it – just to share it. And one day we will. She'll come to understand.'

They moved to the bed, and still clinging to each other, sat on the edge of it.

'It's duty, Kate-ee, but I cannot pretend it is nothing more. I couldn't be happy if I let her down.'

'I know.' And with a water laugh: 'You're a nice guy, Dylan Kitashee. If you weren't I would have learnt to put you out of my life years ago. Guess there's no hope for me, though. I'll just have to go on waiting.'

He'd come to England regularly – and let the gossips say what they liked, he would stay at Bullington. 'Let him sleep with anyone he likes as lone as he doesn't do it in Wyndhamslake.' Words spoken only an hour or so ago, but it seemed a lifetime.

The sunshine streamed across the rumpled bed, its caress warm on their naked bodies. For nine years she'd hungered for this moment. Nothing was changed for them, nothing ever would be.

In the afternoon they drove out to Hartway Height. It was no great beauty spot, but it was quiet. Lying side by side on the parched grass their talk was easy, it seemed that all the pressures had been lifted. She smiled to herself, remembering the morning. No doubt that had something to do with their state of contentment.

'I feel like a cat who's gobbled up a bowl of cream. Replete, content, thoroughly at peace.'

He raised her hand to his lips as they lay there. But this afternoon they didn't make love. Their desultory snatches of conversation were proof of their easy companionship. They talked for a while about Kit and his certainty of his future, about Bertie and his floundering. They talked of Kamma and of Mick. But not of themselves. When he could he would come to her, that they both knew.

'Mick said he'd take Kit straight to his place when they get back from North Garinco. We'll pick him up there,' he threw into the silence.

'He's very English, this son of yours. Do you mind?'

'Kit? Of course he is. You've done well, Kate-ee.'

'Nigel never included him, you know. After the accident, when he left everything to Bertie, Kit had to know about us, about not being Nigel's son. Instead of it driving a wedge between him and his memories he seemed to think even more of Nigel. Said once that he wished he'd known, he would have understood him better. Never a word of criticism that he'd not been treated the same as Bertie.'

273

'Kit is a nice guy.'

She laughed. 'Now when did I last hear that? Ah, now wasn't it just this morning? Didn't I say the very same thing to a certain Dylan Kitashee?'

'Then, my Kate-ee, it must run in the family.'

The very air was silent, the sky a high blue canopy. She raised herself on her elbow, working out which way was south-east. Somewhere far away in that direction, on the other side of the distant mountains, Dad would be cutting the wheat at Higley Creek, Bertie helping him. Bertie, almost a man, learning to do a man's job.

'The young ones went into town,' Mick told them with a chuckle. 'Young Kamma seemed keen to take him on parade. Wanted to be seen with him, wouldn't you guess?'

They imagined her displaying him to her friends, this handsome young visitor from England. They would have been surprised if they could have seen Kit and Kamma. They'd taken the road out of town to Buckleigh Park, never a haunt of the younger set, and except for office workers who went their with their summertime lunch packs, no one else either.

'I guess you're important to your mom, Kit. Sort of head of the family?'

'She's pretty capable. I told you yesterday about the way she runs Bullington.'

'Even so, I bet you'd hate her to get married again.'

He frowned, not sure what was behind the remark. Something must have prompted it from a twelve year old. Was she more perceptive than he'd imagined?

'Mom won't marry again.'

She turned her head sharply to look at him.

'Because of your father, you mean?' But she sounded uncertain. This didn't fit the equation.

'Yes. Mum will never marry any man other than my father.'

They walked on in silence.

'Doesn't anyone ever use this park, Kamma?' he said after a while, believing that she'd forgotten about Katie's thoughts on a second marriage. It was only when she didn't answer that he leant forward and looked at her face as she walked half a pace in front of him. Kamma was crying.

'Hey, what's up? Is it something I said? Is something bothering you?' His voice was so kind. The way he held her back and turned her to face him, his expression of concern, all these things were too much for Kamma. But it was more than that. Right from when she'd met

274

him yesterday she'd had this strange feeling that she'd known him already. Now out tumbled the whole story: she'd always thought her home was safe, not like so many of her friends' whose parents quarrelled or split up. Broken homes, second marriages, a father in one town, a mother in another . . . she knew so many people like it. But not her mom and dad. Why. Mom lectured folk so that they'd learn not to make a mess of things. What hurt most of all was that it was Dad who talked all that rubbish about being in love with someone else, wanting to go away and leave them.

Kit's worried frown deepened. How much did she know? How much ought she to be told? Poor kid. His sister – well almost his sister. He put an arm around her shoulders and steered her towards a bench, grateful that the park was deserted.

Half an hour later, and a lifetime wiser, Kamma took the folded handkerchief Kit passed to her and rinsed it in water from the drinking fountain. Then she washed her face, holding it against her burning eyelids. In a strange, unfamiliar way she felt happy. Later on when she was alone in bed she'd think about it all, she'd try and understand why having a brother – even if it had to be their secret! – took away so much of the fear. Dad's son, just as she was his daughter.

'I'll tell you something,' she announced, 'it may not feel strange to you, you've got a brother already – but it's new to me. And I'll tell you what I think makes it special, shall I? We shall still know each other when we grow quite old. You can't say that with most friends you meet, can you?'

Kit smiled at her.

'We'll make a pact, Kamma. Whatever our parents do, we'll always keep in touch.'

She shook his hand solemnly.

That was the last time she saw Kit alone. The next morning he and Katie drove out of Wyndhamslake.

Kit couldn't guess what she was thinking as his mother drove. If she and Dylan had planned to break up his marriage as Kamma had feared, then surely she would given some hint of it in her manner? But she didn't and said nothing. Yet there was about her a kind of serenity.

The first evening back at Higley Creek he understood the reason. There was to be nothing furtive about her relationship with Dylan.

'He'll spend quite a lot of his time in England now. And he'll live with us at Bullington. She won't divorce him. And he can't leave her permanently because of Kamma. Shara is the epitome of respectability – and that's the way she means to stay.'

275

'Mum, is this a good time for us to talk?' Bertie came upon Katie lying in the sunshine on the patch of grass by the side of the house. In these few weeks he'd acquired something of a Canadian accent. Acquired it purposely, Katie suspected.

'Is it about me and Dylan? Bertie, I know it's hard for you to take. Try to accept – later on you'll understand.'

'That's not what I want to talk about. But since we're on the subject, Mum, I'd better set the record straight. If you'd met up with some guy and gone over the moon for him, then, sure, I think I'd have been put out – for Dad's sake I think I would. But – heck, Mum, remember that dreadful row you and Dad had, the day I found out about Kit? Well, it seems to me if Dylan's Kit's old man, the best thing you could do would be to get spliced.' Then, with a grin she'd seldom seen recently: 'Since you can't do that, I guess you'll have to put up with the next best thing. No, Mum, it's something else I want to talk to you about.'

'Let me guess.' She smiled too. She felt they were closer than they had been since the accident. 'You've looked into the crystal ball and seen what you mean to do with your future? Come on, tell! I knew once you got away from all the pressures of school, suggestions, advice, here in the big outdoors you'd see things straight.'

'And that's what I've done. Mum, would you mind most awfully if I didn't go back for my last year at school? Honestly, it would be a waste of time.'

'Not go back to school? But you've always done well. Later on you'll regret it if you turn up the chance of going on to university.'

'Not go back to school – not go back to England. I've talked to Grandad. He's quite keen for me to stay on at Higley. At least until later when I can get a place for myself.'

She closed her eyes in the warm sunshine. But there was no closing her mind to the pictures that crowded in: Nigel with Bertie astride his shoulders; Nigel riding with him around the estate; Nigel and Bertie packing the Landrover as they made ready for one of their outings; Nigel's hand out of the open window of the car in a "thumbs up" sign to a small boy left at school for the first time. Now Bertie wanted to turn his back on all that Nigel had loved, all he'd taught him, to come here to a land his father had never seen. She could stop it, she could insist that he came home.

'You say Dad talked to you about it?' She played for time.

'He didn't persuade me. He's a great chap. Seems to understand how a bloke feels about things without being told.'

She nodded.

'So what do you say, Mum? I tried to think myself into all sorts of things, you know I did. This time, I didn't try at all. It just seemed to fall into place.'

'If you really want to. You can always change your mind and come home.'

Again that grin. Timidly, he reached out to touch her hand.

'You know, Mum, there's just one thing would make this place perfect. I wish Dad could share it. Sometimes if we have a day's fishing, or when we've been to the mountains, I think that. It's all so – so grand, so large, sort of challenging. Gosh, but Dad would have enjoyed it.'

She swallowed the tightness in her throat. He'd hate to see her cry. But she did allow her fingers to twine themselves around his and feel the answering pressure.

Kamma's eyes had been opened. Until now she'd taken the pattern of her life for granted. Parents who provided a comfortable home, a mother everyone seemed to look to with respect, a father who was regarded as the local success story. After that talk with Kit nothing was ever quite the same again.

In the late fall the Kitashee Foundation opened. More and more of Shara's time was spent there. Dr Kennedy, a psychiatrist, was there three evenings a week, once to lecture and twice to hold private surgeries. The Kamma of pre-Kit days wouldn't have sensed that on those evenings her mother took even more care than usual with her already faultless appearance.

There were some things that went on unchanged – one of them being that when Dylan was away Kamma usually stayed with Mick. It was a snowy night in January. Dylan was in England and wouldn't be home for at least another week. What sort of female premonition was it that made her lie to her grandfather, explaining that Shara would be home this evening after all?

'I like to know you're safely at Mick's,' Shara told her, surprised to find her home. 'Why didn't you go straight after school the same as usual?'

'I wanted to listen to some records Darleena lent me. I'll wait till you've gone before I play them, I like them loud.'

'Dreadful pop things, I suppose.'

'Yes. You'd hate them. I'll play them later, before I go over to Gramp.' She kept her fingers crossed as she spoke.

It all sounded so normal, so innocent. She even did as she'd said and danced with all abandon of any thirteen year old to the blast of the borrowed records. Then she put out the lights and waited – and waited.

The slamming of a car door brought her out of bed and over to the window a little before midnight. Yes, they were both coming in. Well, there was no crime in that. The two sets of footprints were stark in the virgin snow. She got back into bed, sitting up with the covers pulled around her shoulders. Downstairs she could hear movements, the clink of glasses, faint voices. If she crept to the head of the stairs they'd never notice her. She wouldn't put any lights on. What made her so certain that this wasn't the first time he'd been home with her mother? But the idea of her mother having an affair was ridiculous. She spent her life trying to sort out other people's problems that came from that sort of thing. Movements downstairs made her draw back towards her bedroom door. He must be going. But no. He switched the stair light on just as she melted back into her own room. They were coming up, their tread muffled on the thick shag of the carpet. Back in bed she sat up, waiting, listening. How long was he staying? Once she crept along to her mother's closed door. She imagined bursting in on them. But she wasn't brave enough for that.

She was already at the breakfast bar eating cornflakes when they came down in the morning. How dare William wear her father's robe! She hated to see her mother's suddenly heightened colour.

A week later Dylan arrived home. In that week Kamma had stayed with Mick, saying nothing, but with an imagination that worked overtime. What if she stirred up a hornet's nest, brought about the divorce she'd dreaded and found herself put in her mother's custody – and with Dr Kennedy thrown in? But if she said nothing then she'd be deceiving her father just as much as any of them. She wished Kit was here. He'd understand and know what the right thing to do was. She couldn't write to tell him, though, that would be disloyal to her father. He must be the first to know. Ah, that was it! She'd tell him as soon as he got home and leave things to him. Her mother would deny it, she'd do anything rather than be knocked off that pedestal she'd climbed! More scenes took shape in Kamma's mind: herself in Court, swearing to the truth of what she'd seen and heard; her mother denying it; an army of people Shara had counselled marching her out of town.

All Kamma's loyalty was to her father. All her life he'd been the centre of her world. Even so, she felt mean and sick imagining what she might do to her mother. Never had there been such a long week as this one when she waited for Dylan to come.

At a distance of seven thousand miles she'd imagined talking to him. It had seemed simple. Face to face with him it was much harder.

'Did you see Mrs Matheson in England, Dad? Mrs Matheson and Kit?' She asked in what she considered a grown-up, conversational tone.

'Why do you ask?' He sounded irritable. He looked closed in, unapproachable.

'Dad, I know about you and her.' The quick look he threw her did nothing to encourage her. 'I heard you asking Mom for a divorce, I listened. I went to see Mrs Matheson next day, and asked her to go away and leave us alone. Dad, I'm sorry. Honestly, I didn't do it to spoil things for you. I was frightened that you'd go off without me.'

His face softened. She hoped she was wrong, but it looked as though his eyes had tears in them. He mustn't cry! Whatever would she do if he cried?

'Next day Kit and I had a long talk,' she rushed on. 'He made me understand things. I like to know I have him for a brother, Dad. I wish he wasn't so far away.'

'Kit told you?'

'We made a pact that we'd always know each other, even when we get old. I liked that. But I was telling you . . .'

And so she did tell him.

The couples who this evening had benefited from Shara's wisdom had already left the Foundation, home to enrich their marriages from the blue print she'd offered until next Tuesday when they'd come again. The janitor hadn't locked the main door yet, although the place looked deserted.

Recognizing Dylan, he told him: 'Mrs Kitashee is still in the building. I'll tell her you're here.'

'No, don't. I've been in Europe for a couple of weeks. I want to surprise her.'

'She's been giving a talk in the man hall, that's where you'll find her.' A romantic at heart, the janitor smiled, watching him go through the swing doors.

The main hall was empty just as Dylan knew it would be. The only sound was the hollow ring of his footsteps as he walked the length of it. A sign led him to 'Dr W.H. Kennedy. Please ring bell and wait.' He did neither.

'Can't you read?' William blurted. 'No one walks in –'

'Dylan! I didn't know you were back.' Only for a second was Shara caught off guard, then she had the situation in hand. Why should Dylan come here? From the expression in those steel cold eyes, it certainly wasn't because he was anxious to see her! No, there could be only one answer: Kamma must have told him about William staying with her at the house. Sly, wretched child, pretending to be with her grandfather when all the time she must have stopped at home to spy! Perhaps Dylan had put her up to it.

'Pour us a drink, Willie. Dylan, this is Dr William Kennedy. Willie, this is my husband. You remember I told you he's been away in England.'

'Oh, but he knows that.' Dylan ignored William's soft, plump hand that fluttered towards him then withdrew. 'He would hardly have been sleeping in your bed if I'd been at home.'

'Say, now, Dylan,' William blustered, 'I suppose you've got some garbled story from the little girl? Children watch too much television. At that age they look for emotional experience. It's a way of gaining a parent's undivided –'

'You can cut out that claptrap, keep it for your clients. Shara, I asked you for a divorce and you refused. Now I'm not asking you, I'm telling you.'

Coolly, with no trace of emotion, she viewed him.

'You? You who've had a mistress for more years than we've been married, you with an illegitimate son!'

'The choice is yours – the end result will be the same. We can end our marriage with as little publicity as possible, or you can contest my petition, let the town know the sham it's been.'

'How can you talk to her like this?' This time William's hand seemed to know where it was going. It rested on Shara's shoulder as he put a protective arm around her. 'From what she's told me, the poor girl has never had a marriage worthy of the name. It's what happens when you marry outside your own kind.' Standing side by side with Shara, he felt remarkably brave. He'd expected his words to bring a spark of anger to Dylan's cold expression. But he was wrong. Instead he saw amusement tinged with mockery.

'Shara?' Dylan prompted her. 'Which is it to be? I shall see my lawyer in the morning.'

At home Kamma waited. She knew where her father had gone, and imagined various ways the scene might be played out. Pictures danced in her mind. When she heard him return she was almost too frightened to look at him. Mothers almost always had custody of children – and anyway what was one little affair compared with him and Kit's mother? But she wouldn't be taken away from him. If in Court they said she had to leave him she'd fight, she'd make a dreadful scene, she *wouldn't* leave him. And now there was Kit too. Having a brother turned them into a proper family.

She couldn't ask him what had happened and he didn't tell her. But he was in a remarkably cheerful frame of mind.

There was no suggestion that Kamma should have to live with her mother. Indeed, the last thing Shara wanted was the child who'd confronted William and her that snowy morning. In the weeks that followed Dylan and his daughter went to stay with Mike. The Kitashee Foundation took on extra staff, word soon spread that Shara Kitashee was moving east. She found that the very thing she had dreaded could be turned to her advantage. Into the new Foundation that she would set up, partnered by William Kennedy – partly financed by Dylan's settlement – she could bring that extra understanding gained from being a misused wife. And wouldn't her own life be clear evidence of how a woman could live to her full potential even after a man had used her so badly? Her mission wasn't only to counsel couples into enriching their floundering partnerships. It was much broader. It was to guide each one to personal fulfilment.

The lovely and successful Mrs Kitashee – or would it be Mrs Kennedy – would be the perfect example of how a woman can overcome.

Epilogue

The stewardess had finished handing out head-cushions; the lights in the aircraft cabin had been lowered. Most of the passengers had pulled down their blinds, but not Katie and Dylan. The sky was a black velvet background to the diamond sparkle of stars. But they were travelling eastward. Soon it would lighten to a deep blue, the stars would lose their brilliance, the eastern horizon would be painted with the promise of day. Soon they'd be home.

Home? Katie reached out towards Dylan, felt her fingers held in his. Home? Bullington, Wyndhamslake, the forests of the north, Higley Creek . . . where was home? Home is where the heart is, she'd heard say. If that were true, then there was another address to add to the list! Upper Reach, near Radley. Its boundaries marched shoulder to shoulder with those of Kilton Down, the O'Hagon's place. But now Upper Reach belonged to Bertie. She closed her eyes, a smile playing around her mouth. Bertie, a rancher, a cattle breeder. What would Granny Menzies say if she could look down on them and know? A cattle breeder, a cowboy! But Bertie had found himself. At every turn he discovered something that made him love his new land more. Nigel had reared him to be fearless. If Nigel could see him now, surely he'd be glad for him, surely he'd be proud?

Glancing at her, Dylan thought she was asleep. He didn't loosen his hold on her hand.

She hovered somewhere between sleeping and waking. So often they'd flown backwards and forwards across the Atlantic, the eastward journey telescoping the hours of night and hurtling them towards dawn. Her thoughts were flitting in the way they could when sleep is comfortably close, touching on a memory here, hearing the echo of a voice there.

Home? Was it Wyndhamslake? If she'd never left her native land perhaps she wouldn't have appreciated it as she did each time they went back to it. The crisp air of winter as they travelled where the forest tracks were covered by virgin snow, not a murmur, not a sound except for the whisper of their skiis as they glided; the camaraderie of their friends, English, Scottish, Irish, German, Dutch, Chinese, ethnic Indian, but all of them first and foremost Canadian.

Home? Higley Creek, the home of her childhood. Still Ramsey and Lottie lived there, still it was home as it always had been. These days Ramsey had a foreman to take charge, of course he did, yet it hurt to know the changes couldn't be far away for Lottie and him.

Home? Bullington Manor. Always it would be home. The spell it wove around her held her tighter as the years went by. In all its history as home to the Mathesons, surely the years since Grandam had passed the responsibility to her must have been its finest hour? Her mind took another leap, this time back just a few days, to herself and Bertie riding out towards the open range together. Dear Bertie, proud that Kit had gone into practice in Newton Dingley, supporting her in what she meant to do. For two and a half centuries the house had passed through the family. Would the ghosts of their ancestors rise up in horror at what she was going to do? No. Even Nigel, if now he could see the whole picture, if he could read Bertie's heart, and hers and Kit's too, he must know that it was Kit who had such pride in the past, Kit who loved every stick and stone of the place. Dr Christopher Matheson would never fail Bullington.

She let herself sink into thoughts of the Manor. Before her went a procession of residents who'd made it their home through the years. Eva was with them. Out there on the bowling lawn . . . sitting in the shade having tea . . . a hubbub of excitement as they welcomed their own guests for a musical evening . . . and look closer, surely that was Alice Piper? Wasn't that Tom Wadham she could see going up the front steps, his black bag in his hand? No, look again, it wasn't Tom. It was Kit? What odd tricks sleep can play. Even half dreaming as she was, the corners of her mouth twitched as she saw ahead into the future. Who was the young nurse greeting him at the top of the wide stone steps? Kamma. A flight of fancy, for she was still in her first year of training at Oxford. But there was nothing fanciful in the way she'd fitted into the English scene, become part of the family.

It was more than an hour later when Dylan whispered: 'Kate-ee! Look!'

Their seats were on the starboard side, Dylan next to the window. Leaning across him her cheek close to his, together they peered out. So often they'd made this journey together, but the wonder of it never dimmed. Below them there might be clouds, but not here. As far as the eye could see the eastern sky was burnished with the deep gold of a new day.

283

You have been reading a novel published by Piatkus Books. We hope you have enjoyed it and that you would like to read more of our titles. Please ask for them in your local library or bookshop.

If you would like to be put on our mailing list to receive details of new publications, please send a large stamped addressed envelope (UK only) to:

Piatkus Books: 5 Windmill Street
London W1P 1HF

PIATKUS

The sign of a good book